SHAINA PARKS

THE DAWN OF RIKER

Copyright © 2025 by Shaina Parks

All rights reserved.

For permissions or inquiries, please contact: shainaparkswrites@gmail.com

Cover Design: Milbart Design

Map Art: Cartographybird Maps

Edited By: LAPS Editorial LLC

Second Edition: October 2025

ISBN: 979-8-218-69538-5 (paperback)

979-8-218-79266-4 (hardback)

B0FKTRSGWC (Kindle)

Contents

For the dreamers and believers. The ones that long for more and wish for courage. I see you. Make your dreams come true and don't let words of others discourage you. The support of you is what encouraged me to write my story and bring my world to paper.

What dreams you may have, I believe in you.

And for the ones that just want another shadow daddy, enjoy this journey.

NORTHHORN
MORNWIND
VILLAGE
STORMPEAK
VILLAGE
ELDREST
MADORA
WITCH
LANDS
WHITERUN
VILLAGE
DUSTVALE
VILLAGE
CROWNEST
VILLAGE
RAVENWICK
VILLAGE
OAKWOOD
VILLAGE
THE HUMAN LANDS
THE
COTTAGE
ELDKEST

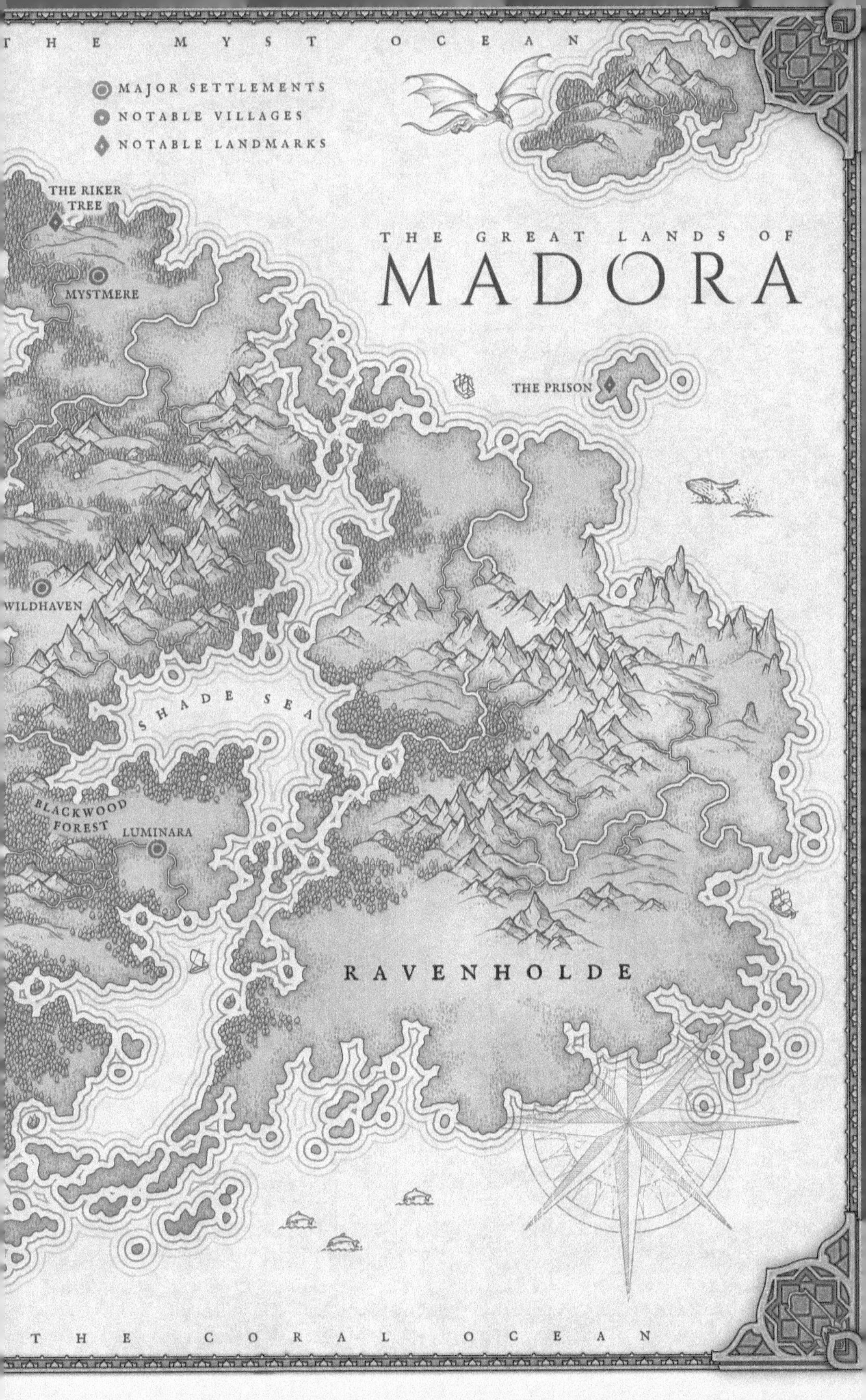

THE MYST OCEAN
MAJOR SETTLEMENTS
NOTABLE VILLAGES
NOTABLE LANDMARKS
THE RIKER TREE
MYSTMERE
THE GREAT LANDS OF
MADORA
THE PRISON
WILDHAVEN
SHADE SEA
BLACKWOOD FOREST
LUMINARA
RAVENHOLDE
THE CORAL OCEAN

NAME PRONUNCIATION

Ellowyn - El-loh-wihn - meaning- Elm tree - elm tree is known to have magical properties

Alina - Uh-lee-nuh - meaning- bright, noble, light

Dealla - Deal-luh - meaning- early invader - protector

Killian - Kill-ee-an - meaning- bright headed - little warrior

Ivarison - I-var-i-son - meaning- iv-yew tree - warrior

Delaney - Duh-lay-nee - meaning- dark challenger

Briallen - Bree-al-in -meaning- primrose

Adriane - Ey-dree-en - meaning- dark one

Ciaran - Keer-own - meaning- dark little one

PROLOGUE

Time. One thing that a Fae believed they would never run out of, being near-immortal. In all her life, Alina had never felt more frightened than in this moment. Her husband, Evander, led the way. She hurried after him, tightening her arms around Ellowyn, a tiny bundle hidden beneath a small blue cloak.

Frantic villagers ran past them through the streets. Alina could almost taste their terror as they fled from the destruction. In the corner of an alley, they pressed their backs against red bricks as they searched desperately for a safe passage. Alina glanced down and saw Ellowyn's fearful green eyes staring back. Tears cascaded down her daughter's cheeks as she tried to remain quiet. Her young mind didn't understand why the village smelled of smoke and blood.

Evander stood to her left, one hand tightly gripping her arm as she carried their child. With his other hand, he unsheathed his sword.

"Alina," he said, his deep voice filled with urgency. "Listen to me: I need you to promise that you will keep going. No matter the cost. Promise me. You must keep Ellowyn safe."

Alina's chest shook with painful inhales, shifting Ellowyn in her arms. "I promise," she whispered, her voice breaking.

"Are you ready? We need to continue."

Alina could only nod as she pulled Ellowyn closer to her chest. Evander kept a hand on her lower back as they rushed through the cobbled path, wading through the panicked crowd.

Deeper into the village, loud, anguished screaming rang out. The air felt heavy, becoming harder to breathe. Soldiers dressed in black infested the streets. It was chaos. They set fire to buildings and homes, and they laughed as they slew fleeing villagers.

The dark soldiers had arrived with Adriane and Ciaran, guests of Mystmere. In return, they destroyed everything in their path. Some of the kingdom's armored soldiers lay face down in the dirt, their yellow-embroidered capes mingling with the red of death.

It had happened so quickly. Alina had been standing beside her father's throne, Ellowyn sitting by her feet. Her parents, King Everett and Queen Amelia, stood on a platform in the throne room with Adriane and Ciaran a step below. Mystmere's soldiers and the dark soldiers were stationed throughout the room.

Alina had been wary about how willingly they had come. They heard of a prophecy: two Fae to rule all Faes. She knew Adriane and Ciaran sought power. Their motive was clear when they stood with the Royals in the throne room. They only pretended to want peace.

Alina watched in shock as Adriane drew a hidden dagger from her gown and struck—slaying her mother before her eyes. Her father's screams echoed off the walls as the dagger found him, Rikeroot entangled and glistening through the blade that Adriane held, covered with the Queen's blood.

Alina knew in her bones that she would be next, and then her daughter. Without another glance towards her parents, she grabbed Ellowyn, Evander following close behind, and darted through a curtain behind the thrones.

They moved through a hidden passage, her muscles tensing at their speed. A dark soldier followed them, but Evander quickly slew him. A wave of weakness washed over Alina as they ran.

The echoing clash of the blades pierced through her mind. The images of her mother on the throne room floor and her father in anguish haunted her.

Neither Alina nor Evander dared speak as they rushed to escape. Panting, they entered the village through a narrow alleyway. Alina shifted Ellowyn in her arms; at only five years old, she wouldn't be able to keep up on foot. Dropping her crown as they went, Evander and she pulled their hoods up, hoping to blend in with the villagers.

The village was in chaos. Adriane and Ciaran's terrorizing dark soldiers were already out.

Alina attempted to glamour them, but her magic only buzzed in her veins. She could feel it fading.

"Evander, I can't glamour us," Alina whispered, terror lacing her words. They might not survive.

"The wine they brought—" Evander began, "it must've been laced. It explains why your parents—" He couldn't bring himself to finish his thought.

Evander was right. The Fae magic that flowed through Alina's veins was becoming muted, a dull ache spreading through her bones, until her limbs felt like they were falling asleep. Evander was human, it wouldn't affect him as it did her.

"Evander." Alina's eyes were wide as she watched a black mist spread down the path ahead. They had heard stories of Adriane and how she could conjure demons that hid in the mist. The Sleroka.

Villagers screamed as they tried to move away from the darkness, disappearing and never coming back through as their screams faded into nothing.

"We can't move through that."

Evander stopped at another wall, his back facing Alina and Ellowyn. Ellowyn's small fists tightly held onto her mother's cloak, burying her face against her chest. Fear filled Alina, knowing that they would have to separate for Ellowyn's safety.

Evander looked to his family, ran his fingers through Ellowyn's brown hair, then looked at Alina next. His hand found her face, his thumb brushing against her cheek as he pulled her in, inhaling her scent as their foreheads touched.

"Switch cloaks with me." He pulled away and glanced back to the mist. "Alina, hurry. I'll take your cloak. Your scent will draw them to follow me. It will give you time to get away. You take Ellowyn." His voice cracked, and he cleared his throat as a tear fell. "Take her and travel as fast and as far as you can go."

Alina grabbed Evander's hand as he tried to pull away. "No," she stammered. "I can't leave you behind. I won't." Her chest tightened as she stared at her husband. Her mate.

The human in a Fae land. He would not survive an attack against the Sleroka.

"I can't do this without you, Evander. Please!" She would have dropped to her knees and begged if she hadn't been holding Ellowyn.

"I love you. I love you both so incredibly much. The life that I have had with you has been more than I could have ever dreamed of having. She needs her mother, Alina. You need to continue without me. Save her for me and for the kingdom. For us, Alina." He brushed the tears that fell from her eyes. Ellowyn looked to her father as he pulled them both into an embrace. "You must be brave for your momma and me. I love you so much, sweet Ell." He kissed her forehead.

Time. Something that she believed they would have more of. Even with him being human, they were supposed to have his lifetime together, to watch their five-year-old daughter grow. It had not been enough. It couldn't be time for them to say goodbye to one another; Alina couldn't accept it. Her mind and heart felt as if it would shatter, unable to grasp this would be the last moment they share.

Once Evander helped Alina pull her own cloak off, he wrapped his thick cloak around his girls. Alina grabbed onto Evander's collar, soaking in the warmth of his embrace.

"I will find you again. If not in this life, then the next. We will have more time together. I know it. I love you."

"As I love you." Alina gasped, bringing him in for one last kiss. "Please—" she tried to beg, vision blurring. "I can't—,"

Evander brushed her cheek with the back of his hand. "Always remember how strong you are. You must remember. Go, now!"

As Evander pulled away, his sword ready as he ran the opposite way from Alina and Ellowyn, Alina felt her heart go with him. Her chest cracked, and an emptiness took over. Evander clanked his sword against the stone as his yells echoed off the walls, attempting to draw the attention and give Alina time to run.

Alina turned away, taking her chance to run with Ellowyn in her arms, who watched over her shoulders, watched as her father disappeared in the invading black mist that took over the street.

The gust of wind dried Alina's tears as she ran, her chest heaving from such agony, as if she was unable to catch her breath. Sobs escaped her lips as Ellowyn cried out for her father.

The mating bond between Alina and Evander dulled before feeling nearly nonexistent. Her magic faded. She couldn't dare look behind her for fear of what she would see of her mate and kingdom as the smell of smoke followed.

With a few strides down the stone path and with Evander's cloak wrapped around the two, Alina and Ellowyn were out of the village and into the forest. Disappearing from their fallen kingdom.

Chapter One

17 years later

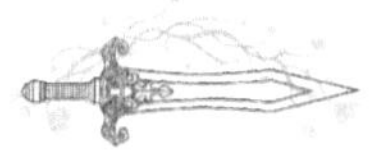

One of the first lessons my mother had taught me was to stay alert and always be aware of my surroundings. As the sun arched behind the trees, the autumn breeze turned brisk, stinging my eyes as I walked the path through the woods. One way led to our arena, the other to the village. My mother and I created the trail when we built our practice grounds years ago.

Years.

It had been seventeen years since we arrived at our cottage, right after I turned five. Our home resided on the village outskirts, just beyond the woods, secluded from others. Just as my mother preferred. My memory was foggy of our life before, but I remembered how it was when we arrived.

The villagers had stared at us with suspicion, whispering amongst themselves. "What cottage?" they asked. No one recalled a cottage in the woods.

Older now, I couldn't blame their wariness. The village we lived near was one of the first settlements erected on mortal land. North of us, through these very woods, was the Fae territory. Our forest acted as the border between mortal and Fae, amongst other creatures, which was the reason the villagers were on high alert with our appearance.

The thick woods separated the two lands that had been grown by the human queen and the Fae queen hundreds of years before, but it didn't stop creatures from crossing. When that happened, humans rarely stood a chance.

Continuing on the path, I pulled my cloak around me, my fingers turning pink as I clenched the hem. Twigs crunched under my feet, and trees creaked against the gust. Then the birds' singing stilled. My breath caught as I took in my surroundings. Ever so slightly, the leaves ruffled from light footsteps.

It came from behind me, to the right. The movement was faint, but I could sense it was following me. My hand went beneath my cloak to my dagger's hilt. I knelt to examine a cluster of red berries growing along the path, using the moment to scan the woods. Acting casually, I tried to locate the threat's exact location.

Only for a moment.

One moment to ascertain what was tracking me.

Deep breath.

To estimate the size.

Closer.

The leaves to my left crunched.

Now!

Pulling my dagger free, I spun and stopped short. My breath hitched as my blade pressed against pale skin.

"Not funny, mother," I hissed. "I should've known it was you."

Her light brown curls shifted as she tilted her head, eyebrows raised with amusement. Those bright green eyes with their honey center glanced down at the dagger still at her throat.

"You're getting faster, Ellowyn. How long before you realized I was following?"

"Just a few moments," I muttered, withdrawing my weapon.

She straightened her cloak with long, graceful fingers, adjusting the bow and quiver slung over her shoulder. Standing tall, she cut an impressive figure against the shadows of the woods, more physically fit than any woman in the village.

When we weren't hunting for food, we were practicing. There was never a day to take a break. It was as if my mother expected us to go into battle any moment. Yet, we had never been bothered during our time living here.

"Well, come on then." She sniffed, rubbing her pink nose as she began to walk down the path. "Dealla will be meeting with us before nightfall."

I sighed as I followed. My mother had always been lovely. I looked so much like her, the curls in our hair, through mine were a bit wilder. The same green-gold eyes and pale skin. But the superior feeling she carried, I would never have that.

The practice arena was built in a large wooden fenced rectangle. Hay bales lined one side, marked with painted targets worn from years of practice. Wooden plates hung from another side, suspended from the fence and nearby tree branches. A leathered practice dummy stood sentinel in one corner, its surface scarred from countless arrows and sword strikes. It had taken us several years to clear the arena and shape it to my mother's exact specifications.

We dove into our usual routine. Standing side-by-side, we worked on our aim, flinging daggers at the targets. Nothing mattered but the center marks; our silent competition had always been to see who could get the most bullseyes.

We were so absorbed that when twigs snapped at the entrance, we both missed our throws.

A third dagger whistled past, striking the target dead center. It clinked against my own blade that I had embedded into the mark moments before.

My mother and I spun around. A woman with a medium complexion stood by a tree, a smirk playing on her face.

"Dealla, if you were trying to hit one of us, we may need to work on your aim," my mother said, moving to retrieve the daggers. Dealla rolled her eyes as she took hers back.

"Oh, I'll be sure to do that, Alina," Dealla quipped, keeping eye contact with my mother, as she threw the dagger once more.

Another bullseye.

Dealla came into our lives about seven years ago. She was wonderful, compassionate, and a good listener, though the villagers stayed clear of her. She carried herself like a guard; face hard, posture rigid, hands near the daggers at her belt. I knew she would strike when the need arose.

Dealla often trained with me while my mother trained alone. She appeared to be in her late twenties, but she fought with a lifetime of experience. While my mother was at the corner of the arena on her own, Dealla worked with me.

"Again," she commanded, her braided black hair swinging over one shoulder as she circled me. Her sharp blue eyes that could pierce armor never left my stance. "Your guard drops on the left. An opponent would notice."

I raised my training sword, muscles trembling after drilling the same movements for two hours. We often used wooden swords so we could practice harder without harming one another. When we used real swords, we took care to aim our hits with precision. Sweat trickled down my back despite the autumn chill.

"Where did you learn to fight like this?" I asked, partly out of curiosity, partly hoping for a moment's rest.

Dealla moved quickly behind me, whistling a faint tune as I turned to strike. She blocked effortlessly, never showing weakness.

Her expression hardened. "Places you hope never to see," she said. Then she lunged without warning.

My arms ached when the night crawled across the woods, grateful for our practice to end. The animals through the woods began to quiet as we packed our gear and headed home. While I led the group, Dealla and my mother lingered further behind.

"I heard whispers in the village today while at the market," Dealla muttered. As if sensing I could hear them, she cleared her throat before continuing, her voice even lower.

I kept my gaze ahead, waiting for the cottage to appear through the trees. I knew when they whispered, they didn't want me to listen. But their voices were too clear to ignore.

"The Wilder Family at the end of the village said they spotted a black-haired female Fae," Dealla said, her tone coated with caution. "In their own words, 'she was what evil would look like.'"

My mother's footsteps stopped. Glancing over my shoulder, I saw her hand gripping on Dealla's forearm. Though the growing shadows of night masked her expression, I could make out the fear that laced her words. "What do you think could be the chance? It's been seventeen years."

They started walking again, Dealla's voice even lower than before. "It will happen one day. Can't hide forever, right?" Dealla said almost in a matter-of-fact way. I fiddled with the bag that I carried as I continued to look ahead. "After all, I found you."

I stopped, unsure if I wanted to continue listening or wait for them to catch up. My mother never made friends with anyone in the village and had never wanted to. When we found Dealla at the entrance of the village one morning, she and my mother had an instant connection. I was happy to see my mother befriend someone, however strange I thought it had been.

The cottage appeared through the trees as night began penetrating its shadows across the woods. Our beautiful cottage. The home my mother claimed belonged to my grandmother before she passed. It was big enough with two bedrooms. Spring and summer were when it was at its most beautiful.

A large garden was gated off on one side, keeping animals from eating what we grew. The horse pasture was on the other side, down a slight slope.

I put my belongings on the steps of the wrap-around porch, with green and white ivy draping off the sides of the railing. When I turned to wait for Dealla and my mother, they were still in quiet conversation.

"What are the two of you talking about?" I asked, my curiosity growing by the second.

"Some town gossip that was overheard," my mother answered with a dismissive wave.

I narrowed my eyes at her. Curious that she would want to know about town gossip when she hated traveling or speaking to any who lived there.

After stewing over it for another beat, I huffed and made my way into the cottage, reminding myself that they didn't know I overheard what had been said.

My relationship with my mother was complicated. We worked well together on daily tasks and practices, but when it came to discussing life or deeper subject matter, communication was limited.

My mother lived by one principle: she never shared the full details, especially of her past. But I wasn't a child anymore, and I could handle more than she thought.

Chapter Two

Every evening, we took turns preparing dinner. Tonight was my night. I always stuck to simple meals, and it didn't take long for me to warm soup, bread, and leftover venison. As I sliced the bread, my mother set the bowls on the table and sprinkled herbs into each.

Spoons scraping against wooden bowls was all that was heard through the dining room. I glanced at both women who sat around the table. Dealla lost in thought, watching her bowl of soup dancing around her spoon. My mother seemed dazed, shoulders tense. I took a breath and decided to break the silence.

"Who was the Fae with black hair spotted in the village?" I asked, very cautiously, with my head down.

"You heard us talking?" Dealla asked, sitting up straighter, but my mother coughed.

I knew very little of Fae or their land. My mother kept information to a minimum, and I never questioned why she seemed to fear them. The rules from the old queen still stood: neither Fae nor creatures were to cross the woods. Humans wanted to live in peace, away from the terror the Fae world brought.

Watching through my eyelashes, Dealla and my mother shared a glance. The hairs on my arm stood on end. My stomach churned as I realized how much truth had always been hidden from me.

"A female Fae. They can be lethal and dangerous, and she sounds as if she may be," my mother answered as she picked at her bread. "Finish your soup, please."

"Why didn't you want me to know she was in the village?" I asked, watching her bread soak up the last of her meal.

"It doesn't concern you."

"I'm not a child anymore. I should know these things. If she made it to the village, she could've come through here." My cheeks burned. My fingers clenched my spoon. If I pushed my mother, she would become dismissive. Dealla sat as still as a statue, studying the wall as if it were suddenly so interesting.

"Do you know who she is? You mentioned the black hair. Why does her hair color matter?"

My mother clicked her tongue, sucking in her bottom lip as she dropped her bread in the bowl. "Ellowyn, please drop it," she snapped. Closing her eyes, she pinched the bridge of her nose as if she were fighting a headache.

"If you think I'll be afraid, I won't be. You do this about everything. Who is she?"

"Ellowyn, I said enough." She stood from her chair, her height towering over me.

"Alina, perhaps—," Dealla began to say, but my mother put a hand up, stopping her.

Her voice became dangerously low as it echoed through the room. "Now is not the time. End of discussion."

A shiver ran up my spine from her icy tone. I pulled my cloak from the back of my chair and stood. My whole life I had to abide by what was and wasn't allowed, and I was growing tired of it.

"I don't understand why everything must be kept secret. I thought it was because you didn't trust me, or I was too young," I muttered, "I'm old enough now. And now, I feel as if I can't trust you." I looked at neither, taking their silence as their reply. "I'm going for a walk."

I left the cottage as quickly as I could. The fury building in my chest needed to cool. I slammed the front door harder than I meant, and it nearly came off its hinges.

My mother's secrets always bothered me, but once Dealla had arrived, it worsened. Were things too difficult and painful for her to speak about? To say that would be enough, but instead, she forced conversations to end.

During the winter months, before Dealla arrived, meat had been scarce, and we'd struggled to survive. There had been times when villagers offered to help when they saw me with my mother, but each time, my mother declined. Once Dealla arrived, we never struggled again. She had been the only person my mother accepted assistance from.

Rules in our household had been set from an early age. We never spoke about our life before the cottage. My mother refused to do so, even when I still tried. When something— or someone — killed my father, we left our previous home. That was all that I knew. Strangely, I couldn't recall a single memory. I remembered nothing of what our family had been like, what my father's name was, or what he looked like. Not even our family name. My mother claimed we were never given one.

My feet moved down our small stone path as I battled through the thoughts until I found myself standing at our old tool shed by the horse pasture.

The worn-down structure had seen better days. Useful to hold our old gardening pots, tools, tack, and blankets for the horses. Pulling the doors open, the dust blew about, making me cough. I shut the door behind me and paced back and forth, kicking the dirt underneath my boots and cursing under my breath. Sometimes I just wanted to scream.

I wanted to scream and escape from this cottage, to travel the world, to see more of what was out there.

Kick.

Not live here for the rest of my life, as my mother seemed determined to do so.

Kick.

That time, my foot slid further, knocking a blanket I didn't recognize off a tattered chest. Had it always been there? Grime caked the surface, and spiderwebs connected the edges to the wall behind it. The moon came through the small window of the shed. And in the dim light, I realized it was unlocked.

Unable to stop myself, I pushed the dusty top open. A few worn-down books lay on top. As I took them out, I found cloaks underneath. Why were these in the tool shed and not inside? I unfolded a faded blue cloak that was fitted for a small child.

Underneath the blue cloak was a heavier black one. Straightening, I held it out, and the bottom seam grazed the ground, its length meant for an adult. The lining for both was a pale-yellow material, with a matching embroidered hem.

My chest warmed at the faint scent — a mix of citrus and cinnamon. My lips curved into a smile as if it were a smell I recognized. I had never seen this before, or had I?

With renewed determination, I made my way back to the cottage with the black cloak folded under my arms. Entering the dining room, Dealla and my mother sat together at the table. Filled wine glasses replaced the dinner bowls. My mother looked at me, wrinkling her nose, before she looked away.

"What's in the tool shed?" I asked. As much as I wanted to pick up our previous conversation, I wanted to know more about the chest. To know why these seemed so recognizable.

My mother glanced at me and out the window. "What do you mean?"

"There is a chest filled with books and two cloaks. Who do they belong to?" I asked, planting my feet firmly on the ground. I wanted answers.

I placed the cloak upon the table. My mother froze, then inhaled deeply as her eyes glazed over and her hands covered her mouth. Dealla stared at the black fabric, stunned into silence.

"Go put it back," my mother whispered, her hands dropping from her trembling lips. Pointing at the cloak, her voice rose, repeating herself. "Go put it back!"

"Who does it belong to?" I asked again, straightening my back as I stared down at her, as she had done to me earlier.

"I thought everything was hidden?" Dealla asked, reaching for the cloak.

But I was faster. I grabbed the cloak from the table, shaking it before me. "They were in a chest. Why would they need to be hidden?"

My mother placed her elbows on the table, pressing her fingers against her temples. She focused on the knots that formed on the wood surface. in front of her as she took deep breaths. "I'll get rid of it."

"It's cloaks and books. Why are you ignoring the question?"

Why did this matter? The anger surged through me as I stood with the cloak in my hand, wanting to know why the scent of citrus and cinnamon seemed so familiar. What — Who — did it belong to?

"My entire life, I've done all you've asked of me without hesitation. What are a few questions, and answers? I just want to know you more; you're my mother." I nearly pleaded. Why couldn't she speak to me as she did with Dealla?

"You are not ready," she said, her voice strained. She didn't look my way, her eyes refusing to leave the table. "I'm not ready."

My lips pressed tightly together. "I don't even understand what that means." I looked at Dealla, hoping for assistance.

"It's not my place, Ellowyn," Dealla said.

As if from sheer will, my mother forced her gaze back toward the window. She was done speaking. Silence stifled the air around me. Hurt and frustration stretched the chasm I felt lay between my mother and me.

Another battle lost.

I placed the mystery cloak back on the table. If my mother wanted to take care of it, then it was for her to do so. Leaving the room, I grabbed my satchel from the hook by the front door and left the cottage.

This time, I walked the path to the garden. It was a sacred place, filled with beauty, growth, and peace. A place for an escape, and during the summer, it was my favorite when the bees hummed and collected nectar and pollen.

I stood at the gate, feeling like something was wrong. But what could I do? Like every other time my mother shut me out, I needed to keep moving forward.

Approaching footsteps came from behind me. I didn't need to turn to know it was Dealla.

"What are you thinking about, Ellowyn?" Her voice was low as she stopped behind me.

"It doesn't matter," I muttered, weariness threading my mind. I looked over my shoulder at her. "she doesn't trust me."

"You know very well that is not what she said. Maybe once you're a bit older and she knows—"

I tilted my head back, sighing heavily. "Dealla," I said, shifting my feet to level my eyes at her. "I may not know your exact age, but you don't seem much older than me."

Dealla clamped her mouth shut, hands folded in front of her, as she nodded with a frown. "I hope in time things make better sense for you.

I'm sorry that you're upset." She closed the distance between us, putting a hand on my shoulder. "They aren't my secrets to tell, but I'm here for you, Ellowyn."

She squeezed my shoulder and turned on her heel to walk back to the cottage. Only taking a few steps, she turned around.

"Ellowyn, the cloak you found—" She hesitated, glancing back at the cottage, then back at me. She spoke fast, yet soft, like she would change her mind if she gave herself another beat to think on it, "The cloak belonged to your father. He wore that very cloak the day he was killed."

My heart dropped to my stomach. Did I recognize it because it belonged to him? The questions went unsaid as I watched her walk back to the cottage. It was hard enough to know I battered my mother with those questions as she fought back with silence. I could not bear any more disappointment. I twisted back around, staring at the garden and the way the moon bathed the land in silver light.

I didn't have a plan, but I breathed in deep and held onto my belongings as if they might run off. Forcing my feet to move forward and fastening my cloak, I trekked toward the village. I didn't dare look back to see if my mother watched me head into the night.

Chapter Three

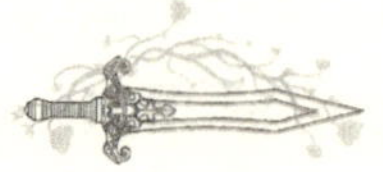

Dim lantern lights signaled the village entrance was up ahead. Candles danced in the passing breeze that threatened to extinguish them. The cold mud crunched beneath my boots as I crossed the threshold. A few villagers hurried past, huddling closer together and averting their eyes when we made eye contact. Their wary whispers faded as they disappeared down a side path.

It had been some time since I'd ventured this way, especially after dark. Not many dared linger on the streets at this hour. The flames, light dimmed by blackened glass lanterns, cast eerie shadows across the buildings and cobblestones.

The human village lay on the eastern side of the human land, south of Fae territory. I found it strange that despite our proximity to the border, the Queen hadn't stationed soldiers for protection. Then I remembered what Dealla had told my mother: The Queen had placed them in villages closer to her castle in Eldkest.

My reflection stared back at me from the dark windows of closed shops as I walked deeper into town. Only one building remained lit at the end of the street. A battered structure with a crooked sign hanging outside: *The Broken Stone.*

The tavern itself looked ready to collapse, but voices carried from the open windows, glowing soft yellow and orange. Smoke rose from the chimney, carrying scents of fire, roasted onions, peppers, and meats. A few horses stood tied to posts as patrons wandered in and out.

The Broken Stone connected to the village inn, the only place I would find open this late. My alternative was a barn full of animals and hay further down the road, but hard, cold ground reeking of manure wasn't ideal.

The door creaked as I slipped inside. More lanterns hung from hooks, filling the room with a warm orange hue, candle wax dripping steadily to the floor. I pulled my hood up, hands trembling as I kept my eyes down. Straw covered the ground, stained with stale ale and speckled with dirt.

Nestled in the center of the room was a large crackling fireplace. And past the crowd, the bar maiden served at the bar. Tables and chairs, most of which were occupied, filled the remaining space.

I kept a hand on my hood as I found an empty table in the back corner. Funny, earlier I had wished for company. Now, with a room full of people, I wanted nothing more than to be left alone.

The wooden chair was unforgiving as I sat, picking at my nails and wondering what I was truly doing here. Debating on returning home for my stupidity, the bar maiden arrived before I could spiral into a breakdown.

She was a plump woman with a tray of ale, blonde hair shimmering with gray streaks in the light. Her eyes danced around, searching for my face under the hood. Her eyebrows rose with curiosity.

"Would you like anything?" she asked. I handed over a coin from my satchel, and she left me with a warm ale. The drink tasted harsh like sherry as it flowed through me, warming my bones against the cold night air.

Each time the tavern door opened, cool air swept through, making the lanterns flicker. I glanced up from beneath my hood, confirming it wasn't Dealla. They had to know by now that I'd been gone too long for a simple walk. When they realized I'd taken my satchel, they'd understand this wasn't just another moment of anger.

Would they let me have my night alone? Or would Dealla search and force me to leave with her? I couldn't decide which would be better.

The table closest to me was occupied by a man and two women, leaning closely together in conversation. I kept my mug in both hands, swishing the warm liquid, hoping it would improve the flavor.

"That's what she said, a Fae with black hair—" came a whisper that drew my attention. I shifted slightly, angling in their direction to hear better over the noisy crowd.

"She's lookin' for another female, another Fae, I think. Seems she's taken somethin' and they want it back." The oldest woman shuddered, her eyebrows pressed together. "She was frightening, I'll tell you that. I've never felt anything like it, talking with her. I wanted to get away from her as quickly as I could."

The second woman's eyes bulged. "You spoke with her?" Before the first could answer, the old man pitched in.

"Nevertheless, they aren't supposed to be crossin' through the woods! What's the point of rules if they think they can do as they please? We don't want them here." He spat on the ground.

"Be my guest and let her know if she comes knockin' on your door," the lady snapped, rolling her eyes as she waved the man off. "Let her search for what she's lookin' for so she leaves quickly."

"She better not come knockin'. The Fae are bad business." His voice rose as he glanced around, fat fist clenched. "Anytime any of us humans have gotten' involved in their affairs, we're the ones who suffer. Don't you remember that soldier? He married one. And last I heard, he was killed. The Fae don't think we will remember, but we do and will."

I shifted uncomfortably, wondering if this was what my mother and Dealla had spoken about. The tavern door opened again, and I dipped my head lower, still afraid Dealla would come.

Once I finished my ale, I crossed the tavern to the bar where the bar maiden stood. She gave me another hard stare, trying to catch a glimpse of my face.

"Are there any rooms available for the night?" I asked, my voice low, refusing to pull back my hood. Some villagers might recognize me, and without my mother or Dealla, I didn't want to risk questions or rejection.

"One room. Payment up front."

I paid the amount before she handed me a copper key edged with the number six and motioned toward the narrow stairs. Given the building's condition, I didn't have high hopes for a luxury room, but if it had a bed, it would do. My eyelids felt heavy, and sleep was all I wanted.

The small size of the room hadn't bothered me. A bed sat against the wall next to a wash station, holding a pitcher of cold water. A tiny round table and chair were near the window, giving a view of the village below.

Once I lay down, I punched the lumpy mattress multiple times to find a comfortable spot. After what felt like only minutes of sleep, the morning sun drifted through the window, waking me.

Strange. My mother hadn't called for me, nor did the usual tree branch scratch against my window. I stared at the ceiling, remembering where I was.

I was a grown woman and felt like I had just run away from home.

Not wanting to leave just yet, I lingered in the room most of the morning, listening to the village wake and come alive from the windows. Chatter wove together into a cacophony of noise. The weekend market must have opened. In one swift motion, I wrapped my cloak tight and tugged the hood low before stepping out.

It was mid-morning, and the market was already full. The dark and empty streets from the night before were now lined with orange canopy tents. The smell of meat wafted in the air. Turkey, chicken, and bacon sizzled atop various fire pits.

The sweet, buttery aroma of fresh-baked bread drifted past as I strolled through the street. Fabric stands displayed bolts of soft and scratchy wool, my calloused fingers catching against the material as I brushed by. Flowers in every color imaginable hung from baskets, filled vases, and spilled from wrapped bundles.

One booth caught my attention — a tent overflowing with flowers and herbs covering every table and filling countless pots. A lady stood beside her wares, motioning at the many varieties. I recognized several as the same ones my mother grew in our garden.

The scents of jasmine mingled with hints of vanilla were overwhelming. Moving further into the display, I found an herb sitting by itself, one we had an entire bed of at the cottage. It carried the same fresh, minty scent as ours, with a tinge of earth and wood. I lifted a hand to touch it.

"Careful with that one!" the old lady said with warning, her gray hair falling across her face like string. "That's Rikeroot. It can cause confusion and dizziness if not handled properly to Fae, maybe to humans too, but I'm not sure."

I glanced down at the herb. My mother had always called it Callaranth. I had never asked much of it before because she always handled it.

"What — this one?" I asked, confused.

"Yes, it can cause side effects—" she paused, glancing around her tent and lowering her voice. "I've been told that it can mute a Fae's power if they ingest it. Create a powder and dip your weapons in it, you can harm or kill them more easily. They can't heal properly with this in their bloodstream. It's a dangerous plant in the wrong hands."

My stomach dropped. We lived near the Fae barrier: perhaps that's why my mother had grown it. She could have known and had it as a precaution, but she put it in our food nearly daily. My mind raced. If this lady was right, what had my mother been feeding us all these years?

"You said you don't know what it can do to humans?" I asked, trying to keep my voice curious rather than alarmed. "Are there any effects if humans eat it by accident?"

The woman's chin tilted back, her brow furrowing as if I'd said something strange. "Eat it? Why would humans eat it? It's not grown in human land. This is a Fae plant, child. You can't find it here in these parts."

"It's rare? Are you sure this is Rikeroot? I thought it was called Callaranth?" I pressed, careful not to mention we had an entire bed of this plant.

"I don't know no plant called Callaranth, this is Rikeroot. I've only come across this plant two other times in my life. Like I said, it's not grown in human land, and this pot is enchanted. We don't have Riker Trees in our land." She raised her eyebrows, studying what little she could see through the shadows of my hood.

"Riker Tree? I'm not familiar with that name."

"Oh, it's something I wish I could see. The Riker Tree is a large tree in the Fae land that blooms year round. Light hangs from it and holds power with magical properties, but I don't know much more about it."

I nodded along, my mind spinning. We had an entire bed of this with no magical lit tree. Either this woman was speaking of another foolish myth that went through the human land, or my mother had this plant confused with another.

"Yeah, okay — thanks," I muttered as I left her tent, my heart suddenly beating faster in my chest, and my head swimming with questions.

My mother never once insinuated that it could have magical properties or that it was dangerous. She had just put it in my food the night before, claiming it had additional flavoring. I couldn't help but wonder if it was the same herbs she put in her own food.

When I arrived back at the tavern, lunch was being served. I claimed the same corner table as the night before and observed the villagers in the room. The group to my right discussed their market purchases, while a man to my left described the fabric selection between bites, grinning as he spoke.

My thoughts wandered to the cottage — sitting at our dinner table, sharing smiles with my mother after a long practice. She would praise my progress and tell me how well i'd performed. I was so proud. The memory made my pulse quicken, and something in the pit of my stomach felt unsettled. I had never spent a night away from home, not even with Dealla.

Yet neither of them had come searching for me. After years of keeping away from others and on constant alert, I couldn't understand why my mother wouldn't be worried. Perhaps she finally realized, after witnessing my readiness for her 'attack' yesterday, that I was capable of being alone while sorting through my emotions.

After checking out, I strolled through the market and headed home when the sun began to set. The marketplace excitement had faded; most orange tents had been packed away, leaving imprints in the grass and dirt. Walking down the quiet path toward the forest, I watched villagers draw their blinds, settling in before nightfall. A few late travelers crossed ahead of me, and an elderly man gestured wildly toward the wood line, speaking with obvious alarm.

"I spotted smoke rising from the woods near the Fae. But you ain't goin' to catch me goin' through those woods to investigate," the old man squeaked to another as they walked by, brushing my arm. "Sorry, miss—"

I broke into a sprint. I bolted past the village entrance and along the winding trail. My feet pounded the ground as I rushed home, praying desperately there would be no smoke.

Racing as fast as my legs could carry me, I was hit by the acrid scent of burning wood. My heart lurched, and I didn't stop. I didn't pause when gray wisps began threading through the trees. I didn't slow until unfamiliar voices reached my ears, shouting commands. My skin crawled. Gooseflesh cascaded down my arms and legs.

Something was wrong. Terribly wrong.

The cottage finally came into sight. Flames crackled throughout the forest, the yelling growing louder as I halted and took in the scene before me. Our cottage. Our beautiful sanctuary was consumed by fire, orange and crimson flames dancing skyward in every direction.

Two large men in black armor emerged from the blazing structure, dragging none other than my mother down the porch steps. With my heart thundering in my ears, I hid behind a tree and watched.

I had to rescue her.

From the edge of my blind spot, a woman — no, a Fae materialized. Her pointed ears poke through her black hair that draped down her back. She might have been beautiful with her angular features if she weren't so frightening to see. A cruel smirk split her red lips as the soldiers hauled my mother closer.

One of the Fae warriors grabbed my mother's hair and jerked her head up, forcing her to meet the female's gaze. My hands pressed against the tree bark, fingernails scraping into the rough surface. I didn't need to be close to see the fury in my mother's eyes. She struggled against the tight grip of the males restraining her.

As the female stepped closer, my mother reared her head back and spat in her face. The female's hand went up to her guard, and she nodded. I barely caught the hand movement. The slap from the guard landed with such force that my mother's head snapped sideways. The sound ricocheted through the woodlands. My mother glowered back at the female. Blood trickled from her split lip, but her defiance remained unbroken.

I looked down at my belt, remembering that I had only a small dagger. My sword was trapped in the smoldering cottage. I wouldn't stand a chance against three Fae without it.

I squinted, attempting to discern words as the soldier with the large dark eyes spoke to his companion. Both their lips curved into twisted scowls, but the roaring flames and splintering timber drowned out their conversation.

But I had to try. The years of training with Dealla and my mother were to prepare me for something like this. Now was my time to show them what I was capable of. Even without my sword. I had hope. I prepared to jump from where I hid when an arm encircled my waist while another muffled the scream escaping my throat. It took a moment before I relaxed at the whispered, "*shh*" in my ear.

Dealla.

I thrashed against her grip but could barely shift under her strength.

"For your mother's sake, you must remain silent," Dealla breathed against my ear.

But why? Why was she restraining me? Why wasn't she assisting my mother? Her friend? My breathing became rapid and shallow. I stared at my mother, and horror twisted my gut.

The female produced a vial from her leathers. One soldier tightened his grip on my mother's arm while the other seized her face. What was in it? Poison? Sedative? My mother fought her captors, trying to wrench away from the glass vial that came to her lips. The Fae emptied the contents into my mother's mouth. Before she could expel it, the guard clamped his gloved hand over her mouth.

The dark-haired Fae's laughter pierced the air, sending chills down my spine. Still in the hands of soldiers, my mother's legs buckled from under her. Her head drooped forward as if she lacked the energy to support herself. My gaze darted from my mother to the soldiers, and when I looked for the black-haired Fae, she had vanished.

I had to try to save my mother. This was my chance before they too, disappeared like the female.

As if sensing my thoughts from where she knelt, my mother glanced in our direction. My heart skipped as she shook her head, silently commanding me to stay put.

"Don't," she mouthed.

I struggled against Dealla's restraint. The moment I locked eyes with my mother, it felt brief and eternal. I watched as the air shifted and a dark hole expanded from nowhere, swallowing the space before them. Pulling my mother with them, the soldiers stepped through, and then the black portal vanished, erasing all traces of them.

Dealla's arm relaxed, and I tore myself away, stumbling. "Why didn't you do something?!" I demanded as I righted myself.

I whirled back, and shock paralyzed me. The woman, female, I saw was somehow Dealla, yet not her at all. I took in her taller frame, and the way her features seemed familiar but altogether different, sharper. Her black hair hung in its usual braid, her blue eyes narrowed. I shook my head and backed away, sticks snapping beneath my feet.

"Ellowyn—" Dealla said, her tone gentle as she raised her palms as if to calm my seething fury. "I can hear your heart racing. Take a deep breath. We don't have time to discuss these matters just yet. We need to move. It isn't safe here, and I don't know if more will come looking for you."

I knew now there was so much. more they hid from me. I had known Dealla for seven years, and not once had she ever looked as she did now.

She was Fae.

I flinched as the cottage groaned and cracked, the roof beginning to buckle under the spreading fire. In the pasture, the horses whinnied in terror, galloping frantically along the furthest fence line from the horse. Darkness crept closer from all sides, and panic seized my chest.

My breath came in short, gasping breaths as I tried to understand what was happening. The familiar world around me was dissolving into fire, shadow, and sounds. Nothing made sense as the first cold drops of rain hit my skin. My heart hammered against my ribs.

I stumbled backwards, turning, then took another step, then another. My feet moved without conscious thought, carrying me away from the destruction.

Everything blurred, unable to focus on anything else. It wasn't until I heard Dealla's voice cutting through the chaos in my mind. "Ellowyn! Stop!" That I realized I was no longer walking, but running, rain streaming down my face as I fled into the night.

I ran until my legs gave out and the tears stopped, and all I could hear were the owls above the trees. Exhausted both in body and mind, I fell asleep within a hollowed tree trunk, only to wake shivering and haunted. My world was broken and whisked into disarray in the matter of a day. My mother was taken not by common thieves or assassins, but by Fae.

Our home was gone. Dealla was not who I had thought she was. As my mind stormed into a million thoughts, I picked myself off the ground and grimaced, stretching my stiff body. The first rays of light reflected off the dew, blanketing the ground and showing me the way back to the path. Bitterness from the smoke lingered on my locks, grazing my nostrils with every move I made, reminding me of what I've lost.

Chunks of black were all that was left, smoke still rising from where the cottage had stood. Small flames brewed on the edges and near what was left of the front porch steps.

I stopped as closely as I could, the heat from the ash still hot. I fell to my knees, my hands covering my face. I couldn't comprehend my questions and what had actually happened last night. Why had my mother been taken by Fae? Why was there a garden bed full of this herb called Rikeroot?

"Ellowyn," her voice was soft as she spoke. Dealla had snuck up on me once again, but this time she kept her distance.

I glanced over my shoulder, Dealla's pointed ears coming through her black hair. "What are you?"

I stood when she didn't answer, ash falling from my pants. I saw the two horses belonging to my mother and me behind her, reins tied to a tree. Each steed was saddled with packs and supplies. Was she expecting me to go, to flee with her? But go where? I had to find a way back to my mother and learn of the secrets she kept from me.

"Do you expect me to go with you? You KNEW this could happen! You and my mother kept everything from me. Look what your secrets cost us!"

"Ellowyn." Dealla's shoulders were tense as she came near, and I backed away.

"I'm having a nightmare. I just need to wake up." I rocked back and forth, wondering if pinching myself would wake me up.

"This isn't a nightmare." Her feet shifted as if she hesitated to come closer. "I'm Fae and a guard of the Fae kingdom. I'll explain more when I can. For now, we need to move." She motioned toward the horses. "Our provisions are packed and ready. We just need to go."

I bounced on my heels. No way did I want to go with her. I hardly recognized the woman I had known for seven years. Did I truly know anything about her? It seemed that I even had the right not to trust my own mother.

"How have you looked one way but now different? Do you expect me to go with you so willingly?"

"I took my glamour off so you could see my true form. There was no reason to hide it anymore." I wanted to ask more, but she stopped me. "I'm sorry, Ellowyn. I truly am. I only did what your mother asked, as I'm a guard and must follow orders. I'm begging you to come with me. I'll explain what I can and answer your questions. I promise."

I stilled. "Your promises don't mean much to me right now. How am I supposed to trust you after all this?" I shook my head. "I'm going to search for my mother."

"You have to learn for yourself who you can and can't trust, but for the last seven years I've done everything to try to help you. I'm here to protect you." She paused.

During the time she had been with us, she had been loyal to, at least, my mother. My mother had seemed to trust her. She had kept *her* secrets, and now she knew why my mother had been taken.

"You need help navigating Fae territory. Let me help you find your mother. You can trust me just as you always have."

I pursed my lips. What other choice did I truly have? I didn't know anything about the Fae territory. Without giving her an answer, I moved closer to the horses, but then my eyes fell on the herbs in the garden, and I made my way over. If Rikeroot was toxic to Fae, I needed it.

"Is this Rikeroot?" I demanded, as I tugged on a pair of gloves and pulled as much as I could stuff into a satchel. I held it up for Dealla to see who backed away.

"Yes, that's Rikeroot." She untied the horses and brought them closer to where I stood in the garden.

"Is it dangerous for Fae? For humans?"

"It's not truly dangerous for humans. We tell humans it can be dangerous for them to keep them away from using it on Fae. It's a dangerous plant that dilutes magic if ingested and absorbed in the bloodstream. It can harm or kill."

I cut it into smaller pieces, and Dealla followed me as I filled an empty satchel that hung in the shed, then attached it to my hip with my other satchel.

"What are you doing? How did you know it was Rikeroot?"

"I'm assuming my mother was growing this for a reason?"

"As a precautionary measure. She used it when it was necessary."

"What does that mean? Who was she using it on?"

"Ellowyn, please. We need to move. We're wasting time, and it's not safe." She handed the reins to my horse, and I pulled myself up onto the saddle. I took one last look at what was left of my home. A farewell to the life that I had. The home where I had grown and learned. I hesitated, but if I wanted to find my mother, I had to continue.

As we rode north toward the border I'd never crossed, I gripped the reins tighter. Whatever waited in Fae territory, whatever dangers lay ahead — none of it mattered. I was coming for my mother.

Chapter Four

My mother had been someone whom I could always count on. When I was younger, we made a trip to the village, and I tried talking with some of the village children. They had run in the opposite direction, whispering amongst themselves. I couldn't stop the tears from falling, but my mother had been there to console me, letting me know that I was special.

I tightly gripped the reins. My mind raced, wondering if my mother knew we're coming for her.

Dealla had been like that too – reliable, caring. She'd found us food during that brutal winter when we nearly starved, given me my first real dagger, and taught me to throw it true. When my mother grew distant, Dealla listened. But now I knew it was built on lies. What she was, where she came from. Everything. How many other deceptions hid behind her concerned glances?

When Dealla's head tilted in my direction, glancing from the corner of her eye, I caught sight of her pointed ears. How had I never noticed? Anger flared in me. She'd promised to give answers, but hours had passed in utter silence. Was there any truth? Her friendship? The care she showed me? Each memory I'd treasured now felt stained, leaving me to wonder what truly had been real.

Everything was changing. The air felt different, warmer and alive with something I couldn't name. The trees were becoming thicker, and the smell of pine and honey became richer. Just like everything else, I was entering territory I didn't understand, guided by someone I didn't know — Dealla.

She wasn't the human I thought her to be; she wasn't even human.

Arriving at a small stream, we stopped to stretch and give the horses a break. While they drank, Dealla's eyes burned into me, but I kept my back to her, pretending to adjust my saddle. My chest ached from the hammering of my heart as memories of what happened flashed through my mind — my mother's split lip, the dark portal that swallowed her, Dealla's pointed ears.

When we remounted, I gripped the reins so tightly that my knuckles turned white. Questions were endless: Why had those Fae wanted my mother? She was a human who lived in the woods. What could they possibly—

"Are you feeling okay?" Dealla finally asked, cutting off my thoughts. The woods began to clear, revealing ahead the beginning of the Fae land.

"Fine, just a bit sore," I answered, but she nudged the sides of her horse, picking up the pace, and I had no choice but to follow.

"Welcome back to Madora," Dealla whispered as we went through the last section of trees and entered a field outside the woods.

Back? The words hit me like she punched me. I'd never been to Madora. My hands trembled as I stared at the open field in an impossible shade of green, full of wildflowers that glowed in the afternoon light.

Dealla pulled on her reins, and her hand went up.

"Killian," she said, looking ahead through the field. I followed her gaze to a single tree further out with a handsome male standing in the shade. I could make out his pointed ears and jade-colored eyes so clearly. When had I ever been able to see such details from this distance? Then a smile crept across his full lips.

Dealla's horse took off in a gallop toward him. Just before she reached him, she pulled the reins hard, jumping from the horse before he fully stopped.

In a swift motion after landing, her arms were around the male as he spun her, his grip tightening around her waist. I tried not to watch as I made my way over, feeling like I was intruding on a special moment.

"Ellowyn," the male said, his voice deep, looking over Dealla's shoulder as I neared. "It's a pleasure to see you again. Although, I wish it were under better circumstances."

My eyes found Dealla's. Being welcomed back into Madora, and now hearing from another Fae that I had once known him? I clenched my jaw, another reminder of how much had been hidden from me. Dealla melted in his embrace, and I felt even more like an outsider in my own life.

"I don't remember you." My eyebrows furrowed.

"This is Killian Faklan," Dealla said, her cheeks a shade of pink as Killian let her go. "He is my mate."

"Your mate?"

"Yes. A mate, in a way is what a husband is to humans, with a much deeper meaning. There is a strong and deeper bond, and when you accept it, you are as one."

My mother told me very little of Fae and what she knew. One thing had been of other creatures having mates, like soulmates were to humans. Another being with whom they believed they fully belonged.

I couldn't recall his name and wondered why he never came to the cottage. "I can't recall you mentioning him before."

Killian's eyes widened as a hand went to his chest. "I'm hurt!" he said sarcastically.

Dealla rolled her eyes and smacked his arm.

"There were many times I wished I could have told you about him," she said, her expression softening before she shook her head and scanned the open field. "Let's continue moving. We need to make sure nothing is tracking us. The Rikeroot is beginning to leave your system, and it's causing your scent to grow stronger."

My blood turned to ice. "My scent?" The pieces clicked together with horrifying clarity. "You said Rikeroot only affects *Fae*! I thought it was only toxic to fae and not humans? And my mother—" My voice cracked. "She's been putting it in our food for *years*."

Dealla's shoulders slumped as she returned to her saddle. "Ellowyn, I'm sorry. Your mother gave you Rikeroot to suppress your magic and maintain a glamour. She's been doing it for the last seventeen years. When I found you both, I begged for her to stop, but she made me swear—"

"No." I shook my head violently, that wasn't right. "You're lying. I'm human. I'm human. The herb doesn't work on humans. The woman at the market and you told me that!"

"Feel your ears," Dealla said quietly.

I was certain she was playing some sort of cruel joke as I stared at her. But her expression remained serious. Killian watched with something that looked like pity in his green eyes. My hands trembled as I reached for my earlobe. Nothing unusual, but as my fingers traced higher, toward the tip—

Sharp. Pointed. Just like Killian and Dealla.

My skin burned. The reins fell as both my hands flew to my ears. The world tilted sideways. Bile rose in my throat as my chest constricted, stealing my breath.

"It's called a glamour," Dealla continued gently. "Your mother used her abilities, combined with the Rikeroot, to hide your true nature. You were so young when she ran away. Alina thought it would keep you safe; humans outside Madora don't exactly welcome our kind, so she hid her Fae identity and yours."

"No, I'm human," I whispered, repeating to myself again, then louder, voice breaking. "I'm human!" I was imagining this. I had to be. I was having a wicked nightmare that I couldn't wake up from.

"You're half Fae," Killian said matter-of-factly. "Your father was human; your mother is full Fae."

The words hit like physical blows. I stared at the two Fae before me, trying to focus as they began to blur and spin. My breathing came in short, sharp gasps.

"We need to move," Dealla said, already nudging her horse forward. "Once we stop for rest, we can talk more."

Still reeling, I followed automatically, and only then did I notice Killian had no supplies or horse. I frowned through my shock. "How are you going too—"

He winked at me, and with a shift in his shoulders, his form shimmered and collapsed. Where once a tall Fae had stood, now a large gray wolf with shades of white that traveled from his snout to his belly padded beside us. Those same jade green eyes stared at me with unmistakable amusement.

I screamed.

"Killian!" Dealla roared, "At least *warn* her!"

The sun dipped below the hills as we moved, my legs aching from riding through the day. My hand flew to my growling stomach as if it would help silence the noise. I didn't want to be the reason for us to stop due to a queasy stomach and body aches. Nor did I know what could possibly be tracking us.

When my stomach growled again, Killian still in his wolf form, looked at Dealla, and they shared a glance. I watched Killian run further ahead, his body moving gracefully before he disappeared into the distance.

Dealla slowed our walk as we waited for him to return. I watched the horizon, admiring the land that I was supposed to fear, yet now I was traveling through.

"I think we've made a good distance and should rest for the night," Dealla said as Killian returned. He motioned for us to follow, guiding us to a small cave opening that he deemed safe. When we came to a halt, he shrugged again and returned to his Fae form.

As Dealla and I dismounted from our horses, our eyes met. Her jaw tensed as she looked away and began to unpack the horses.

I rocked on my heels, processing what had happened within the last twenty-four hours. This couldn't be real, and the anger was still humming. The last seventeen years of my life had all been a lie. How could I not have known I was half-Fae?

I had pointed ears.

A physical part of my body had been hidden from me. We had never owned a mirror, but I had always assumed it was the lack of needing one or not being able to afford one.

It was hard not to watch when Killian morphed from wolf to Fae and back, collecting firewood for our fire and fresh water while patrolling the area to ensure we were safe. A bit of excitement filled me, wondering if I was capable of such a thing. But that didn't make sense, I didn't have magic.

Magic. Why were humans so keen on keeping it at bay and not wanting what it could offer? They had forced themselves to be secluded from such a life. There had to be a reason. A reason why they feared and loathed Madora.

Killian set up a small fire and prepared for dinner as Dealla rolled out cots. I watched as they worked in tandem, like this was something they had done so many times before. Not wanting to stand and watch with a miserable look on my face, I went to my saddlebag and found feed and water for the horses.

My horse was smooth as I rubbed the top of her velvety nose. It was the first day of travel, and I already felt helpless, unable to stop touching my pointed ears.

"Ellowyn," Killian said. I gave the horse another rub before turning to settle down beside the fire.

As I took a seat on a log, Killian handed me a plate of bread, cheese, and slices of meat. The flames cracked as I picked at the plate, afraid to eat what had been offered. As the fire crackled, Killian watched, even as my stomach growled painfully in protest.

"I didn't do anything to your food, I promise," he said softly. Dealla took a seat next to him as he reached to take a piece of cheese from my plate, tossing it into his mouth. "See? I promise I would never do such a thing to you."

I sighed, picking up a piece of meat. Killian watched, his eyebrows rising as I brought it to my mouth. I dropped my hand to my lap and looked at him.

"What's wrong?" he asked Dealla, turning his head toward her.

"You're staring at her like a mother hen. That's what's wrong." Dealla said, rolling her eyes as she scooted closer to him.

Killian rubbed the back of his neck and chuckled. "Apologies, Ellowyn. Dealla cures her meat like no other, and I couldn't help but be curious about what you thought of it."

My mouth had already begun salivating by the toasty umami aroma. I shoved the piece into my mouth; I was so hungry that I didn't care how I looked.

After some time of us eating, Killian's eyes darted back and forth between Dealla and me.

"Oh, if someone doesn't say something now," he muttered, causing Dealla to shake her head.

"What would you like to know?" Dealla asked, placing her plate down at her feet as she took the last piece of cheese.

I snorted. "Everything would be a great place to start," I said, doing my best to keep the sarcasm away as I pointed to my ears. "Who am I really? What happened before I was five? I can't—" I shook my head. "I can't remember anything about where we came from and how we arrived at the cottage."

Dealla's chest rose as she inhaled, her hands on her knees as her eyes drifted toward the cave's opening, out to the land of Madora.

"I'll start from the beginning," Dealla said. "Shade Sea divides our homeland, Madora, from Ravenholde, which Queen Adriane and King Ciaran rule. They are old, powerful, ruthless, and feared by many. They believe Fae and humans should never unite and procreate and that it's a disgrace."

"Why would it matter to them if humans were on a land that they didn't rule?" I asked, my elbows resting on my thighs as I listened.

"The late King and Queen believed all who lived in Madora should stay united in peace."

"They were seen to be unfit to rule Madora by Ravenholde's rulers," Killian added, between the last bites of his cheese.

"Adriane and Ciaran saw it as a weakness." Dealla clenched her hands in her lap, knuckles whitening. "They wanted to rule Madora but always failed to obtain it."

"Until the prophecy," Killian said.

Dealla nodded slowly and sighed. "Yes, the prophecy only fueled their ambition."

"What prophecy?" I couldn't help but ask.

"There was a prophecy long before you were born that we learned—" Killian began.

"Killian," Dealla interrupted.

"She has the right to know."

"Agreed," I said through clenched teeth. "No more secrets. I have the right to know." After we stared each other down for several heartbeats, Dealla looked back at the fire.

"You're right. I just don't want it to be too overwhelming," Dealla said, drawing in a slow breath. "The prophecy involved three. Two to conquer. One to end them. Adriane and Ciaran believed they were the conquerors, and conquered they did. But being 400 years old, they were not impressed that a halfling could be their downfall."

"Two ancient, power-hungry Fae who think they were destined to rule the world," Killian said, poking at the fire with a stick. "Honestly, they sound like every tavern drunk I've ever met, except with pointed ears and more teeth."

Dealla shot him a warning look, but I felt something loosen in my chest — the first feeling that had felt remotely normal all day.

"What? I'm just saying, if I had 400 years to conquer two kingdoms and the best I could manage was terrorizing a five-year-old, I might reconsider my choices."

"So—" I paused, furrowing my brows and gathering my thoughts. "They believe that I'm the one in this prophecy? Why me? Aren't there other halflings?"

"They know it must be you," Dealla answered. "It has been nearly 200 years since there has been a halfling. You're the only one known in existence right now."

My pulse quickened. Was my night in the village fate? Even so, my mother was captured by the lunatics who justified their actions with a thread of words. I crossed my arms across my chest, trying and failing to feel safe. "They attacked Madora because they found out I existed, and that's why my parents fled?"

"Adriane and Ciaran were summoned to our kingdom because attacks on Madora were believed to be orchestrated by them," Dealla said, her face illuminated by the fire. "You were five years old when they arrived at Mystmere, your home, after agreeing to come and negotiate peace. Once they arrived, Dark Soldiers overran the streets while the King and Queen of Ravenholde attacked the royal family. Your parents took you and ran to try to save you, to give you a chance at life."

"They were coming for you, Ellowyn." Dealla's voice was quiet, each word deliberate. "The attack on Mystmere wasn't random violence. It was a hunting party with an army behind it. When I realized Alina and your father ran with you, I tried to follow, but I was attacked. When I made it through the village, I couldn't find you. Days later, Adriane announced to anyone that would listen that she killed your father, who tried to defend his family. Ten years, I searched for you both. I knew you had escaped, even if others didn't believe it."

I felt the blood drain from my face. "A five-year-old halfling. They brought an army to capture a five-year-old."

"No, to kill a five-year-old," Killian corrected grimly, then caught Dealla's sharp look. "What? She deserves the truth, not this sugar-coated nonsense."

"You were not just any five-year-old." Dealla closed her eyes. When she opened them, they were filled with a different sort of seriousness. "I was your mother's personal guard," she said quietly. "I failed to protect her then. I won't fail to protect you now."

I leaned back and tilted my head. "What do you mean, personal guard?"

"Your grandfather and grandmother were King Everett and Queen Amelia, King and Queen of Madora. Your mother was their daughter, the crown princess of Mystmere."

The words hung in the air like smoke. My lungs forgot how to breathe. The dinner felt as if it spoiled in my stomach. I covered my chest with a hand, as if it could stop my heart from racing.

If she were a princess, and I was her daughter...

Dealla and Killian looked at one another, muttering words that I didn't hear. I couldn't speak as Dealla stood and came over to me. She knelt before me and placed a hand on top of my own.

"You are Princess Ellowyn of Mystmere."

Chapter Five

*R**oyal. Princess.*

Two words I couldn't stop repeating. How could I be a princess to a kingdom I couldn't remember? Forced to forget, forced to fear what lurked in the shadows.

The next morning, my body felt heavy and worn. Moving was a struggle. The weight of such a devastating secret pressed against my chest. Seventeen years of lies, and my body was not settling into the truth well. My stomach churned, and pressure pounded between my temples.

My mother was a princess. I was a princess. Princess of Mystmere. We were the missing royals that some assumed to be dead. Now, I had returned to Madora while my mother remained captured by the two murderous Fae who plagued the land.

The black-haired Fae from the village had to have been Adriane. Searching for my mother and me, she had been so close, within reach. My mother had run from her kingdom to protect me, and I knew she would never willingly give up information about me.

The morning was quiet as we continued. Dealla made sure to keep away from prying eyes as we traveled. Killian left in his wolf form, moving further ahead to investigate and ensure our path was clear.

Silence stretched between us, broken only by the rhythm of hooves on packed earth. My temples still throbbed, and the queasiness in my stomach had only worsened since the morning.

"You're quiet," Dealla observed, her voice gentle as she guided her horse closer to mine, "More questions?"

I wanted to say no, to let the silence linger between us, but words tumbled out anyway. "How exactly was this hidden from me? I feel weak, like this has just drained me. I don't understand any of what is happening, and I'm exhausted." Before I gave her a chance to answer, another question bubbled to the surface, and I blurted. "You mentioned my parents were mates. What does that actually mean?"

Dealla drew in a slow breath, her gaze fixed on the path ahead to where Killian had disappeared through the trees. "Let's start with your last question," she said. "Understanding that will help the other pieces fall into place."

"It means they were bound — soul to soul." Dealla's hands tightened slightly on her reins. "Alina and Evander were mates, as Killian and I. When she lost Evander, a part of her died with him." She winced as if the thought of losing a mate physically hurt her. "She changed."

I thought of the way I'd seen Dealla look at Killian the night before, with a sense of security that I couldn't resonate with.

"If you meet your mate and accept the bond, your life becomes intertwined with one another," she continued, "Losing one is devastating and unimaginable."

"I don't remember anything about my father," I said quietly. "You know she wouldn't speak about him or what life was like before the cottage."

"Your father's name was Evander," Dealla said, a soft smile playing on her lips as she recalled a memory. "Killian knew him well. They were often side by side during the time before the attack. He was a wonderful man and a fierce fighter. Even for being human, Killian was always impressed. He could have easily called him a brother."

My chest twisted at his name. *Evander.* The name my mother never spoke of, and the one I had never heard while growing up. Even as my heart reacted to the sound of it, my mind remained filled with darkness, a void of no memory.

"Fine. I understand hiding this from me when I was young, if she was trying to keep the trauma from me, but once I was an adult? She gave me what you consider toxic, and you let her. What was the point of our training if I had other ways to protect myself? I thought we did it because she was just a bit crazy."

"It was one thing that felt normal to her. She practiced nearly every day before the attack, and it kept her mind from drifting. I believe it was her way of beginning to prepare you without fully admitting to it." Dealla paused. "You had such powers at a young age, and there are Fae with tracking abilities, the ability to track magical sources and pinpoint where they come from. It's a rare ability, but we were afraid Ciaran had one."

"I don't have magic, though." I put my hands out, as if magic would come pouring from my palms.

I couldn't believe such a story: I've lived in Madora. I was half human, half Fae. An old creature. And the lies and secrets that my mother had fed me? All to hide from two wicked Fae.

"It's there, and I've seen it," Dealla said. "At a young age, it can be difficult with abilities because it can be wrapped around our emotions. When you lost your temper, it didn't always end well." Dealla fell silent for a beat, looking down at her hands. "Alina didn't want to risk you being found after she fled, which is why she gave you Rikeroot. I don't know how she obtained it and how she grew it; she would never tell me. As you grew older, it became harder. I begged her to stop by the time you were a teenager. But when she noticed that your hearing, speed or strength were increasing, she would give it to you."

I slowed my horse to a walk, needing to process. "That's how she could glamour me?"

"With your magic so muted, you had no protection barrier to prevent her from using her own abilities to glamour you. She even altered your memories, which is why you can't remember what your life was like before you left Madora."

I sucked in a breath, bringing my horse to a complete stop. "I can't remember my father or my life because she forced me to forget?" I seethed, anger and bitterness growing again. "How could she play god with my own life!"

My hands shook as I tightened my grip on the reins. The anger felt different now. Heavier, like it was pulling something up from deep inside me.

"With the Rikeroot leaving your system," Dealla spoke carefully, watching my reaction. "It may be why you're feeling physically weak. Your magic may be trying to awaken, so it could be tiresome. Your memories may begin to return, but I don't know for sure. I do know your senses are going to return. They will heighten, and you must be careful."

"Yes. I guess we have to make sure I don't harm anyone, especially the one who tried to kill me," I said.

Dealla did not smile at my remark. The serious look on her face made my sarcasm die in my throat.

When you would lose your temper, it didn't always end well. The idea of hurting someone — anyone — made my stomach clench. "What happens if I can't control it?" I asked, my voice barely above a whisper.

"I honestly don't know what will happen," Dealla admitted. "You've had your magic diluted for seventeen years. We will take each day as it comes."

Great. I was potentially a ball of magic, waiting to explode and free itself after being bottled up for seventeen years. My fingertips tingled strangely, though I couldn't tell if it were from gripping the reins too tightly or something else entirely.

I urged my horse forward, and Dealla fell back into her watchful silence. The miles passed with the only sound of hooves and creaking leather.

"Where are we going?" I asked, midday after lunch. I hadn't spoken much since our last revelations. There were still so many questions that burned to be asked, but each time I tried to voice them, the pressure stopped me.

"Madora is divided into several courts. Lord and Ladies reside and maintain their section of land. We're headed to Luminara first. Lord Durin and Lady Celia were once allies to the royal family. If their loyalty remains with the crown, they may have information about your mother. We can discuss our next steps there too." Dealla's eyes searched our surroundings, her back straightening.

"Do you think it's wise to stop and trust them? We should just keep searching for my mother."

"We were able to trust them in the past. We can only hope that they've remained loyal. There is a chance they might know where Adriane and Ciaran's guards may be. If so, we have to hope your mother is with them."

Killian came running toward us in his beast form. Mid-leap, he transformed into his Fae form.

"All clear ahead. If we stay at a steady pace, we will be there by tomorrow afternoon."

Dealla looked over her shoulder at me. "We will ride through the evening. We will stop as soon as you need us to. Just say the word."

I nodded, hoping that this court, Luminara, would have a warm bath where I could soak my aching muscles. I needed a moment to escape from myself and process the thoughts of the new world surrounding me. My life, my body, nothing felt like it belonged to me anymore. I still waited to wake from this nightmare.

The air warmed as we traveled north. Sunrise painted the horizon in a beautiful shade of orange, streaked with purple and pink. I rubbed my eyes, adjusting to realize I was still on my horse with a body behind me. My head whipped around to see Killian sitting behind me, his arm around me to hold the reins.

"Good morning, sleepyhead," Killian said. I stared wide-eyed as his arms tightened to grip the reins. Dealla rode up from behind, keeping pace beside us.

"I'm still in a nightmare, I see." I muttered, rubbing my eyes again to adjust to the soft light.

Killian chuckled, handing me the reins and jumping down from the saddle. He immediately shifted to his beast form, moving ahead of us. Dealla and he looked exhausted, with dark circles under their eyes from staying up through the night.

"You started to drift. I didn't want you falling from your horse. Let's stop and rest."

Dealla swung her leg over her horse and hit the ground. Killian returned shortly after, taking the water canteen Dealla offered once he shifted to his Fae form.

"We should be arriving shortly," Killian said, after taking a swig. "We need to be careful, just as a precaution. The entrance to Luminara has a particular enchantment to keep unwanted guests from their court. If it's not used properly, you'll walk past Luminara and never know it exists." Killian grinned. "You'll see, it's fascinating."

We didn't linger long, wanting to move quickly. Madora was brighter and more alive than anything I'd ever seen in the human lands. The grass shone a vibrant green, trees grew impossibly tall, even the dirt below was a rich, pretty shade of brown. Our surroundings had been mostly green hills and fields, with occasional farmhouses that we stayed clear of.

When my legs began screaming from the constant pressure of the saddle, Dealla stopped with her hand raised.

"We're near the entrance," she muttered, glancing at the sky. "We need to walk on foot from here."

"Here, let me help," Killian said, spotting me as I pulled my legs over the saddle.

A lack of energy I couldn't explain ran through me. Mentally exhausted, worry eating at every bit of me. I feared for my mother. I had to stop myself from questioning whether she was alive. If Adriane and Ciaran were as terrible as claimed, why wouldn't they just kill her? What was expected of me in the meantime?

"Do you have any idea where they could have taken my mother? Will they—" I paused, afraid my words would turn to vomit. "Will they kill her?" I forced the question out, my legs trembling.

Killian and Dealla shook their heads as we navigated the rocky terrain.

"We don't know. There are many places they could have taken her. We'll start at Luminara and hope they know where Adriane and Ciaran are headed. Then we'll continue to the neighboring villages."

"The problem is that not all Fae can fade. Those who can often can't move far — especially with a companion. It drains too much energy." Killian said. I furrowed my brows with more questions.

"Fading is an ability to move from one place to another," Dealla clarified. "I have the ability to do so, but it's very draining, and I can't travel far when I do it. Killian can shape shift, but he can't fade."

"Is that how they took my mother?" I asked, remembering Adriane and two soldiers dragging her through a black hole before they vanished.

"What Adriane is capable of is a bit different. We don't completely understand her ability, but she can move through time using her mist," Dealla muttered.

We continued walking up the cliff, the terrain growing rockier as we climbed higher, pulling the horses with us. We moved slowly to prevent slipping. Dealla and Killian never removed their hands from their swords' hilts, eyes scanning the area, staying alert.

Time crawled as we climbed through rocks and rubble. I scanned the sky when I heard fluttering and whooshing sounds above. Heavy beats — wings? — and gusts of wind suddenly surrounded us. A silhouette appeared against the sun, diving straight toward us.

The rush of air sent dirt swirling as a winged male Fae landed ahead of us.

Golden wings spread wide from his back, matching the gleaming armor and horned helmet he wore. Deep brown eyes narrowed at us. Soft chestnut hair was visible at the edges of his helmet.

"Who do we have here?" His voice rumbled deep as his wings spread wider. He straightened from his landing, staring at us like his prey.

"We came to ask for shelter before continuing our journey," Killian answered, placing himself in front of Dealla and me as she handed me her reins. Killian was large and muscular, but this golden-winged Fae stood taller and fiercer.

"Who are you to make such requests?" he sneered, his eyes moving between the three of us. Dealla stepped closer, her hands raised in front of her.

"I am Dealla Faklan, and this is my mate, Killian. We met you long ago in Mystmere."

The winged male studied me, not dismissive yet. Unease crept over me when he pointed in my direction.

"Who is your companion that you hide behind you?"

"We do not mean to offend. We just do not know who we can trust," Dealla answered, positioning herself in front of me, her hand moving back to her sword.

"Trust? You will not tell me who travels with you, but you expect me to allow you into our court? To shelter and feed you? How could you wish for us to trust you if you don't trust us?"

I tried to keep my head high, breathing in the warm air. Would the beginning of our journey be such a failure? This was going to be exhausting, and we had no time to spare with so much at risk.

Tell him.

"This is Princess Ellowyn, daughter of Princess Alina."

His wings snapped tightly against his sides, causing a gust of wind to hit us, my hair blowing around my face. He stepped closer to investigate while Dealla and Killian moved protectively around me.

"Princess Alina and her daughter were murdered seventeen years ago," the guard said, his voice quiet.

"You know very well who I am. We met you when you were in Mystmere, and I am Princess Alina's guard. Who else would be at my side if not her daughter? If they were murdered, Adriane and Ciaran would be on the throne."

He huffed. "I suppose we shall see then." He waved his hand, and another winged Fae landed nearby. I stared at the sky to see if any others flew above us.

"Take their horses to the castle," he ordered to the newest sentry, motioning for us to follow.

"Many of the land protectors have special abilities — they can bind, fly, or shift to different forms," Killian whispered. He stayed on one side of me, Dealla on my other.

We followed the winged male, whose wings were tightly tucked against his body. The terrain flattened as we approached a female statue. Her arm stretched out, her palm facing the sky. My eyes narrowed at the statue's hand.

"Take hold," the male instructed.

The earth whirled and melted when I grasped it. Pressure crushed against my chest like I was being squeezed in a giant fist. I couldn't see straight, trying to watch as everything ended as quickly as it began.

"I suppose I should've warned you," the winged male said as my feet touched solid ground once more. My hand covered my chest, and I gasped for air.

"You get used to it with time." Dealla rubbed my back as Killian came to my other side.

"Maybe you won't find it fascinating," Killian said with a grin, "Not a way you're used to traveling."

Once I could breathe again, I straightened and took in Luminara. The rocks and sandy terrain were gone. A brick bridge extended in front of us, lined with pink flower bushes leading to a small castle. Sunlight gleamed against the dark blue roof, and light beige walls filled with open windows. Green ivy climbed the walls, blooming with white flowers. Trees hung low with drooping branches as we walked across the bridge.

Just beyond the bridge lay a small village. Some residents slowed their walking to watch us, taking notice of the new intruders in their court as we were led to the Lord and Lady.

"It will be okay," Dealla whispered. I was sure she could hear my pounding heart. "This is just a precaution for them." She glanced at Killian, eyebrows raised.

The winged Fae didn't speak as we followed. He pushed open iron gates with panthers welded in the center, leading to the castle entrance.

"Aldric, who do we have here?" a clipped voice called from the top of the steps.

The female was beautiful. She walked down the castle steps, her long, pale blonde hair bouncing in curls that shimmered in the sun. Her features were sharp, pale blue eyes studying what lay before her. Her gray-blue gown flowed up the stone steps, and jewels wrapped around her torso reflected the sunlight.

"Lady Celia," Aldric said with a small bow as the female smiled. "Intruders. They seek shelter," he answered, sounding annoyed as he looked at us. Lady Celia stepped closer, studying our state — dirty from travel and tired from lack of sleep.

"Dealla?" she asked, looking back at Aldric with a glare. "Don't you remember her from our visit to the kingdom?"

He shrugged, "I'm sorry, my lady. I do not recall."

Dealla bit her cheek, her eyes narrowing.

"Lu, could you please request for Lord Durin?"

A figure who had stood in the shadows near Lady Celia came out. She was tall with tinged blue skin. With a nod, she quickly went up the steps back into the castle.

"Come. Let's move to a private room of the castle," Lady Celia said, turning on her heel to walk back up the stairs after Lu. Aldric gestured for us to walk as he followed closely behind.

Chapter Six

Our footsteps echoed off the castle walls as we strode across stone flooring, down a wide hallway lined with doors on one side and windows on the other. Before the group reached the set of tall wooden doors at the end of the corridor, Aldric swooped past us and opened them for his lady, gesturing for us to follow in.

Gray pillars lined the edge of the walls with large filled bookcases, and the smell of dust and old pages settled over me. My shoulders slightly eased. No signs of chains or a cell. In the center of the room were dark-colored chairs in no particular order.

"Please, take a seat." Lady Celia offered with a smile. I hesitated, unsure if I wanted to comply. When I did, Dealla and Killian stood behind my chair, instead of sitting down at the chairs next to me. Lady Celia stood beside the chair directly across from us.

The wooden doors opened again, and additional guards entered, some with wings like Aldric's. Then a tall Fae male entered, his silver hair brushed against his jawline, wearing dark leathers and a sword at his hip.

"My lady," he said, bowing his head at Lady Celia. She smiled brightly at the lord who came to her side and quickly gave a small kiss on her cheek. "I am Lord Durin," he said, bringing his gaze to me. "It's a pleasure to meet you. I have once met your companions." He looked at Dealla and Killian. "It's a pleasure to see you both again."

Both gave him a small nod. Guards stood near the entrance of the room, and Aldric positioned himself by the wall behind Lady Celia. Was this going to turn into an interrogation? Lady Celia and Lord Durin shared a look before focusing on us.

There could be consequences if any of us spoke poorly and they weren't on our side. But at the same time, right now, I had a hard time knowing who I could trust. I had been lied to, and my true identity had been hidden from me. A ruthless Fae captured my mother and forced me into Fae land. What had this court done in those seventeen years? Just because they were once faithful to the crown didn't mean they still were.

"It's a pleasure to meet you. My name is Ellowyn," I said when no one else spoke. "We're looking for my mother. We've been traveling the last few days and hoped to rest before continuing." I glanced down to see how much dust from the rocky terrain lingered on my clothing and skin. I mumbled, "Perhaps a warm bath and clean clothing would be nice."

Lord Durin smirked. "Of course, a warm bath could be arranged." He raised his eyebrows at Lady Celia. "However, we must first look at who you are and why you've come to Luminara."

I hesitated. If they didn't believe I was Ellowyn Kelgrove, who would I be? Why would someone claim to be a hunted princess?

"I don't understand," I said as Lady Celia approached me, her palms up. "May I?"

"Sure?" I questioned. Was she going to pull me from the room and hurt me? Her cool hands brushed against my own. I tensed under her touch but allowed her to pull me up from the chair. Her pale eyes narrowed before she closed them. I winced, feeling a rattle through my mind, shaking it off as if it were a chill. It lasted only a moment before Lady Celia opened her eyes, baffled.

"Your memories are hidden. I cannot see through." She glanced at Lord Durin. "I've never had that happen before." She released me, and her stare went to Dealla. "May I try with you?"

Dealla walked around my chair as I took my seat, and Killian moved closer, his eyes never leaving Dealla. Lady Celia's pale hands held her tightly. Everyone in the room was quiet as they watched. Once Lady Celia opened her eyes, her hands went to her lips and tapped. Dealla stepped back to her original place behind my chair.

"What they claim is true, Durin. This is Princess Ellowyn, daughter of Evander and Princess Alina." She hummed to herself, pleased. "She's been alive all this time."

"How?" Aldric snapped, his gold helmet now missing from his head, hair pulled away from his face. Lady Celia cut her eyes at him, and he retreated to his post.

"Pardon Aldric. It's clear why. King Ciaran and Queen Adriane wanted to cease hope and try to spread lies that they killed the royal family. Not everyone knows of the prophecy and what it entails." Lady Celia frowned. "It's concerning that you may be the one who is supposed to end this."

"What's that supposed to mean?" Irritation wrapped through my words. I had just learned what had been kept from me; now a prophecy lingered above like a dark cloud.

"You are still but a child compared to some who have battled these monsters for some time." She strolled to my right like a predator circling its prey. I refused to play the part. Keeping my eyes forward, I focused them on the furthest pillar behind Lord Durin. "You do not know of your Fae heritage from what I could gather, or your power if you have any."

She walked back into my peripheral vision, turned her head toward me, and again appraised me like some trinket. "Pardon my bluntness, but what could you be capable of? I speak out of concern for my fellow Fae and others of Madora." She stopped beside Lord Durin and both stared at us.

Exhaustion weighed on me like a dozen anvils. Lady Celia wasn't wrong. How could I know if I was capable of facing the rulers who had slaughtered my grandparents and father and then captured my mother? I'd only just learned what I was. How could anyone expect me to know what I was capable of when I wasn't even sure who I was anymore?

But the way she said it — what could you be capable of — like I was a child playing dress up in my mother's clothes. The dismissal in her voice and the way she circled me like I was beneath her. Something hot flared in my chest.

"Pardon me, if I may correct you," I began, my temper rising, despite my exhaustion. The anger felt good, cleaner than the doubt, "If I'm a princess of Mystmere, daughter of Alina, the Fae and others of this land are my subjects, just as much as they are yours in this court, if not more. I will stand for what needs to be done because that is what is right and what will bring my mother home. For the last seventeen years of my life, this is what I've trained for."

My voice grew stronger as I spoke, the words coming from somewhere deeper than logic. "These monsters have destroyed the family I once had and can't remember. I will not let them destroy what is left or anything else."

I stood from my chair, nearly knocking it over as I rose to my feet. Dealla and Killian followed, flanking me. I had to believe the words I spoke, or no one else would. For a moment, the air in the room felt changed, like the moment just before lightning strikes.

Lady Celia's eyes sharpened, studying me with new interest. But her expression remained a bit guarded, calculating.

"What a wonderful speech," she said slowly, keeping her voice neutral. "Your mother could give stirring speeches too." She paused. "Words are easy, child. Adriane and Ciaran have had four centuries to perfect their cruelty. They've killed and destroyed throughout their own villages as well as Madora's. Turned Fae against Fae, witches against Fae."

She tilted her head, like a hawk examining prey. "What makes you think passion and seventeen years of human combat training will be enough?"

The question was like a physical blow. My moment of confidence wavered, but I forced myself to hold her gaze. "I don't know if it will be enough," I admitted, my voice quieter but steady. "But I know I must try, because if I don't, who will?"

Something flickered across Lady Celia's face — surprise, maybe respect. She exchanged a glance with Lord Durin.

"Interesting," she murmured. "Honesty rather than bravado. Perhaps there is more to you than first appears." She stepped closer, her pale eyes never once leaving mine. "Fine. You may stay. Rest, eat, recover your strength. But understand this, Princess. This does not make you ready to face the monsters who destroyed your family and the monsters that they can conjure. You have much to prove that you're ready, other than having noble blood and good intentions."

"What kind of proof?" I asked, though I wasn't sure I wanted to know the answer. What if I couldn't give her what she wanted to see?

Lady Celia gave a small smile, but it didn't reach her eyes. "I suppose you'll have to figure that out, once you have a better understanding of what you're truly capable of. We can discuss more tonight and tomorrow."

"We cannot stay long," I said quickly. "We need to continue our search for my mother."

"We understand," Lord Durin interjected. "Just enjoy a warm bath as you requested and dine with us this evening."

Lu entered and requested we follow her to our rooms, but I could feel Celia's calculating gaze on my back as we left.

Chapter Seven

Lu led us down a long corridor where laced embroidered drapery was pulled back, revealing open windows. Sunlight bathed the space, warming my skin. Fae portraits hung over the stone walls as we climbed up marble stairs. I inhaled deeply, breathing in a mixture of lavender and mint and trying to ease the tension in my shoulders.

Lu guided Dealla and Killian to one bedroom while mine was directly across the hall. It was more lavishing than I had ever seen before. The village inn could easily fit in the room more than once. Glass windows and a door led to a balcony, overlooking the river that passed through the village and bridge.

"I'll draw your bath," Lu said, sunlight hitting her soft blue skin as she walked through a door offset to the side. I could hear the water running as I turned on my heels to see the bathroom she had entered. When I turned again, the large canopy bed was in front of me. My hands brushed against the bedding, and my body ached for comfort and sleep.

Was Killian and Dealla's room just as nice? What had our castle been like before we were forced to leave? It had been my home for a short period of my life. I had been so young, I wasn't sure I would remember much even with my memories.

"Your bath is ready for you, Princess." I turned back on my heel to see Lu coming from the bathroom. "I'll leave fresh clothes on the bed for you." She took a small bow and left.

Not waiting, I stripped my clothes, relieved to be out of them after three days of travel. The smell of eucalyptus consumed me as I entered the bathroom and shut the door behind me. I noticed the gray-colored walls, which had gold leaves reflected through the paint. On one side of the room was the bathtub, across from a large vanity sink with a golden mirror.

My eyes darted away from the mirror and back to the tub, where the water awaited. I wasn't ready to see what stared back through a mirror. I wouldn't like what I would see, a reflection of someone I wouldn't recognize. Someone who felt betrayed, who still mourned over the loss of an entire family. Even the ones that I was unable to remember.

I dipped my toes in the tub, feeling the perfect temperature, and my aching legs felt the instant relief. The eucalyptus scent consumed me as the water rushed to meet my skin as I lowered myself in. My eyes closed, the warmth relaxing me, and I rested my head against the back of the tub. My first moment to myself since I had left the human lands.

The fresh, minty scent reminded me of the large fields we had traveled through. such beauty in this land I had seen as of yet, and it was odd. How the plants had such brighter colors and how they thrived compared to the vegetation in the human land. It seemed humans constantly struggled to survive and live, while the Fae lived wonderfully. Even the bath water I rested in seemed to stay at a perfect temperature. How was that possible?

A gnawing tug burned inside me, consisting of everything that had happened in the last few days. The dreams and wishes of wanting to grow from the cottage and explore more of the world that was around were shattered. Secrets, lies, and twisted truths, I didn't know what was real and what hadn't been real. The confidence in myself just days ago, the voice that told me to take the step away from the cottage, had vanished. I needed that strength so desperately now to keep myself together.

"Ellowyn?" Dealla's voice came from the other side of the door.

Some time must've passed. As I stood, droplets of water fell, and I glanced around for a towel, anything to dry myself off.

The mirror stared back, the reflection catching me off guard. The glamour my mother had placed was truly gone, and a stranger stared back. Pointed ears peeked through my wet hair. My bottom lip trembled. Who was I?

I looked down at myself, studying my pruned fingers. They seemed a bit longer. I raised my fingers, noticing even my movements had become quicker, finding the pointed ears once more. My chest tightened at the feeling.

"I'm in the bath," I finally called out when Dealla knocked again.

"Dinner will be served soon. We've been requested." She paused. "Will you be finished soon?"

My body would surely begin to shrivel if I stayed in longer. Although, I didn't want to stay in the bath. I would rather crawl into the bed that awaited just outside the bathroom door than go to dinner.

I didn't want to leave the bathroom, but I had a feeling that Dealla would come barging in and rush me out if I didn't leave willingly.

I brushed the tear that fell down my cheek. "I'm coming out," I called out, my voice cracking.

I took the robe that hung nearby and entered the bedroom. Dealla sat in a chair by the open balcony door. The breeze coming through brushed her dark hair over her shoulders as she faced me.

At the end of the bed, Lu had left an ivory blouse that went under the soft green dress. Flower embroidery hemmed the sweetheart neckline that wasn't revealing. The fabric flowed through my fingers toward the ground as I held it, perfect for the warm air of Luminara.

Once I was dressed, Dealla helped lace the back, and we chuckled at the awkwardness we both felt. I couldn't remember the last time I had worn a dress, and she had never helped me in such a way before. The dress brought out the green in my eyes.

"How is that?" Dealla asked as she finished the lacing. I looked over as I turned to her, realizing she wore dark trousers and a gray tunic.

"Why are you wearing that when I'm in this?" I said, patting at the fabric. There was a softness against my skin, but it didn't mean that I felt comfortable.

"I'm not supposed to look nice like a princess when I'm a guard." Dealla smirked, but then it faded. "Is there anything you would like to speak about?" she asked, her voice full of what I imagined regret sounded like as she raised her eyebrows.

"I'll be fine, Dealla," I whispered. I didn't believe myself. She winced, and I knew she blamed herself. "I wish I knew what to do and how to handle this. How am I supposed to be a princess of a kingdom that I know nothing about? The village by our cottage hated everything to do with Madora. My mother trained me never to trust anything that came from this land."

"There were awful humans in the village, just as there were wonderful ones. Madora is the same. We have our good and bad. Although I never learned much about the human queen she always hid within her own territory."

As I sat at the edge of the bed, Dealla joined me. She took one of my hands and rubbed the back side with her thumb. "I will be with you every step, as will Killian. We will serve and protect you. I'm your guard and will help you learn anything you wish to know, and we will find your mother."

My lips turned downward, shaking my head. "You're not only a guard, Dealla." I squeezed her hand tighter. "You taught me everything. How to fight, how to think, and how to survive. When my mother seemed lost in her thoughts, you were the one who was there with me." my voice broke again. "I don't remember my father or my grandparents, but I remember you and everything you've done. You'll always be family to me."

Her blue eyes brightened, and she smiled, pulling me into a side hug. "I hold you very close to my heart, and I will do my duties as your guard." Giving my shoulder another squeeze, she added. "Are you ready?"

"No." I took a deep breath, exhaling deeply. "How can we be sure that we can trust them after all this time?" I asked. Dealla may have known them before, but anything, anyone, could easily change directions like the wind. Just like my entire existence.

Feeling hurt and completely betrayed by my own blood, could I trust another so easily? I felt uneasy with what was happening, especially after how Lady Celia spoke and questioned my very existence earlier.

Dealla rubbed my arm. "It seems as it was before. Lady Celia is a very complex female, but from what I understand, she has always despised Adriane and Ciaran. To be honest, I believe many despise them. They are cruel, but they are feared."

"I'm finding it hard to trust anyone at the moment."

There was a knock at the door. "Pardon me, Princess," a voice called out.

Dealla's eyes darted between the door and me, like she wanted to say more. Then she grimaced, getting up and opening the door. Aldric waited as Killian stood nearby.

"I'm here to escort you to dinner, Princess," he said, his voice neutral as he spoke.

"Thank you, Aldric," I responded, trying to sound polite, as I felt the tension that he wanted us out of the court he protected faster than we could move.

He kept quiet as he led us down the marble stairs and a corridor toward the great hall. His golden wings were folded tightly into the curves of his back. Not once did he look to make sure we followed.

Dealla and Killian walked together a few steps behind me. Walking as guards would for royalty. It left an unsettling feeling in my stomach from the lack of familiarity.

"Can you walk with me?" I whispered to Dealla. Being between a winged guard and two others, I didn't like the confined feeling it gave.

Dealla shook her head, whispering back. "This is how it's supposed to be, Princess. You're our leader."

I swallowed hard to avoid the discomfort I felt in my stomach. I raised my chin slightly higher and straightened my back, hating the dress I wore. I wasn't a leader, but I would act like one if it meant getting us out of here and back to searching for my mother.

I peered through the windows of the corridor that overlooked the river. Other Fae walked around the village, horses meandered in pastures, and guards flew through clouds above.

Aldric opened a set of brown doors that sat below a stone arch, leading to the great hall. Our footsteps echoed through the room. Dealla and Killian continued a few steps behind as we neared a large table. Plates of food filled the center: steaming venison and chicken, bread, and colorful fruits and vegetables I had never seen before. Hunger set in. My mouth watered as I looked over the table.

Lord Durin sat in the head seat while Lady Celia sat to his right. Aldric narrowed his eyes as he glanced around the room and then toward us, before bowing his head and leaving the room.

"I'm happy that you accepted our dinner invitation. Please take a seat with us," Lord Durin said as he stood from his chair. Two servants entered with goblets and pitchers as I moved closer to the table.

I took in the surroundings of where we were. Half covered with large curtains, the night sky peeked through the room's large window. The stone floor shone, reflecting the lights from the iron chandelier that hung from the ceiling. A stone staircase was at the other side of the room that led to a small platform and a door which I assumed was locked.

The growing hunger in my stomach took over any sense I had.

"Please join us as well, Dealla, Killian. We have much to discuss and to learn while we eat," Lord Durin said. I turned my head quickly to see that they had begun to move toward where the other guards stood.

"Princess Ellowyn, please come sit by me," Lord Durin requested.

I caught Dealla's eyes, motioning for her to sit at my side. Their hunger had to match my own.

"Thank you, Lord Durin," I said quietly, taking the chair to his left.

"Please, call me Durin. No need for such formalities at all times. It can be such a bore."

"Yes, Celia for me too. I grow tired of hearing Lady so often throughout the day," she said as she began serving herself from the food at the center of the table. It was quiet. I glanced down the long table of empty seats, then began filling my plate with food, too hungry to ask who else might've filled those seats.

"What are your next steps?" Durin asked, as he finished a bite of his chicken. "We were wondering if there were—"

The hall door opened, and Aldric rushed into the room. He looked even more irritated than when he had brought us into Luminara.

"I apologize for the rude entrance—" Aldric began.

"Sorry, I'm late." A soft voice came directly behind him. Aldric narrowed his eyes at the beautiful female who entered the hall. Her silver hair was pulled half up as the longer strands brushed against her shoulders. Hair the same color as Durin's. Her gray eyes looked like a storm was brewing as she took notice of us together at the table. "And for interrupting."

Her pointed ears poked from her silver hair as she raised her eyebrows at her mother. The similarities between mother and daughter were there, with high cheekbones, but her almond-shaped eyes and hair were just like her father's. She wore black trousers and a light green tunic, a similar shade to the dress I wore.

She looked young compared to the other Fae that sat at the table. Fae were immortal, but they seemed similar in age as I looked at each of them. Now that I knew Dealla and my mother were Fae, I didn't even know their true age.

Celia shook her head as she dismissed Aldric, and he took a stand near the hall door. She raised her arms out to the empty chair at her side. "Come sit next to me."

"Delaney," Durin warned, annoyed, and she shrugged her shoulders.

"This is our daughter, Delaney." Celia said, as Delaney walked over. "This is Princess Ellowyn and her guards, Dealla and Killian."

"It's nice to meet you," I said. Delaney bowed in my direction before she took a chair across the table.

Her lips curved. "The pleasure is mine, Princess Ellowyn." She took a piece of bread from a basket. "Have my parents bored you to tears yet?"

"Delaney." Durin was clearly annoyed with his daughter, but she only shrugged her shoulders again.

"Delaney is our free-spirited daughter," Lady Celia said, her smile showing her perfectly white teeth. "She seems to enjoy getting a rise out of her father and hopes to become a warrior."

"To continue with our conversation, we requested that you join us for dinner to learn of your plans," Durin began, putting his goblet down and not looking back at his daughter. "You want to search for Princess Alina, but how do you know where to begin?"

I tilted my head toward Dealla, hoping that she could answer.

"Please, speak freely here at this table," Durin said, taking notice of my glance.

"We have not discussed it yet. We hope to do so while we are in Luminara," Dealla answered.

"What do you hope to do?" Celia asked, and Delaney picked at the meat from her plate, looking interested. "As well as the plan after you've found her?"

"After we find my mother, we can figure out what the next plan should be," I replied. Finding my mother was the only thing I could manage; I couldn't think of what it would mean if we didn't find her in time.

"Once word has spread through Madora that you've been alive after all, riots may begin," Celia began. Delaney positioned herself higher in her chair at this, listening more intently. "Others have wanted and waited for an opportunity to move against Queen Adriane and King Ciaran since they attacked Mystmere. A rebellion. Adriane and Ciaran continue to go back and forth between their land and Madora; they are never consistent with where they are or stay. We do not know what they're doing or what's happened to Mystmere."

Eyes glittering, Delaney chimed in. "My mother filled me in on what happened when you arrived. Adriane and Ciaran's soldiers will be coming for you. Others who want to stand against them for what they've done to our land may look for you too; they will want to stand and fight with you."

"Our plan first must be to find Princess Alina," Killian said. "Once we find her, we will discuss what the next course of action will be. She is the next in line for the throne. She will be Queen of Madora." He looked concerned as he spoke, and I didn't miss the glance he made in my direction.

When I looked back at Durin, my eyes adjusted, looking for a sign of mistrust. A sign that they may be hiding anything, but Celia looked at her lord and nodded.

"We would like to offer assistance," Durin said, just before Celia spoke.

"We have always supported Madora's royal family, never Adriane and Ciaran. They will rule Madora over my dead body," Celia said, and Durin flinched at her words.

I watched the lady sitting across from me. Dealla and Killian both believed that they were trustworthy. But from our current visit, I had felt belittled by their guard and put down by Celia while Durin watched. She placed her hands in front of her, lacing her fingers together.

Your memories are hidden.

"When you touched my hands and said that my memories were hidden, what was that and why?"

She looked taken aback at the question, eyebrows raising. After several days, I had to adjust, and even with Dealla's words of encouragement, I still wouldn't trust anyone so easily. For all I knew, they were only speaking what they believed that we wanted to hear. Anyone could lie as easily as my mother had to her own daughter.

"At my touch, I can see memories. I can sort through them and find information that I'm searching for." She waved a hand of hers out as she spoke. "If I know they have been somewhere or spoken to another, I can see the memory as if it were my own."

"Why weren't you able to see anything when you touched me?" I wondered out loud. What could be the cause of the blockage?

"I'm unsure. I've never touched another and was unable to see anything like you before. I have had others that could block, but as I pry deeper, I could see through cracks. Yours was a solid barrier that I was unable to penetrate in any direction."

"Could it be because I don't remember what happened to me before the attack?"

"No. I couldn't see even from yesterday, or once you arrived at Luminara. Your memories are blocked, hidden away."

From seventeen years. of having the truth hidden from me, could it have broken my mind? Caused this barrier where I would never regain memories of what my life was like?

"So, what you're saying is, Ellowyn's mind is more secure than most royal treasuries?" Killian said, giving a sly grin and looking at me from the corner of his eye. "That's pretty impressive."

There was a pause as looks went toward Killian. He continued eating from his plate without taking notice.

"You asked me for a chance to look into my memories to ensure we weren't lying about who I was and to gain your trust. Now it is my turn: How do I know that we can trust you and your court?"

"We've been allies with Luminara for a long time, Ellowyn," Dealla said, her brows furrowed, looking at me in question.

"Yes, but things change. It's been seventeen years since the attack, but no one else has tried to make a move? Why don't Adriane and Ciaran sit on Madora's throne today?"

"It's why we keep watch of the barriers of our court," Durin spoke, his voice low, and I wondered if I had struck a nerve with my questions about being trustworthy. "If you enter our terrain, our guards know from the barrier spell that was once granted to us. We know if anyone enters or leaves."

"There was one village that tried to stand against Adriane and Ciaran, and they were quickly burned down; nothing was left for the survivors." Durin took a sip from his goblet before continuing. "They fled and found refuge elsewhere. Others have attempted to make a stand but have gone missing."

"As for the throne, there hasn't been much of an explanation of why they aren't on Madora's throne, until now."

Durin looked at me. Celia had been quiet as her husband spoke, her lips pressed tightly together while Delaney hung onto every word.

And although I figured I knew the answer and it was because I was now in Madora, I asked anyway. "Why is that?"

"Your mother and you," Celia cut in. "She would be next in line to the throne. If not her, then it would fall to you. If you believe in the prophecy, they cannot be on the throne of Madora if you remain alive."

"Delaney," Durin said, raising a hand toward his daughter.

Delaney placed her fork down in front of her. "I would like to offer my assistance in your search for Princess Alina or anything you may need. I'm here and want to help protect Madora."

Dealla and Killian didn't seem surprised, but my eyes darted from the silver-haired female and back to her parents. Was this a trap or a way of seeing more of what they think we could be hiding from them?

"Why would you offer and not stay at your home?" I couldn't help but ask, being the daughter of a lord and lady, I assumed it came with duties and importance to their court.

"I've never enjoyed being confined in a court that I cannot leave the walls of. I've trained consistently for the last fifteen years. I've also studied and understand the terrain of Madora and would be more than happy to help you through it." Durin nodded in agreement as Celia pursed her lips, nearly looking as if she were biting her tongue in disagreement with her daughter.

"I've heard stories of your training and how skilled you've become in the last few years, but you've only had training." Killian rubbed his chin, staring at Delaney. "If you want to compare, I can turn into a wolf. What's your trick?"

Dealla tapped Killian's arm, but Delaney didn't hesitate as her long fingers drummed the table, brows pressed together. "I'm more than capable. I have trained with the best warriors in our court, and they have years of experience. I'm sure if Princess Ellowyn can handle being in a new land, I can handle it just the same."

"Ellowyn has trained with me every single day since I've been with her and trained with her mother before that," Dealla said defensively. "She is more than capable. I also don't see how she has much more of a choice in this matter, but *you* do."

"I only meant to get out of her home," Delaney corrected herself. "I know we're capable of this." Dealla took a deep breath, her shoulders still tense.

The gnawing tug came back once more. It was refreshing to know that Dealla believed in me. Believed that I was capable of handling what was coming. If only I could believe in myself as she did. I had to be capable of continuing. The hurt and anger I felt couldn't prevent me from finding my mother.

I would find myself again, one way or another. But even in that moment, I felt broken and in pieces.

Chapter Eight

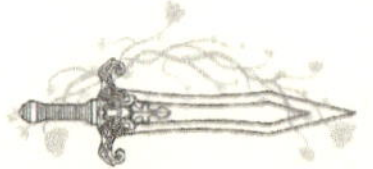

The cottage had always been warm and welcoming, but there were times I'd felt trapped in those woods. There were times when fear clouded over me at the thought that I would be there for the rest of my life. Under different circumstances, Delaney was right, I would've been thrilled to explore a new land.

Perhaps, if my mother hadn't been taken, I would have accepted it more easily that I was a princess. The princess who had been missing from her land for seventeen years. Surely she would've eventually told me? When we didn't age as years went by, there would've had to have been something.

After Delaney offered her assistance to join our group, dinner seemed uneventful. I retired to my room, exhaustion swooping over me like a heavy cloud. As soon as my head hit the feathery pillows, I fell asleep.

The next morning, I strolled the grounds, enjoying the small peace before we left. Luminara was a beautiful court. The satchel full of Rikeroot was in my hands as I twisted the buttoning of the opening. It gave me something to do as I walked through the grassy path between flower beds. So many different shades of colors.

Pinks, whites, violets, and oranges, it nearly glowed from the afternoon sun. The long stems brushed against my body as I moved toward the center of the garden. It was so quiet and peaceful, nothing like what the inside of my mind sounded like.

When I made it closer to the heart of the garden, I found Dealla and Killian sitting at a round table with trays of food in front of them. When Dealla spotted me, her smile didn't fully reach her eyes.

I released the satchel as I sat with them and began to lightly tap at the top of the table. "If we're to leave tomorrow, we must discuss more."

"Especially now that we have another companion joining us." Killian added, popping a grape into his mouth.

Dealla sighed. "Are we comfortable with her traveling with us?"

"I heard about her training while you were in the human lands. She's been working with warriors since childhood. Determined to become one herself. Lady Celia initially refused. I suppose she hoped Delaney would outgrow the want." Killian shrugged. "She's still young, though."

"Young, how? What are everyone's ages anyways?" The question had been nagging me. Neither of them looked much older than me.

"Delaney is twenty-five years old," Killian said. "practically a toddler for a Fae." Killian and Dealla exchanged grins. "We're both 160. Your mother is 155."

My jaw dropped. Sitting across from me like life had only just begun, yet they had already lived multiple human lives.

"Wait." My voice came out strangled. "Are Fae and other creatures actually immortal?"

"Not exactly. We're long-lived, but we can still be killed, just like humans. When aging stops varies for each individual, and many develop enhanced abilities as well." Killian leaned back in his chair.

"Enhanced how?"

"All Fae are faster and stronger than humans, with accelerated healing," Dealla said. "Beyond that, abilities differ. As I was telling you before, Killian has his shifting ability, while I can fade between locations. My combat skills surpass others too. And Killian is one of the best patrollers of the kingdom, as he has heightened abilities with tracking and surveying."

"What about me, being half-Fae?"

"When halflings were here, aging followed the same pattern. It's hard to know for sure about longevity since Adriane and Ciaran wiped them out," Killian said. He tilted his face toward the sky and closed his eyes.

My stomach lurched. "They were killed for being halflings?"

"Yes." Dealla's voice dropped to nearly a whisper. "That is why there haven't been other halflings in so long. Fae became terrified of risking relationships with humans. Eventually, humans fled Madora and created their own territory."

"Adriane and Ciaran are ruthless." Hatred darkened Killian's tone. "400 years of power have only fed them hunger for more. When the prophecy surfaced, it triggered a massacre. They slaughtered every halfling they could find. At first, they tried to keep it quiet, making their deaths look like accidents or an ambush that had gone wrong."

He scratched at the scruff on his cheeks before continuing, "We couldn't prove their involvement. They covered their tracks, not wanting others to know they were targeting halflings.

"Once there weren't any halflings left, Madora still wouldn't crown them. That's when your great-grandfather and great-grandmother negotiated the human alliance for separate lands."

Killian paused, drawing a deep breath. "It was rumored that a witch cursed Adriane and Ciaran for what they had done. With a curse that prevented them from touching another that resided on human lands."

My mind raced, remembering Adriane and her two guards, how they held my mother, and Adriane never once touched her. The guards had even slapped her across the face after my mother had spat in Adriane's face. Could the curse be true? Had we both been safe in the human land?

Now, in Madora, that protection was gone, and I was more at risk.

"Then your mother met Evander." Dealla added softly, breaking me from my thoughts. "A human who became her mate. Incredibly rare for Fae and humans to bond that way, but he was special."

"Then I was born, another halfling in the Fae world." A princess halfling, heir to the crown that Adriane and Ciaran coveted. "What if the curse is true? Adriane never touched my mother when she captured her. She made her guards do everything."

"There would have been a point in your life that you would've had to return to Madora regardless. They will never stop until you or they are dead, Ellowyn. I hope someday you'll understand your mother's fear, even if it consumed her." Dealla pinched the bridge of her nose. "She thought she could forget herself in that fear and hoped that if your magic was gone, you'd be safe."

Yes. Fear that built walls between us, that made her feed me Rikeroot. She had trained me, but I could've been prepared for this, if not more, if I'd known the truth.

"What about Delaney?" I forced the words through the tightness in my throat. I had to stop speaking about my mother to rid the lump I felt. "I can understand her wanting to get away from her home. However, I'm not exactly in a trusting mood, and what if this isn't the right decision?"

Killian went back to the tray of fruit in front of him. "We have to hope and stay alert as we travel."

I straightened, ready to face the most challenging journey of my life. One that would hopefully lead me back to my mother. "What shall our plan be?"

Stars glittered above the garden table when our planning ended. Hours had passed as Killian and Dealla detailed Madora's courts while I did my best to keep up with the information. Most remained loyal to the crown, kindling hope in the chest. Only Eldrest posed concerns; their lord had once been furious when my mother chose a human over his son to marry. The relationship between the lands had soured, and when he died and the son became the new lord, repairs to reconnect never had the chance to occur.

From Luminara, we would travel west to Oakwood Village, a common stop for travelers. It was the first village that resided close to the human lands and was well stocked with necessities for travelers. With many visitors passing through, the village was a hopeful source for useful gossip. If Adriane, her soldiers, or my mother had been spotted, we might come across information there.

Traveling anywhere through Madora, we would have to be careful as we moved toward Mystmere. Was I ready to see the home that I once had? Not knowing what conditions it could be in or what my life may have been like if I had lived there as a child, I found myself having to stop myself numerous times from spiraling.

We would stop when needed, travel through some of the more common villages to gather useful gossip, and replenish our supplies when we were low. Even if there were many Fae who would support us, there was always the concern of others who didn't.

I only wanted to stop when it was absolutely necessary. I didn't know where they would take my mother, what they would be doing, or how long she would last. What if we were too late? We knew nothing of what Adriane and Ciaran had planned, and since my mother was in their hands, every moment mattered.

Exhaustion weighed on me as I returned to my chambers. I'd just slipped into the soft night gown Lu had left when there was a soft knock at the door. Dealla must've forgotten something important about our plans.

I cracked the door open. Delaney stood there, silver hair braided away from her face. Her ivory tunic hung from her shoulders as if she'd been tossing in bed before she decided to come here. She gave a tentative smile as my eyes narrowed.

"Hi, Princess. May I come in for a moment?"

I hesitated, glancing longingly at the pillows calling to me. But adrenaline began coursing through me instead. Why was Delaney here?

Opening the door wider, I watched her enter and examine the vanity as if the hairbrush and mirror held secrets.

"Can I help you with something?" I perched on the bed's edge while she settled on the vanity chair.

"I just wanted to come by and see if you were ready to leave tomorrow." Her silver eyes appeared darker in the lamplight, thoughts dancing behind them.

"Yes, I believe I'm as ready as I can be. Are you?"

"This was your first time leaving home that you remember, isn't it?" She twisted to face me. "My mother mentioned some details. Are you scared? Because after what happened to Mystmere, I haven't been allowed to leave Luminara."

"I've been frightened since leaving my cottage." The admission slipped out before I could stop myself. "My mother and I...We argued the night before she was captured," I continued as if I'd opened a well and couldn't seem to stop. "I've been upset and hurt, learning about secrets and hidden truths. Then guilt consumed me for how I left things."

The buried fears crashed over me like a tide. What if that had been the last time I saw my mother? Such sorrow gnawed at my insides. If I hadn't stormed off, maybe everything would have unfolded differently. Adriane and Ciaran slaughtered my grandparents and wanted me dead. Why would they spare her? Unless they held another plan and used her as bait to lure me in.

"It won't be the last time," Delaney said, taking me away from my spiraling thoughts. Her voice carried a quiet conviction. "You'll see her again, I'm sure of it."

I wanted to believe her, yet uncertainty tightened around my throat. I didn't want to fall into that fear. I couldn't let it poison my judgment, not until we knew whether my mother lived or died. Silence stretched between us until Delaney spoke again.

"It must be difficult to trust after everything I'm sure you've learned the last few days. I came here hoping to earn your trust, to be friends." She shifted in her chair, voice dropping. "If you'll let me."

My chest ached at the word – *friend* – something I had always wanted but never had. Trust wouldn't come so easily, but she sought me out with hope and genuine desire. I wanted to believe the offer.

"That would be nice," I said after a pause.

Her eyes brightened. "Ask me anything you may like to know," she said with a smile, crossing her feet and her hands folded over her knee.

"Are you afraid to leave Luminara?"

"There's excitement mixed with sadness to leave. I'll miss the beauty of my home." Her fingers drummed against her knee, gaze distant. "But it has felt so long that I've waited for a chance to leave. Now that it's here, I'm grateful. I want to make a difference, so that we make one, and bring your mother home."

I want to trust her. I want to have a friend.

"As long as we can trust one another, I believe we will succeed."

"Yes," she murmured, voice growing hoarse. "I think we can help each other in many ways. I'd be happy to help you with training too."

Standing from the chair, she smiled, silver eyes warming. "I'm exhausted now. We better get to sleep if we're leaving early. I don't know how the others will feel if I stay up late before my first day with your group."

I chuckled, imagining Dealla's annoyed look if we both appeared exhausted in the morning. That wouldn't start any partnership well.

Chapter Nine

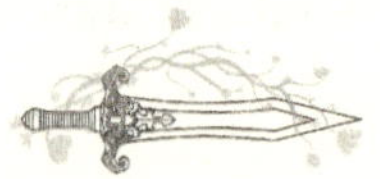

Orange, yellow, and red hues painted the sky. The colors spread across my open balcony as dawn crept through. The curtains swept across the floor as a warm breeze came in, bringing scents of fresh bread and florals that I didn't recognize. I snuggled deeper in the covers, not ready to leave the warmth and comfort of the bed. I wasn't sure of the time when someone began knocking on the door.

Wishing I could sleep a bit longer, it felt as if I hardly slept. My dreams were more like nightmares, following me everywhere; a darkness plagued through every street, every corner, seeping through the cracks of each stone and brick.

"Ellowyn, are you awake?" Dealla's voice came through the door, following another soft knock.

I groaned and pulled the blanket over my head. "Five more minutes?"

The bedroom door creaked open anyway. "We need to leave soon." Her voice held that gentle but firm tone I'd come to recognize, the one that meant no arguing.

Rolling over in the sheets, I squinted at her silhouette in the doorway. She was dressed in traveling leathers, hair braided back. "You look like you've been awake for hours."

"Warriors rise with the sun," she said with a small smile. "Get ready. Lord Durin wishes to see us before we depart."

The great hall buzzed with quiet activity as we entered. Servants moved between the long table, bringing in bread, fruit, and pastries that made my stomach rumble, despite my nerves. Delaney sat hunched over a steaming mug, the bright demeanor she had last night subdued.

"Good morning," Delaney mumbled as we entered, not quite meeting my eyes.

Killian dropped into the chair beside me with his usual easy grace. "Well, someone looks thrilled to be leaving paradise," he said, eyeing my expression. "What's wrong? Afraid you'll miss the fancy soaps?"

Despite my worry, I almost smiled. "The soap was pretty incredible."

He grabbed a piece of bread and tore off a chunk of it. "Maybe we should ask Lady Celia for the recipe. You know, for when we're camping in the woods and desperately need lavender-scented bubbles." He grinned as he popped the chunk of bread in his mouth.

Dealla rolled her eyes, but a subtle smile crept on her lips as she looked at Killian. Each of us sat quietly at the long table for some time, enjoying the cherry-filled pastries.

I took another bite, my insides humming from the filling. All of us lost in our own thoughts, I looked to the windows. The curtains had been pushed open, letting the sun illuminate the halls happily, despite the roaring nerves brewing in my gut. I listened to the birds chirping beyond the windows, giving myself something else to focus on.

"Good morning," Lord Durin's voice boomed as he entered. Lady Celia walked beside him, holding a small velvet cushion with something glinting on top. "Princess Ellowyn, I hope you slept well." They both bowed their heads slightly in my direction.

"Good morning," I answered quickly, pulling myself up in my chair, unsure what was expected of me in return. But what made me sit straighter was the servant who entered after. They walked in a ceremonial way, carrying a sword across both palms, the blade catching the morning light.

My pulse quickened. What was this? We weren't here for just farewells and breakfast.

"Princess Ellowyn," Lord Durin said, approaching with measured steps once he took the sword from the servant. I twisted in my seat to face him properly. "Before you venture into the unknown, we would be honored to equip you properly."

The sword was beautiful in a way that made my breath catch. The pommel held a turquoise stone that seemed to glow with inner light, and the dark gray wrapping on the grip looked both elegant and practical. But as he held it out toward me, my hands trembled.

This wasn't the old, dented blade that was left in the rubble of the cottage. This was a weapon meant for a real battle.

"I couldn't accept, you've already let us stay in your home," I objected, but Lady Celia put up a hand, a faint smile curved at the corner of her lips.

"We insist. It has been an honor to welcome our princess back. If you truly believe that you are capable of what is to be expected, you need to be equipped with a weapon. These items have been left untouched for too long," she said. And although the pressure of her statement lingered, I heard the kindness in her voice that was lacking the night before. "It's the least that we can do."

"I-I'm not sure I'm ready for this." I whispered, my fingers hovering over the hilt.

"None of us ever are," Dealla said quietly. "But readiness comes with practice, not waiting."

When I finally grasped the sword, it felt both heavier and lighter than expected. The metal against my palm hummed, almost warming at my touch. My reflection stared back from the polished blade, wide-eyed, uncertain, but undeniably Fae with pointed ears now uncovered.

"It's never had an owner, so you can name it what you wish," Lord Durin explained.

"Name my sword?"

"Yes, we name our swords, as there are times we can connect and channel our powers through them," answered Dealla. I turned to face her with my new weapon in my hands. "It will always answer to you." Her hand fell to her own sword at her hip. "My sword name is Voidbringer."

"The bond between warrior and blade is sacred," Lord Durin said with an encouraging nod.

Killian leaned back in his chair, still picking at the breakfast food. "I've always wondered what would happen if you picked a terrible name? Can you change it later, or are you stuck introducing yourself with, 'This is Mr. Stabby, my trusty sword'?"

Despite my nerves, I snorted with laughter. "Mr. Stabby?"

"Mr. Stabby, the Blade-Bringer, Mr. Stabby, the Beast Slayer." He grinned, "The possibilities are endless."

Dealla elbowed her mate's ribs, earning an oof. He didn't seem to mind as he flashed her a grin, and she rolled her eyes, biting her lip to hide the smile.

Lady Celia stepped forward, still holding the cushion. "For you, our daughter." Her voice caught slightly as she lifted the bracelet. Copper bands twisted into diamond shapes, centering on a labradorite stone that shifted from blue to green in the light.

Delaney inhaled, her voice but a whisper. "Grandmother's bracelet?"

"Enchanted for protection," Lady Celia said, fastening it around Delaney's wrist with careful hands before embracing her. "Wear this at all times."

"You truly believe it's enchanted for protection?" Delaney asked when she pulled from her mother and touched the stones now on her wrist.

"Yes, as long as you believe in its power, you shall stay safe."

We were truly leaving. Trading soft beds and safety for unknown dangers in a land where ancient enemies hunted for me. I had to trust the three who traveled with me fully. Dealla and Killian knew more of Madora, and I knew they would do everything to keep me safe.

"Where will you begin your search?" Lord Durin asked, his expression growing serious.

"Oakwood Village," Dealla replied. "If Princess Alina passed through or was taken through any settlements, someone would have noticed. We'll listen to gossip, gather what information we can."

It felt strange as I placed my new sword at my hip. "Thank you." I looked up and met the gazes of Durin and Celia, hoping my sincerity came through. "For everything. I know this puts your court at risk."

"Standing for what's right will always carry a risk." Lady Celia said. "But some things are worth the risk." She glanced toward Delaney.

As each of us came together, Celia bid a farewell to her daughter with a tight hug, and Durin gave her a swift nod.

"We will be ready when Mystmere needs us," Lady Celia said before we turned and headed out of their home.

The end of the bridge, leaving Luminara, seemed to hover ahead. Beyond the bridge stretched the wild lands of Madora. Long winding roads, no guards other than those who traveled with me, and no safety. It was endless miles of land and forests, where anything could be waiting.

I looked back once more at the towers of Luminara, before the distance would cause it to fade from sight. I breathed deep, and then trekked onto the path that would lead me to my mother or whatever fate awaited, that I may be foolish enough to enter. My hand held onto the pommel of the sword at my hip, feeling heavier than it had before.

None of us knew how this would end, but the rush to find information and to remain inconspicuous was what we would start with. After learning from Dealla that Adriane had creatures she could conjure, it was another gut-wrenching feeling that made me worry. A beautiful land plagued by her personal demons.

But there was still hope. Hope that roamed through Madora that Adriane and Ciaran would be taken down one way or another. When Dealla had been with us at the cottage, Killian had used the time to travel through villages. Just before my mother had been captured, there had been gossip from villagers who believed my mother and I were alive.

It was the reason Adriane and Ciaran weren't on Madora's throne, after all.

After three days of hard travel, I learned that leaving Luminara's comfort was one thing and surviving without it was entirely another. My legs ached and shoulders burned from my pack, and every evening I found myself checking my satchel for the Rikeroot, like a talisman I wasn't sure how to use but couldn't bear to lose.

The aching feeling in my feet made me regret the decision to leave the horses in Luminara. But the frequent stops for feeding, watering, and letting them rest would have only slowed our progress, and I knew it was better for us to travel on foot.

"Again," Dealla called, raising her sword.

We'd made camp in a small clearing, and despite my exhaustion, Dealla insisted on nightly training to strengthen muscle tone. I lunged forward, aiming at her left, but something felt different. My strike came faster than

I intended and had a much harder impact. When our blades met, the vibration shot from my hands to my shoulders with surprising force.

"Your hits are getting stronger," Dealla said, lowering her weapon with a concerned glance.

I tried to keep my expression neutral, even as my heart raced. "I don't think that I feel much different." The lie tasted bitter on my tongue. Every morning when I woke, I felt as if my limbs had stretched in the night. When I stood, the ground seemed slightly further away, as if I were at a greater height. Even the clothes felt tighter across my shoulders and arms.

"You may not notice it yourself," Dealla said, moving into a defensive stance, "But I can tell. Rikeroot has been in your bloodstream for years. Your true nature is only starting to reemerge. It will take time to grow used to the changes in your actual strength and power."

Actual strength. Words that sent a chill down my spine. How strong was I to become? What else would change within me?

"Again," she repeated, but gentler this time.

The next morning brought more of the same as the days before, endless walking through increasingly wild terrain. We'd fallen into a rhythm the last few days: eat breakfast while breaking down camp, lunch while moving, and stop only when someone desperately needed rest. Madora was large, and we had much to cover while we made our way.

The path we'd begun to follow had grown fainter, barely visible now in the gathering dusk. To our right, a forest pressed in closely together, not the friendly woods around the cottage, but something darker. The trees stood like black sentinels, branches so thick they blocked light from penetrating through.

Delaney had taken point again, the confident stride kept me from asking for rest as my legs began to feel like lead. But suddenly she froze, pointed ears twitching, making us stop. When she glanced back at us, she pressed a slender finger to her lips.

"Something is following us," she whispered.

The words hit like ice water. I suddenly felt cold, not even daring to breathe. In the sudden silence, I could hear what she heard. A soft rustling that didn't match the wind, but a rhythm that suggested footsteps trying to keep pace with our own.

Dealla and Killian's heads snapped toward the sound, hands moving to their weapons. My own fingers found my sword hilt, and for the first time since receiving it, I was grateful for its weight as the jewels brushed against my fingers.

"There is more than one," Killian said, scanning the other side of our path. "We need to move quickly, or they will gain on us." He studied the dark woods to our right, then back to our group. "Enter the woods, and we can split to try and confuse them."

"That's suicide." I said quickly. "I don't want to be separated."

"And that's Blackwood Forest," Delaney hissed, flustered as she held her sword. What was tracking us moved closer. Their grunts and hisses grew louder.

"What's wrong with the forest?" I demanded. I turned to look between the forest and where the noises were coming from.

"There are rumors about the creatures that reside in it," Delaney explained, the grip on her sword tightening. "Dark things that hunt in packs."

"We don't have time, Ellowyn." Dealla interrupted. "Stay close to Killian. Delaney, come with me. I have an idea. We must move quickly, so don't go too far in; we will be nearby."

Dealla took hold of Delaney's arms as she tried to object and rushed into the black trees, disappearing.

"Killian!" I whispered, fear clutching my chest as I tried to breathe.

"Move quickly, as Dealla said. Stay as close to me as you can. I'll keep you safe, I promise. Just have your swords ready," he said softly, but I could see the fear in his eyes. At least the calmness of his voice kept me from further panicking.

We moved swiftly into the forest. Dark roots snaked through the ground like veins, while massive trees stretched wildly toward the sky. They cast such deep shadows on the ground that I couldn't even see my own silhouette on the forest floor. It wasn't long before twigs began to snap under heavy feet, and a huffing noise came through the brush ahead.

"There you are, little half-breed." The voice was so malicious that it sent shivers down my spine. A gray, disfigured being emerged from the brush. It was something that might have once been man or Fae, now a twisted nightmare. I sucked in a breath. It walked slowly, elongated arms and fingers, seeming designed to slash flesh, swaying at its sides.

"We've been looking for you," it spoke again, words dripping with venom, saliva slipping from its protruding teeth.

"Well, that's unfortunate to hear," I said, grimacing at the creature's appearance as I moved closer to Killian. Lowering my voice for only Killian to hear, I asked, "Where are the others? What is this thing?!"

"A creature of Adriane's." Killian answered, his eyes narrowed as he heard another noise.

The creature was repulsive. If this was something Adriane was capable of conjuring, what was happening to my mother? We had to find her.

"You do not belong here," Killian said with his sword in hand, waving it in a circle, ready to charge against the vile creature.

The creature only chuckled as its dark eyes leveled at Killian. "There is no use for you, traitor. I'll feast off your bones when we're finished with her."

Traitor?

"Not if I kill you first, right along with the one that conjures you out from the pits of hell," Killian roared, his sharp canine teeth visible.

Seeing Killian in such a way made the hair on my arms rise.

Then it happened so fast. The creature bolted toward us. The air caught in my lungs. I clenched the sword in my hand, preparing to strike while holding in the scream that built in my throat.

Just before the creature reached us, a white beast jumped from the trees and snapped its jaw onto the creature.

Adriane's creature howled as it rolled onto the ground with the white beast. Killian reached around my back, pulling me toward him as an arrow came flying from above, straight through the creature's eye. It squirmed for a moment, just before it lay lifeless in the dark forest.

The branches above our heads creaked, and Dealla, with her bow in her hand, jumped down beside us. I looked down at the dead creature. It was hard to tell if the dark ground was made by the shadows cast by trees or the black blood.

There was another snap in the dark woods, and Dealla pulled me toward her, nearly causing both of us to fall to the ground. Killian slashed his sword, cutting a second creature in half that had tried to attack.

"What are those things?!" I shouted, backing away from the horrifying mess at our feet. The other beast that had attacked the first creature began to walk toward us.

It had a body as large as a lion. Gray eyes stared at me. White fur covered its body with brown spots around its hind legs. And white tusks extended from its mouth with teeth that looked to be as sharp as talons. Then, just as Killian had done with shifting, Delaney was now standing where the gray creature had been.

"Those are Norwags. One of Adriane's creatures." Delaney answered, wiping black blood from her chin. "There is also a creature she calls, The Sleroka, which we all should hope never to encounter."

Great. I didn't care about the dead Norwags now.

"Why did you not mention you could transform into that?" I asked, but Delaney didn't answer.

Delaney swiveled her body a second before I could make out the new noises, coming from the forest's depths. I squinted, noticing a figure that looked to be a horse, galloping toward us. "We need to go. NOW!"

Snatching my hand, she pulled me into a run, with Dealla and Killian following, we raced through Blackwood Forest. Risking a glance over my shoulder, I saw hooves pounding against the earth and dirt flying everywhere. Branches whipped at our faces as we ran, and I counted at least five figures pursuing us.

The forest edge was within reach, and we bolted as quickly as our legs would carry us. The sound was so close that I didn't dare look behind me. The wind burned my cheeks with how quickly we moved. Just as we passed the last row of black trees, I felt a breeze against the back of my head, as if a hand had been close enough to grab me. Delaney grasped her chest, painting, once we were back on the path.

I turned back toward Blackwood Forest and froze. Seven massive figures stood at the forest's edge, larger than horses, with powerful equine bodies but human torsos rising where necks should be. Their faces were stern, ancient, and watching us with barely contained fury.

"What are those?!" I whispered, my pointing hand dropping immediately as I met their hostile stares.

"Centaurs," Delaney said grimly. "We entered their forest without permission." She sighed heavily. "It's a grave insult, made worse by the fact that we just killed creatures and left the bodies. They aren't fond of Fae. Now they have another reason to hate us." She shook her head.

It was hard not to remain on high alert as we continued, but something felt different.

Adrenaline still pumped through me, tugging at my chest. It was different from what had just happened, the near excitement and horror residing. I couldn't quite figure out what I felt, as if I were only waiting for something else to happen.

"Wait, stop." I finally whispered. I took a drink from my canteen, hoping the feeling would pass and my chest would calm.

I was afraid to stop for the evening after what had just happened.

"What's the matter?" Dealla asked, looking in every direction. Even she was on high alert.

"Something just feels off. I don't know how to explain it." I looked down our dark path. "I don't think we're alone."

Dealla exchanged glances with Delaney and Killian.

"We can scan the area," Killian said, looking at Delaney. "In our beast form, we can cover the space quickly."

Dealla shook her head. "Let's continue together for now. Stay alert." She gripped her sword at her hip.

We continued through the night, the odd feeling growing with each step. The moon provided our only light, casting silver reflections on a river that meandered alongside our path. Exhaustion weighed on all of us, but none of us felt safe.

The sensation I couldn't name pulled at my consciousness, like a thread being tugged deep in my chest. It wasn't the same as the fear I felt from the creature or the adrenaline from our escape. This felt like ... anticipation? Recognition?

"Something seems wrong," I whispered, stopping so suddenly that Killian nearly ran into me.

The others halted, hands moving right to their weapons. In the distance, quietly and closing in, footsteps. A presence that made the air itself feel charged.

"GET DOWN!" a powerful male voice roared, echoing over the hills, sending chills through me. I turned to see a hooded figure with a hand stretched out in front of him, just as my peripheral vision caught sight of another disfigured creature running at high speed.

Delaney, Dealla, and Killian crushed against me, using themselves as a cover to protect me as we fell to the ground. A horrifying shriek rang out, not from pain, but from something deeper. Agony.

The gray creature withered on the ground. My heart pounded between my ears as I realized it was being consumed by flames from the inside out. Its screams lasted far longer than necessary before it finally collapsed, smoking and silent.

The three jumped off me quickly, swords drawn. The male who had shouted approached with measured strides, unhurried despite the chaos. The tugging sensation I had felt moments before faded, replaced by something else – a prickle of unease.

"At last," he said, pushing his hood back with an air of impatience. "Do you have any idea how tedious it has been tracking you lot?"

I may have stumbled over if Dealla and Delaney hadn't stood so close. My heart raced, but not entirely from fear. He was stunning in a way that seemed almost unfair. His dark hair fell past pointed ears, and his piercing blue eyes reminded me of winter glaciers. He towered over me, his broad shoulders filling the leathers beneath his dark cloak. There was something sharp about his expression, something that made my skin prickle, even as I found myself staring.

"Ivarison," the voice from one of the others spoke harshly.

Ivarison.

Ivarison.

Why did that name tug at something in my memory? Why did he smell like ember and petrichor?

"Dealla. Killian." His tone was flat, almost bored. "And you must be Delaney of Luminara." His gaze swept over us dismissively before settling on me with uncomfortable intensity.

"Why were you tracking us?" Dealla demanded, sword still raised. Her shoulders were rigid with tension I'd never seen before.

Ivarison's mouth curved in something that wasn't quite a smile. "Word travels fast when a hidden princess surfaces. The princess's capture wasn't exactly subtle. Rumors have been traveling." His tone held an edge that made me flinch. "I've been following your trail because someone needs to keep you alive long enough to be useful."

Useful. That word stung.

"Useful for what?" I asked, finding my voice despite the way he looked at me. Did he know who I was?

"For ending this war, obviously." He spoke as if I were slow, and yet his voice sounded like velvet. "Unless you'd prefer to let Adriane keep torturing your mother while you stumble through Madora killing Norwags."

"Why would we trust you?" Killian growled, his grip tight on his sword.

Ivarison let out a sharp laugh. "Trust me or don't. I'm not here to coddle your feelings or earn your approval. But those creatures won't stop coming, and clearly, you need someone who can kill them efficiently." His eyes flickered to the smoldering corpse. "Though that took far longer than it should have."

"You arrogant–" Killian started forward, but Dealla's hand shot out to stop him.

"I don't believe I need to justify myself to any of you," Ivarison continued coldly. "Except perhaps–" His gaze returned to me, and something in his expression shifted, not exactly softer, but less cutting. "I'm Ivarison Miralen. Lord of what is left of Wildhaven, before Adriane destroyed my home."

"Oh, I-I'm Ellowyn," I managed to say, hating how I sounded like a nitwit.

Ivarison glanced sidelong at Dealla and Killian, raising his eyebrows as Delaney kept her stance near me.

"You mean Princess Ellowyn," he corrected, stepping closer. "Although, I'm not sure it's safe for you to be out in the open like this." He took my hand before I could react. If my heart raced any faster, I was sure it would be gone from my chest. His calloused fingers were rough against mine. When he pressed his lips to my knuckles, a soft zap.. Magic? – attraction? – shot up my arm.

He released my hand quickly, as if he felt it too, his jaw tightening.

"Just Ellowyn." I breathed.

"We don't need your help," Dealla said, her voice deadly calm. Too calm for my liking at this moment. "We've managed fine."

"Have you? Because from what I've seen, you've been stumbling from one disaster to another. Blackwood Forest? Did none of you consider that entering Centaur territory might have caused a complication?"

Who was he to accuse of naivety?

"How long have you been following us?" I asked, unease crawling down my spine.

"Long enough," His tone was maddeningly vague. "You're moving too slowly, making too much noise as you move–"

"Enough," Dealla snarled, cutting him off.

Killian sighed as he moved closer to Dealla, "We need to continue and do not have time to waste." He lowered his voice, but not enough that I couldn't hear. "His power could be useful."

"We could use the help," I added, ignoring Dealla's sharp look. "We don't even know if my mother is.." I trailed off.

"We have to hope that she is alive." Killian said. He touched my arm, giving it a gentle squeeze, but the comfort was not enough to soothe my thoughts.

For the first time, Ivarison's expression softened slightly. "She's alive. They won't kill if they plan to use her as bait to lure you in."

So, I wasn't the only one who thought it.

"How would you know that?" Killian asked suspiciously.

"Because it's the oldest trick in the book. And they're old." His words came out flat. "If you want to reach Princess Alina before they decide otherwise, you'll need all the help you can get."

Dealla stared at him for a long moment, her jaw working. "Fine. But I'll be watching. One wrong move–"

"You'll try to kill me, yes. I'm terrified." Ivarison rolled his eyes; his sarcasm was cutting. "I'm sure you could if you truly tried, but I'm not the enemy here. If you're done being dramatic, we should keep going."

"You were once a concern, and I have not forgotten that," Dealla snarled, not taking her eyes away from him. "Let's move."

As we began our journey again, the tension was suffocating. Dealla positioned herself where she could watch Ivarison, who seemed utterly unbothered by her hostility. In fact, he almost seemed amused by it.

Delaney's eyebrows furrowed as we stared at each other and then at Ivarison.

"What concerns did he cause?" I whispered to Delaney as we fell into step.

She shook her head, eyes troubled. "I don't know, but for her to act that way, whatever he did.." she trailed off, glancing toward Ivarison's broad back. "We just need to be careful, Ellowyn."

I nodded, but I couldn't shake the memory of that jolt when he'd touched my hand, or the way his harsh expression had softened just for a moment when he looked at me.

He was beautiful and dangerous. The worst possible combination.

Chapter Ten

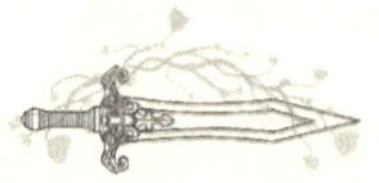

The question of when to stop weighed on all of us. After facing two Norwags and Ivarison killing the third, tension was high. When adrenaline drained out of me, and my eyes grew heavy, we finally stopped.

"I'll take first watch," Dealla said, even though, in the dark, I could see her glancing at Ivarison. Killian offered to take second to make sure Dealla rested.

Each of us pulled our cots out, Delaney settling on my left, while Ivarison began to set up on my right. Killian ignited a small campfire, warming some meat for us to eat quickly, before getting some sleep. With one final bite of his food, he shifted into his gray wolf form and circled the area once before coming back to rest.

Each faint sound of twigs snapping, the fire crackling, or animal noises that came from the nearby woods had us jolting to check and ensure we weren't under attack.

When I finally went to my cot, Delaney quietly moved into hers, shifted around, and closed her eyes. I took one more look at our new member of the group, who was moving into his own cot, when Dealla moved in. Putting herself between us, she stared off at the horizon. Her watch began.

Each time I drifted off to sleep, the fear of being under attack came in nightmares. The sight of the horrid creatures chased me, their sharp teeth leering above my throat, waiting to feast. When creatures didn't come after me, it was a black mist. It invaded every escape I tried to take, wrapping itself around my body and choking the life out of me.

I jumped awake, still feeling that mist around my throat. I took a deep breath and loosely grabbed my throat to ensure nothing was constricting me. Morning was creeping in. Killian sat nearby on watch, glancing over his shoulder to where Dealla slept between Ivarison and me.

When everyone woke, we began our journey. The dewy grass brushed against my boots. Delaney stayed close to my left, Dealla and Killian following behind us, while Ivarison stayed ahead to the right of me.

They hovered over me, waiting for a potential ambush. I felt trapped, feeling claustrophobic with the way they kept me surrounded. With each shift I made, they were just a shadow away. I often had to pry my eyes away from Ivarison, who hadn't spoken since the night before.

What had he done to make Dealla so on guard? How could Adriane conjure the monsters that had tried to attack us? I couldn't stop thinking of those sharp teeth and the odd-colored skin when I remembered Delaney attacking in a form I hadn't known of.

I inched my way closer to her, "So, back to my question from yesterday. You can shift into a panther?" I hoped the topic could keep me from thinking of the Norwag's saliva dripping from its sharp teeth.

"Similar to a panther, yes. My shifting abilities came from my father." Her eyes rolled as she said. "He can shift, but his form is just a bit different and larger than mine." She lifted her hand, claws of her beast form protruding from her knuckles. Her smile broadened as my eyes widened.

"That's incredible," I mumbled. I looked at my own hand, as if claws would start coming from my own, wondering how it would feel to have such an ability.

Luminara's warmth gave way to cooler air, the sky turning gray as clouds gathered overhead. I crossed my arms over my chest, rubbing my forearms for warmth, when something in the sky caught my eye. High above in the distance, something massive was flying.

"What's that?" I asked. My eyes burned from lack of sleep as I tried to make out the shape.

The rest of the group looked up, Delaney sharply inhaled.

"Dragon," Ivarison replied. My eyes darted from the clouds to him. This was the first time he'd spoken since he found us. "There aren't many left in Madora anymore. Another problem that Adriane and Ciaran caused. Nearly extinct because she only wants her own creatures lurking." He paused as he watched the dragon, and before I refocused my gaze on the dragon, Ivarison looked directly at me. "I'm sure because of that, dragons wouldn't hesitate to turn on us if you went too close."

Suddenly, the fascination of the dragon came crashing down at the chance of being a meal for one. It was almost more terrifying now as I watched the dragon fly through the clouds and disappear.

If dragons were near extinction, what did it mean for me to see one? If I were the last known halfling to be in existence, was this a bad omen?

For the remainder of the afternoon, I stumbled over my own feet, combing the sky for the dragon again.

CLASH.

Dealla's sword came hard against my own, nearly missing to block her hit. After having Killian and Delaney watching, now I had to get used to the dark-haired male who watched. He sat nearby, his feet crossed. My cheeks heated, noticing his eyes were trained on my every move.

I didn't want to be watched. I wanted to focus on the practice without him judging every movement.

"That's good for today," Dealla said, barely out of breath. She sheathed her sword, and I walked over and grabbed my water canteen. Sweat beaded my brow, and I was thankful I could relax.

The fatigue I had felt before Luminara was less of a hindrance the last few days of travel. Feeling more energized than the day before made me wonder how long I could keep being who I thought I was. There hadn't been a moment when I felt ready to accept whatever power lingered beneath my skin. It was hard enough to accept what my mother had taken from me.

"Why don't you practice with magic?" Ivarison asked, as if he heard some of what I was thinking. I hesitated, but then relaxed, realizing his head was tilted toward Dealla.

After glaring at him for a long moment, Dealla admitted. "We've never worked with magic."

He leaned back and narrowed his eyes. A deep blue light danced across his fingertips.

"What do you mean, you haven't worked with magic?" he asked, his voice grave as he stood, the blue magic flaring a bit brighter. "You've never worked with magic to help teach her, or she hasn't shown them to you?"

"I don't have magic," I said simply, rolling my shoulders and placing my sword back into its scabbard.

Dealla opened her mouth to object, but Ivarison cut her off.

"Of course you would say that. Denial is easier than responsibility," Ivarison said incredulously. "When you were only a child, I heard of the potential you showed. You're the daughter of Princess Alina and granddaughter of King Everett and Queen Amelia. Their power runs through your veins."

Delaney and Killian crept through the campsite to prepare the cots for sleep. They both lingered only for a moment before stepping away, hesitation in their steps as if they couldn't decide if the conversation needed to be interrupted.

"If you must know, Princess Alina gave her Rikeroot during their time away," Dealla confessed. "She glamoured and hid everything from Ellowyn. She didn't know who she truly was."

Ivarison's brows rose the more she shared, and I wondered just how far they would go before he spoke with disbelief. "This entire time they were missing, she forced her to forget her kingdom? Her powers? Everything?" He closed his eyes, taking a deep breath to calm himself, his blue magic shifting around clenched fists. "Seventeen years of Rikeroot and coddling. Remarkable that you can even hold a sword."

"It doesn't matter how you feel about this," Dealla spat. "What's done is done. Alina did what she believed was best for her daughter. At least she still trained every day."

"It would have been beneficial to prepare her for what is inevitable." Ivarison paced the ground like her mother would when listening to things that needed to be done. "Train her, teach her to control her magic and the abilities she has. In her state, she might as well be thrown into the battlefield like a snack to a beast."

I rubbed my temples, glaring down at the jewels decorating my sword. Looking over, Killian and Delaney had stopped setting up camp to listen.

Dealla scoffed, "Oh?" she folded her arms across her chest, a challenge blazing in her blue eyes. "I suppose you would know what it's like to be fodder."

"Enough!" I snapped loudly, my arms crossed over my chest as irritation burned within me. Their bickering was the last thing I wanted to listen to.

Dealla and Ivarison went quiet, the tension between them still crackling. Dealla looked stricken, as if she had just realized she was making decisions about my life without including me.

"I train with her as often as we can so that never comes to pass," Dealla started as she glanced at Killian and then back at Ivarison. "I can already tell that her strength is increasing. When her magic manifests, we will work with it."

I pursed my lips. It felt wrong not to mention the warmth that flowed through my body, but I was scared. Still trying to grow used to feeling stronger and faster, I could not deal with something new. Something different about myself. Not yet.

"Your magic is limited, Dealla. I can help her." He peered over at me. "If you would allow me."

My cheeks heated, betraying me again.

"Absolutely not," Dealla snapped, her teeth flashing at him as she stepped between us. "I've seen what your magic does. I do not want you near her. I'll find someone else if needed."

"It is by her choice. Not yours, Dealla. It would be wise to remember that."

I stepped away as Killian moved closer. There had never been a time that I had seen Dealla act or speak in such a way to another. Her sharp canine teeth were drawn out as if she would rip him apart. She was frightening. Yet, her anger did not faze Ivarison, who rolled his eyes, smirking at her.

"You've turned a potential weapon into a liability. Congratulations." He turned back to look at me. "I'll be here to assist when you're ready. It's not easy to control power when you don't understand and know how to, or when you're being caged." He glared at the rest of the group as he spoke the last bit.

My eyes darted between Dealla, whom I had known for nearly a decade, and Ivarison, the Fae I had only just met with powers that could burn a creature from the inside out. Dealla only wanted to do what she thought was best, and I didn't want to disrespect her wishes. But would it be wise to turn away help when we needed it most to find my mother?

I swallowed, saying my next words with extra care. "*If* I manifest magic, I will be the one to make the decision."

Ivarison bowed his head, and Killian murmured words to help cool Dealla. I turned and plopped beside Delaney, who offered a comforting smile, remaining quiet. Gazing up to the night sky, I wondered about Ivarison's powers and the history Dealla and Killian seemed to know. What had he possibly done that made Dealla so skeptical about trusting or not wanting to speak with him?

Dew glistened at the hilltop where we stopped to rest. Oakwood Village stood quiet and calm below, the morning sun peeking over the horizon and casting the roofs in a yellow glow. Agreeing it would be suspicious if five travelers roamed the empty streets, we waited till the village woke and the streets filled with others.

"Pull your hood up, Ellowyn. I don't want to take a chance of someone mistaking you for your mother," Dealla said, just before we entered the village. She looked at our surroundings as I did what she asked.

Crossing the distance with wariness and excitement, I looked up to the tall, tan homes and shops lining both sides of the road. Ivy hung down the brick buildings, and windows were cracked open. I inhaled, the smell of baked goods whirling around.

"Oh, something smells delicious," I muttered, Delaney nodded in agreement, inhaling the scents.

"Stay close together," Dealla muttered, her lips pursed.

I only nodded, looking over the tents of clothing that shone and shimmered. Dazzling beads that looked as if they held enchantments as they reflected from the morning light. My eyes were widening at the small creatures that were being carried in the arms of others. The white fur poking out, with their large, pointed ears and noses. The creatures I had seen in Madora were so different compared to the farm animals I had seen in the human lands.

Continuing further down the street, I realized it was full of Fae. Pointed ears that came through hair and hats. I felt my own pointed ears, still feeling so mundane. My walk slowed as we walked the stone street, passing other Fae with bluish green skin, similar to what Lu had.

Then I stumbled, looking down to the ground to see a scaled tail. Shades of vibrant blues and purples, and as my eyes followed to see where it came from, I did a double-take. One of the Fae, with bluish-green skin, had a tail that hung from under a dress.

"Oh, I'm sorry," I said from under the cloak.

Delaney tugged on my cloak to pull me away as the Fae walked off. "Stop staring," she hissed, a smirk playing on her lips. "They won't enjoy being watched. They are called Scaletails. They travel through the lakes but live in the ocean."

There was so much to see of Madora, so much more to learn.

Delaney continued at my side as we continued through the village. Dealla was in front as Killian and Ivarison walked behind. Ivarison kept the hood of his own cloak over his head, covering his face.

"Delaney," I whispered, after checking that the other three were a bit further away from hearing and using the street's growing noise to drown out my voice. "Do you know anything about Ivarison or why Dealla and Killian don't seem to like him?"

Delaney jutted her lips out, thinking. She leaned in to whisper. "I don't know what it is between the three of them, but I heard the gossip that runs through Luminara that something happened between Adriane, Ciaran and him. Something terrible that they were angry enough to destroy his home and land." She dropped her voice so low, I had to step closer. We were so close, I could feel her breath against my skin. "You saw what he could do. He is capable of destroying someone with a snap of fingers; he isn't someone to provoke."

I glanced back at Ivarison, and although I couldn't see his face, his hood was in my direction. I quickly turned as we hushed, not daring to speak of anything more, in fear that he was listening. I learned how terrible Adriane and Ciaran were. What had he done that caused them to attack him?

We drifted through the village, splitting apart and regrouping as we listened to others as they gossiped. I caught fragments of conversation, crops not growing quickly enough, shadows that lingered on the edges of a forest in the west. The entire time, someone from our group remained close, a silent reminder that I was never truly alone.

The afternoon sun was already slanting low when hunger drove us toward the small tavern at the heart of the village. The moment we walked through the arched door, warm air hit us, thick with the scent of roasted meat, ale, and unwashed bodies.

We squeezed around a table barely meant for four. Ivarison and Killian looked like giants crammed into children's furniture, their broad frames making the wooden chairs creak ominously. I bit my lip to hide a grin at the look on them as I found myself wedged between Delaney and Ivarison. Hyperaware of how his presence seemed to take up more space than physics should allow.

The stew arrived steaming, and I wrapped my fingers around the warm bowl, letting the heat chase away any chill that settled in my bones. As we ate in silence, I looked around the tavern that buzzed with life; merchants arguing with one another over prices, farmers complaining over the weather, and a couple clanking their glasses of ale together.

For the first time since Ivarison joined, Dealla looked at ease. Her shoulders dropped as she leaned into Killian's warmth, her constant furrowed brows softening as she spoke quietly with him between her bites. As he stole glances at Dealla, his lips twitched upwards. I felt a pang of something, envy, maybe, for never having that sort of feeling with another.

Ivarison took glances around the tavern. My arm brushed against his as he had turned, still hiding under his cloak.

"Careful, you'll spill the soup." Ivarison's voice was barely a breath against my ear as he had shifted to scan the room. His arm brushed mine, and I swore I felt sparks where our skin touched. 'You're staring."

Heat flooded my cheeks, and my entire body burned. "Sorry," I whispered back, then immediately wondered why I was apologizing in the first place.

Delaney picked at her plate, her gaze toward the ceiling as her head tilted, clearly listening to our exchange with interest.

Ivarison went still beside me, the casual survey of the room sharpening into focus." Killian," he muttered, so quietly I almost missed it. "Back corner. We have company."

Each of us tried not to look at once.

At the corner of the room, a male sat at a table alone and watched us. His arms rested on the table, fingers tapping. For being Fae, he looked older than those surrounding him. The sun came through the window, his brunette hair glistening with white.

"Let's go," Killian whispered. "If he wants something, he will follow."

"Wait, what if this is a trap?" I asked, hesitation in my voice. What if this Fae was a soldier of Adriane and Ciaran? We needed to find information about where my mother was, but we couldn't risk walking into anything without a plan.

"Don't worry, we will be careful, but we must see if he knows information that we could be searching for." Dealla answered. But my heart was pounding.

Our chairs slid against the floor. I looked at the table one last time before we walked through the exit to find that the male had vanished. The streets were still crowded, and instead of continuing through, Killian guided us toward an empty alley that went to the back of the tavern.

Killian knew well. As we moved around the corner, the Fae male leaned against the brick wall, waiting. His arms crossed over his torso with his head tilted as he watched us approach.

"I know who you are." His voice was raspy, and I didn't like the way he pointed a finger toward Dealla and Killian. He didn't look so threatening now that I had a better look. His clothes were tattered on his slim body, and I wasn't sure he would make it through any sort of battle if he tried to fight any of us. "I'd been in Mystmere when the attack happened all those years ago. I saw you two slaughtering sentries."

"What do you want?" Killian demanded, gripping his sword's hilt.

None of us moved, waiting for what the male planned.

Was he foolish to try to attack? I stepped forward, wanting to stand near Dealla and Killian if this male was going to try anything. The hood of my cloak slipped, revealing my face. The male's face lit, as if he had just seen the greatest gift he could have been blessed with.

"I heard a rumor that Princess Alina was finally captured." He pushed off the tavern wall, stepping forward. "You have to belong to her, girl. You look just like her." he sneered, that finger now pointed toward me.

My throat tightened as I swallowed. He knew my mother had been captured; did he know more? I wanted to ask, but as Dealla slipped in front of me, a voice came from behind.

"If you have information you wish to share, speak now before I cut out your tongue," Ivarison snarled.

Killian moved in, as if waiting for the male to make his first move.

He chuckled, unafraid. "From what I understand, she won't see daylight where she's headed. Shame really."

"Tell me where they are taking her." I stepped forward, brushing off Delaney's hand. I reached for my sword, and a wicked grin split on his lips. "You will be rewarded for information."

Did I have anything to give at this moment? No, but he didn't know that. The old Fae shook his head lazily, putting his hand up in a mock surrender.

"I have no energy to attack you, girl."

"A token for a location," Ivarison offered, though it sounded more like a command than a suggestion.

The Fae picked at his fingernails, as if this conversation dulled his mood, and sighed. "Some of her Dark Soldiers passed through the outskirts of the village just days ago. Looked to have her locked up, so good luck." He looked up with a sneer painted on his features, and I knew he was lying or withholding information.

Before I could ask, there was a jangle at my side. "And what else?" Ivarison snarled, holding the bag of tokens loosely in his hand.

The Fae grinned, and I could see now that one of his canine teeth was missing. "They were headed toward Whiterun Village."

Two tokens flew across the alleyway from Ivarison. "Be gone and forget you saw us here." he said. The male caught it mid-air and disappeared, rounding the corner.

Away from the alleyway and into the village streets, the crowd began to disperse. I didn't trust the information the Fae had given us. I had seen in his beady eyes that he knew more than what he told us. If he had seen soldiers, had my mother really been with them?

"How do we know we can trust that information? There was something not right with him." My hands were restless as I broke a twig off a tree we passed, breaking it into small pieces in my palms.

"Oh, what do you mean? He looked trustworthy enough," Killian said, raising his eyebrows with a small grin. "We could at least travel to Whiterun Village to see if we can spot anything," he said, turning more serious.

"We're chasing ghosts based on rumors from villagers that may or may not be trusted. This is such an excellent plan," Ivarison said, annoyingly, under his breath.

"We won't know unless we try. This could mean we are getting closer to finding her," Dealla said, gripping my arm lightly and giving me an encouraging squeeze.

I sighed, looking up to see Ivarison watching me as his hood came partially down. I bit my lip, unable to say anything as he lifted an eyebrow.

Chapter Eleven

Dawn crept across the hills in gray whispers. Fog clung to the ground. We slipped from Oakwood Village's inn while the streets were empty, our footsteps muffled on wet cobblestones.

She won't see daylight where she's headed. The informant's words haven't stopped ringing in my mind since yesterday. Whiterun Village – our only lead, our only hope.

The path ahead wound through a grove of twisted oaks, their branches reaching like gnarled fingers. I was scanning the tree line when I saw him.

The odd male that gave us our only source of hope. Leaning against a tree like he was waiting for us. My hand shot out, stopping Dealla mid-stride. "Wait." My voice came out sharper than intended. "It's him, the Fae from yesterday."

Four pairs of eyes followed my gaze. The informant's lips curled into a sly smirk. He touched two fingers to his forehead in a mock salute, then waggled them in farewell.

"Princess," he called out, his voice carrying easily across the morning stillness. "It would seem the soldiers suspected someone would be in search of their prisoner. They offered more than two simple tokens." He hefted a bag of what I assumed to be gold.

My stomach dropped. "It's a trap."

I knew it. I said over and over to myself, maybe this is what my mother had always meant when she said you couldn't trust anyone in Madora.

Black armored guards appeared from behind trees. A dozen. Maybe more.

"I should have killed him," Ivarison snarled. Blue magic sparked along his fingertips, and shadows began bleeding from his skin like smoke.

"Ellowyn, I know you're capable, but I don't want to take any chances. Stay behind me," Dealla barked, already drawing her sword. "Killian, left flank. Delaney, right. Ivarison–"

"I know what to do," he cut her off, darkness coiling around him.

She scowled at him, looking back at their assailants. "Protect your princess."

Nerves settled in my stomach, my breakfast turning sour. Each of them circled me, swords in hand. There were more than a dozen soldiers.

Then they charged.

Delaney moved like liquid silver, her blade singing as it cut through the air. The first soldier's scream was cut short as her sword went in between his armor. Blood sprayed across the grass, and she was already spinning toward another.

Ivarison didn't bother with his sword at his hip. He raised his left hand, and black shadows lashed out from him. The soldiers it touched suddenly dropped in front of him, their bodies twisted in ways that made my stomach heave, then crumpled to the ground, lifeless.

What kind of magic could do that?

Steel rang against steel as Killian and Dealla fought back-to-back, their movements perfectly synchronized. There were too many of them. They pressed forward with inhuman determination, their helmet slits revealing nothing but darkness.

My sword was in my palms. When had I drawn it? My fingers ached from gripping the hilt so tightly, everything happening so fast.

Multiple soldiers attacked Dealla and Killian, their stance never faltering, but then, between the four of them, a soldier broke through, his blade aimed at my chest.

Time slowed. All the time spent training with Dealla came rushing through me as I focused. I lifted my new sword, meeting his strike with a clash so forced that it sent a heavy vibration down my arms. The impact pushed me back a step, my shoulders screaming with protest. Through the opening of his helmet, I saw.. Nothing. No humanity stared back.

Then he swung again, a vicious curve toward my head. I ducked and spun, just like Dealla had hounded into me countless times with training. But this wasn't training. This male was looking to kill. Kill or be killed. The thought hit me as I stepped into an iced lake. I had never taken a life. Even now, staring death in the face. I wasn't sure I could cross that line. What if.. His blade came toward my ribs. I parried desperately, the force sending him stumbling backwards.

Off balance, he was now vulnerable.

Strike now!

I raised my sword, muscle memory taking over. One strike against him and it could save my life, but I hesitated. Steel punched through the soldier's chest from behind. Killian's blade emerged from the soldier's front before he jerked it free from the wound. The soldier collapsed in a heap of black armor and spreading crimson.

Around me, the battle was ending. I could only hope the villagers didn't hear the clashing of swords so early in the morning and believe their village was under attack. Delaney wiped the mess from her blade while Ivarison stood between a circle of twisted corpses, shadows still writhing near him. Dealla and Killian, side by side, lowered their weapons, breathing hard.

"Is everyone–" Dealla began.

I looked to see why she had stopped; her eyes were wide with terror. She opened her mouth to scream.

There was a breeze through the air behind me.

Fire emerged beneath my ribs as a warmth of heat soaked through my skin and my shirt. I grabbed the side of my stomach, red filled my palm, glistening like a handful of rubies.

My sword clattered to the ground as my knees buckled.

"ELLOWYN!" Dealla's voice seemed to come from underwater, distant and distorted.

Ivarison was at my side before I even saw him move, his sword already splitting the soldier who stabbed me in two. The male crumpled, but I barely registered it. The world spun, tilted, and my chest felt like a boulder rested on it.

"Stay with me, Ellowyn," Ivarison commanded, his hands covering mine over the wound. "Don't you dare faint on me."

I tried to focus on his face–those beautiful blue eyes, but the edges of my vision kept blurring.

"I'm.. bleeding a lot, aren't I?"

He didn't answer me, "Where did that bastard go?" Ivarison's voice turned deadly as he looked up at the others.

"Through the trees, that way," Dealla answered, pointing at the trees as she rushed over. "But Ivarison–"

"Hold pressure here," Ivarison said, pressing Dealla's hands over the wound as he released mine, causing me to gasp.

Then he vanished.

"Ellowyn," Dealla stammered, as I groaned from the pressure of her hands.

It felt as though I was in a daze, and time became distorted. Delaney's voice sounded muffled as she asked questions that I had forgotten how to answer. Killian's hands were searching through Dealla's bag, looking for anything that might help. The taste of copper in my mouth and the growing cold that seemed to seep through my bones.

"I took care of it." A jingle of what sounded like gold rattled near me. Was that Ivarison? When did he return? There was more mumbling that I couldn't make out, the sun blinding as I tried to open my eyes.

"Is it bad?" I asked, even though I could hear how weak my voice sounded. My hands stayed on my wound, pressing tightly against it with Dealla's hands over mine. I became lightheaded as I leaned forward to try to get a better view. I cried out as the pain seared and my vision blurred again.

"Stop! Don't move!" Dealla cried out.

"Move!" Ivarison snapped, pushing Dealla's hands away from the wound and returning underneath mine.

I found Dealla's face focused on my abdomen; the color on her face was drained. I was dying. I should be terrified, but instead, there was an anger that settled in me, and I was pissed. I hadn't even been capable of staying alive long enough to find and save my mother. My eyelids were growing heavy. Was this it? The pain was easing. Maybe I don't have to figure out who I'm supposed to be after all.

Dark shadows crept around the edges of my vision, but something else was coming through. Swirls of blue light, dancing behind my closed eyelids like flames.

Well, that's peaceful.

They pulsed in rhythm with my heartbeat, and with each breath I took, they grew brighter. What was this? The blue wasn't just in my vision, I could feel it warming me, flowing through my veins like liquid starlight. It gathered beneath my palms, tingling against my skin where my hand pressed against the wound.

"What is that?" Delaney whispered, now near me at my side. "What are you doing?"

"That isn't me," I heard Ivarison say. His pressure was still around my abdomen, but this time it didn't hurt.

The shift of their feet in the dirt sounded closer, and I could hear every pebble crumbling under their boots as it echoed painfully in my ears. I forced my eyes open again, flinching at the brightness. Everyone stared down at me with wonder and fear. But they weren't looking at my face; they were looking at my hands.

The warmth of my blood began to grow cold in my hands, and the bleeding seemed to slow. I glanced down, my vision clearer, and saw what Delaney had asked about.

My hands glowed the very same blue that I had seen just moments before. My skin felt like tiny bugs were crawling at the wound as it was repairing itself, stitching together like thread. Were my hands on fire? What was this?! I tried to shake my hands as if it would smother it out.

The blue began to fade from my fingers as I waved my hands, and where the wound had been, a faint pink line now appeared.

"Wha-What was that?" I could only whisper, staring at my hands as if they weren't my own. The fingertips that had looked to be ignited in blue looked perfectly ordinary now, but I could still feel an itch of that impossible power.

"Your power," Killian answered. The word hit as if it knocked the wind out of me.

Your power. There was something inside me that I had only scratched at the surface of. Something that had just saved my life and that I didn't understand.

"Your grandmother had an incredible healing ability. You may have inherited her gift. Most Fae heal quickly, but it doesn't typically work in this way, especially when stabbed with a Riker blade." Killian had continued, as he scratched his head and looked at the blood that was beginning to dry.

"You may be fascinated by my shifting ability, but having that sort of healing ability is more fascinating," Delaney said, shifting on her knee as she knelt, looking at me with a grin.

"Oh, if she hadn't been fed Rikeroot and known of her ability, we wouldn't have had to watch her nearly bleed out to death," Ivarison snarled, as he raised his blood-covered hands. Dealla shot him a glare. "A power like that doesn't just disappear. It waits, and now it's beginning to emerge."

Dealla rubbed her face, sighing heavily. "You brought yourself back from the edge of death," Dealla corrected, her voice thick with emotion. "Ellowyn you... We thought we were going to lose you."

The weight of nearly dying crashed over me. I'd really almost died. I had felt myself growing distant, slipping away from everything around me, and surrendering myself to the darkness that was flooding me. And then something inside of me sparked. Something I didn't want to accept, but it had refused to let me go.

"We need to start moving before the villagers wake and find this mess," Killian said, looking over the mangled bodies of soldiers that were piled around.

This was what I was warned of and what I was going to have to face going through Madora. At the beginning of our trip, I had nearly died. I would not let myself go down so easily again. If I were the one mentioned in the prophecy and the reason why Madora faced the wrath of Adriane and Ciaran, this was only the beginning.

We moved quietly as I tried to ignore the difference I felt in my body: how warm it felt and the strangeness that flowed through me. My feet dragged as we traversed through a thick grove of trees, moving toward Whiterun Village. Even if the male Fae had set us up for a trap, the village was the only information that we had learned of.

It was hard not to stare down at my hands, seeing if the blue magic would reappear. Checking to make sure nobody was looking, I looked at my hands again to make sure this hadn't been a bad dream. There was still dried blood that followed the lines of my palms and in between my fingers. The pink faded line was still on my stomach. I had healed myself. Now, could I save Madora?

Now everyone knew I could no longer deny that I didn't have power. I tried to will the power back to my fingers, but nothing happened. I felt for the warmth, tried to imagine it again as what it had felt as before, but I was unable to figure out the way to conjure it.

When you lost your temper, it didn't always end well.

Dealla's words rang through me. How could healing powers cause problems? What more was there that hadn't come to the surface yet? The question was burning through me. Did my companions wonder the same as they watched over me to ensure that I was okay?

The horizon was tinted blue as the lingering clouds drifted, and I watched, trying to distract myself. I wondered if another dragon might come by to avoid the fear that more soldiers might come instead. A dragon was something I would have never thought to look for when at the cottage.

The beautiful home of ours that was burnt to ashes. I glanced around, hearing Adriane's laugh as I had that very night. So clearly as if she were somewhere nearby. Adriane's black hair was glowing with the reflection of the growing fire. I had just sat there and watched as they forced my mother to drink the vial. There was a clash of swords echoing in my mind, echoing through me, and the hesitation I had made about killing the soldier.

Lost in my thoughts, I startled when a hand touched my arm. Instinctively, I grabbed the forearm to steady myself, preparing myself in case someone was coming after me.

Ivarison winced, glancing down at where I held him. "Dealla was calling for you."

I looked over my shoulder at Dealla, "I'm sorry, what did you say?"

Her eyebrows furrowed. "Are you ready to stop for the evening?"

I nodded, looking at Ivarison, who was still near me and wincing.

"I need you to let go now," he said calmly.

I jerked my hand back not realizing I had still been holding onto him. Immediately, my eyes went to his forearm, seeing an outline of my hand pressed against his skin. Was that blood I had gotten on him? No, the blood left on my hands was dried and stained. It was a burn.

"W-What was that?" I asked quickly, trying to look.

He jerked his arm away to cover it with his cloak as he stepped away. "There wasn't anything."

The others had their attention on us, as they too had seen the mark. He rolled his eyes as he shrugged his shoulders. "You may have burnt me. Slightly. It's fine."

He pulled his arm back from under his cloak and rubbed where the mark had been, already fading away. "See? I can heal myself too."

"Why didn't you heal Ellowyn?" Delaney asked, coming closer.

"My healing abilities only work on myself. I heal almost immediately." He glanced at Dealla with a smirk on his face as she only scowled back. "Which is why it's so difficult to kill me."

"I burnt you." My chest tightened with guilt; even if he could heal immediately and I hadn't caused damage, I had lost control over what was flowing widely in my veins. "I'm sorry – I didn't mean to do that, I don't know how –"

"Yes, anything is bound to happen when you don't know the possibilities of the power that is wanting to find a way to escape. This is why you should train using it." Ivarison paused as he stepped closer, that blue magic of his flickering at his fingertips. "Your emotions are going to control every ounce of it and heighten it. If you don't learn to wield it, it will control you. I've lost control more than enough times."

Ivarison glared over at Dealla and Killian as if this were their fault. The power he seemed to love reveling in made it sound easy to conjure, to use. It wouldn't come so easily when it had been muted for seventeen years.

If I didn't accept his offer to help, I would have to accept help from another, but who? Luckily, I had burnt someone who could heal immediately and not have any consequence to what I had just done, but if I lost control and hurt one of the others in my group? I couldn't think of that or a chance for that to happen.

Stopping for the evening, Delaney and Killian shifted to patrol and hunt. I wanted to rest, as exhaustion and hunger hit me, looking down at myself, seeing how filthy I had become just from our battle and travel.

Dealla walked with me to a stream that was near our evening camp. She took a spot close by, but further away to have privacy. I wouldn't have minded one of those lavender-scented soaps now from Luminara.

My hands reached out toward the water as it erased the blood that had soaked my hands. I moved in a bit further, letting the water crash against my skin, taking away the show of what we had just faced earlier in the day. The light faded pink spot now on my abdomen was a reminder that this was life or death, and I was being hunted. I jumped at each movement I heard, the shifts from Dealla through the trees where she rested. I could not fail, I could not let myself falter.

"We can take a break tonight from training," Dealla said softly, as we left the river. "I think you had enough of it today."

I was afraid to sleep, unsure if there would be other soldiers who would find us through the night and try to attack. So instead of immediately resting after dinner, I learned more about fading. The power that Dealla had, as well as Ivarison.

"Why don't we use fading to travel?" I asked, resting in the cot nearby the others. Delaney had fallen asleep. I was surprised. Her heavy eyelids had begun to drift shortly after dinner.

"I have limitations. I'm unable to travel far distances. If I travel frequently and bring another with me, it exhausts me and could have consequences," Dealla said, and she glared at Ivarison as he spoke.

"I can go longer distances, but for me only. To bring another with me would still take time to get through, and after some time, it does get exhausting." Ivarison sounded bored again as he turned in his own cot.

"I'll take first watch," Killian said. I began to drift to sleep and wondered if I would be able to fade. Wondered if it was an ability that I would want to have when I was afraid of what else I was and what I could be capable of.

I hit the sword away from my shoulder, nearly missing Delaney's hit as her silver hair whirled around her.

The evening before we arrived at Whiterun Village, I practiced with Delaney as Dealla and Killian stayed by the fire in a discussion of our travel. As I didn't know the land of Madora as well as they did, I asked Dealla to make our course. Even when I was furious at the secrets she hid, I trusted her for this.

"You need to move faster. Shift your feet so your opponent won't catch you off balance." Ivarison snapped, slouched nearby as he watched us spar.

Delaney was fast and was nearly as skilled as Dealla. It was remarkable, given the age difference and her level of experience. Dealla had trained me as well as she could have, but when I had Rikeroot in my system, there had been limitations.

"Never let your guard down. Be aware of your surroundings at all times. Hesitation like that is why you nearly bled out yesterday," he spoke again, as Delaney glared once at Ivarison and then back at me as her sword sliced through the air for a hit.

"I suppose you would rather her torture her opponents and burn them alive?" Dealla called, pulling her attention from Killian.

"That might be a quicker way to end a fight, though." Killian said, chuckling. Ivarison's shoulders stiffened, and my focus went back to Delaney, who patiently waited.

I exhaled hard, trying to fill my lungs with air and to tune his voice out. But he watched every step. Delaney moved with no hesitation, and I knew she wouldn't take it easy on me. I didn't want her to.

Our swords continued to clash as Ivarison's voice echoed through my ears. The heat rose in my cheeks as my irritation grew. My arms grew heavier as my sword swayed back and forth from hits. He was right. I would have a chance of being hurt again if I didn't move faster.

I couldn't hold it any longer, and I suddenly roared with my hit, Delaney's sword smacking against my own so hard that it sounded as if it had cleaved in two. She fell to the ground as her sword was thrown from her. What had I done? The power seemed to radiate against my bones as Dealla and Killian jerked back up to see the commotion.

Delaney's shocked eyes matched my own as we both stared at my sword, hissing steam. Her lips broke into a cheesy grin.

"That was incredible!" Delaney jumped back to her feet. "The power of that hit, I'm surprised my sword didn't break."

The sweat beaded at my forehead as my chest heaved. Ivarison watched as I narrowed my eyes, "Was that good enough for you?" I asked, gritting my teeth.

"No." He glared. "You just got lucky."

"Lucky?"

"Delaney could have seriously been hurt just now, and that uncontrolled power is just itching its way out, isn't it?" He jumped from where he had been resting in the dirt and dared to move a step closer. "Do you feel it? You're a disaster waiting to happen."

I was shaking, the heaviness in my breathing not improving. Wanting nothing more in that moment to practice with him, in hopes that he would be the one who could be injured instead.

"Power without control is just a tantrum with consequences. Ask anyone who's lived through one of mine," he said, he didn't blink as he stared.

"Why don't you just go over there and away from us?" Delaney snapped at Ivarison, coming in between us. "Shoo."

Ivarison glared at her, his chin rising some. At first, he didn't balk, his attention moving back toward me before he reluctantly walked away toward the fire and faced away with a grunt.

What a jerk.

Chapter Twelve

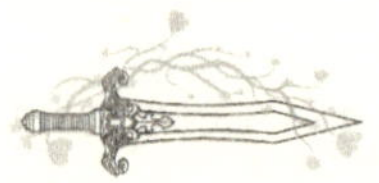

My blanket was ripped off me, the sudden chill making me cringe. I grunted as my sword was slammed into my chest.

"Ellowyn, wake up!" Delaney hissed, shaking my shoulders. Did she just smack me?

"What? What is it?" I exclaimed, suddenly alert. Purple painted the sky with waves of yellow as I looked around. The others were missing from our camp.

"Something – someone – is tracking us. The others are pushing it away now," Delaney said, flustered. She gathered our belongings and threw my bag into my lap. "Come on, Whiterun is only a half day's walk, they will catch up to us."

"What? No! I'm not leaving the others. We need to stay together," I hissed. I was suddenly wide awake, pulling my bag over my shoulder.

"They are going to kill me if you get hurt." She huffed. "Let's go, and we will try to find them."

Adrenaline pumping, we raced through the woods. The sun peeked over the horizon, hazy light filtering through the trees as I stayed alert for any abnormal sounds around us.

With the light crunch of leaves under our feet, we stopped, trying to listen for anything around us. Delaney's arm brushed against my own as we listened.

A hand came up to Delaney and pulled her over, as I unsheathed my sword. I would not hesitate again. Just before I swiped, Killian let go of Delaney, ready to duck from my hit.

"Easy now!" Killian said, his sword in hand, ready to block. "We told you to continue toward Whiterun, and we would catch up."

"I know," Delaney said frantically, taking a look around, hearing snarls through the trees, and then back at me.

Killian put a finger to his lips, lowering his head to look through the low branches of trees. He pointed. Just ahead in the woods was a Dark Soldier.

But the soldier froze, his body turning in the direction where we hid. I wasn't sure any of the three of us were breathing. Killian's arm went out toward me in protection.

Then a long sword sliced across the soldier's back. Ivarison. Through the shadows he emerged. When he walked to us, I could see new blood on his once clean tunic.

"You don't listen very well, do you?" he asked, glaring at Delaney and back to Killian. "There is a small camp with at least a dozen soldiers. We need to move."

Our heads snapped to our right at the sudden shouting that was coming toward us. Dealla was running at full speed in our direction, and the sound of soldiers was trailing behind her.

"Stay close, Ellowyn!" she shouted. We sprinted through the woods away from the soldiers. I held my satchel of Rikeroot in my hand as we ran, contemplating how I could use it now.

My feet nearly stopped moving as a soldier began to shift, clothes tearing as gray, battered skin emerged, arms stretched into gnarly limbs, nails lengthened into skin-shredding talons.

"They are changing into Norwags!" I screamed. The others looked back, mouths gaping and eyes widening.

We watched in horror as each of the soldiers transformed into Norwags. Swords in hand, we positioned closer together as we could see them trying to corner us, trapping us.

"Get down, Ellowyn!" Delaney pushed into me, and we both fell and tumbled further, as a Norwag burst through a nearby bush separating us from the group.

"There are too many!" Killian shouted. He thrusted his sword through one. Every Norwags' dark eyes were on us. We were trapped.

I froze, seeing just how many surrounded us. Sharp talons and teeth of the creatures reached for me and the others, looking for anything they could latch onto.

There was darkness and suddenly Ivarison blocked my view. Black shadows flowed from his body, wrapping around one Norwag.

Delaney turned to her beast form and struggled to keep them back. Dealla and Killian were surrounded by multiple, fighting further from where we were. She met my eyes and mouthed something I couldn't understand. Then, she grabbed Killian, and they vanished. My eyes darted everywhere. My heart thundered against my ribs more.

Shit! Did she just leave us?

"Where did they go?!" I gripped my sword as one of the horrid creatures lunged. But Ivarison was there again, his shadows blocking the Norwag before it could reach me.

I couldn't do anything but watch as he fought them off, one after another. Then Dealla suddenly reappeared. Alone.

Where was Killian?

Her breathing was labored. Seeing that Ivarison and I were furthest away, she rushed toward Delaney's beast form. A Norwag charged straight for them.

"Delaney!" I screamed.

Dealla's arms wrapped around Delaney's form. They both vanished just as the Norwag's claws swiped where Delaney had stood.

I blinked. Disoriented. Ivarison kept moving, shadows flowing around us like a protective barrier. I felt useless. I couldn't even catch my breath.

Then Dealla was at my side, pale and looking like she might collapse. A tree crashed behind us as another Norwag barreled through.

She pulled me into her chest, shouting at Ivarison. "Fade thirty marks before Whiterun. Finish them here!"

He nodded over his shoulder, darkness enshrouding him.

Dealla squeezed her arm around me, and the land before me spun. As soon as I closed my eyes, our feet hit the ground. Dealla let go of my waist and clutched her chest. Her sword clattered to the ground.

"Dealla?"

Her eyes rolled back, and she collapsed.

"Dealla!" I shrieked, catching her as we both went down. Delaney and Killian were nowhere near us. I pressed my fingers to her neck, searching for a pulse. Nothing. I shook her shoulders, then smacked her cheeks. Still nothing.

"Dealla!"

Shortly after Killian and Delaney found us, confirming there were no signs of soldiers or Norwags pursuing us, Ivarison arrived. Finding an area obscuring our presence, we made camp.

The campsite was quiet as the fire crackled. Killian sat beside Dealla's cot, where she slept. Hours had gone by since she fainted. I hadn't let her go until Killian found us, after patrolling to ensure we were safe where we were.

Now, I sat near the fire to keep warm. Delaney poked at the fire with a stick as Ivarison paced nearby, muttering to himself.

"Are we not going to talk about how Adriane can shift her soldiers into Norwags?" Delaney cried, her eyes wide, throwing the stick in the fire.

"What happened?" I finally asked, as Dealla began to stir.

Killian moved closer to Dealla, pulling out his canteen. "I was on watch and could hear movement through the woods. They may have caught our scents and were searching. Dealla, Ivarison, and I led them away from camp while Delaney was supposed to get you to safety, but.." He glanced at Delaney. "You ended up running right into where we ended up anyway."

Dealla's eyes fluttered but remained closed as Killian helped her sit up to take a sip of water.

"Will she be okay?" I asked, watching her struggle to stay and raise her arms to hold the drink.

"Everyone has limits," Killian said, his hand steadying hers around the canteen. "She drained herself pulling us to safety."

"It was foolish." Ivarison's voice cut through the camp as he stopped his pacing and came closer to the fire. "I could have helped move us out. Instead, she nearly killed herself. Even a young Fae knows what happens when you push beyond your limits. Especially fading back-to-back like that."

"That's enough," Killian snapped, rising to face him. "What's done is done."

"Yes, for now," Ivarison hissed.

I glared at him, but I knew he was right.

"What did you do after we left?" Delaney asked Ivarison, handing Dealla some bread and meat. "You were the last one there."

"I killed them so they couldn't follow. Dealla cleared everyone out so none of you were accidentally caught in my shadows."

My throat went dry. I had seen those shadows leaving him just before Dealla pulled me away. The way they'd started to engulf the area. It reminded me of the mist that haunted my nightmares, but different.

One thing was certain: I couldn't allow Dealla to risk herself that way again. Not when I should be capable of protecting myself. We had to find another way. We had to.

Chapter Thirteen

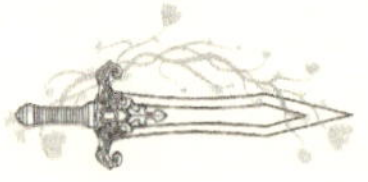

Dealla refused to rest once she was awake, snapping that there wasn't time to waste. She was right, but I still felt guilty as she pushed herself to travel.

Whiterun Village was smaller compared to Oakwood. We arrived midday, and each of us was more wary this time around. Crows hopped through the paths. The streets were narrow. Villagers walked closely side by side, whispering and staring.

Some of the villagers looked just like humans, except for their pointed ears. A few were naturally much taller, hunching over to fit through doorways. But it was their expressions that made my stomach clench – hollow and drawn out.

"They were here," Killian muttered, moving closer to Dealla. "I can smell the stench of the soldiers and fear from the villagers."

Fear. It hung in the air like smoke. I wondered if this is what every village throughout Madora would look like now. Broken Fae, waiting for the next blow.

I moved closer to Dealla, wanting to help if she needed it. Delaney moved closer with us, as I peered through the hood of my cloak, I noticed we were missing a companion.

"Where is Ivarison?" I asked, looking through the streets and nearby tents.

"Hopefully, he ran off," Dealla mumbled under her breath, not bothering to search. I suppose she was still angry about what he said when she woke.

We continued our way through the streets, but I glanced occasionally in search of him. We stopped at some shops, lingering in our conversations. When we tried to speak with shop owners, we received short answers before they moved quickly onto other customers.

Each dismissal felt like a sting. I understood the fear well, but watching others scatter through the village reminded me of how helpless I felt. They were mother's subjects – my subjects – and they were too terrified to even look at newcomers. What kind of princess would I be if I couldn't get them to trust me?

We left the seventh shop with no luck finding information from anyone.

"They indeed came through here, but no one saw Princess Alina." Ivarison reappeared, his lips turned downward.

"Where have you been?" Dealla asked, her arms crossed over her chest as we walked down the steps back into the street. Ivarison's hands found his pockets, eyebrows arched.

"One of the shops near the entrance of the village. A female owns it, so I offered some generosity to help her. Her mate was killed by soldiers some time ago," he sneered.

"Oh, really? What kind of generosity was that you gave her?" Delaney piped, her eyebrows raised to her hairline, but then Ivarison narrowed his eyes at her.

"Not the generosity you're thinking." He shook his head. "I offered to fix some of the problems in her shop, if you must know."

"Oh, how very kind of you." Dealla rolled her eyes.

"That was kind of you. Did you gather any other information about where the soldiers could be moving?" Killian asked, wrapping Dealla's cloak around her.

"I only learned that they came through several days ago. Making threats. Demanding and stealing supplies they needed. They made it clear that if demands weren't met, they would kill every single villager, starting with their young." A vein protruded from Ivarison's temple.

The cruelty of those words made me sick. Threatening children to get what they wanted – is that what Adriane's rule was like? I had seen how the villagers flinched when we approached, how they didn't want to talk. How many other villages had already suffered the same fate?

"We have someone listening," Ivarison snapped, looking ahead at a Fae female with curly, golden hair.

As the group spun around, each hand went to the hilt of their swords. The narrow street had grown more crowded. Villagers pressed in all directions, but three figures stood apart from the rest. They had been watching us as we spoke.

The curly-haired female stepped forward, soft brown eyes darting nervously between us.

"Are you Dealla Faklan?" Her soft voice whispered as she glanced at the crowd. Two males flanked her, close enough to be protective, but far enough to avoid looking threatening.

Dealla's body tensed. She shifted subtly, putting herself between the strangers and me while keeping me within arm's reach. "I'm sorry, but do I know you?"

"No, I suppose you wouldn't," she said, her voice still a whisper. "We were in Mystmere for some time, selling fruits and vegetables at the market. You were often there with Princess Alina and purchased some from our stall."

The crowd began to slow, heads turning our way. Too many ears, too much attention. Dealla's hand stayed at the hilt of her sword as she scanned the growing circle around us. The two males must've noticed our defensive positioning and shifted closer to their companion, not aggressive but alert.

"I wanted to ask," the female continued, taking another glance nervously. "Is it true that Princess Alina has returned? I never believed she was dead."

Fear flickered in Dealla's eyes. Was this another trap? She looked over the crowd, hand gripping her sword. Without a word, Delaney, Killian, and Ivarison tightened their formation around me. I was trapped in their circle of protection once more.

Even if it were necessary, it was still suffocating. We were attracting exactly the kind of attention that we didn't want.

"We stand with Mystmere. We want you to know that there are still some of us willing to fight for it. The rest are just scared, but we are willing to take a stand against the wrongdoing." One of the males spoke, his voice deep and proud.

I stepped forward, but as Dealla blocked me with her arm, the hood of my cloak slipped. The female's eyes narrowed as her gaze fixed on my face.

"You look just like her," the female whispered, her hand rising as if to point before she dropped it back at her side.

My heart hammered against my ribs. She knew. I could see it in the way her eyes examined my features, how she glanced at my companions standing guard around me.

"Princess Ellowyn, forgive me."

The title was like a blow. This was different from when Lord Durin and Lady Celia spoke it. Different from when Ivarison's mocking tone said it. She wasn't just someone searching for her mother. She was the princess the Fae of Madora longed for. Hope. The weight suddenly pressed down on my shoulders.

I hesitated, weighing out our options. She seemed like a genuine female, but we'd been wrong before. But with so little to go on, and each day that passed was another day of building doubt on whether my mother was still alive, I took the risk.

"The soldiers that came through," I spoke carefully, "did you hear anything of where they were headed?"

The female and one of the males exchanged glances before looking at their other companion. The second male had remained quiet, watching with sharp green eyes.

"I was out in the woods when they arrived," he said finally, taking a cautious step forward. "They came from the east path. Some continued west while others stayed to terrorize our village. But the ones that headed west had a wagon. Large, wrapped in iron, covered with witch runes I'd never seen before." My heart lurched. A wagon. Locked and hidden from sight. "I couldn't see what was inside it, but anything they'd go through that much trouble to secure.." He shrugged grimly.

I looked at the others, hoping that they believed my mother may have been in that wagon. If she was, she was still alive.

"You didn't see any clues of what could be in it?" Delaney asked, her voice low as she tried to keep the passing villagers from our conversation.

"I only overheard that they were meeting with others to take the wagon to their next location, which was to go west and to keep hidden."

My heart leaped. A wagon that was locked with iron and runes. It had to be my mother. But then the thought of her being trapped in some cage, alone, most likely hurt, made my breathing shallow. How long had she been trapped in there? Could she have..? I forced the negative thoughts away.

"They could be meeting with Adriane. She can't do anything on human land if rumors are true," Killian said, trying to unravel what could be happening with the enemy.

"Yes, but why are they traveling like that? Why not immediately take action or head straight back to Ravenholde?" Dealla whispered, biting her lips as she was in thought.

As we parted ways with the three, we thanked them for the information they'd given. Hope shone in the eyes of the nearby villagers who had listened, the terror that had consumed them vanishing into something brighter.

But terror rushed through me, not just for what I'd witnessed here, but for what lay ahead. The hopeful looks the villagers gave me, as if they believed I could save them, made my confidence waver. I had hesitated to take down a single soldier just days ago. If I hadn't somehow healed myself, I wouldn't be standing here.

If we failed to rescue my mother, it would be expected of me to step to the throne. I'd be the last of the royal family. But I wasn't sure I could ever be what they needed me to be – what they deserved.

With Whiterun Village behind us, Delaney fell into step beside me as we began to travel through Woodlawn Forest. The others walked a few strides ahead, their voices a low murmur.

"You've been quiet," Delaney noted. "Are you alright?"

I dragged my feet as we ventured deeper into the forest. Whether from the constant travel or the fear that sat deep in my chest, I couldn't tell. I was afraid of failing my mother, afraid of failing Madora, afraid of failing my traveling companions.

"I suppose." I rubbed my temples, my eyes hurting. "Do you ever feel like you'll never be good enough? What if we don't find her?"

Delaney frowned. "I think there are many of us that feel that we are never good enough. I also believe that it is normal for us to question ourselves. It's the actions you make during that time that matter." She nodded toward Dealla, Killian, and Ivarison. "Together, I have hope we will find your mother."

I wanted to believe her, but the words stuck in my throat.

"You know," Delaney continued, absently spinning her small dagger between her fingers, a habit I'd notice during our walks, "I wanted to be something more than just the daughter of the Lord and Lady of Luminara. My mother had expectations." She shook her head. "I'm not exactly the daughter she expected, and I never will be."

Delaney seemed to know every detail of what she wanted, even with every strand of her silver hair that was clipped away from her face.

"Is that why you train so hard?" I asked.

"Partly. But also, because I refuse to be helpless." Her gray eyes met mine. "Neither should you."

Something in her tone, not pity, but an understanding, made my chest pull. After the lies that were kept from me, I'd been afraid to trust anyone. But Delaney had already protected me, trained with me when Dealla couldn't, and pushed me to be better.

"Thank you," I said quietly. "For believing I can do this when I'm not sure what to do."

She smiled, her elbow tapping against mine. "That's what friends are for."

Friends. The word felt precious and so fragile.

It felt like an eternity had gone by as we continued to make our way through villages, searching for hints of a wagon that didn't seem to exist. Each village was different from the last. Some had welcomed us, seeming to know we were coming. Words must've traveled from families who lived in other villages we passed through.

News spread that Princess Alina had been captured, and her daughter was searching for her. Princess Alina and Princess Ellowyn survived the royal assassination seventeen years ago. They were alive.

Fear mounted each day that more Norwags were searching for us. But since the last attack in the woods, we had not seen more. It was unsettling. Why had they vanished? The paranoia was high with any odd movement or noise we heard while traveling.

After another dead end in a village North of Crownest Village, we stopped early for the evening. Dealla and I began our practice, both exhausted and mentally drained. We fought, swords colliding and feet twisting through the dirt as we twirled against one another.

"Again," Dealla snapped. Irritation radiated from her as my own thoughts clouded me. She pushed, her breathing ragged. My muscles burned even with the increased strength that I felt had grown since our journey began.

The Rikeroot effects faded out of my system. My sight was sharper as I focused on Dealla's movement, I pivoted, twisted, and blocked her hits. But there was an ache that lingered in my chest, a pressure that waited for an escape. I hoped that once we found more information about my mother or found her, it might ease.

We didn't stop at the last village we came across. Even though supplies had begun to diminish, Killian and Delaney patrolled and hunted for our dinner while Dealla and I trained. Ivarison sat on a log nearby, a book in hand. It didn't stop him from watching over the top of the book, though.

"Again!" Dealla shouted as I whipped around her. The power of my strike vibrated down my arms as our swords collided.

Again and again.

Dealla blocked each hit that I gave, eyes focused on the sword.

"Faster!" Dealla said through gritted teeth, stopping her sword from hitting my flesh.

Dealla was as frustrated as I was and it showed. The hope of finding my mother was fading, but she wasn't the type who would give up so easily.

"You need to move faster! You're moving too slow, and you'll get hurt again!" she said angrily, blocking my next hit.

I couldn't help but grow frustrated with her as she shouted. I had seventeen years of practice, but with power that was muted. Dealla was over a hundred years old and a skilled warrior, which, according to Killian, was one of the best of Madora – of course she would be stronger and quicker.

"Stop yelling at me!" I shouted back. Sweat beaded my brow. I wouldn't back down, even if my shoulders screamed from the constant swaying of my sword. A warmth built, moving toward my fingertips. I exhaled, containing the anger that was aching to be free.

"Perhaps you should keep moving then!" She came at me multiple times without a breath. My feet nearly flew from under me to keep up. Sweat stung my eyes as my entire body felt like it was pulsating. I screamed and attacked. With my sword over my head, I swung with all that I had against her strike.

Dealla's eyes widened as she gripped her sword, diving to the ground and rolling in the opposite direction from me. As she pulled herself from the ground and knelt to look at me, she gaped.

My eyes followed where she looked. The blade of my sword was engulfed in flames, and my hand was covered in the swirling flame.

I immediately dropped my sword in shock, panic filling me as I suppressed a scream. When the sword left my palm, the fire extinguished as I shook my hand. I hadn't felt the flames that covered the sword or my hand. How could I get it to go away?! The blaze began to fade, looking over every inch of my hand, I searched for burn marks.

"That was... Impressive." Dealla moved closer to my sword and tapped to see if it was hot. "But you need to control when that happens, not let it control you. Focus on containing it."

Dealla picked up my sword, my eyes looking warily over the blade. What if I ignited it again and couldn't get it to stop? How dangerous could this ability be if it came when I was defending myself, but couldn't control the outburst, ending up harming someone I care about?

A book snapped shut, breaking me from my thoughts. Ivarison jumped to his feet, and the log he sat on wobbled and turned at the force. "Containing it is not what she needs to be doing. She needs someone pushing her. It's been weeks since she's been off Rikeroot, has it not? She must get used to her power's presence, flowing through her, feeling it at her fingertips," Ivarison ground out in exasperation. I wasn't sure he was taking full breaths.

"She's doing fine," Dealla snapped.

"Coming from one whose abilities don't match the powers that she has to harness," he snapped back. Closing his eyes, he pinched his nose bridge. "I can sense her magic. I know we all feel something."

I searched for the others, but Killian and Delaney still had not returned. Dealla's fists were clenched at her sides.

"We've only seen a sliver of it. Giving her such advice will not help her. Only fear suppresses it now," Ivarison said and pointed at me. "Unless you plan to slip her Rikeroot because your fear of her exploding is greater than your hope she'd understand and learn to work with it?"

Now I was beginning to get pissed.

"How dare you–" Dealla began to shout.

"ENOUGH!" I shouted. "You're both acting like stubborn children while I'm the one who needs to figure this out."

As I stood in between the two, Ivarison's tall frame towered over me as he stared at Dealla. Her lips pursed as she stared back at him. I didn't know if they would start attacking one another, but I wasn't about to let members of our group start turning on each other either.

"Your power doesn't tie into your emotions, nor have the chance of submerging everything around you, Dealla. How can you help someone train if you don't understand how to pull the ability out of you and use it to your advantage?" Ivarison tried to keep his voice contained, but he still growled. "She questions if she does this correctly and then hesitates because she is unsure of herself."

How could he possibly know that?

"She's doing great," Dealla countered, speaking like a patient tutor. "This is new to her. I don't want her to feel overwhelmed. It is going to take time for her to understand how to handle everything new to her."

"This is why I prefer swords to feelings. Stop coddling, Dealla." Ivarison sniped. "We don't have time! Princess or not, she's a liability until she learns control."

I stared at the sky for a moment before looking back down. I was too exhausted to argue. I walked away, leaving them to their bickering, and went to my cot, placing my sword at my side. Tuning them out, I stared at the beautiful sword that had become my own. If my powers were emerging and I had no sense of control, I would have to accept his help even if I hated to admit it because of how infuriating he was.

When they both grew quiet, I turned slowly to see why they had stopped. Dealla and Ivarison stared at one another, assessing each other to see if either one would attack or back down first.

"Ellowyn, grab your sword," Ivarison instructed. Dealla crossed her arms as he never took his gaze from her. Dealla glanced through the woods, as if she were waiting for Killian to come through.

I picked up the sword and stood up, swinging it around my hand and raising my eyebrows in question.

Ivarison moved closer to me. "I'm not going to apologize." He wrapped an arm around my waist, and my body went rigid. "We will return shortly."

There wasn't enough time for me to register what was happening as Dealla rushed toward us. Her eyes widened just before we faded in front of her.

The world swirled. I gripped Ivarison's cloak as if I would fall into oblivion if either of us let go; his muscles flexed beneath my touch. His ember and petrichor scent filled my nostrils as I took in a deep breath and held tightly. When I started to wonder how long we'd fade for, our feet touched solid ground.

Chapter Fourteen

I shook Ivarison's grip from my waist and stumbled back, my heart hammering. We weren't anywhere near camp. The meadow stretched around us, grass dotted with various colors of wildflowers, and ancient trees towered overhead. It should have been beautiful, but all I could think about was Dealla panicking right now.

He actually abducted me. Just grabbed me and faded us like I was some helpless child who couldn't make her own decisions.

"Take me back. Now, Ivarison." The growl that left my throat surprised me. Raw and dangerous in a way that I've never heard from myself before.

Ivarison stood there with his hands shoved in his pockets, completely unmoved by my fury. "No."

My body shook from his flat refusal. Ivarison rolled his shoulders back, watching me. He didn't listen to anyone; surely, he wouldn't listen to me now. I turned my back on him, not knowing where I was, but I wanted to get away from him.

Before I could take another step, he was in front of me, blocking me.

"Get out of my way," I seethed, eyes narrowed.

"No," he said simply again, rolling his eyes.

I saw red. My hands clenched into fists. I didn't know what I was doing, and before I could reconsider, my hand was in the air. My palm stung as it made contact across his face.

Ivarison's head snapped to the side. He looked at me from the corner of his eye, a smirk playing across his lips. Then the smirk dropped, and he was furious.

"Feel better yet?" he asked with a growl.

Not even close.

A growl escaped his throat and I took it as a challenge. I wasn't afraid of him. Why would I be when I was already running for my life? I raised my hands again, but just before I made contact, his calloused palm caught mine.

"Am I supposed to be afraid of *you?*" he whispered.

He gripped tightly, then yanked me closer to him. He closed his eyes, inhaling deeply. When his eyes flashed open, they were dark as he smirked again, this time with a form of amusement.

"Take me back!" I shouted in his face. I jerked my hand away from him. His eyes were still boring down at me.

"I'll take you back after we work on several things. I think being away from your babysitter may be beneficial. Dealla watches over you as if you were but a child," he chided, rolling his eyes as he released me and returned his hands to his pockets.

I stepped away as his ember scent wafted across my nostrils. "It's always been that way. She doesn't want to see me hurt again."

"You mean with your mother?" Ivarison looked off as he began to pace back and forth.

"This isn't your business." I turned from him, looking away now, truly debating about running.

"You don't want to talk about how your mother kept your life hidden?" Ivarison began circling me, his voice deceptively casual. "Took away precious memories?"

"Shut up." I turned away, but his words already crawled under my skin. He had no business bringing any of this up.

"Kept you away from your home?" Another step closer. His tone was deliberate, pointed. "From remembering who your father was? Your family?"

"Shut up." What was he playing at? *I wanted to punch him.* My hands started to warm.

"Then stole your magic, the very thing that makes you who you are?"

The heat in my chest flared. "STOP IT!"

Birds took flight from the trees around us.

Ivarison stepped closer behind me, voice dropping to a whisper, "She isolated you like a dirty secret, didn't she? Made you forget a part of yourself like she erased every memory of where you came from." He was so close, I could slap him if I turned around. "Threw away everything and hoped you'd never remember who you really are. Who, exactly, are you, *Princess?*"

"Don't you dare–" I whipped around, but he already stepped back. My skin felt like it was burning from the inside out. Anger rose, and my body warmed as I studied his movement. My mother had done what she thought necessary for protection. It didn't matter what others thought of how she handled it. He continued to circle me, then he stopped and looked over.

"Do you feel that?" he asked, a ruthless smirk playing on his lips as he pointed at my hands.

I looked down. Blue and red flames danced across my fingertips, beautiful and terrifying. The magic hummed through my veins like liquid fire, demanding release. For the first time since this journey began, I felt... powerful.

"That is the feeling you need," he said, watching me with intense focus. "Your blood and magic are bonding together. You need to learn to control that without needing anger to summon it."

"You bastard," I snarled, but I couldn't look away from the blue magic. It responded to my emotions, flickering brighter when I focused on my fury, dimming the moment doubt crept in.

"Thank you," he said, as if I meant it as a compliment.

The moment I tried to analyze what was happening, the magic began to fade. My fingertips returned to normal, pale and powerless.

"Take me back to the campsite."

"I'll take you back as soon as you can manage something with your magic. I know you feel it there. You feel different, and it's just itching to seep out." He towered over me, staring me down.

"I don't know what you're talking about," I said, crossing my arms, fingers tapping against my forearms.

Ivarison rolled his eyes, not falling for my feigned ignorance. "You can't lie to me." He wiggled his long fingers, and shades of blue danced. "I'm waiting."

His lips pursed, and he furrowed his eyebrows slightly. I looked at my own hands, and the blue flames were long gone. "Focus on bringing it back. Think of the emotion you just had."

"It was satisfaction from punching you in the face," I said, my face burning as he bit his lip.

I closed my eyes and thought of the soft colors after I was stabbed, their brilliances dancing in my thoughts. The colorful swirls had distracted me from the pain and helped me focus on the warmth they gave. I opened my eyes, hoping, but my fingers remained bare.

Ivarison wiggled his fingers again, his power seeping out. I didn't have a moment to react when he pushed his palm toward me. His power crashed against my chest, sending me sprawling backwards in the grass.

Pain shot through my ribs. I gasped for air. But underneath the hurt, something else stirred. It wasn't only anger, it was determination. He wanted to see what I could do?

Fine.

I pushed myself up, every muscle screaming in protest. When he moved toward acting again, I chose to fight back.

"Come on now." His voice echoed in my head without his lips moving. The invasion made my skin crawl. Did he just move into my mind? Did he have such an ability that made him even more dangerous?

When his hand moved toward me, I dodged. My hands clenched as the heat ran through my veins. I reached for the burning sensation in my chest, the fire that wanted to find an escape. If he wanted to see something, I'd show him exactly what happened when someone pushed me too far.

Heat charged through my veins, and I released. My hands blazed with blue flame as I aimed for his smug face. He jumped back just in time, but my magic caught the edge of his cloak. His eyes glistened, and he raised his hand toward it, and the fire vanished.

"I didn't mean for you to catch me or the meadow on fire." He rubbed his forehead as he coughed. It nearly sounded like a laugh.

"Maybe you should be afraid of me. I should've aimed better for your face." The blue flame vanished from my hands.

"You couldn't hurt me," he said with that infuriating chuckle. "It was adequate. But your form is sloppy, your focus is scattered, and you're more likely to set yourself on fire than defend anyone."

The assessment stung more than his physical attack. I was dizzy from adrenaline, from magic, from the realization that he was right. I had done it. I'd actually used my power on command.

But I was furious. I reared my arm back. I just wanted to get one more hit in. But he was ready.

He snatched my hand, squeezing so tightly I cried out. He looked at me with those deadly blue eyes.

"You can hate me if you wish," Ivarison said, his voice losing its mocking edge. "But I'll be the one to keep you alive, Ellowyn."

He pushed me back, releasing my hand. I stepped back further, flexing my fingers. The magic was still there, humming just beneath my skin, waiting.

He let out a deep sigh that sounded more like a frustrated growl.

Maybe I did hate him. But I couldn't deny what had just happened. For the first time since this nightmare began, I felt like I might have a chance.

Even though setting his cloak on fire was not what Ivarison had in mind, he kept his promise to bring me back. I couldn't summon the magic again, partly from exhaustion, partly because I hadn't truly tried. My body felt wrung out, my emotions too raw to focus.

As the world swirled around us, I pressed my face against his shoulder to fight the nausea. The moment our feet touched solid ground, shouting erupted.

"WHERE IS SHE?!" Dealla's voice cracked like a whip.

My eyes snapped open to see her charging toward us, blade drawn, murder in her blue eyes. Delaney and Killian stood frozen behind her, faces paled with shock.

Before I could speak, Ivarison pushed me behind him as darkness engulfed me. But when my eyes adjusted, I realized it wasn't his shadow magic. It was feathers.

Massive wings had sprouted from his shoulders, shielding around me. Each dark gray feather faded to brilliant orange tips – a beautiful shade.

"I'm going to hurt you," Dealla snarled.

The wings shifted, allowing me to move to the open space with hands raised. "I'm fine!"

Relief flooded their faces, but Dealla's fury didn't diminish. Ivarison tucked his wings back into his shoulders, and they vanished as if they'd never existed.

"If you ever touch her again–" Dealla started.

"Oh, enough. I've only been here to help." Ivarison's voice turned cold. "I've let you threaten me enough now. Do not forget your standing. I'm a Lord, and you're a guard." His canine teeth gleamed as he snapped, longer and sharper. "You cannot teach her what she needs to learn. You're only holding her back."

I watched them square off: Dealla had her sword half-raised, Ivarison's irritation on full display, Killian stepping up to be a mediator while Delaney stood frozen by uncertainty.

Something inside me snapped.

"Both of you, shut up!" I ordered, my hands raised in frustration. "I've had enough. I don't know what happened between you, but enough of this childish nonsense."

Dealla's eyes widened in shock, but I wasn't finished.

"Dealla, I'm an adult. You cannot control everything I do, and you cannot stop if I were to train with him." The words tasted bitter, but they needed to be said. "And you," I pointed at Ivarison, still wanting nothing more than to hit him again – "Lord or not, taking me away doesn't earn any trust from the group. Even if I weren't a princess, it breaks any trust."

I stepped between them, my hands shaking from residual anger from our training session. "We need to be working together and communicating. This–" I waved my hands in the air to what was around us, "will get us nowhere. We're supposed to be searching and saving my mother, and instead, you two spend every moment tearing each other apart! Your arrogance and stubbornness will get her or one of us killed!"

Silence fell like a stone.

"Nothing to be said from anyone now?" I seethed, tapping my fingers against the hilt of my sword.

Ivarison's jaw worked. Dealla finally lowered her sword but refused to look in my direction, her shoulders rigid with hurt.

"You're right, working together and communication are key, Ellowyn. We need to do better." Killian said, before he turned to murmur something in Dealla's ear, too quiet for me to hear.

When the malformed circle of our group remained quiet, Delaney stepped in.

"Agreed. We need to work as a team." She looked at me with determination and resolve. "I'll help you in any way you need me; that is why I'm here."

I nodded gratefully as she took my arm, guiding me away from the others, toward the edge of our campsite.

"We will figure this out. Don't worry," Delaney said, handing me a plate of leftover meat. "Perhaps they just need time." She shrugged and sat beside me.

Across the campfire, I watched our fractured group. Killian had let Dealla go, who now sat staring into the flames with hunched shoulders. Ivarison had walked away to the opposite side of camp without another word. He glanced up, his blue eyes finding me. The hardened stare he often had relaxed for a moment. He blinked before looking away.

The cool night air hit while the fire crackled and crickets chirped. My blanket rubbed against my skin as I stared up at the stars. Dealla and Killian surprisingly let Ivarison take the first watch for the evening. It didn't stop the death glares from Dealla, though.

I twisted and turned for what felt like hours. Black mist filled my nightmares, never coming close enough to see what lurked through. When I pushed myself up from my cot, Ivarison sat with his back to the fire as he watched over the dark horizon.

He had caused such a panic for what he'd done. I could still see Dealla's eyes as we faded away. What would she have done if I hadn't returned?

I wanted to understand the desperation that Ivarison had for me to learn these abilities. The fire had felt incredible when it happened – powerful. I had never felt more alive, as if I were finally whole. But that was what terrified me. What if I couldn't control it around the people I cared about? What if I became like the mist in my nightmares? Dangerous and consuming?

Training with Delaney and Dealla had been tiring enough; I didn't know if I would be capable of handling more. A faint tug pulled at my abdomen, pulling me to ask questions. As I hesitated to talk to him, my feet decided before my mind could. I pulled the blanket tightly around me, tiptoeing my way over without waking the others.

"Trouble sleeping?" Ivarison asked. He shifted his hood to look over at me. The moon was bright enough that I could see his face and the shadows smearing under his eyes.

"It's the same nightmare every time I close my eyes." I rubbed my tired eyes. "I'm still pissed at you."

His lips formed a fine line. "Clearly, but I won't apologize." He studied my expression with those calculating blue eyes, as if trying to look for me. "Might I ask, which part are you speaking of?"

I massaged my temples, a small ache forming behind my eyes. Was he the cause of the headache? "For taking me away. I know you saw her fear. Dealla and I watched Adriane capture my mother, and we couldn't do anything when it happened. She may be just a guard to you, but they were best friends, and she is family to me. Imagine how she must have felt, seeing me disappear in front of her too."

Ivarison opened his mouth to say something, but then closed it, thinking better of it. He bit his lips as I studied his reaction. "I'm only thinking of what's best for you," he finally said, "You have to learn to control your abilities. I'm not worried about how Dealla feels."

"Why worry over what's best for me and that I learn?"

"Because you're Madora's princess." He glanced toward the sleeping forms of our companions, then back at me. His hand came from under his cloak, and some of his magic danced as he moved his fingers.

"I've done many things that I'm not proud of. When my emotions were heightened, it was harder for me to control my magic, and it caused damage. Sometimes it was catastrophic. I don't want that to happen to you." He cleared his throat. "Or to anyone. You're not like me."

"What did you do? Dealla *strongly* dislikes you." I hugged my knees tighter from the chill. "I mean, you're a jerk." I said, not hiding my smirk, to which he scoffed. "But you must've done something horrendous for her to find everything you say treacherous – someone who is supposed to be our ally."

He dropped his hand, magic extinguishing as he rubbed his cloak's hem. "That is not something I wish to discuss."

No matter how much I wanted to know, I wouldn't push him. Especially not after I had told him what my mother had done was none of his business. His past wasn't mine either.

"So, you have wings?" I asked, remembering the gray feathers and hoping that if I talked for a bit longer, I would get tired enough to fall back asleep.

That stupid smirk appeared on his lips. "Yes. Fascinating, right?"

"But how?" I blurted out. "Delaney and Killian can shift into animals. How would one know they're able to shift?"

"Every Fae and creature is different. Dealla has incredible strength." He glanced back behind him. "I'll deny I ever said it, but she is one of the best warriors of Madora. Fae are known for strength, speed, and immortality. While some of us have these gifts of power, others don't. You don't know any of this?" His body shifted toward me, tilting his head to look at me.

"Dealla and Killian have tried to fill me in while we've traveled. It's overwhelming trying to learn so much." I paused, thinking of the abilities I was beginning to experience in myself. The abilities I had seen were healing myself and the fire. What if those were the only things I was capable of, and I couldn't fully control either after being muted for so long?

"Being a halfling, I can't possibly have that much power. I worry that when I fight, I won't be able to control myself, and I'll lose myself."

"Denying it will not help you learn how to harness it. Not trusting it to flow within you will only make it volatile when you have an outburst. Just as you tried to burn my face off." He gripped the bottom of his cloak where my magic burned a hole through. "We all have to adjust to change. This is just one of many that you will need to adjust to."

"Are your wings something more? Some of Luminara's guards have wings, but they didn't disappear like yours."

"I'm able to turn into a large beast that can fly. That's where the wings come from. I can summon them and use them to fly if I like, just as Delaney and Killian can summon their claws."

"A large beast? What sort of beast?"

He was quiet for so long, and I thought he might not tell me. "Large enough that you could ride me," he answered finally.

The words hung in the air between us, and I felt heat creep up on my neck. Before I could stop myself, I choked on a laugh. His lips curved into that infuriating smirk.

"What's so amusing?"

"Nothing," I said quickly, but a chuckle escaped anyway. It was the first time I'd seen him truly smile, and it changed everything about his face. The harsh angles softened as his eyes warmed, and suddenly I understood why people might find him charming instead of just intimidating.

My pulse quickened in a way that had nothing to do with fear or anger. This was dangerous territory – finding him as attractive as I did. But there was something about seeing him without his usual arrogant mask that made my chest tighten.

Beautiful, I thought before I could stop myself.

Something flickered across his face as if he were surprised. His head tilted slightly, like he was listening to something that I couldn't hear.

"I don't know about beautiful," he mumbled.

Ice flooded my veins. "What?"

He paused, running a hand through his dark hair. "This is going to sound intrusive."

A chill ran down my spine. "What are you talking about?"

He shrugged, then stared toward the night sky. "At times, I can enter others' minds and communicate. It's difficult and an invasion of privacy. It's not something I can always control, and your thoughts especially like to sneak through every so often."

"What? How do I manage that when I'm not meaning to?"

"Your power. When I say that I can sense it, it's because I know it's there. An ability like that is something that shouldn't be shared with others either."

I paused, thinking of the meadow when I heard him. I *had* heard him.

"I thought you needed a boost of encouragement," he muttered, but something cold settled in my stomach.

"You mean I could accidentally read someone's mind without meaning to?"

"It's possible. That's another reason why you need proper training." His voice carried a weight that I hadn't heard before. "You worry that you won't be able to control your abilities, and it is dangerous to keep yourself untrained."

My eyes were growing heavier as I tried to process. Not only could I hurt people with fire, but I could potentially invade their privacy without knowing I was doing so.

"I haven't done it to anyone else, I don't think?" I questioned, trying to recall if there were any moments.

"Not that I've noticed. But Ellowyn–" he leaned forward, his expression serious, "this is why I don't want to leave training with just Dealla. She means well, but she doesn't understand the risks."

The realization that he could have heard private thoughts made my face burn with embarrassment. Of all the things he could accidentally overheard, my traitorous attraction to him was definitely not something I wanted to share.

"You've never told anyone that you're capable of doing that?" I quickly asked, hoping he didn't just hear my last thoughts.

He shook his head. "It's not something I wish for others to know, and I would like to keep it that way. I also can't do it with everyone."

I nodded, understanding he wanted privacy. "I don't think I'm ready to train with magic just yet." The words felt heavy, but I needed him to understand. "Every time I've used it, I've been angry or desperate. What if that's the only way it works, and I can't access it without losing control?"

"Ellowyn." His voice dropped in a warning tone, but there was something else now, something that sounded almost like concern.

"I'm not refusing forever," I said quickly, standing up. "I just need time to understand what's happening to me and process everything." I gestured between us, meaning the mind-reading and the complicated mess of trust and fear.

"Time is something we may not have," he said softly.

"Then, that's a risk I'll have to take."

Not giving him another chance, I returned to my cot. I turned away from him and tried to give my mind and body the rest it so desperately needed. But I could feel him staring at my back as I began to drift to sleep.

Chapter Fifteen

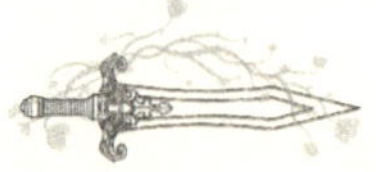

It was hard not to lose sense of time, days turning to a blur. After traveling through Woodlawn Forest, our journey went south and passed through smaller villages. But when we browsed through Crownest Village, we heard of the gossip that Dark Soldiers had been seen, heading toward Ravenwick Village.

Venturing through green rolling hills and more forests, the trees began to glow in beautiful shades of orange and red, as if autumn approached.

Four courts split Madora, plus the kingdom of Mystmere. Traveling toward Mystmere was no small feat. Stopping at small and large villages that filled the land while searching for signs of my mother and avoiding being attacked again was exhausting. But where were they? Why hadn't we been attacked again or used my mother as bait?

"I'm concerned about why there hasn't been news about my mother," I said sitting by the campfire. We had stopped to rest for the evening, our stomachs full of the dinner that Killian had managed to obtain for us. He left the camp again to patrol and keep watch while we rested. "What are Adriane and Ciaran waiting for? Why are they keeping my mother hidden from us?"

Ivarison leaned against a tree, watching the fire, arms crossed against his chest. Dealla and Delaney were near the fire, sitting together on the ground.

"I've wondered the same," Dealla said. The fire crackled, orange light hitting their faces.

"They could be trying to see what your abilities are. To see what you're capable of and the way to strike," Ivarison said sharply. "They aren't seated on Madora's throne for a reason, and they're trying to figure you out."

It wasn't an exact answer, and it still didn't help me feel better. Since Oakwood Village, the soldiers knew we were following their whereabouts. They hadn't left soldiers there without reason. They were left to attack. Were they really watching to see more?

Training with my abilities would have helped me see what more there may be. Ivarison hadn't brought up training with him again since the evening he had taken me. But he watched, each evening when I trained with Dealla or Delaney, nearby and observed. He bit his lips at times as if to stop himself from speaking, and I knew he waited for me to take the initiative.

I had tried multiple times to pull magic out of me since our evening in the meadow. There had been times when I noticed a difference when I held my sword, my hands humming as I grasped the grip. A pale shade of blue would appear at my fingertips, but I hadn't been able to do more before it snuffed out.

The night before we arrived at Ravenwick, Delaney and Killian left to patrol the thick forest surrounding us. As Dealla gathered sticks for our fire, I watched Ivarison pace back and forth, ever so often glancing over his shoulder toward the forest.

I tapped my fingers together, searching for the heat of my magic to pull it out. Tuning into the sounds around me, I noticed the birds had gone quiet, and all I could hear were faint steps behind me. Something heavy was ambling through the forest.

"Dealla," Ivarison called out, turning toward her. "Did Killian say where they were going?" he asked. His hands were in his pockets as he continued to pace, watching the forest. I could still hear the steps, and it was coming closer.

"East of here–" Her words were cut short as she spun around. Ivarison's head turned toward me.

My eyebrows shot to my hairline as I looked at Dealla and Ivarison. But as I began to turn, thick arms wrapped around me, and I crashed into something hard.

The sound of splintering wood erupted from the forest edge. Dealla's blade sang as she drew it.

"Ellowyn!" Dealla shouted. Ivarison's familiar scent filled my nostrils. He pulled me from the Norwag that crashed into our camp along with several Dark Soldiers. He pushed me behind him, away from them.

"Keep her safe!" Dealla shouted. Her sword whistled as she swung, bringing down one. Blood dripped from her blade as she continued to the next.

"Stay behind me, and try not to do anything stupid!" Ivarison shouted. I stood with my back to his. I watched the woods to ensure nothing else would come crashing through.

I would have smarted back off at him, but something was in the underbrush just ahead, hiding in the shadows of the forest.

The world seemed to slow as a Norwag came out, stalking, drool dripping from its sharp teeth as it cackled. My sword was on the other side of camp beside my cot, and there I stood, defenseless, unable to pull any source of power.

"Ivarison!" I shrieked more than I meant. He twisted around, pulling me to his side. Raising his other arm, darkness poured out of him as the Norwag reared its hind legs and pounced.

Ivarison bellowed a challenge that made my ears ring, his protective grip never wavering as shadows rippled out of him. The shadows wrapped over the Norwag in mid-air. And it released an ear-piercing screech, causing me to cover my ears.

Another Norwag screamed as Dealla plunged her sword through its thick gray hide. It fell to the ground with a resounding thud, and the dirt beneath its carcass turned black with blood.

I looked up at Ivarison. He inhaled before releasing a deep sigh as he glanced at me. His grip was still tightly around me as he scanned the camp, ensuring there were no others.

"Ellowyn," Dealla said, her voice slightly ragged as she breathed hard, her sword still in hand as black and red blood dripped.

"I'm fine," I said breathlessly, waving her off as Ivarison released me and stepped back. "Not even a scratch."

Dealla took my hand, pulling me closer to check for herself. Ivarison hadn't moved when Dealla looked at him. "Thank you for protecting her."

"Of course, I'm not the enemy here. I will protect our princess." He paused when Dealla pursed her lips.

I hadn't battled, and yet I was still breathing heavily as I watched trust build between the two of them.

Delaney and Killian dashed into the camp moments later, eyes widening as they saw the scattered soldiers and Norwags.

"We don't understand how they slipped through our patrol." Delaney's words came out in a rush, her breathing ragged. "We never saw or heard anything!"

"I dropped our dinner after hearing the fight," Killian said, looking over Dealla, and she shook her head at him. "Looks like we missed out on the fun."

"We were able to manage," Dealla said as she sat on a log to catch her breath.

"We should move then, just in case others come and find this mess," Killian said, kicking one of the dead Norwags.

What did that mean for us if they could slip through our patrol? As Dealla was known for being one of the best soldiers of Madora, Killian was known for his skills with patrolling. If they had slipped through him, did that mean we weren't even safe at night?

"Where are we again?" Delaney asked as we passed several small cottages and dry fields that lacked vegetation and care.

The village entrance rested between large, open iron gates. Two serpent statues sat on each side with onyx eyes. Nothing looked welcoming. The smell of ash lingered in the stale air. Broken branches hung from trees, and small gardens where workers picked through very few vegetables growing in dull garden beds.

The mid-morning air was chilly as I rubbed my hands together. This village was one of the worst we have traveled through. There was a guilt that hung in my stomach, unable to believe that anyone still lived in such a condition.

"Ravenwick. It was once large, but a section of it was burnt down," Killian answered. Ivarison glanced around, pulling the hood of his cloak over his head, then reached for mine and pulled it over my own head.

"Stop there," an unknown voice ordered.

Our feet stilled on the path. Some of the nearby Fae scurried away as two soldiers emerged from between two cottages and approached us.

"This can't be good," Dealla muttered as she exchanged a worried glance at Killian. His hand moved to the hilt of his sword, waiting for more from the soldiers.

"You have been requested at the manor. Follow us," one of the soldiers directed us as the other watched, taking notice that each of our hands was at our swords.

"We only just arrived. Surely, we haven't caused trouble already. Who is requesting us?" Killian asked, but the soldier straightened himself.

"You may ask questions once you're there," he spoke with his jaw clenched, his tone demanding.

"Be prepared for anything, right?" Delaney whispered and winced, taking my arms into hers.

"Come," the soldiers ordered, leading the way. The second soldier walked behind our group.

We walked deeper through Ravenwick, cutting through a rocky path, broken bits of buildings lay at our sides. The paved path gave way to dark gravel, leading to a small, beautiful manor – out of place compared to the rest of the village.

The manor rose before us like a jewel in a wasteland. Pristine white stone walls were unmarked by soot, gardens bursting with impossible color against Ravenwick's withered landscape. Even the glass in the tall windows gleamed, while every other pane we'd passed hung cracked or boarded over.

Who lived here? How could they let their village have such a horrible way of living, yet they lived so ravenously as others suffered?

"Dealla," Ivarison muttered as he moved closer to whisper, "You know who this village belongs to."

His words made me glance at him. Who did this village belong to? Were we in trouble?

"Well, this is cozy," Killian muttered, glancing around. "Nothing says, 'friendly chat' like being escorted by soldiers with snake–"

"Silence!" the commanding soldier snapped.

The soldier led the way into the manor. We walked through a stone corridor foyer, our steps echoing off the high ceiling. The walls were empty, no portraits or lanterns hung.

As we walked slowly, the soldier behind us pushed Dealla to move faster.

"Don't you dare touch–" Killian's black, long claws, pointed like talons, came through his hands, widening toward the soldier who had pushed her. Dealla shook her head as she grabbed hold of his arm.

His jaw tightened as he glared at the soldier, but continued to follow the leading soldier, who led us into the room that may have been the hall. There was a long table inside with chairs scattered about. Drapery hung from the windows, pushed to the side to give the room little light.

"Stay here," one of the soldiers said as we moved to the table. The soldiers turned on their heels and left, shutting the door behind them.

The room was quiet as we searched, looking for an exit. The fireplace at the end of the room and several higher windows were the only other way.

Perhaps Ivarison would be able to stretch his wings and fly us through the window if we couldn't fade out.

I turned to face him, but he shook his head. A familiar pressure touched the edges of my mind – gentle, questioning. Through our connection, I felt his reluctance, his certainty that escaping through the window would only make matters worse.

"We need to get out of here quickly," Ivarison said, Dealla turned toward him. "I cannot be here."

"We have to move as quickly as possible if we want to fade out–" Dealla was interrupted as the doors of the room reopened.

A young female and male Fae walked in, striding over together. Their features held similarities. The female wore her brunette hair in a tight braid, while her brothers fell loose around his shoulders. Their amber eyes moved across our group with predatory calculation, sizing us up like hunters evaluating prey.

As they approached, Ivarison had gone to the back of our group, his face in complete darkness under his hood. I tried to focus, to reach him the way he'd reached me before.

"Why are you hiding? What's wrong?" I tried to ask, but his mental walls felt like solid stone.

"The twins," Killian murmured, glancing back toward our group, his eyes stopping on Ivarison. The twins had never been mentioned. Who were they?

"Mara and Kai," Dealla greeted, as if she knew what I was questioning. "It's been some time since we've seen you. We didn't know you'd returned to Ravenwick."

The soldiers accompanying the twins took up their posts just outside the door of the hall. A heaviness settled in the pit of my stomach, burning through my bones, telling me these two could not be trusted. Something was wrong. If Adriane and Ciaran's soldiers had been spotted heading toward Ravenwick, where were they now?

"We prefer to keep our comings and goings private these days." Mara's voice was light as she sat in a chair at the table. "Though, apparently, not private enough."

Her twin brother positioned himself behind her chair, wrapping his arm over the top edge.

"Why didn't you come out for us?" Killian asked, "You sent soldiers to collect us instead." His tone was colored with displeasure from being ushered about like a criminal.

"We heard rumors about Princess Alina's capture." Kai studied our faces, searching for confirmation. "Judging by your presence here without her, I'd say the rumors are true."

"And why not come greet us yourself? Why the secrecy?" Dealla asked calmly, but her jaw muscles flexed.

"It was better for you to be seen with our soldiers than us." Mara said, not glancing at Dealla.

"Will we have a problem with these two?" I tried to ask Ivarison mentally again, searching for a way to get through his barrier. I flinched, feeling the pressure of being pushed back, before a nudge soothed the pressure.

"Yes, most likely." He responded, his voice low and tense. I didn't turn to look back at him, afraid of putting attention on him for whatever seemed to bother him.

"How is it better to be seen with soldiers than you?" I asked, growing less fond and more alarmed as each moment went on.

Mara arched an eyebrow, sitting straighter in her chair, trying to look under my hood. "I don't seem to know a few of your guests. Who are your traveling companions?"

Killian's eyebrows rose, looking at me. My chest tightened as I weighed the options. If they already suspected who I was, denial would only make us look guilty. But revealing my identity might be the key to getting information – or would it be a trap? Either way, hiding wouldn't help me find my mother.

"Delaney of Luminara," Killian introduced. Delaney slightly bowed her head in response. Then Killian looked at me, narrowing his eyes as if he were silently trying to tell me that he didn't believe it was a good idea. I nodded in response, pushing my cloak's hood down. "I would like to introduce you to Princess Ellowyn Kelgrove."

Kelgrove.

The room around me seemed to pause as I was pulled into a corridor that stretched longer than the hall. My last name rang in my ears, and I noticed another male standing in the corridor with me. A distinctive smile that was oddly familiar, and as he looked at me, he laughed. It reminded me so much of my own.

"*Ellowyn.*" He had a voice that could soothe any worry. It was comforting and made me feel as I once felt when I was home.

"Princess Ellowyn," the twins repeated in unison.

I blinked, breaking out of the trance, and tried to remember every detail of what I had seen: the smile, the tone of his voice.

Who was the male I had just seen?

"Yes, daughter of Princess Alina," I answered.

"The rumors are true, then? Princess Alina was captured, and you're looking for her?" Kai asked while Mara stared at our last companion. She inhaled deeply, and her nose wrinkled.

"We heard that some of Adriane's soldiers were headed toward Ravenwick. If you have any information, it would be greatly appreciated if you could share," I said. Mara kept her eyes on Ivarison, and I did not like the darkness that grew in her eyes.

If she doesn't take her eyes elsewhere...

I had to contain the heated feeling growing in my palms.

The twins exchanged a long glance – as if a silent conversation passed between them. It made my skin crawl. When Mara finally turned back to us, her expression had shifted to practiced indifference.

"I'm bored," Mara finally said, playing with the ring on her finger.

Dealla stepped forward. "If you know anything, you will be rewarded. We will leave immediately, and you won't see us again."

Mara huffed.

"Do you believe us to be fools?" Kai snapped. The sudden change in his demeanor caused Killian to step closer to me. "You may not ask now. However, regardless of whether you save Princess Alina or not, there will be war. When it comes, you will come and ask for our allegiance, then ask us to fight for your cause."

"My only concern is rescuing my mother." I didn't want to think of war. I didn't want to think of going into a war for a world that I did not fully understand. I could only focus on one thing at a time, and now, it was surviving to save my mother.

"And if you accomplish that, and this war arrives, will you disappear again? Leave Madora to pick up the pieces while you retreat to whatever haven you've been hiding in for seventeen years?"

Delaney spat on the ground toward the twins, and I wondered, for just a moment, if she would have spat in their faces if I asked.

I wish she could.

"You will not disrespect your princess," Delaney snapped. My chest warmed. It was clear that Mara and Kai weren't worth the time that we were wasting to find the information they may or may not have had.

"If there isn't information that you can share, then we are finished here." I insisted. I wouldn't fall for the accusation. They wanted to get a rise out of one of us, and I wouldn't let it.

"Who is the companion that hides underneath his hood?" Mara stood from her chair, moving closer as she pointed to Ivarison, not looking at me. "How very rude of him," she said, her eyes narrowed as her finger still pointed toward the hidden male.

"Are you such a fool that you have forgotten all manners, and you dare to ignore your princess?" Killian asked, blocking Mara from stepping closer to Ivarison and me.

Something wasn't right with the tension that was growing. Ivarison had been so quiet, I had nearly forgotten he was standing behind us.

Kai's lips curled in disgust. "Why do you ignore the question regarding the one hidden under the hood?"

"No one of importance. He hides under his hood because he is too ugly to look at," Killian answered. His shoulders were too tense as he tried to huff out a laugh.

Delaney's arms came around mine again, pulling me further away from the twins as Dealla and Killian stood in the front.

"Take his hood off, or I'll do it myself," Kai threatened, pulling a dagger from his hip.

"We've come in peace, Mara and Kai," Dealla said, "You have shown enough disrespect to our princess, and this will not be tolerated." She held a palm out to keep the twins from approaching closer. The guards watched every movement, just outside the door.

Ivarison put a hand toward the twins, still not speaking. The twins watched and waited. Ivarison put a hand on his hood and paused, just before he pulled it down.

It happened so quickly.

There was no hesitation in the twins. Kai raised his dagger above his head as they both ran to attack Ivarison. Delaney pulled me from harm's way with one hand, the other already holding her sword. Dealla and Killian took hold of the twins, pinning their arms behind their backs.

Ivarison's hands were up, and black shadows rushed out from him. The door to the hall slammed shut, blocking the soldiers. Through our connection, images flashed unbidden: flames consuming a village, screaming echoing through smoke. The memories weren't mine, and the guilt that crashed over me nearly brought me to my knees. What had he done?

"I'll kill you!" Mara screeched, her voice raspy from screaming. Soldiers pounded on the door from the other side. "I'll kill all of you for bringing him here!"

"Threatening a princess in front of Kingdom guards. You must be a fool," Killian growled, holding Kai tighter, making his dagger fall to the ground with a sickening clank.

"We didn't know that you were in Ravenwick, Mara. We were only passing through." Dealla hissed as she held the female.

Kai was rigid as he stared at Ivarison.

"I promised I would find a way to end you, and I will one day," Kai finally spoke, trying to pull from Killian's grip, which only tightened.

Delaney and I stood closest to Ivarison, Delaney's sword was held at the ready if they escaped Dealla and Killian's vice grips.

"Will you both step aside if we let you go so that we can leave in peace?" Killian asked. The twins glared at one another before Kai nodded.

The moment Killian and Dealla loosened their grip, the twins tried again to reach Ivarison. Delaney had waited, ready, but before she had the chance to react, Ivarison's hand curved out in front of him, and the twins froze in place.

"Enough of this," Ivarison roared, his deep voice carrying the weight of absolute certainty. "I could end you both right now." He clenched his fist, and the twins flinched as one. "Tell us about Princess Alina. Now."

It was not a question. He gave a demand that they would obey or die. When Ivarison moved his hands, the twins wrenched in pain.

"Ivarison," Killian warned. "you cannot kill them. It will get you nowhere."

"I could have ended this in half the time," he snapped. His eyes narrowed at Killian, as if to tell him of what he could or couldn't do.

"Let Mara go," growled Kai, gritting his teeth.

"I don't believe that you're in any state to make threats or commands. As your threats are what landed you here." Ivarison's grip tightened on Mara. Her brows pressed tightly together, her breathing hitched, gasping for air. My heart raced, waiting for one of them to talk.

Kai's eyes widened at his sister. "We were told that Alina had been taken prisoner. She was locked away in such a way that she couldn't use her power," Kai said as he hissed in pain.

"And?" Ivarison asked, the muscle in his jaw ticked.

"They were taking her to a prison that Ciaran built, headed toward Dustvale Village and then North."

Ivarison studied Mara closely, then at Kai. "Are you sure that's all you know?"

The banging at the door of the hall intensified as soldiers tried to break through.

I could sense Ivarison's power, very vaguely. He was slipping through their minds to see the truth. I stepped away, wanting the feeling to fade as I could feel his power come through me, and the heavy darkness like shadows brushed against my skin.

"Yes," Mara shouted through clenched teeth, her face reddening. "We don't know anything else!"

Ivarison tightened his grip. The twins screamed and were slammed against the wall. Guards continued pounding against the door, trying to break through the magic that held the door shut.

"Ivarison!" Dealla shouted as Mara and Kai grabbed at their throats as if they could pry his magic away.

"You're helping Adriane and Ciaran, aren't you?!" His shout made me jump as he stepped closer.

"You must stop. You cannot kill them!" Killian said, blocking his view of the twins. "Now is not the time for this. We must get out of here."

"Ivarison, let's move," I coaxed. Delaney followed the step I took closer to him.

Ivarison snarled, then exhaled heavily. His grip was still tight against the twins as he gritted through his teeth. "Fine. As soon as I release them, they're going to try to kill us."

"If we don't go far, I can fade with them both." Dealla grabbed hold of Delaney and Killian. "I trust you will take Ellowyn?" Dealla asked, her voice stern as she gave a piercing glare. "Move out now!"

The muscles in his jaw loosened as I looked up at him, his gaze finding me.

"Grab hold of me," he whispered. There wasn't time to ask any more questions, so I wrapped my arms around him while he kept his arms raised toward the twins to keep them in place.

"You'll regret this." Kai's voice was hoarse as he spoke.

Dealla vanished, holding Killian and Delaney.

"You're right, I already do." Ivarison glanced through the room. I felt his magic being reined in, loosening. The doors of the hall burst open, and the guards rushed in.

Shadows wrapped around me, disorienting me. Then I could hear Mara's shattering scream as we vanished before them.

Chapter Sixteen

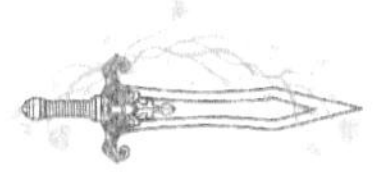

We fled as quickly as we could from Ravenwick to escape the twins' wrath. The air grew chiller as we continued Northwest. We stopped less, and the days blurred as I tried not to think of the conditions my mother could be in.

"Why is it so cold?" I pulled my cloak tighter, missing Luminara's warmth and the mint and lavender breeze that once filled my lungs. Now, crisp air hit our lungs, and browning leaves surrounded us.

"We're near witch territory," Killian said from ahead. "The village that we're stopping at is near their land."

"There really are witches?" I asked. Dealla and Killian had mentioned the prophecy, but I hadn't thought much more of the witches with the other information I had tried to absorb.

"The witches do not bother others as long as they don't bother us," Killian answered. He wiggled his fingers as if he were casting a spell, then sobered. "We haven't seen any since Ciaran torched their land many years ago. It's mostly destroyed."

"Was Lyra a true witch? My parents fed me stories of her to scare me when I was a child." Delaney asked, rolling her eyes at me. "Unfortunately, I was more fascinated by the story than frightened." We both chuckled.

"If you met Lyra, you'd understand fear," Ivarison said. "I met her once, and I would be fine never to cross her again. She's why Ciaran set their land on fire."

"Why is she so frightening?" I asked. What could she be capable of that made Ivarison wary?

"Do you always talk this much during travel?" Ivarison huffed.

"Oh, she's capable of trapping you in your worst nightmares and driving you into insanity," Killian rambled, shooting a glare at Ivarison. "She wouldn't need to harm you physically; you'd do it yourself. I've never seen her do it, but I once heard she could melt skin off your bones." Killian shuddered at the thought, then stopped at Dealla's sharp look. "I don't know if it's true. They don't enjoy Fae company, and most fled after the burning."

"Could they've just escaped through other parts of Madora?" I asked.

"There are books of them in Mystmere," Dealla said. "If we reach there."

If. The words hung between us.

Despite the drop in temperature, the grass still shone a beautiful shade of green beneath our feet, blooming flowers dotting trails and over tree roots. Orange leaves blazed overhead as we followed the stone streets, welcoming us into Dustvale Village.

"Hello," a female said as she passed by, her skin texture resembling that of moss and smooth bark. She was taller than most. I tried not to stare as I watched her walk.

The village felt more welcoming than any of the others we had entered, which made it harder not to stand guard. After Oakwood and Ravenwick, even a welcoming hello felt like a trap.

"Princess Ellowyn?"

Each of us tensed.

A dark-haired female stood behind us with others beside her, eyes bright and eager. "Are you the daughter of Princess Alina?"

My companions shifted closer. I quickly looked at the others, alarmed. I studied each of the villagers, looking for weapons, hidden threats, and escape routes.

"Please, just call me Ellowyn. We're passing through in search of my mother. Have you seen or heard anything about her whereabouts?" I asked, still glancing about. I refused to be caught off guard.

"We're honored by your return." The female's brown eyes never left me. "You met a relative in Whiterun, and I couldn't believe it. You look just like your mother. I heard she was taken to the North. We have tried to listen for information, but Madora has gone quiet these last few days."

"Quiet how?" Dealla's hand remained at her belt. Delaney and Ivarison were closer at my sides, trapping me in between them.

"We try to stay alert to what is occurring throughout Madora. We haven't heard of the whereabouts of Adriane and Ciaran, nor their soldiers." The female paused. A look of concern spread from her brows to her lips, and she tentatively rested a hand on Dealla's arm.

"You must be famished. Please allow me the honor of offering you rooms and a warm meal. We can speak privately there."

A male Fae joined her, taking her hand. "It would be an honor if you could join us."

My mind raced. Could this be another trap? How many times had we been attacked and survived? How many more until one of us doesn't? Ivarison caught my eye, reading my panic.

I couldn't make a decision; I didn't want to take the chance. Ivarison looked to Dealla and Killian, some silent communication passed between them.

"That would be wonderful," Ivarison said. His hand brushed my arm. "Breathe. We will be careful."

The couple guided us through the streets where apple trees were heavy with fruit, bordered by gardens. Homes with Fae standing near their steps and fences, watching as children's laughter echoed from tall grass fields.

Children. The first children I'd seen in Madora. The jovial sound made my chest ache with longing for such freedom.

"Here we are." The female opened a purple door, revealing a dining room with gray marble floors and a large oak table surrounded by matching benches.

We walked cautiously, hesitation in our movements.

"You need not be afraid of us. We want to help and support you." The female smiled. "I'm Xantara, and this is my mate, Asher."

"Thank you." I stepped forward, claiming my position as the group's head. I prayed to the gods that our decision was not a mistake. "I'm grateful."

She bowed her head. "We have rooms upstairs. You'll need to share, but each has a private bath. This is our small inn, though we don't receive many visitors anymore." Sadness flickered across her face. "One day again, I hope. I'll prepare dinner if you wish to rest and wash up. Asher can lead you up."

Upstairs, I chose to room with Delaney, while Dealla and Killian shared another, leaving Ivarison to the room across from mine.

"You can bathe first," Delaney said once the door closed. "I'll keep an eye on things here."

The room wasn't very large. Just enough room for a king-sized bed with gold framing and curtains. A vanity sat near a closed window, and two maroon chairs that clashed against the blue walls.

I didn't linger in the hot bath for long after I cleaned the dirt and grime from my skin. The time was enough for the water to soothe my travel-sore muscles and the constant pull in my chest.

"Does this seem strange to you?" I asked, emerging from the bathroom. "Such hospitality from strangers?"

Delaney shrugged. "It's common to have this sort of welcome when you're royalty."

Royalty. The word still felt foreign. Princess of Madora. A realm where I had been stabbed, hunted, and nearly killed on multiple occasions. Was that to be expected of royal life? I wasn't too impressed.

"I'm sure it will take time to get used to," Delaney said as I frowned at the thought of this new life.

A soft knock interrupted us.

"Hello, dears," Xantara said as Delaney opened the door. "It has been some time since we've had guests and could offer services." She carried a small basket. "May I come in?"

Delaney looked at me, and after I gave a slight nod, she opened the door wider.

"Long before I met Asher, I was a maid in Mystmere," Xantara said, walking in and setting a hairbrush and perfume bottles from her basket on the vanity. "It was before your mother was born. I knew your grandparents. Queen Amelia was so very lovely, you have her eyes."

She held up the hairbrush. "May I? I used to do this for your grandmother. What a surreal moment, I must say, having her granddaughter here in my home."

Delaney slipped into the bathroom as I took a seat, and Xantara began brushing my damp hair.

"What was she like?" I only knew of my grandmother's cottage and her healing abilities. *If* that was even her cottage. And now, I learned I had her eyes.

"She was wonderful and very beautiful, just as you." Xantara's voice caught. "I was her maid, but she treated me like a friend from the moment we met. She treated others as her equals. I was with her for nearly a decade before I met Asher. It was hard for me to leave the kingdom, but I knew she was in good hands. Shortly after, Princess Alina was born."

"She had healing abilities, but did she have other powers?" The powers I had experienced came from somewhere, and I hadn't known what each of my family members had been capable of. I hadn't even asked about my mother's abilities and wasn't sure I wanted to know just yet.

"She helped protect the Riker Tree and had extraordinary healing powers. She could mend many types of wounds just by touch alone, rarely needing herbs for assistance."

Dealla has mentioned the Riker Tree, but I don't know much about it." I glanced at my satchel with Rikeroot; it never left my side unless I was sleeping or washing.

Xantara's eyebrows rose. I didn't want to go into detail about what and why I didn't know about things. She certainly didn't need to know about my forced amnesia and the seventeen stolen years.

"You should ask the others you travel with. The Riker Tree is sacred to our land, massive and believed to be the source of our magic. Queen Amelia had helped guard it. I don't know what happened to it after your family's tragedy."

I closed my eyes as she worked, misting sweet perfume over my drying hair. The sultry scent hung with my questions of who my grandmother had been, who the male I had a vision of might be, and whether any of us would survive long enough for me to learn the truth.

Chapter Seventeen

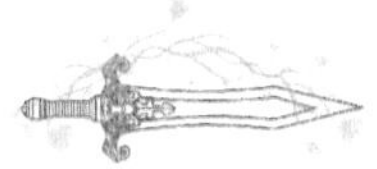

Our stay with Asher and Xantara lasted just long enough to rest and replenish supplies, but not a moment more. We couldn't afford to linger; we needed to continue our search.

Xantara had insisted on serving every meal herself, sharing stories of my grandmother between courses and walking me through the village to show everything they had accomplished through their time. Breakfast was unusually quiet the morning we were set to leave. Asher had left early to help another in the village while Xantara gathered our belongings.

The purple door burst open. Asher stumbled through, his tan face pale.

"We're under attack!" He managed to spit out, lunging for the cupboard under the stairs and pulling out swords for Xantara and himself.

Time seemed to still. Outside, screams erupted. Villagers ran frantically across the open door and through the streets.

"Through the back!" Xantara hissed. Asher took the lead, guiding us as we grabbed our bags and fled.

"That forest path leads north," Asher said breathlessly. He looked directly at me. "It's Dark Soldiers. They are coming for you. You best move quickly and take care of yourself."

I nodded, my throat tight for words. The soldiers had tracked us here. Dustvale Village was under attack because of me. Dealla's words rang through my ears: *They won't stop until you're dead – or they are.*

We moved fast, watching panicked Fae running through smoke-filled streets. Steel clashed against steel. Villagers screamed. I didn't look back, but the acrid smell of fire followed us.

There were children in the village.

The children.

"Wait!" I stopped short, the group nearly colliding with me. This was my fault. I had to help. "We have to go back. There are children in the village. I cannot let them die or get hurt because soldiers are hunting me!"

Ivarison looked back at the village, his jaw tight. "I'll go, does anyone care to join?"

Killian kissed Dealla's cheek. "Stay with them," he said to Delaney, then clasped Ivarison's shoulder.

"Keep her safe," Ivarison snapped at Delaney and Dealla. Before I could object, Ivarison and Killian vanished.

Dealla took my arm, forcing me forward alongside Delaney. "Come now, Ellowyn. They will make sure they get to safety."

Dozens of soldiers rushed through the streets, slaughtering anyone who crossed their paths. Blood gleamed on armor as death followed in their wake.

"MOVE!" Asher roared, cleaving his blade through a soldier's armor. The gentle innkeeper had become a protective warrior.

Dealla and Delaney flanked him, blocking soldiers from reaching Xantara and me.

You will not be afraid.

You have power.

You will not be afraid.

Over and over, I chanted as we pressed forward, hoping that it would spark the magic within me. If I had the power, now was the time. I had to protect my subjects. If I could conjure anything, I could end this. The soldiers wouldn't know what hit them.

But nothing came. No flame, no power, no salvation.

Dealla and Delaney slew our enemies with ease. Dealla twisted, taking the last soldier down that Asher had fought. Xantara gripped my hand as we ran faster. I hoped Ivarison and Killian were safe with the children.

There was a low rumble, and the earth shuddered. Heat and force slammed into our backs, launching us forward. Swords flew from sweaty hands, clattering against the dirt. Xantara's grip never left mine as we landed on hard stone together.

I rose, vision blurred, ears ringing. Xantara pulled my arm.

Move. *Move!*

"ELLOWYN!" someone cried out. Delaney's sword flashed as a soldier emerged from the woods.

Through the muffled chaos, Xantara suddenly threw herself in front of me, her hand crushing mine.

Her eyes widened.

Our joined hands shook. We looked down at her abdomen, where a sword tip protruded, glistening in her blood.

I couldn't hear my own voice as I screamed. Her hands pressed against her stomach as the sword withdrew. The soldier came for me, but Dealla was faster. Asher caught Xantara as she fell, then cried out as an arrow buried itself in his chest.

A white blur ran by me, Delaney in beast form, reaching the path of Dark Soldiers before any of them could react. I turned away, not wanting to watch as she tore them to shreds. But it didn't stop me from hearing her growling, thrashing, and dying soldiers' screaming.

I dropped beside Xantara. Asher held her, ignoring the arrow jutting from his body. Delaney shifted back, kneeling with us. She examined the wound, then hissed after sniffing the blood on her hands. "Rikeroot. I can't – there's nothing we have that could heal this."

"No." Panic clawed at me. "This is my fault, maybe I could try. I healed myself before," Dealla tried to pull me from Xantara.

Asher's head hung low, tears streaming down his cheeks as Xantara writhed in pain.

This was my fault.

I pushed Dealla aside. "I have to try!" I sobbed, placing my hands over Xantara's and closing my eyes. I searched and searched for that blue flame, the magic, any source of power. "PLEASE, ANYTHING!"

I cried and cursed at myself.

Nothing. I couldn't do anything.

Xantara's hand moved to come on top of mine, pressing tightly against her bleeding wound.

"Listen to me, dear." she spoke weakly, as if there wasn't much air left in her to breathe. "This is not your fault. Do not blame yourself. If I had known this would happen, I wouldn't change a thing."

She squeezed my hand as I sobbed. A stranger who had welcomed me into her life like family. Who had filled me with stories of my grandparents, whom I would have never known, and shown such kindness and generosity.

"Do not dwell on the what-ifs, Ellowyn. You're strong, with a kind soul. You must remember that. Do not be afraid." His voice faded. "You will make it through this. You must, and I believe in you."

Asher slumped beside her, his breathing labored. "Leave us here. Continue north. We will be fine together. I will not go on without her."

"No, we can't leave you both like this."

"You must go." He coughed, blood speckling his lips. "The arrow also has Rikeroot. I can feel it spreading." His hands found Xantara's face. "I don't have much time left, and I will not live without her."

"Two hundred years," he whispered. "I love you. I'll see you again soon."

A hollowness spread through my chest as I watched Xantara fade. She gave Asher a soft smile before her heart stopped, her eyes fixed on his face.

Asher held Xantara close to his chest, roaring to the sky as he pulled the arrow from his chest. I would never forget his agonizing scream. Just as Asher threw the arrow down, Ivarison and Killian reappeared.

Ivarison grabbed the arrow and hissed. Blue flames consumed it to ash. We waited, not leaving Asher alone as he faded. Around us, soldiers lay dead, and Delaney ripped apart the last few she found lingering. I clutched my chest, watching Asher whisper final words of love before his heartbeat stilled.

Mates. Together even in death.

I couldn't pull myself from the ground. My legs felt heavy. I couldn't bring myself to move. Dealla tried pulling me up as I wept.

How was I supposed to do this?

"Ellowyn, we must go." Dealla's voice seemed far away. "Come now."

"I can't– I can't breathe–" I clawed at my tunic, trying to loosen the fabric around my throat.

I couldn't. Do. This.

"Dealla–" Ivarison's warning came too late. The panic rising within me brought the power I had tried to summon earlier, now burning out of control in my chest, searing my skin. "Control yourself, or you're going to announce to every dark creature that may be around exactly where you are."

My hands glowed blue. I couldn't stop it. I wasn't even sure what Ivarison said.

Ivarison's arms wrapped around me. I couldn't feel his pull as he faded us away, letting go immediately and stepping back. Dealla appeared with Delaney and Killian moments later, their lips moving, but I heard nothing.

We were safe. The village wasn't. I could still smell their beautiful homes burning and their screams as they were slaughtered.

Were the children safe?

Was this my reality?

This was my reality.

Others would die for what they believed in, for my family. They would die for us. I hit the ground hard, my knees striking the dirt, my fingernails clawing the soil until earth packed beneath them.

Asher and Xantara.

"This is my fault. The village, they were killed because of me!" I wasn't sure if I was crying or screaming.

Would I be forced to run while others died? Why did I get to survive when they didn't? I couldn't handle that such a welcoming village was nearly destroyed because I had traveled through it.

"Ellowyn–" Dealla's voice was still muffled. "You need to breathe. We will be okay."

I heard her, but I couldn't breathe. My body shook as I closed my eyes, wanting the pain to fade as more cries escaped. All the grief since watching our cottage burn and watching my mother taken. Was she even alive?

"Ellowyn!" someone shouted.

I wanted an escape. I wanted this to end.

"Ellowyn!" There was the voice again, but it sounded as if it were underwater.

My eyes opened and saw swirls of blue and black. A cloud engulfed me, creating a barrier between me and the world. I could hear Killian and Dealla shouting through the darkness as I sat and wept for the ones that had been lost and suffering. For my family, I'd never know. For my father and grandparents. My mother – she was lost. I had stopped counting the days since my mother's capture once we had hit a month since her capture. Was I left with nothing?

"Ellowyn," Ivarison's voice cut through clearer than the rest. "Relax your mind. Take deep breaths."

"I can't. I can't." The lump in my throat was choking me.

"Let me through. Let me come to you."

I could see him, trying to push through the darkness surrounding me, his face twisted with pain.

"Ellowyn–" he winced and cried out as he continued to push.

"Ivarison, stop!" Dealla yelled, trying to pull him back, but he brushed her off.

I watched him struggle, skin cracking then healing instantly as he fought through whatever this barrier I created.

"*You have to let me through–*" his lips weren't moving as I heard his pleas. I didn't know how I created the shield, but I focused on him, wanting him to come in. The pressure against my mind and the shield were a part of me. It pulled at my stomach as he broke through, gasping.

He grabbed my shoulders, then gently cupped my face, his glacier-blue eyes meeting mine.

"You're safe."

I shook my head. "The others aren't. They died because I was there." I choked on a sob.

"We saved all the children because of you. They're safe. We were able to protect them and move them out." His thumbs brushed away my tears. "Breathe with me. In.. Out..."

I followed his rhythm, inhaling deep breaths and exhaling slowly. After several times, my shaking began to subside.

"This isn't your fault. They will pay for what they've done." His voice steadied me, his hands never leaving my face. The protective barrier began to dissolve. I could see the others standing nearby, waiting. "You're okay. I've got you."

He rubbed my arms, holding on as Dealla came closer, her expression grim.

"Help her, Ivarison. If she is willing, help train her." Dealla's voice was leveled but strained. "I promise not to interfere if that is what Ellowyn wishes."

Dealla pulled me into the tightest hug she'd ever given, her hands smoothing my hair as she held me.

For a moment, we shared unspoken fears of what the future looked like. What would happen if we never found my mother, or if we found her too late? The pain flowed between us, the shared grief bound us together just a little stronger.

Chapter Eighteen

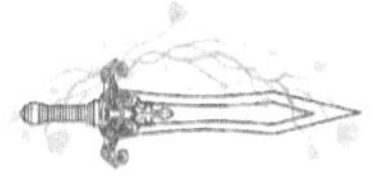

Power. Be strong, Ellowyn.

What kind of Fae princess would I be if I weren't able to figure out a way to wield my power? The magic ran through my veins, yet I couldn't conjure it willingly.

"You're overthinking it." Ivarison's patience had worn thin after days of failed training sessions. He'd conjured his blue fire dozens of times, showing how easy it was while I managed nothing.

I rubbed my temples, fighting the urge to throw a rock at him. "Of course, it's easy for you."

I paced away, kicking dirt until my boots turned white, heat rising in my cheeks.

"It's never easy. The Rikeroot is not what's stopping this – your mental shields are." His fingers raked through his dark hair, jaw tensing as piercing eyes fixed on me. "You don't seem to be truly trying, love."

My shoulders shuddered at the endearment. "Yes, I am! Maybe my mind knows I'm not capable of what's expected of me. I didn't ask for this. Lost memories, people dying because of me."

Ivarison crossed his arms, an eyebrow rising. "Self-pity won't help your kingdom."

"I can't protect myself or others. How am I supposed to help an entire kingdom?"

"Madora has a name and it's yours. You need to get over your fears and do what must be done. Maybe your mother was right to keep you hidden."

"You're a prick!" I shoved past him, then whirled back. "Is this all you want from me? To rid the monsters that no one else has been able to do so?"

He didn't respond. He rubbed his face, looking through the trees. His jaw remained tight.

I didn't want a kingdom relying on me, not when I would only fail them. If my mother had told me the truth, prepared me, perhaps this could be different.

"Where are you going?" Ivarison called out as I headed toward the woods.

"Away from you."

"You cannot go alone."

"Watch me," I snapped back, leaving him standing alone as he huffed.

He didn't follow as I disappeared into the trees, needing distance from his arrogance. That damn scent of his lingered everywhere; woodsmoke and the freshness of rain. I couldn't focus, even when the world was frantic around me.

I walked in a straight line so I could retrace my way back. Ivarison wouldn't lose me. He would come searching, eventually. I hoped.

I took my time being alone. It was hard to find a moment for myself while we traveled and had to watch our backs constantly. Orange and yellow leaves fell around me as birds sang overhead.

"The beast came through here–"

My heart caught in my throat, and I stopped in my tracks, listening to the direction of the voices.

"I saw tracks. Let's keep moving so we can kill it," a nasty voice came just ahead. I ducked behind low-hanging branches.

Two Fae males slowly walked through the brush, swords at their hips, and bows on their backs. Filthy and reeking, they wore dark armor beneath their cloaks. Adriane's soldiers.

They continued, muttering under their breath at each other.

It had been a mistake to go off on my own. Worse, I had turned from my path when I went to hide. Now, I had two soldiers to stay clear from and whatever beast they were hunting.

"Ivarison?" I tried to call out mentally to him, hoping if he could hear me, he could guide me back.

How long before I had reason to panic? He wouldn't let me wonder for long. I hadn't been able to do what he asked during our training. How could I navigate back to camp?

I forced myself to stop spiraling, knowing it would only escalate my panic.

The forest grew quiet, except for the crunching leaves underfoot. A rustle nearby made me hide again, hoping it was Ivarison searching for me.

I moved to a large tree, pushing through branches and spider webs until I froze. I had found what the two Fae hunted. Only it wasn't just a beast.

I grabbed my chest, breathing heavily as I suppressed a scream.

She was beautiful. How could something so beautiful be killed for only existing? Just as I was hunted for being a halfling.

She rested amongst the trees. Her golden eyes, flecked with purple, met mine. Black pupils outlined in honey-gold. Scales rippled across her body in black and turquoise, her belly deep obsidian.

Dragon. Of course, I stumbled across one while alone. Ivarison's words hung over my head: *Dragons wouldn't hesitate to turn on us if you went too close.*

Shit.

She growled low – a warning. I couldn't yell or run for fear of bringing attention to us.

"W-wait. Wait." I stammered, letting go of my sword and raising my hands to show I meant no harm. I listened and could still hear the Fae through the woods. "Can you understand me?"

Her head tilted slightly. This was ridiculous.

"Two soldiers are hunting you. I think they are soldiers of Adriane and Ciaran. They will slaughter you if they find you. You must go, now!"

The dragon's growl seized. Golden eyes narrowed as her head rose higher.

"THERE'S THE BEAST!" The two soldiers burst through the thick brush, their swords ready. Their fists clenched as they walked closer, then noticed me and stopped.

"Move out of the way, wench," one huffed, but I wouldn't allow it. As long as I stood there, I wouldn't let the soldiers take another life, dragon or not.

"No," I said, my voice low as I stood in front of the dragon, hoping that she didn't get pissed.

The soldiers looked at each other and laughed.

"Fine, we will kill you both." They advanced. She began rising, and if she attacked, I would be caught between them.

"NO!" I roared, voice ringing through the trees as I raised my palms at the charging soldiers.

The ground shook and cracked between my feet, forming fissures across the earth. The deep cuts in the earth stopped where the soldiers stood. They looked down as the ground below their feet crumbled beneath them. Unable to keep their footing, they fell. The ground opened deeper and deeper until their shouts cut off abruptly.

I dropped my hands as dust rushed up from where they'd fallen. The ground swallowed them whole.

I stared at my hands, then at the gaping hole I had created.

Slowly turning to the dragon, I found her golden eyes had softened, watching me. I hadn't realized she was larger than the small manor that the twins lived in.

"You should go," I urged, my voice shaking. Would she attack me?

But then she did as I said. Her wings unfurled, creating a large gust of wind. The leaves of the trees swirled, and my hair whipped across my face as I watched her fly toward the clouds in the sky.

"Where the hell have you been?!" Ivarison hissed when I made my way out of the woods. Pacing marks scarred the ground where he'd waited, and his face went pale seeing my expression.

"I got lost. Someone was in the woods, and they were searching for something." I was still mad, but I was more shaken by what I had done to the soldiers than our squabble. I sat on a log and took a swig from the canteen.

"Which is the reason why you shouldn't have gone off like that. I couldn't hear you –" He stopped, looking toward the sky. "Get up, we need to move."

"What?" I started to protest but I heard it too, something was coming fast.

Wingbeats pounded overhead before something heavy struck the ground, shaking the earth beneath our feet. I coughed from the dust that whipped about. The beautiful dragon I had saved landed in front of us, studying Ivarison and me.

"Stay behind me," Ivarison said, drawing his sword. The dragon huffed, sending smoke in his direction.

"No, wait! I think it's okay, I just met her." I ignored his gaping expression as I walked closer to the dragon. "I'm happy that you're safe."

"What in gods' name were you doing? What do you mean you *met* this dragon?" Ivarison demanded, sword still drawn but lowered.

The dragon leaned forward, her head large enough to have been the size of my cottage. She huffed. Her warm breath washed over my skin. It felt like I was dipped into scorching water, making my eyes water.

"Thank you," a warm, welcoming female voice filled my mind.

"What was that?" I looked at Ivarison.

"You saved me. I wanted to express my gratitude."

A dragon was speaking to me.

"How am I hearing you?"

Ivarison watched, eyes darting between us. I had never seen him look so dumbfounded.

"I choose to communicate with you. I understood you when you warned me and stopped them from attacking. You took a chance to save me when you didn't have to. Perhaps that was very foolish of you, but you still risked yourself. I've never seen that from your kind."

"I'm only a halfling, human and Fae."

"Yes, I know who you are, Ellowyn Kelgrove."

"You know who I am? What's your name?" The ground shook as she settled, bringing her head down so we were closer. The black scales on her back shone as the sun came through the clouds.

"Briallen, but you may call me Bria."

"You've been in Madora for how long? How have you befriended a dragon?" Ivarison asked, and Bria watched the sword in his hand.

"Oh, are you jealous, Ivarison?" I asked, rolling his name off my tongue. "Put your sword away."

His eyebrows shot up, but he placed his sword at his hip. "Yes." He dared step closer to Bria. "She's magnificent."

Bria huffed more smoke in his face.

"Oh, I might like him if he compliments me more," Bria said as she inhaled his scent. *"He seems different."*

"What do you mean?" His scent always did linger.

"Something is unique about both of your scents. Perhaps since you're a halfling. I haven't been around many Fae in my lifetime. Other than a few I've eaten." She paused at my horrified look. *"Only when provoked, and they tried to kill me. I protected myself."* I bit my lip to hide the grin.

"What did she say?" Ivarison asked, crossing his arms in front of him, looking annoyed that he wasn't in the conversation.

"That you smell," I answered, now grinning wider as he rolled his eyes.

"What happened in the woods? How did you meet her?"

I sat back on the log, adjusting my shoulders. "Two Fae males were hunting her, and I tried to go in the opposite direction, and that's when I found Bria."

"Bria," he muttered, testing her name.

I nodded, "When the two males found us both, they tried to attack her. I don't know exactly how I did it," I looked down at my hands before I continued, "When I threw my hands up, the ground cracked open and swallowed them. I don't know if they're even alive now."

He studied me carefully. "Well, we won't go find out. If they were trying to kill her, they deserve what you did." He closed his eyes, huffing out a laugh. "Risking your life for a dragon that could burn you alive or eat you? Brilliant strategy. Looks like you may be capable of saving others after all." I crossed my arms, glaring at him. "We've been gone from the camp for some time. We need to return."

I gazed at Bria, taking in her fascinating beauty and terrifying power. Those sharp talons and teeth that were larger than my hands.

"It was nice to meet you, Bria," I said quietly, wishing we had more time to speak with her.

"I would like to help you, if you'd allow. I know you are searching for your mother. Fae and humans aren't the only ones suffering from what Adriane and Ciaran have done."

"Ivarison, she wants to help." Excitement bubbled up inside me. "We have others traveling with us too, as we search for my mother. Have you heard anything about where Adriane may have taken my mother?"

Ivarison cleared his throat, "Bria, may I listen to your thoughts?" he asked, "I don't want to intrude if you do not wish."

Bria nodded, and Ivarison's eyebrows furrowed as he concentrated.

"I have not heard a word of Princess Alina's whereabouts, but have overheard her being captured. I may learn more as you travel, though it has been some time since I encountered another dragon. As you search for your mother, I will search for others of my kind. Perhaps, they would have information."

Anything would be useful," Ivarison said, "We only know of a prison that Ciaran built, but we don't know where. Your assistance could be invaluable." He paused, "We should get back to camp first and tell the others before you arrive."

"I would love to help you find others too," I said, hope building in me. We had a dragon on our side.

Chapter Nineteen

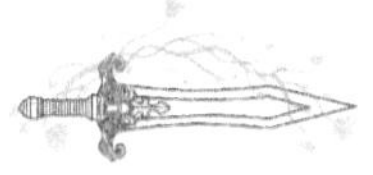

Fire crackled as Dealla, Delaney, and Killian sat together. We were gone longer than usual because I ran off. Dealla looked up, orange flames illuminating her face, eyebrows raised in question.

Our training area wasn't far from camp. It wouldn't take Bria long to arrive. What would the others think when she appeared?

I could sense her somewhere above the clouds. The connection she had gifted me allowed me to sense her presence and hear when she chose to speak. It was fascinating, but I didn't want Bria staying if she wanted to search for others of her kind.

"What is it?" Dealla asked as Ivarison released me after we returned. Was it that obvious? I'd never been very good at hiding emotions.

Ivarison looked skeptical as I watched him from the corner of my eye. Before I could answer, powerful wingbeats created gusts of wind overhead. Dealla, Killian, and Delaney darted from the fire so fast I barely registered their movement. Bria landed at a respectful distance, taking in the three that stood at my side.

"This is Bria," I said with a sense of pride, moving closer.

"Ellowyn!" Killian grabbed my arm.

"Her name is Bria," Delaney repeated. While the others looked alarmed, Delaney grinned widely.

"Yes, Ivarison and I just met her. She would like to help us during our journey."

"How could you know that?" Killian remained rooted in place.

"I'm able to speak and hear her," I replied as if this were a normal thing.

All that was heard was the trees rustling against the breeze. Dealla, Delaney and Killian stared wide-eyed at the towering dragon. I moved closer after Killian let me go, standing beside Bria's massive legs.

"You were supposed to be training," Dealla said, breaking the silence as she looked at the quiet Ivarison. "Have you been doing that?"

He rolled his eyes. "No, I've been sending her out to collect dragons. I suppose it's a relief she wasn't set aflame."

"Don't worry over the questions they may ask. Fae and dragons have not trusted one another in ages. Focus on continuing your magic training and mastering it. Being connected to a dragon may amplify what's within you."

I bit my lip. I couldn't conjure my magic so willingly. What would that mean for our connection?

Bria kept her distance while the others adjusted to traveling with a dragon. She had done well by keeping herself hidden since staying concealed while near us would have proven challenging.

"I've been replaced, you've found a better patroller!" Killian cried out jokingly. I smacked his arm. Bria couldn't enter the villages, but she would fly above and look for suspicious activity.

As we continued our journey, Bria still looked for other dragons. She'd been alone ever since her parents had been killed long ago, unable to find another like her.

"Is having a dragon traveling with us a good idea?" Dealla asked quietly, while we walked to our next destination.

"Why wouldn't it be?" Delaney countered. "Not only can she see from above, but she can see things we may miss from the ground. She could scorch enemies if needed."

"Yes, but dragons are dangerous and unpredictable. How are we supposed to move through villages or enter Mystmere?"

"*I'm hardly unpredictable when you're able to communicate with me.*" Bria grumbled with annoyance.

"They're only unpredictable because you're unable to communicate. Bria and I understand each other just fine." I adjusted my satchel strap. "She's done nothing wrong and genuinely wants to help. She'll fly above us when we're in villages and stay hidden as she did before I met her."

"And once we get to Mystmere?" Killian asked, scanning the clouds to see if he could find her.

"I am a Princess of Mystmere. Bria is my friend, and I welcome her with me."

No one said anything else about it after that. We would benefit from having her on our side, just as Delaney mentioned: early warnings of soldiers and reconnaissance ahead. It could ease the fear we'd carried since Oakwood village.

The air turned cold and icy as we neared Northhorn. Snow covered the land that was larger than Luminara. The lord and lady had supported the royal family before, and we hoped that hadn't changed.

Northhorn was the last court before reaching Mystmere, and the thought was frightening. I couldn't remember what the kingdom had been like. Once my home, and the place we had lost everything.

Bria flew off on her own to hunt; the amount of food we carried did nothing for her appetite.

"What do you carry in that satchel that never leaves you?" Ivarison asked during another frustrating training session. Pushing my limits, my stomach growled in hunger, and I hadn't managed to do anything, yet again.

The day before, I felt a warmth flow through my veins, but I was unable to accomplish anything. I hadn't told the others what Bria had told me about powers being amplified. I had healed myself, protected myself, and opened a hole in the ground. I had seen so many different glimpses of what I could do, but I couldn't understand where to focus to help conjure.

I touched the satchel at my waist, expecting him to snatch it.

"It's Rikeroot, my mother grew it. I grabbed some from our garden before we started our journey."

Ivarison looked surprised. "She grew Rikeroot? How?"

"Everything in our garden grew well, no matter the time of the year. The Rikeroot never died like other plants."

"Of course it wouldn't. It has magical properties." He paused, eyes staring off. "Rikeroot only grows near the base of the Riker Tree. It's impressive she could cultivate it elsewhere. I'm interested in how she did so. But why do you carry it with you?"

"It's considered poison, right? If all else fails, I could use this."

He huffed a laugh, his shoulder shaking as he shook his head. "What will you do? Shove it down your enemies' throats? Make powder to dip arrows and swords at the most crucial moment?"

"Come closer and find out," My hands never left the satchel.

His expression turned serious, power rising. I knew he was capable of far worse before I could ever get the bag opened.

"I'm not your enemy, love."

"Stop calling me that," I snapped, trying to go back to the lesson and lighting a campfire. I wanted to set his cloak on fire instead.

"You should have had this lit by now." He brushed off his sleeve with a glare.

"If you would shut your mouth, perhaps I could focus."

He pulled his sword from his belt, pointing it toward me. "Should I try gutting you to see if that sparks a flame?" His tone was harsh, eyes narrowing dangerously.

He wasn't serious, was he?

"Stop it." I stepped back as his towering height followed. He came closer enough that I felt his breath.

"Make me," he breathed.

My heart and mind raced as I stepped away from him. I hadn't been able to do anything he asked. What made him think I would now? Power surged, but even if he attacked, I couldn't stop him.

I sensed what Dealla wouldn't admit. From the moment we met him, they were afraid of him. He was nearly impossible to kill, thanks to his healing ability, plus whatever other abilities he was capable of.

"He can't survive if I bite his head off." Bria growled, listening from wherever she was. *"Focus, Ellowyn, the power is within. He is testing you, and you're failing. Concentrate."*

I tried to mute her in my head as I stepped closer, refusing to show fear. He spun his sword hilt, watching me as if I were prey. My hand dropped from my satchel. Even if I tried to use it, he was right. I would never have time to use it in real combat. But I would stand against him.

I grabbed my sword, letting my power surge through me. I felt the speed and strength. I wanted to move around him.

He would not frighten me.

I spun my sword mockingly, striking his. With newfound speed, I attacked him directly, which he blocked with ease.

I raised mental shields, making sure he couldn't penetrate my thoughts. Each hit of mine, he blocked and countered. Twisting, turning, and diving.

I blocked his hits but felt weak against him. His power was there behind every strike, every time our blades collided and vibrated with force.

"STOP IT!" Our blades crossed, bringing us inches apart. His blue eyes flickered to my lips – and with that error, I kicked him in the stomach and sent him sprawling. Dust billowed from his impact.

He returned to his feet just as quickly as he fell. My chest heaved from exertion, sweat beading my brow. I moved swiftly, striking with precision, forcing him to block each of my attacks.

There.

I felt my entire body ache for the release as magic roared and turned hot under my skin. Blue waves danced along my fingertips, and it was beautiful. My sword began vibrating as I attacked once more, and he staggered back from the power behind my hit.

His eyebrows rose as he smirked, but he wouldn't back down. His own magic danced along his fingers, igniting his blade.

"STOP IT!" I growled, my canine teeth scraping against my lips as if I were turning more Fae. I felt graceful in my movements, like I was dancing, as we sparred. He wasn't listening. He continued to push and push.

I imagined blue magic lighting up and flowing down my sword blade. A familiar warmth spread across my cheeks as flames covered my sword. It was moving as I asked.

"JUST LEAVE ME ALONE!" I wouldn't back down. Perhaps this was his way of showing me the magic within that needed the release.

His sword blazed brighter, and he swung. Our blades met and crackled, creating such a force that we were both thrown backwards. The world spun as darkness encroached.

I was going to be sick.

It lasted a moment. I sat up with blurred vision, regaining focus. The grass felt different under my palms. The cold weather had vanished. Looking around, I realized Ivarison was gone, and I couldn't sense Bria.

Somehow, I had faded. My heart fluttered as I tried to understand how I had left and how to return.

But I was not alone. Ahead lay a camp of soldiers, and there were nearly two dozen of them. Tents and campfire smoke rising. Each of the soldiers looked over at me as I scrambled to my feet.

Dressed in black, they glared at me with cruel, smug faces. Dark Soldiers. How bad was my luck?

They shouted at one another, pointing and alerting. Could they know who I was? How rewarding, the princess they sought appeared right before them. Searching for an escape, I noticed it was an area we recently passed through.

They were tracking.

"*BRIA? IVARISON!*" I cried out, hoping that one of them could hear. "*Ivarison! Bria, help!*"

Soldiers advanced, and I knew I couldn't handle so many alone. My sword was beside me as I gripped dirt in my clenched fist.

"*He is coming! I'm too far away to reach you!*" Bria's voice was frantic.

I would not cower. Not now.

Would he find me in time?

Soldiers filled the horizon ahead. Air hitched in my lungs. Was this my last breath? I would take down as many as I could. They hesitated as they approached, faltering as their eyes widened.

The earth shook behind me. A roar cried out, sending birds fleeing in terror. That was all I needed to hear.

I turned to see what loomed. Shadows filled my vision as my eyes adjusted to the sun.

A sweet, earthy smell mixed with embers. My heart skipped as a large beast appeared. Dark gray wings with beautiful yellow and orange tips. His head resembled a mix of a lion and a dragon with arched horns above his ears. His mane flowed from his neck to his stomach. The rest of him was scaled, and his tail ended in white.

Ivarison.

He stomped in his form. Oh, he was magnificent. Blue eyes found me, looking me over. His roar filled the sky, like thunder from brewing storms.

My heart beat so loudly, I was sure he could hear my grateful sigh. The ground shook as he leaped, swiping at the first soldier who dared to approach. In that same moment, the soldier was no more.

"SHE'S MINE!" roared Ivarison, transforming back to his Fae form. Darkness surrounded him, his sword in hand.

He was absolutely terrifying. Wings spread wide behind him, and eyes so dark, they looked black as obsidian. I gripped my sword, knuckles white. His wings brushed against me, shielding me from harm behind him.

Had I been fully human, I would have missed his movements. His sword slashed through the air, slicing each opponent as they came. Bodies fell before they could ready their swords. One rushed toward me faster than I could react, but I didn't hesitate. I wouldn't let fear consume me.

I twisted away from the lunging sword as I swung mine. I felt the tip pierce flesh and slammed it deeper. The soldier fell, red spilling from his abdomen as I pulled my sword free. Blood dripped down my hands.

Bile crept up my throat. A second soldier came for me, but Ivarison was quicker. He raised his hand, and the soldier's arm twisted at an unnatural angle, his face horrified as he tried to scream, but no sound escaped. His back broke as his torso twisted, and then his face hit the ground.

Soldiers lay scattered in the grass. Blood, bodies, and swords painted it red. Ivarison stood without a scratch, hands at his sides as he looked at me, chest heaving. He paused, blinking as darkness faded from his eyes, returning to the crystal shades of blue.

"Now will you listen to me? Your magic, you had it there moments ago." His voice was a whisper as his wings vanished. He took a piece of cloth and wiped his blade clean.

I was going to be sick. My hands shook as I covered my mouth.

"You need to learn to wield your power. It would have been beneficial just now. Ellowyn–" His voice was honey as he spoke my name. "I felt your fear of dying."

I couldn't say anything. My heart was beating so fast. I looked from him to the red grass and scattered bodies. I told myself over and over again: it was them or me.

I knelt, trying to catch my breath, fingers clawing the ground, dirt piling under my nails. A soldier's blood has smeared across my knuckles.

My chest burned. Bile rose, and I vomited. It was the first time I had taken a life. Sure, I had accidentally caused the ground to collapse underneath the two soldiers, but they had threatened Bria.

This was different. I had pierced flesh. I felt my blade go through flesh and hit bone. How could I ever be okay with taking a life?

"Ellowyn." Ivarison's voice was firm. He knelt at my side, away from the mess. Grass blades were all I could focus on, trying to avoid the lifeless bodies. He lifted my chin.

"Eyes on me." His eyebrows rose as I found his blue depths and felt myself getting lost in their ocean. "Take a breath."

He demonstrated, having me follow.

"This will never be easy. You have to remember that in battle, it is you or them. If you don't, you'll be the one dead." He shook his head. "I don't want that. I want you here and breathing."

"You almost sounded like you cared there for a second." I breathed out, still following his breathing as he narrowed his eyes.

His hand dropped as he stood, warmth leaving my skin. He offered his hand to help me stand.

"You have to learn to trust me. Can we try to do that and help one another?"

I nodded, not sure I could speak or how I could help him. My throat still burned with defeat pounding through me. Even if I trust him, would that help? Each day of traveling without finding my mother or any additional information made my chest cave in. I was drowning in lost hope.

"Yes," I finally spoke, his warmth radiating through me as I took his hand and stood.

"Try not to disappear like that again." His voice was stern, but there had been panic in his eyes when I had seen him in beast form. "You're a princess. We can't have you vanishing again."

I rolled my eyes, wanting to object. I was no princess. He grabbed my elbow as I turned away.

"You're on dangerous ground, Ellowyn. Adriane and Ciaran have spies roaming Madora. They will try to figure out what you're capable of and use it against you. That is why I believe your mother is still alive. They are waiting, and they will use her against you. That is what they do."

"You wouldn't listen! I asked you to stop!" My head shook in frustration, fixing a blazing glare on him. I looked at where he held my arm. "It wasn't like I was trying to vanish. How would you know what they have done – what they do?"

He flinched, letting my arm go as his focus wavered. He rubbed his jaw.

"It's one of the reasons why Dealla and Killian were so wary when I arrived and offered assistance. I was with Adriane and Ciaran for a time when I was younger, before I knew of their true tendencies. Once I learned, I left. Now is not the time to discuss this. It's in the past." He folded his hands in front of him. "I was trying to find ways to help you. Clearly, that wasn't a good option."

I stepped back, eyes narrowing.

"Don't think that this conversation is over," I snapped. I would learn about his time with them. He had helped me and saved me, but Adriane and Ciaran had killed my father and grandparents, then captured my mother, and caused countless deaths at the hands of their soldiers.

"Of course," he said, not looking at me.

"And what did you mean when you said, 'She's mine'?" His frightening roar echoed in me with such intensity.

He bit his lips. "I was only trying to protect you. When a Fae claims another, it's stating they are their other. The claim means they should no longer be targeted. I was challenging them to fight me and me alone. I suppose the two that came after you didn't want to follow those rules. I shouldn't be surprised."

He shrugged, then moved closer and pulled me in without warning.

"Why would you do that?"

He stared down for a moment as if he would say something. The space between us tightened, and the air changed as we faded back to the others. Bria sat on the grass, waiting, watching me closely as Ivarison let go.

He took a step, looking as if he fought for words and about what to say. But then he turned and walked to the other side of camp, saying nothing.

"Practice makes perfect, Ellowyn. Try not to startle us like that again." Her voice rumbled, nudging closer to me.

Chapter Twenty

My dreams were haunted by my sword going through flesh and bone, followed by black mist chasing me through dark forests, waking me in cold sweat. After accidentally fading myself, I could feel my body making shifts and adjusting. I felt more aware, focused, and magic flowed warmer under my skin.

Conjuring blue flames to dance through my fingers came easier now. The fire moved against my skin without burning. I still struggled to throw or use it to my advantage, but it was progress.

"You're still not trusting me, love." Ivarison said. I rolled my eyes. Bria sat further down the meadow, watching birds fly above just before snatching one mid-flight. She hadn't let me out of her sight since I faded.

"Excuse me if I have trouble with trust after what happened to me and what you've told me." I snapped, sitting cross-legged on the cold ground. My cloak did little against the chill. I focused on a pile of sticks, willing them to light aflame.

I closed my eyes, hoping imagination would light them, but nothing happened. No matter how I tried and what process I attempted, I couldn't produce smoke, let alone a hint of heat.

Ivarison positioned himself behind me, watching and waiting for my ability to appear. I could feel it, could he sense it too? A part of me wanted the power to fade away so others wouldn't rely on me. Another could fulfill this so-called prophecy and end Adriane and Ciaran.

Because if I failed, what would happen to Madora?

I tried imagining blue flames dancing at my fingers and flowing at my palms. My fingers drummed against my knees, anger building as I was at the end of my patience.

"Perhaps we could try a different route, Ell," Ivarison whispered, sitting beside me, his leg brushing mine.

"What?" My voice cracked. My mind spun, envisioning a man smiling at me.

I blinked, seeing Ivarison before me again. My hands covered my mouth, eyes wide.

"What is it?" Ivarison looked toward Bria, whose head turned without sensing danger.

"What-What did you say?" I asked, fingers still grazing my lips.

His head tilted. "Your magic. Perhaps we should try a different approach."

I shook my head.

"Ell? I thought you didn't like me calling you, 'love'."

"Only one person has called me that before," I whispered.

My father. I'd just remembered my father. I could see the memories my mother had taken from me, suppressed thoughts I had not been able to access. The glamour she placed on me was fading – vaguely but surely – and I could see clearer. I remembered his last moment, the warm embrace before his goodbye. I remembered my mother carrying me and running from the village as he ran into the black mist. I inhaled sharply. The mist that haunted my nightmares.

Ivarison's voice brought me back. "You can remember him?"

"I was only five when I saw him last. I don't remember much, but yes." My eyes began burning. "He called me Ell."

I closed my eyes. His sandy blond hair was brushed neatly over to the side as he stared lovingly at my mother. He looked down at me, taking me and lifting me in the air, hugging me tightly when he caught me. I was so small in his arms, giggling and smiling.

"I met him once when your mother brought him to Mystmere. I was there with my father on court business." Ivarison spoke quietly as I brushed away an escaped tear. "He was a good man."

I gaped, head tilting as I stared at him. "How old are you?"

Ivarison narrowed his eyes as he teasingly said, "I'll have you know, some might find that to be a rather rude question."

I squinted my eyes mockingly. "Well, I'm just speaking to you. So?"

He huffed, rolling his eyes. "I'm 250 years old."

My head turned slowly, eyes growing wide. "Wow, I suppose that explains why you're often so cranky. You're an old Fae."

"I'm not cranky. The ignorance of others just astonishes me. I've lost my patience." He waved dismissively, biting his lip.

I was nearly grinning as we stared at one another. I couldn't deny how handsome he was. His crystal blue eyes made me feel as if I was drifting on a glacier, drowning in the sea. Stubble from days of travel shadowed his sharp jawline.

He broke our eye contact, looking off with a smirk. "Do you smell that?" He pointed at the pile of sticks. "You nearly lit it."

I looked over. Smoke rose above the brush. With a little more concentration, flames erupted.

The air turned freezing as we neared northern territory. Snow crunched with each step of our boots, icicles hanging from tree branches. We continued into the mountain court, trekking up another peak that wound around a frozen lake.

Thankfully, Northhorn didn't have flying guards. Bria was able to stay in the skies undetected. The last thing we needed was a dragon crashing through a guard patrol.

"Lord Eirwen and Lady Serene reside here," Dealla quietly said, watching our footing on the icy path. Another Fae walked ahead of our group as Dealla stepped in front of me. "Hood on."

"You would think it would be more guarded," Delaney observed, noting the apparent lack of security compared to her home, which was heavily protected; no one entered or left Luminara without notice.

"Other than Mystmere, I don't believe anywhere else is as guarded as Luminara," Killian said.

Delaney shrugged, eyebrows creased. "Mother doesn't like unwanted visitors. Although sometimes, I think it has more to do with my father too."

"Smart woman," Killian added with a grin. "I once tried sneaking past Luminara's guards as a dare. Spent about two days hanging upside down from the gates as punishment. Dealla had to cut me down."

"You deserved it," Dealla muttered, but her lips twitched with suppressed amusement.

"Yes, I was young and ignorant."

"Correct, but you're not so young anymore." Dealla glared at him as Killian gaped at her insult.

Though the village path was layered with snow, I could feel uneven bricks beneath the white fluff as we walked. Snow-covered roofs and icicles hanging from home frames surrounded us on both sides. Orange luminance from the hanging lanterns warmed the scene as the sun set.

At the end of the village, a frozen waterfall cascaded off to the side while the curved brick path led to a gated manor. The high-peaked roof was also snow-covered. Stained-glass windows glowed with candlelight. High arches framed two large black doors.

I wrapped my cloak tighter, trying to escape from the winter air. I hated being cold. I wondered if the small blue fireball I was learning to conjure could warm me or if I would set myself ablaze.

"Should we try to meet with Lord Eirwen now or wait?" Dealla asked, her voice low amongst the crowd.

I didn't like waiting. Our journey to find my mother had already been complicated and long enough. Each passing day was frightening – what could or had happened to her? I clung to Ivarison's belief that she was still alive, even if only used as bait. We had to learn if there was any information that could come from this court.

We walked down the snowy path. Killian suggested the tavern for warmth, but as we made our way, Delaney nearly gasped as she collided with a hooded blue figure.

"I apologize, I didn't see you there." Delaney straightened her cloak and helped the other to stand.

"Hello," came a female voice. She moved in closer, causing each of my companions to move closer to guard me.

The hooded figure stood near my height, raising her head to reveal fair skin, rosy cheeks and pink lips, spreading into a soft smile.

"Lady Serene?" Ivarison whispered, glancing around the street. The female pressed a finger to her lips.

"Shh!" Her emerald-green eyes glistened as she looked at our group. "I wondered when you'd arrive. I've walked through this village the entire week, waiting." There was no thrill in her voice, only irritation. "It's been rather cold, and I've had to hide like this so I'm left alone."

"Colder than my personality after a week without ale," Killian muttered, earning a sharp elbow from Dealla.

"Are you alone?" Dealla asked, "Do they realize that you're gone?"

She rolled her eyes. "Eirwen wouldn't let his lady out unguarded. My guards are about-" she waved a hand out, "hiding and watching. Finding you has been a priority, but we wanted to be inconspicuous. We don't want attention if others are watching you. Were you followed?"

"There was increased dark activity near Stormpeak Village, a bit south. Nothing closer," Bria called out.

"The last sighting of any Dark Soldiers was nearby Stormpeak Village," I answered, relaying Bria's information.

"Lead the way, my lady," Ivarison said, gesturing to our group to follow. The few hidden guards Lady Serene had mentioned came out and followed, keeping their distance. We walked toward the manor. Two additional guards stood at the large front doors, opening them as we approached.

Our footsteps echoed against the dark marble flooring of the foyer. A chandelier hung high from the arched ceiling, lit with specks of white like stars in the night sky. Doors lined the walls as Lady Serene led us upstairs to a room with a lit fireplace and sofas.

"Ah, I was wondering when you would return!" A deep voice came from the other side of the room.

A handsome Fae, whom I believed had to be Lord Eirwen, sat at a table, legs propped up with a book in hand, turning to face us. "And with friends!"

Pale blonde hair, nearly white in the light, fell across his face. His nose was pointed, face square. Most peculiar were his mismatched eyes: one crystal blue, the other a deep jade.

"I suppose introductions are in order," Ivarison spoke, breaking the room's silence as Lord Eirwen stood.

"Indeed, thank you, Lord Ivarison. I am Lord Eirwen of Northhorn, and this is my lady, Serene. Welcome." They gave small nods in greeting.

"You've met Killian and Dealla. This is Delaney of Luminara and Princess Ellowyn."

Lord Eirwen and Lady Serene moved closer together. "Princess Ellowyn, it's a pleasure."

I nodded. "Thank you. It's nice meeting you both."

"I'm pleased you made it here safely, I presume?" Lord Eirwen asked, glancing around at each of us.

"We've had situations along the way, but nothing we weren't capable of managing. Thank you for having us," Ivarison said. "When Lady Serene found us, she mentioned you'd been waiting."

"Why is that?" Dealla interrupted.

Lord Eirwen's smile was so warming it could easily make you smile in return.

"We've heard of your travels since you've arrived in Madora," Lady Serene stated. "Have you forgotten us already?"

"What's that supposed to mean?" Killian asked. "Do you know what is happening outside your court? Considering we almost died about five times in one month, I'd say we're making quite an impression," Killian added dryly. "Though preferably not the 'please try to kill us' kind."

"That's not what I meant," Lady Serene snapped, but Lord Eirwen raised a hand.

"Serene, please." He gave her a stern look, taking her hand and kissing the top. She backed down. "What my lady means is we've always been allies to the royal family. We're neighbors to Mystmere and have assisted when needed. We want it known that the notion has not changed. Adriane and Ciaran must be stopped, so Madora can be restored."

"He may have information about your mother. I'm traveling further through the court, I won't be long." Bria's voice came. I could feel the cold air pushing against her scales as she flew, making me shiver.

"Be safe," I said in return.

"Why isn't your court more guarded? How do you know who is walking through your village?" Delaney asked. The thought clearly had not left her regarding the Northhorn's minimum protection.

"My villagers know I would not harm them, but enemies learn quickly how impactful I can be," Lord Eirwen answered.

"What do you mean?" I asked.

Lord Eirwen smiled, glancing at the table, and Lady Serene stepped away. As he placed his palm down, a chill swept through the room. The fire within the hearth flickered, and the table turned to solid ice. I staggered back, feeling the temperature drop more than I had ever experienced.

"I have a gift with snow and ice. I can freeze an entire ocean if I wish." He grinned. "It's why my court is filled with snow. I enjoy it." He paused, relief escaping him. "I'm happy the rumors were true that your mother and you survived."

"I forgot how impressive your power is," Killian said, though his teeth were chattering. I pursed my lips to keep myself from laughing. "Reminds me never to get on your bad side. I'm already cold enough to freeze my–"

"Killian," Dealla warned sharply.

"--sense of humor," he finished innocently.

"Yes, and now we're searching for where they may have taken my mother. Have you heard anything about her whereabouts? Any sightings of Adriane and Ciaran?" I asked.

"No, I'm sorry," Lord Eirwen answered. "Several weeks ago, some of their soldiers were spotted deep in our northeastern forest. I sent guards to patrol the area more, but nothing was found."

"What's northeast of here?" Delaney asked. "We have maps in Luminara, but I don't recall seeing anything."

"Once you get through the forest, there are several docks. They aren't typically used because the water is often frozen."

"We must figure out what they intend to do. Ciaran has a prison that we don't know anything about, and it's rumored my mother was being taken there."

The room fell silent. Why hadn't we found them yet? After seeing what the Dark Soldiers and monsters were capable of, I knew Adriane and Ciaran were far more capable of worse. What kind of condition would my mother be in if we did find her? If I failed and was killed during this, the prophecy stated Adriane and Ciaran would become Madora's ruler. I couldn't let that happen.

"It's getting late," Lady Serene interjected. "We would like to offer our residence while you're here. We have plenty of rooms available. We can meet in the morning to discuss more to assist and look over maps."

A small female entered, wearing an apron over her light blue dress.

"This is Efa. She'll take great care of you and show you to your rooms, if you'll stay with us."

Chapter Twenty-One

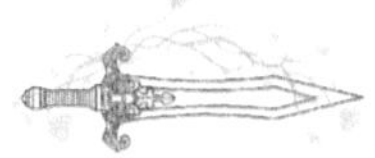

From my room's window, I could see across the village. The manor perched higher on the mountain, moonlight reflecting off the snow below. The best view came from the tower just down the corridor, where I leaned against the railing overlooking Northhorn.

At the village center, music played softly as villagers swayed to the melody. Unfrozen water rushed down the brick path to the manor, a continuous burble at the bottom. Ice popped and cracked on tree branches. I pulled the blanket that I took from my room tighter around my shoulders.

Northhorn seemed both mundane and majestic, as if magic ran through the snow and sparkled in moonlight. The human village I had lived near had been so unappealing compared to Madora's beauty. Below, villagers danced with joy-filled laughter.

I had never had that. I imagined what it must feel like to be so carefree. One hand traveled to my pointed ears. I found myself reaching for them often, still questioning if this was real. It's hard to comprehend that they had been there, but hidden by glamour.

Whenever my abilities began to show, my mother would give me Rike-root – again and again. Between doses, if only I had a mirror, I might have seen. So many times, it had been close to surfacing.

"Ellowyn, love." A soft, quiet voice came from behind. My hand dropped from my ear.

"Stop calling me that," I snapped.

He smirked, approaching the railing to look over the village. "Have you heard from Bria?"

"I spoke with her earlier. She was flying through the mountains, searching." I answered. He nodded, watching the villagers dance.

"I am here. Unfortunately, with nothing to report." Bria's voice was grim before going quiet again.

"They seem so blissfully unaware our world has gone to shit." Mockery coated Ivarison's voice as he rolled his eyes, fingers gripping the railing tightly.

"Do you find it humorous?"

He sighed, looking up at the stars as if they were more appealing. Millions twinkled like they danced with the villagers beneath.

"No. I wish I could find humor or dance as they do," he muttered, and I wouldn't admit I felt the same.

Searching for my mother had been constant since leaving the cottage. I had been angry over what had happened, what my mother had done to me, and Dealla never speaking of it. We needed to find my mother, but anger could not coexist with the hope of finding her alive. I would deal with that later.

"It's hard to think you'll never smile or be happy again," I muttered, holding the railing by him.

A growl escaped Ivarison's lips as he placed his hand on top of mine. I hesitated at the zap of power flowing between us, just like the night we met. I thought to pull away, but the warmth was welcoming, his calloused hand was nice against my own.

"You'll find reason to be happy again, Ellowyn." His blue eyes filled with warmth. The darkness that often haunted them was gone, and I wondered if he believed the same for himself.

"I hope you do too, one day." I hesitated, biting my lip. "What is it with Dealla and Killian? The twins? They wanted to destroy everything in their path because you were in that room."

"Ah–" His hand dropped from mine.

"*Wow, you ruined that moment,*" Bria mocked. I hushed her; I wanted to know.

"Perhaps that is a conversation for another time." His jaw clenched as he looked away. "It's getting late."

He turned to leave but looked over his shoulder, his eyes looking me over, strands of dark hair falling over his face. "Goodnight, *love.*"

I growled. A small curve touched his lips as he departed. At least he could find humor in teasing me.

Once back in my room, the warmth and firm mattress felt luxurious compared to the travel cots we had been using. It was difficult pulling myself from the sheets the next morning – cold air hitting my bare skin, making me pull the covers closer.

Efa brought us to the dinner area for breakfast the next morning. The room was filled with the scents of sausage, bacon, bread, and fruit, which colored the table. Lord Eirwen and Lady Serene did not join. Only after we finished did Efa return, asking us to follow.

"Have you heard from Bria?" Dealla whispered as we walked down a corridor. We had not seen much of the large manor, but a cold winter breeze followed us as we moved.

"Just a good morning. Yesterday, she reported soldiers were spotted near Stormpeak Village. When she returns, I'll venture out to her," I whispered, rubbing my hands for warmth. "I'm worried about how quiet it's been since Dustvale. Something doesn't seem right."

"I've wondered why we haven't seen Adriane or Ciaran too," Dealla whispered, moving closer as we followed Efa. "It isn't like either of them to hide, but it's as if they're waiting for something. We're getting closer to Mystmere, and I'm afraid of what will come as we move closer."

Expressing my concerns didn't help the weight that seemed to lie on my chest. Dealla agreed, afraid something was wrong and more was to come.

Efa opened the door to another room, the smell of dust and old pages greeting us. The large fireplace crackled, its red and yellow flames lighting the space. It was a small library, with bookshelves filling every inch. Near the fireplace was a long table with books and papers, and Lady Serene was hunched over stacks of parchment.

"Good morning. I hope you slept well." Lady Serene said as Lord Eirwen emerged from behind a bookshelf.

"We apologize for not joining you for breakfast. We've been up for some time, handling matters in the village," Lord Eirwen said, clasping his hands in front of him. "We've been viewing old maps of Northhorn to see if there is anything we may have missed regarding where the soldiers could have gone." He paused, placing a map back on the table. "I know you want to keep moving, and we do not wish to keep you. I wondered, and this may be bold, but what are your plans? Will we be going to war?"

None of the others spoke as Lord Eirwen looked directly at me. Of course he would ask. I was the princess of Madora.

"Lord Eirwen, I've been away from this kingdom most of my life. It's not my decision alone. My goal right now is to find my mother. Alive." I paused, remembering Asher and Xantara, envisioning children in the streets, blood and screams echoing in my ears. My body tensed before coming back to reality. "Once my mother is found, we will discuss what needs to be done against Adriane and Ciaran. What they have done cannot continue. Too many innocents have died because of them."

"Have you returned to Mystmere yet?" His tone turned low.

"We haven't made it back there yet. None of us has been there since the attack." Dealla looked at Ivarison, who only nodded.

"I sense there is something you are not telling us," Killian said, head tilted.

"Yes, there is. I have not returned to Mystmere myself. However, I have sent guards to see if Adriane and Ciaran may have tried returning or to see what remained. They are not on the throne of Madora, which we know, but–" He glanced off in thought.

"But?" Dealla pressed.

"No one can enter the kingdom. We do not know why," Lord Eirwen said. Killian and Dealla gaped slightly. "It was as if there was a barrier. My guards said it was like walking into a wall. The horses wouldn't go near it."

"What could that mean?" Delaney asked. "Who could place such a barrier?"

"Could it be because of the prophecy? It stops Adriane and Ciaran from entering since Ellowyn is still here?" Dealla asked, glancing around the room as if one of us might know the answer.

"I don't think so, and it couldn't have been Adriane or Ciaran," Ivarison said with certainty, turning to Dealla and Killian. "Was anything else in the kingdom capable of a barrier that large?"

Dealla looked lost, her eyes glancing toward the ceiling in thought. "No, I don't believe so. I honestly don't know."

"What if we can't get through?" I asked, wondering who else might be in the kingdom. Would it be someone else we would have to fight, or someone wanting to help?

"We will find a way, Ellowyn," Killian said, though his voice wavered as if he didn't believe in his words. "We will tear it down if needed."

"But what if it's protection rather than a trap?" I countered. Xantara's words crossed my mind: The Riker Tree is believed to be the source of our magic. I turned to Dealla. "You have said Madora does not accept Adriane and Ciaran. Xantara told me the Riker Tree is where our power is believed to be drawn from. What if someone else is guarding it?"

"Bria."

Delaney and I trudged through the snow-packed woods to where Bria hid. After a day of searching for her kin and other soldiers, she returned. The others remained at the manor, not wanting to draw attention by all of us vanishing.

Clicking sounds pulled our attention to our right.

"Over here," Bria announced. Large trees surrounded her, and her dark scales helped her stay hidden in shadows as she lay still.

"No luck?" I asked as we approached her, sitting in the snow with her head lowered. She shook her head, sending snowflakes flying. Delaney pulled her cloak over her face, shivering.

"Hey!" Delaney cried out, laughing as she uncovered her face.

Bria broke a large branch with her mouth from a tree above. The log was wide enough that it could simply crush Delaney and me. She took it in her talons and mouth, snapping it with ease, breaking it into smaller logs, and placing them in an open area.

"Light it," she instructed as she laid the logs down.

"You sound like Ivarison," I muttered, rolling my eyes. Every spare moment was practice. "You could just light it for us. That would be much quicker."

"Yes, that would be much easier, wouldn't it? Light it." Different shades in her eyes speckled as she narrowed them, nudging me closer to the logs.

Delaney watched, keeping quiet as I refused to look up in embarrassment. Tension built in my arms as I thought of flames. I focused, wanting to burn the logs with my touch, to watch yellow and orange embers grow.

But something felt different – stronger, more volatile. The magic surged unpredictably, making my fingertips tingle almost painfully.

"*Oh, look at you, Little Spark,*" Bria said. I opened my eyes to smoke rising from the pile, the sudden engulfment in flames as warmth hit our freezing bodies.

Delaney smiled. "You're doing great!" she said, rubbing her hands near the fire.

"*Little Spark?*" I asked.

"*Oh, I'm not allowed to give you a nickname, but you'll let Ivarison?*"

My jaw clenched, face reddening. "*You know very well I don't care for his nickname either.*"

She chuckled across our connection.

Little Spark fits you, your temper, and because I'm a fire-breathing dragon."

"You could have lit the fire too!" I snapped as Delaney glanced around the woods, and I heard the crunch of snow.

"*How will you learn without practice?*" Her head jolted sideways after she shook, shaking the ground as she rose. Delaney turned, looking alarmed and standing in front of me. "*Both of you, move closer at once.*"

"What is it?" I asked, taking Delaney's hands, pulling her closer to Bria and me.

Delaney put a finger to her lips, pausing as we listened to the approaching footsteps. Soft movement through snow, crunching lightly. It came from the manor's direction, but none of the others were to come out while we were here. Bria lowered her head as she watched, a growl creeping out.

"Oh, this is a pure delight." Lord Eirwen's voice came from behind trees before he stepped into view, hands clapping as he soaked in what was in front of him.

"Lord Eirwen." Delaney's voice held a hint of hesitation, her hand resting near her hip. There would be severe consequences if we struck him in his own court.

But Bria didn't care as her growl gave him pause. He raised his palms.

"I mean no harm, I promise." He dared to inch closer. Bria was nearly straddling us as Delaney and I stayed side by side.

"She's magnificent. It has been a very long time since I've seen a dragon, never up close like this. Tell me, which of you connected with her?" he asked excitedly, eyes wide with pure joy.

"I have," I answered, hand on my own sword. I wasn't sure we could stand a chance against him with his ice power.

"I sensed something different about you when we met." He looked dazed. "A few of my guards spotted you leaving the manor. I had to make sure you weren't doing something I needed to be aware of, being in my court, after all." He paused, examining Bria. "From my understanding, dragons are near extinction and haven't connected with others for centuries. How were you able to befriend one?"

I stepped forward, Bria moving with me. "I tried to help her and protect her when two of Adriane's soldiers tried to kill her. She found me afterwards, and we connected."

His throat made a sound of approval as he nodded excitedly. "She's helping you?" I nodded, and Bria extended her head, sniffing his scent. "Have you flown with her?"

"Why does he ask?"

"She wants to know why you ask that."

He looked even more excited now. "So, the legends are true. If you connect, you can communicate."

"Yes." I was growing impatient. What would he do with this information? What if we had to battle through the manor to escape his court?

"When others connected in history, they used to ride their dragons. We had dragon riders." He smiled and chuckled. "We have a saddler in the village. Yes, he's only done horse saddles, but he is the best there is in Madora. If anyone could create a custom dragon saddle, it would be him. We could have the saddler create one for you."

"Her name is Bria. She doesn't belong to me. We're only helping one another."

The thought of riding on Bria was frightening – the height she could reach, the fear of falling.

"Even without a saddle, I would never let you fall. It isn't a bad thought to have. The option could be useful if we needed to move quickly together or in battle."

When I didn't answer, Delaney said, "We do not want to put Bria or others in danger by bringing her into your village."

"Oh, no, no. She wouldn't fit in our village, would she? Our saddler would need to be discreet. He'll be paid well and knows to keep quiet or face dire consequences. He will come to her."

Bria nudged my back, wanting me to agree.

"As long as he agrees to discretion. But we must move quickly. We cannot linger. I need to continue the search for my mother." I stated my terms, hoping I would not regret this agreement.

Lord Eirwen nodded. "Let's go have a discussion with him." He put out a hand for us to walk with him.

"Little Spark," Bria called, causing me to turn back to her. *"Your magic felt different when you lit the fire. Stronger but less controlled. We should discuss that with Ivarison."*

The last thing I wanted to do was have that discussion with him. But she was right. Something was changing, and I wasn't sure if it was good or dangerous.

Chapter Twenty-Two

Creating a saddle proved more complex than expected. Even with the Fae's ability and magic combined, the saddle-maker and his assistant needed a considerable amount of time and effort. The maker looked older than Lord Eirwen, and I couldn't help but feel bad when he had to come back multiple times for measurements.

Extremely wary of the dragon, he took measurements around Bria's legs and wings, then had to climb on her back for the remaining dimensions. She obliged, helping with a lift of her foot. She was gentle, and with time, his hesitation eased.

The waiting was stressful. Time was precious when every moment could be spent on our search. Delaney and Killian spent most of the time in the library, studying the maps Lord Eirwen offered.

Once the maker finished the chestnut-colored saddle, we met early morning and snuck through the woods to where Bria kept herself hidden. The saddle slid on and fit the grooves of her back like a glove. It was made similar to a horse saddle, but tougher and wide enough to saddle a dozen horses together, and could accommodate multiple riders. Two angled pommels were set in the front seat for hand placement. A harness strap wrapped around her chest, securing the saddle.

"A dragon saddle. Because what you really need is to be more visible to our enemies," Ivarison said, shaking his head. I glared at him before ignoring him and returning to Bria.

"How does it feel?" I asked Bria while everything was strapped in place. The maker stepped back to marvel at his masterpiece.

Bria stretched her wings, casting a shadow over us as she adjusted her legs to test movement restriction.

"Perfect fit. No restrictions. This is marvelous."

"She said it fits perfectly, and it's marvelous." I told the maker, who smiled happily and bowed at Bria.

Bria knelt beside me. *"Get on,"* she demanded, with a huff. I stepped back, unprepared for an immediate test flight.

"I believe she would like for you to test it," Dealla said, shifting her weight nervously.

"If you don't, I'll go." Delaney said, ready for a flight.

"Go on. I'll follow. If you can't hold on, I'll catch you." Ivarison rolled his shoulders as large wings emerged from his back. My eyes widened at the sight. I wasn't sure I would grow used to watching any of them transform into beasts, or how casually everyone treated something so extraordinary.

My body hesitated as I pulled myself up with the maker's help.

"No need to worry about falling, these harness clips will prevent that," he explained, pointing to the strap. "We added extras if others fly with you. Grip these pommels, and slip your feet into these grooves so they aren't dangling."

Oh, thank the gods.

"This is beautiful," I said, admiring his craftsmanship. "This was such a wonderful thing for you to do, and I'm truly grateful."

The male beamed. "It was truly an honor to make it for our princess."

"Go, we will see you back at the manor," Killian said as Dealla pursed her lips.

"Are you secure?" Bria asked as I clipped in and the saddle-maker stepped away.

Bria's head turned to glance at me before she stood, towering above the snowy trees that glistened from the sun rising over the mountain. I inhaled, the crisp air filling my lungs. Her powerful strokes sent snow falling from branches as she began to rise, ground shrinking below.

A cold breeze hit my cheeks, and I took in sharp inhales. With each wingbeat, my legs tightened against the saddle. My grip tightened around the horns of the saddle, my knuckles turning white.

"Relax, Little Spark. I will start easy until you grow used to flying. You're safe. If anything feels wrong, you must speak. We work together."

I looked ahead. Pink and yellow tones filled the horizon as the land around began to wake. My lips trembled at such a breathtaking view that I couldn't let slip away despite the dangers lurking below. Deep breaths, doing as Bria asked.

I trusted Bria, and we worked together.

She moved through the clouds in the opposite direction of the village, and I sensed something approaching. Bria's head turned as I looked. Ivarison's blue eyes in the form of his beast flew beside us, his large wings gliding as his mane flowed in the wind.

"I can't say I've done this with anyone before." I heard Ivarison's voice as he flew closer.

"You look incredible," I said, immediately wishing I hadn't. He seemed to grin, oddly endearing from his beast form as lips curved over sharp white fangs.

"He looks just darling," Bria snipped.

We didn't speak again as we continued flying. I sat straight, arms extending at my sides as I closed my eyes, feeling the winter breeze beating against me. The fear of flying, gone. I could get used to this, already loving being secluded from the troubles lingering back on land.

My legs wobbled once we touched ground. Ivarison landed nearby, his body shaking as he returned to his Fae form.

"It's been a bit since I've just flown. Therapeutic and refreshing." He looked between Bria and me. "How was it? Did you have any complications with the saddle?"

"I don't believe so. It will be an adjustment, but I enjoyed it." Excitement rang in my own voice.

With time and patience, we'd take small rides to get used to each other. I worried about what other dragons might think of Bria's saddle. It was large enough that it would take more than just me to remove it from her.

"It will be nothing that I couldn't handle. Having a rider once was common for dragons. This may be a new beginning," Bria said.

It was hard to keep her from my thoughts, unless I focused on shutting her out. But now that we could fly together, this was another advantage we had.

After dinner, I twisted and turned in the silk sheets – another restless night. Most nights when I fell asleep, dreams turned to nightmares. I could feel my sword piercing flesh, see black mist seeping toward my skin as malicious laughter overpowered other noises. There were times that I even saw my mother in conditions I hoped never to see.

I jolted from bed, grabbing two thick blankets. I tossed one over my body as I left the room. The brisk night air filled the corridor as I walked to the tower balcony, which I had enjoyed nightly at Northhorn.

Small snowflakes fell, and below in the village, the lights were dimmed and the streets were quiet. I went to the railing, placing one blanket on the ground to lie on. Maybe watching the stars would give me a sign of what to do or put me to sleep.

"Ellowyn?" A tired voice from the tower entrance. Caught in my thoughts, I hadn't heard his approaching footsteps.

Ivarison looked pale as he approached.

"Do you often lie on floors?" he asked, holding his cloak.

I rolled my eyes. "Only to watch the stars."

"Interesting. Does it work?"

"Does what work?" I shifted to look at him clearly.

"Working through thoughts or distracting you from them?"

I placed my arms behind my head, turning back to the thousands of twinkling stars dancing above, each staring back.

"I suppose. It's the only time I can quiet my thoughts. I haven't done this in a long time."

"Mind if I join you?"

My throat betrayed me as I gulped. Loudly. I moved over to give him space on the blanket. He kept space between us. Quietness settled over us as we stared up at the sky together. Counting the stars would be impossible. I took a deep breath, and there it was again: His scent hit me like bricks.

"Do Fae have a heightened smell?" I asked. All I could smell was embers and petrichor again. That rich, wonderful smell. I sensed him stiffening, head turning slightly toward me.

"Are you hinting that I need a bath?"

My lips curved as I playfully hit his arm.

"Yes, I suppose we do. A higher sensitivity. Things are amplified, more than what I'm sure is normal for a human. You aren't used to what your Fae senses give you. It will improve, and you'll get used to it, even your taste."

"You don't stink. You smell rather nice and it's always the same," I mumbled. He didn't say anything as he quickly looked back to the stars.

I closed my eyes. What would happen to us and my mother? What was to come? I could no longer think of how long it had been since she had been captured. She still had to be alive, but the time she had been missing gnawed at me. I couldn't lose hope yet. I wouldn't.

I shifted on the blanket as the sun began rising.

The sun was rising.

I blinked, eyes adjusting to the warmth hitting my skin. My head rested on something hard as I glanced up to see a sleeping Ivarison and his arm wrapped around me. I had used his chest as a pillow.

I quickly sat up as he woke, arms dropping.

"I fell asleep. Ivarison–" My voice cracked, but he sat up before I could continue. My heart raced. I knew he could sense it as he offered his hand to help me stand.

"I'll see you at breakfast," he said, his voice scratchy from sleep.

I pulled the blankets from the ground, afraid to say anything else as I left the tower for my room.

I nearly ran.

"Are you avoiding me after this morning?" Ivarison asked as we stood together in the woods near Bria.

I focused on the line of wood he had placed in the snow, the bark dark against white. I studied every groove, instead of looking at the male behind me, waiting for an answer.

"I haven't been avoiding you," I said quietly, lighting the first log and focusing on the second.

"Look at that, you're getting better. Almost competent, even." He placed another piece down. I focused on showing him who was almost competent. "Try something else with the wood."

The piece broke into shreds as he moved away to be missed. He huffed as I wigged my eyebrows at him.

"You won't look me in the eye and haven't spoken to me since this morning."

"We're speaking now," I focused harder on how the bark caved in with the next piece, with little splinter pieces sticking up from knots.

Bria's eyes went back and forth watching us.

He was right. I had avoided him since we woke up together in the tower. I felt awkward. It hadn't been intentional. But I had to admit that having someone hold me was nice.

"There is nothing to feel awkward about. We only fell asleep."

"Stay out of my head," I snapped, not taking my eyes from the logs. "I cannot focus if you keep talking."

"I wasn't in your head – I can see it clearly on your face." He paused, putting another log down. "You need to learn how to handle distractions. You won't be able to stop mid-battle to focus."

He was infuriating. I took focus from the log to his face – those perfect shades of blue eyes staring, watching. He hesitated at the look I gave him, just as I wished I could slap him to shut up.

Embarrassment filled me, something zapping through my fingers as I narrowed my eyes at him.

His hands instantly went to his face. "Ow! What was that?" The red mark faded against his cheek.

I covered my mouth, suppressing my laugh. I didn't know how to tell him what I had done, so I returned to the logs. He kept his mouth shut as I looked at the bark once more. They lit and exploded into splintered shreds.

I ducked, hand blocking. Ivarison grinned as he looked at the shield I had thrown around us, protecting against the flying wood.

"Excellent!" he said, his grin never leaving his face.

It felt like hours passed as we focused on what I could accomplish. Pushing me to do more and keeping me away from fading. He knew I wasn't ready after what had happened the first time. Instead, we focused on strikes, arrow hits, and discussed turning Rikeroot into powder for my dagger and sword. When we finished, I was able to light an arrow just before releasing it.

It was an incredible feeling. Beginning to understand how to wield the power flowing through me. I felt drained and couldn't remember how we made it back to the manor. I skipped dinner, going straight to my room, where I quickly enveloped myself in the soft blankets and the warmth of the crackling fire.

"What did you do to her?" I heard Dealla ask at my door. I laid with my back toward her, eyes too heavy and burning to stay open.

"Stop coddling her. She can do anything she puts her mind to when she believes in herself. She needs to eat and drink when she wakes to replenish." Ivarison was nearby, and I heard a metal tray placed on the bedside as he continued with frustration. "Tell me, how draining it must have been to constantly hide things when she should've been taught years ago what she's been shielded from?"

A dark void filled the room as it went quiet. He had made it clear that he didn't believe how things had been handled. How my magic had been made useless, to have fed me lies to cover truths.

"I never had a say in the matter. I'm only a guard of the kingdom, after all. I tried speaking with Princess Alina about this, but she was heartbroken. She lost everything: her family, her *mate*. She couldn't handle the pain and then the chance of losing her daughter."

Ivarison huffed as the door began closing. "Yes, and look where that got her." Their footsteps echoed down the corridor as I drifted to sleep.

When I woke, the sky was filled with light pink and red as the horizon began waking. I'd slept through dinner. My stomach growled in protest as I glanced at the tray Ivarison had left. I took bites of bread, then wrapped myself in a blanket to keep the cold air away.

Leaving my room for the tower, the sun began cresting the horizon as most were still asleep.

Freezing air hit as soon as I entered the balcony. Pink overtook more of the sky as I stood against the railing. My stomach continued growling as it tugged at me. I glanced over, a figure in the shadows sat watching.

"Good morning," Ivarison muttered. "Did you sleep well?"

He stood from his corner and came to the railing.

"I suppose I am well-rested after yesterday. Do you ever sleep?" I asked quietly. His fingers grazed mine as he gripped the rails. I pulled my hand from his. "You're freezing! How long have you been out here?"

"Most of the night, I couldn't sleep," he answered, eyes fixed on me.

"Here," I took some of the blanket from my shoulder and pulled it over his tall frame. He didn't object, his body pressing at my side, forcing me to inhale that scent.

"You still smell nice," I muttered under my breath, gripping the blanket together.

"As do you."

Standing side by side, we were so close. So close I could feel his breath hitting my hair. I sensed his stare still fixed on me as I watched the warm tones growing through the sky, lighting up the balcony. I looked up. The sky's pink reflected off his creamy skin as my eyes traced his full lips, back to his cheeks, then up to his blue eyes.

Eyes I could get lost in. Eyes I could drown in.

"I don't think I've told you how beautiful you are," he muttered so quietly, I almost couldn't hear.

My breathing hitched. I couldn't think. *Was I breathing?*

I've never been close enough with anyone to receive such a compliment or have more. Nervousness filled me, and I forgot how to put a sentence together.

Ivarison's hand came toward my cheek and brushed a strand of hair from my face. His hand traced my jaw, his head leaning toward mine as he inhaled. I could see every detail. His perfect skin. His blue eyes glimmered with lighter specks in the center. He looked like a god before me; his tall muscular body could easily overpower my small frame. I wanted to let him.

His fingers lingered against my jaw, his thumb brushing my lips. I licked my lip, tasting salt from his finger. His eyes were frenzied, unable to take any more.

His lips came against mine, filled with such hunger. I returned the kiss. I pulled him tightly against my body, wanting to feel more of him against me. His scent, his body. I didn't care that we stood in the middle of a tower. Everything about him was intoxicating and made my body tingle. I wrapped my arms around his neck, and his hands wrapped around my waist. Our kiss deepened. My skin burned where he touched me, as my hands ran through his dark hair.

Sweat beaded off my brows as I tumbled from my bed, feet stuck in the sheets as I fell onto the cold marble floor. A moan escaped my lips as I pulled my ankles from the twisted sheets and stood. Where was I?

The bedroom in Northhorn Manor.

It felt so real. My lips were still warm.

It had only been a dream.

A dream.

Chapter Twenty-Three

"What's the matter?" Delaney muttered during breakfast. The hall was filled with the farewell feast Lady Serene and Lord Eirwen had prepared. The smell of bacon, sausage, cinnamon, eggs and fresh bread was delicious.

"I don't want to talk about it right now," I mumbled between bites. "Just an odd dream I had."

"Oh, do tell. I'm interested." She twisted in her seat, popping a strawberry in her mouth.

"Later," I whispered, catching Ivarison watching us from across the table. My cheeks heated, and I dropped my eyes to my plate, ensuring my mental shields were up.

"There is something I wish to discuss before you depart." Lord Eirwen announced, taking Lady Serene's hand. All eyes shifted toward the head of the table.

"Before you leave us, I would like you to know that when war occurs, we will be there for our kingdom, and Northhorn will fight alongside you. We want the peace and respect our land once had. We want to see our royal family returned and our realm restored," Lord Eirwen stated.

I breathed in, feeling the heavy weight of the land relying on me: the support and higher chance of bringing Adriane and Ciaran down. With Luminara and Northhorn's support, we could have a real chance.

"Thank you. I appreciate all that you have done for us during our stay," I responded, searching for the correct words. "I shall keep that in mind when that time comes. My goal at this moment is to find and rescue my mother."

"They took your mother to try to find a way to control you, Ellowyn." Lady Serene spoke, her head dipped down as she spoke.

"The only way this will end is if we end their reign. They're guilty of too much." Killian said.

I bit my lip. Knowing that this is what Madora wanted: to end the reign of the Queen and King from Ravenholde that had plagued the land, who destroyed all they could. Was I ready for that, though? Coming to terms with my abilities, connecting with a dragon, and two courts that were supporting us, would I be capable? I had to be.

"I believe you should continue to Mystmere," Lord Eirwen offered. "Even though my soldiers were unable to pass through, they've claimed there have been disappearances – instances where others had gone through but never came back. You're the princess. Perhaps you would be able to find the way." Lord Eirwen flexed his jaw as he looked at Lady Serene.

"There is one more thing," Lady Serene said quietly. "We know some of the history between Kai and Mara." She glanced at Ivarison, her eyes dark. "The twins have caused problems for some time now. They jump between locations, but we fear they may be up to something and working with the enemy."

"The twins are how Dark Soldiers knew you were in Dustvale. They reported you. You must be careful. As long as Lord Ivarison is with you, we fear they will never be on your side."

"What happened between Ivarison and the twins was a terrible mistake and an accident," Dealla stated. Ivarison nodded.

"I will not force him away because they've made the wrong decision. They're not allies of Mystmere. It was clear they had other motives when we met them, even before they knew Ivarison was with us." Anger filled me. It was the twins' fault that Xantara and Asher were killed. "Ivarison has been with us and helped us during our journey. As long as he wishes to stay, he shall."

Ivarison said nothing, but I could feel his eyes burning through me. Lord Eirwen bowed his head, face grim as I refused to look around the table. I still couldn't look at Ivarison without thinking of the dream.

"*Oh, dear Little Spark,*" Bria said with a chuckle. I bit the inside of my cheek. "*It was only a dream.*"

"We shall take care of them when the time comes," Killian said lightly.

Yes, the twins would be dealt with.

I still had not learned what happened between the twins and Ivarison to cause such hatred, the whole reason Dealla and Killian were wary when he found us. He had admitted to once being with Adriane and Ciaran, information that he could've kept from me but hadn't. I knew what he had done for me since joining, even if he did often piss me off by doing and saying what he pleased.

"Tread carefully, Princess Ellowyn. Dark Soldiers have been lingering near Mystmere. They will be waiting for you," Lord Eirwen cautioned as we bid farewell.

Leaving Northhorn was quiet as the weather began warming and snow melted. The pleasant temperature was welcoming after being bundled in cloaks and trudging through snow. Bria flew ahead, checking in periodically as she stayed alert for soldiers, wagons, or other signs.

I was growing nervous about returning to a place that had once been my home. A kingdom that belonged to my family. My stomach was in knots as I tried remembering what it had been like. Memories of my father and grandfather were faint. We didn't know what condition Mystmere would be in, and my stomach lurched with fear that it was in ruins.

With Lord Eirwen's information, we could find ourselves stuck at a barrier, unable to move forward. Killian left once and returned with no sighting of soldiers or Norwags. Mystmere was a lingering hope that we might find answers, but the silence was deafening. If we arrived at a dead end, it was hard to think what that could mean for my mother.

"Do you know what happened between Ivarison and the twins?" I whispered over to Delaney. We walked closely together as we normally did, while Ivarison stayed ahead with Killian and Dealla behind us.

Delaney frowned. "No, but I've been curious since that happened."

My lips turned downward.

"Speaking of him, any more dreams?" she whispered, grinning.

"Stop it! I shouldn't have even told you," I violently whispered, looking around. Her teasing hadn't stopped since I told her, and I still couldn't look at the male.

"Care to tell me why you aren't looking at me again? You haven't looked at me since we left Northhorn." Ivarison claimed as we stood together in a cleared area with small boulders scattered around our feet. I could hear the chuckle that came from Bria as I hushed her.

It wasn't exactly true. I had looked at him plenty, but the moment he caught me, I looked away. I couldn't. The dream had felt real. I could still feel the warmth of his hand on my skin when I woke. I didn't want this. I couldn't. Was the dream telling me what I was lacking or telling me something more subconsciously?

"Nothing is wrong," I answered quietly, glaring at Bria where she sat atop the dirt area that turned to grass. Her chuckle rang through my ears as smoke puffed from her snout.

"Ellowyn, you look as if making eye contact may burn your eyes from your skull."

He moved closer as I gripped my sword, focusing on lighting it with magic. I would rather watch blue flames consume my sword than stare at him in embarrassment.

"I could ask Bria. Maybe she will tell me what is bothering you. We cannot afford to fall back to barriers after everything you've accomplished."

"*Don't you dare,*" I glared at Bria.

I rolled my eyes at Ivarison and turned my back to him, but he grabbed my forearm and forced me to look up. His grip loosened, but I didn't fight – I didn't think I wanted to.

"Have I done something to upset you?" he asked, his voice low. I could see Bria from the corner of my eye, shifting. Watching.

I inhaled deeply, an earthy scent filling my senses.

"*I suggest he release you,*" She threatened.

"Bria said she's going to eat you if you don't let me go," I said so quietly that I hardly heard my own voice.

"*That is not what I said.*"

"*Close enough.*"

"No, she won't. Tell me."

"It's nothing. It's more of an embarrassment that is my own problem."

His hands shifted, eyebrows rising, waiting. His eyes never left mine as I slid my sword back to my belt.

"Do tell, love." he said when I refused to say more.

"We fell asleep on the balcony, then I had a dream. It's just embarrassing."

He released my arm. "I don't understand why that would be embarrassing."

"It's embarrassing because we–" I paused, not wanting to say more. "We were close. We kissed, and it felt like it was going to lead to more." My cheeks felt like they were on fire, knuckles white as I clenched them into fists.

"Why would that be embarrassing?"

"I've always been secluded, Ivarison. I've never been with someone in that way," I admitted. My heart raced while feeling like it dropped to my stomach. I had craved for more, even when it was only a dream.

"Ah, I see." He took a breath. His scent lingered from the proximity. "There is no need to be embarrassed. Even in a dream, I'm sure I would have satisfied and treated you well."

I gaped, unsure my cheeks could burn any hotter as I smacked his arm. He laughed – a laugh that lit up his face, his perfectly white teeth showing as he closed his eyes. How could I not dream of a Fae like him from his beauty alone? But then his arrogance had to ruin it. My hand went to smack him again, but he caught it mid-air and stopped laughing.

"You found a reason to laugh," I whispered. The corner of his eyes slightly crinkled as he looked at me.

"I suppose I did. It's perfectly okay, love. Come on, let's try something different today." He hesitated as he removed his hand from mine, asking Bria to come over.

The ground vibrated as she moved closer and gave him a soft growl. "Let's go airborne. Try working your magic while in the saddle.

Bria looked alarmed. *"I'm not positive that's a great idea."*

"I could at least try. I wouldn't mind being in the air for a bit."

Ivarison had been listening. "If it's something you prefer not to do, we can stay on the ground."

"Why?" Bria snipped.

"Lord Eirwen told me tales of dragons and riders. He seems a bit obsessed with dragons. Riders could merge their powers with their winged companions."

"I already have trouble connecting with my own power. How would that help by trying to give more?"

Bria's feet shifted in the dirt, head bowed.

"You told me that you could amplify my power. Is that what you meant?"

"I can sense how powerful you are and will be when you allow yourself. Being connected to me will amplify what you have, but it can also increase what you're capable of. You could be stronger than most, if not so already." Her voice was strained.

"If you aren't already stronger than Adriane and Ciaran, you would be with that ability. You would be stronger than anyone in this realm," Ivarison said.

"I suppose the only way to shut him up would be for us to go. Let's try, Ellowyn. The moment anything seems wrong, we will come back down."

Ivarison smiled, shifting into his own beast form and propelling himself into the air.

Bria flew us through clouds, cool air hitting our skin as my hair whipped behind in the wind. The breeze felt nice against my skin.

As we rose, it grew quiet. Noises below faded, and only the gust of wind from the flaps of wings was heard.

Ivarison's large wings came near us as Bria pulled away, daring him to keep up.

"Play nice," I called out, chuckling as Ivarison stayed close. He let out a small roar, unafraid of Bria's size. My arms reached out to my sides, wind hitting every inch of me as if I were flying with them.

"Now what?!" I asked. The sun was starting to set, and we would have to return to camp soon.

"Try connecting with me. Focus on the magic flowing through your veins when you call to it. Once you feel your own power emerging, we can try merging."

I looked over my shoulder, holding tightly to the pommels as I found Ivarison. I would fall to my death if I slipped. The wind pressed harder, and my hand shook on the horns.

It was time. I had to let it escape.

"Little Spark, I do not know what will happen if this works. I've never had a rider or seen another do this."

No pressure.

"I trust you. We're in this together." I could hear the wobble in my voice, confidence slacking.

I shut my eyes, pulling the warmth of my magic throughout my body. Blue swirls of power emerged. My magic, the abilities I was capable of if I just wasn't afraid. I opened my eyes, Bria ascended until everything on the ground was too small to make out. Hairs on my arm stood on end as I took heavy breaths and brought my right hand closer to my body. The heat radiated through me as my fingers and palms glowed blue, traveling further down to my wrists.

Ivarison watched as I tried not to be self-conscious, not knowing what I was doing, and afraid this was all a show and nothing more. I needed to truly handle my power if I wanted to find my mother and defeat the enemies that caused catastrophe in our lives.

"Focus on the connection. Focus the power you feel to let it merge within."

I did as Bria asked. I wanted this to work. I wanted to accomplish something more. My mental shields stayed up as I felt the tingle of pressure against my walls, searching for a way to enter. I tilted my head as I focused, trying to find a place to let it through. Bria flew in circles, keeping quiet as I worked.

Nothing happened.

Nothing.

I reached for her scales to see if physical touch would help, but there was only darkness.

"Relax and loosen your mind, Ellowyn." Ivarison's tone was encouraging as he flew nearby. *"Breathe and think of your barriers that keep me out. Focus on bringing enough down for Bria to feel and be allowed in."*

I watched Bria's head bob as she flapped her wings, noticing how her spikes down her neck flowed like my hair. In that moment, my sight trailed down her spine, imagining magic connecting us. Warmth shocked through me like the world would burn beneath if I touched it. Bria tapped against my mind, and I built a door for her to enter.

We were in flight and flying against the world.

"Let it be free," Bria said. I felt pressure throughout every bone, needing release, begging for it.

This power was mine. I had to let it be a part of me completely for our journey to succeed.

There was a roar from the clouds, nearly deafening as we flew. A darkness surrounded us, and it wasn't from the sun setting. My hands let go of the pommels, feeling slick from the building condensation. I reached out, as I let power fly out of me while I screamed.

The pressure in my chest loosened, the emotions that had built since my cottage burned started escaping: from the worry I may never see my mother again, to the hurt from learning the lies I'd suffered from, to what lay on my shoulders from a prophecy.

Again and again.

There was so much pain in my chest, it begged to be set free.

"Wonderful, Little Spark. Now, fully release it."

Tension built, and I pushed my palms out, raising them over my head and throwing them hard to the sides. Ivarison dodged, nearly rolling mid-air to fly through lightning.

No. Not lightning. A bolt of fire had emerged from me. Blue fire burst through my hands, and wind pushed against us as Bria shifted her weight and turned. I focused, another strike coming.

I had done it. I would no longer question myself and what I was capable of.

Chapter Twenty-Four

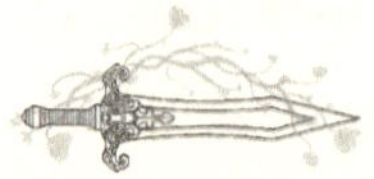

Ivarison didn't mention the extent of what I had accomplished when we returned to camp, nor did I. It felt like a private moment between Bria and me, and I wasn't quite ready to share or relish in the victory. What if I were not capable of it again?

A bolt of fire had exploded from me. I could still feel the tingling sensation in my palms. The strength that had traveled through me was something I'd never felt before. I could master the ability and pull that fire bolt against an enemy, I could take out more than one.

I began welcoming it. The strength was there even when I was found, and Dealla felt the difference when we practiced. She struggled with some of my hits as my speed increased.

I needed a way to keep the fear from my mind that was constantly creeping to the surface. During our travels, I began to ask more questions: how Killian and Dealla met, what positions they helped in Mystmere. I learned as head guards of the kingdom, Killian was the best patroller, and Dealla had been assigned as my mother's guard, requested by the princess herself. Many feared Dealla because her ability was a force of nature. She wasn't only recognized for her fighting capabilities or how she seemed to dance in battle, but also for what she did for the ones she loved.

The heaviness in my shoulders seemed to grow as I feared what could happen to each of the ones I traveled with. They were all at risk for being at my side. I thought of Adriane, her black hair in the wind as she had laughed at my mother before they vanished. Her dark eyes had been like tunnels of darkness, and I wanted to hurt her for what she had done.

Our feet dragged through the dirt, dust filling the air as Dealla and I sparred. I blocked her again and again, focusing on her blade. I threw myself into strikes as the hatred for Adriane overpowered my judgement. I hit and struck, keeping up with Dealla's speed, my sword warming as it crashed against hers. A zap of power escaped my fingers.

It hit Dealla's sword. The sound of our last strike boomed through the woods like thunder, knocking Dealla off balance. She staggered backwards. Birds screeched, taking flight from branches.

"What was that about?" Delaney asked, wide-eyed as light vanished from my sword.

"I-I don't know. It was an accident." My sword was in my hand, humming as it radiated, and my fingertips rubbed against the turquoise jewels.

"Take a breath, you're doing wonderful," Bria said calmly from somewhere through the trees as she hunted herself dinner. Then came the sound of crunching bones.

Clouds across the sky darkened as if a rainstorm would hit us at any moment. My mind continued to race. Adriane and Ciaran took everything because of their desire to rule Madora and destroy every halfling known to exist because of a prophecy.

My father. My grandparents. Due to their greed, I hadn't had the chance to know or learn from them. The length of time we had together would never be enough. My family's death drove my mother to do unthinkable things in the name of love. She took the love that had been there for my family, my identity. Now, fear consumed me with the state of what she might be in *if* we found her.

"Ellowyn." Ivarison's voice came from somewhere. I couldn't look away from the sky as he moved in front of me. The others had moved closer to the campfire, watching the dark clouds that were gathering. I lost my grip of my sword and heard it clatter to the ground. My hands hung low, palms up to the sky. I hadn't realized what I was doing as magic escaped from me, colors dancing and flowing.

"Ellowyn," Ivarison spoke again. His palms came under mine, holding them steady.

I couldn't completely focus as more clouds swirled in waves. My palms glowed with the same waves. He leaned into me, brows furrowed, an unspoken request hanging between us as he took a deep breath.

My fingers laced into his, and I breathed with him. His ember smell hit me like waves, calming me as I focused on trees moving in the wind, seeing a small bird sitting on a nearby branch.

The bird was a beautiful shade of blue, nearly silver – like, staring at a sea I could get lost in, just like Ivarison's eyes.

"Deep breaths," he said quietly, taking another breath with me. As I exhaled, he held his in. "Good, love."

Ivarison's hand squeezed mine, his lips forming a small smile as the clouds calmed. The worry was apparent from the others. Dealla watched with a grim look, her eyes dropped to our hands, then looked to Killian. I just wanted to rest; my mind was exhausted.

Nervousness built as we moved closer to Mornwind. So close to Mystmere, we didn't know what condition it would be in or if we'd ever pass the barrier. While stopped at a nearby river, Bria flew further ahead, looking for soldiers or markings of traveling.

"I see nothing," She sounded annoyed as she searched.

"Killian hasn't seen anything during his patrols either."

Delaney and Killian took turns hunting as Dealla prepared our camp-fire. Ivarison and I left to train, but I wasn't in the mood for any of it.

Among an area of hills with boulders, we both sat comfortably on the largest one. His thigh brushed against mine, heat radiating from him as he pulled his cloak off his back. I watched his shoulders stretch.

"How did you figure out you could transform?" I asked, imagining him extending his feathered wings.

"I was young when I summoned them for the first time. I was angry. My father was capable of doing the same, but his form was a bit different. As I grew and my magic progressed, I tried focusing on a beast form like my father's. One day it happened. It took time to transform back and forth the first few times. Now, it's like blinking." He shrugged, and his gray wings spread behind us, the tips brushing against my hair.

"Could a halfling have the ability?"

What would it be like to turn into another? To have wings and fly with Bria and him?

"Anything is possible. Your mother and grandfather could shift. I think you have many abilities, you just have to learn what those are."

My heart felt like it skipped a beat as I stared at him. "My mother can shapeshift?"

He nodded, looking away, realizing what he had given away.

Why did this feel like it was another source of betrayal? Did I know who my mother truly was? "Dealla didn't tell me."

"I don't think she was keeping it a secret, but perhaps holding onto hope that your mother could tell you things herself when she thought it was safe."

I watched him from the corner of my eye. He was right. My mother was bound to have more to tell me. Gods, she kept an entire life and world hidden from me; there had to be more about my father too. I didn't know my mother as well as I thought I once had, but I also didn't know myself much more either.

"It's frightening having these abilities. I've never had others rely on me, and now I have an entire kingdom. They side with me because they believe I can help them." My voice shuddered as I spoke, staring at the hills, focusing to keep my eyes from burning.

"Perhaps it's because they sense they can trust you. They would say it if they didn't believe in you. I believe you're capable of anything. You just have to believe that yourself."

I huffed. "Ivarison, what happened with the twins? Dealla and Killian?"

"You just ruined another moment," Bria barked.

"What?" I snapped back. I couldn't stop myself; the wonder consumed me. He trained and traveled with me, yet I didn't know much about him. I wanted to trust him. I felt that I could, but the way others were with him made me question myself.

"I pondered when you'd ask again." His voice was low. "Some things are better left unsaid. It was a very hard and complicated moment that I don't enjoy speaking about." I began to object, but he held out a hand to take mine, his warm palm brushing with mine. "I can show you instead, if you'd allow."

I nodded, unsure of what he meant.

"Close your eyes," he whispered.

A warm sensation floated through my mind as I closed my eyes. It filled my body, and I began to see everything he wished for me to see, as if he was projecting his own thoughts as my own. I saw myself through his eyes, sitting in front of him as my hair fluttered in a light breeze, just before he closed them.

A cool breeze touched my skin, and I saw a river flowing close by. Ivarison was at my side, but it didn't look like the Ivarison who was holding my hands. His clothing was different, lighter leathers with a sword in hand, wings gone. His hair was messy, as if he had been running and battling through the surrounding chaos.

We stood on a brick path that went toward a small castle. For a moment, I saw the beauty of where he had brought me. Different shades of flowers bloomed, wooden fences with animals, and homes in various colors lined the alleys.

It was over as quickly as I took it in. Smoke smothered the air from colorful buildings blazing with fire. Roofs caved in as villagers fled their burning homes. Horses galloped freely through the streets, soldiers attacking others, and corpses lay across the streets.

Ivarison stood in the middle of the path. Fae ran and shoved past him. The fear and screams were terrifying to hear. He looked back at the castle – his home – with widening eyes as ash fell from the sky.

Ivarison had just seen his father slaughtered in front of him, and now his mother and younger brother were running for him, hands together as they raced from the castle.

Their screams for Ivarison were screams that I would never be able to forget.

"MOTHER! GARETH!" Ivarison screamed with such agony, chills ran down my spine, and the hair on my arms raised. He tried to move toward them, his terror radiating inside me.

Something was wrong. I could feel it as I watched. The earth rumbled at our feet, and there was a hissing noise.

Ivarison's mother held tightly onto Gareth as they rushed down castle steps, shoulders tensed as she looked over her shoulder, then back at Ivarison. She stalled. Ivarison froze, eyes so wide the whites showed. His mother grabbed Gareth tightly, holding him to her chest. She looked at Ivarison and mouthed, "I love you, so–" then the castle behind them exploded. Bricks blasted into the sky, and fire burst from the walls.

Everything turned red. Flames engulfed the castle and path, down to the steps. Ivarison's face was red from screaming, then the pressure of the explosion reached him, forcing him backwards. All I could smell was burnt sulfur and charcoal, feeling the heat against my body and wet tears streaming down my cheeks.

Everything turned black, then there was a faint light that flickered. The scenery had changed as I looked around at our current location. I stood in a high peak tent where Ivarison rested on a cot. His eyes opened, and he jolted up, looking around the unfamiliar area, black soot over his face and leathers.

He moved, knocking into another soldier as he rushed from the tent, trying to adjust himself from stumbling. The soldier held onto Ivarison as he shouted for his mother and Gareth.

"Where are they?!"

I could still smell the smoke and the ash on my body as the soldier held a grim stare, telling Ivarison that they had been killed in the blast.

Ivarison, dried blood from wounds that had healed, let go of the soldier and ran. I followed him as he dashed through the woods toward where his home had been. He stopped, catching his balance on a tree, gasping for air.

"Lord Ivarison–" a female voice spoke. The sound of her footsteps grew closer through the woods he had run through.

"Come back to camp, Ivarison." a male said as he and the female came closer. They looked so familiar as I tried to study their faces, not knowing who they were.

Ivarison only stared ahead, seeing what was left of his home.

Nothing. There was nothing left.

The tree Ivarison gripped broke in half. He pulled his hands away from the crushed bark and began ripping the armor from his chest as if it would help him breathe. His shoulders slumped as power seeped through him, black and blue filtering through his hands.

His home was in ruins.

Black shadows came from everywhere. They seeped from his fingers, his arms, his back.

The female and male who had tried to lead him back to the camp gasped. Even through the darkness of the trees, I could hear their movement as they had turned to escape.

My hands went to my chest. Darkness swirled around his waist as his knees fell to the ground. The world stopped as a rumble came from him. His head fell back, releasing a scream that shook the earth. Everything went black.

I thought the visions he was showing were over, but his eyes opened, and he blinked frantically. Further shouts were heard as he saw what he had done. Everything left was blackened and burnt. Nothing was left alive as shadows still fell from him and fire burned on his palms.

"WHAT HAVE YOU DONE?!" Mara shrieked. "YOU MONSTER! YOU KILLED THEM! I'LL KILL YOU!"

A burst of wind hit Ivarison and me as he broke our connection. Our actual surroundings appeared back in place as I opened my eyes. We were standing. He yanked his hands from mine, tears filling my eyes.

"I lost my family in a battle with Adriane and Ciaran; they destroyed my home and court because I wouldn't be their ally. The twins and their family had come to help, and in turn, I killed their parents. I was so blinded with rage and fury that I lost myself and lost control. I hadn't realized they had followed.

From that night, things only grew worse as I tried to find Adriane and Ciaran. Anytime I heard they were back in Madora, I went for them. Dealla and Killian had to deal with the mess a few times."

"How could you–" I shook my head, trying to understand what anyone could see in such despicable beings. "How could you be on their side in the first place?" I took a tight breath, afraid to know, then asked, "What made you see they couldn't be trusted?"

He closed his eyes. A vein in his forehead protruded as he opened his eyes and looked at me. His gaze darted all over my face.

"I considered them friends at one point. I had stayed in Ravenholde for some time. My father wanted to know more about them, and they didn't seem evil when I first arrived. Slowly, I began to see what they were doing and what they were capable of.

"Once they saw the power I had, they wanted me to join. They attacked multiple of their own villages, killing their own subjects. Adriane killed her parents and sister to become Queen of Ravenholde. She will not admit to it, but I know that Ciaran and she did it. They wanted others to fear them.

"When their land began to die, they wanted Madora, and that's when I learned they were killing halflings. I didn't agree to help, so they retaliated to teach me a lesson."

I took his hand back, tightening my hold when he tried pulling away.

"You're not a monster, Ivarison." I said.

"You don't understand." He tried to pull away again, but I held firm. "It's partially my fault for what happened to Mystmere, to your family. I taught Adriane everything she needed to destroy your family."

My grip loosened as I stared, not understanding how it could be. His mouth parted, but nothing came out.

"I don't understand," I said, chest pounding. "What do you mean it's partially your fault?"

"Adriane couldn't fully control and conjure the mist. I taught her how to control it, make it spread in the way she can, and use it to travel. Before, she could only conjure her creatures, but even then, they weren't as they are now. I taught her how to move and travel through it."

He tipped his head back to stare at the sky. "I led them to Mystmere. It wasn't only the call from the King that led them. They were waiting for me, because I didn't join them. They wanted to kill me. If I had known what they were planning with their mist and what she would do, I wouldn't have taught her. I should've known and been able to read her, but she has her own ability with the mind and keeping hers locked."

I took a deep breath. I felt sick. I was going to be sick.

"He does seem to have regrets with this. Take a moment." Bria said.

I could only close my eyes and take a deep breath. When I reopened them, he wouldn't look at me. I still felt like I was going to be sick. How could he carry this with him for so long?

"How could you keep this to yourself?" I breathed out, my lips quivered. "You lost your family, your home. What happened with the twins' parents was a mistake. I don't hold that against you. I don't believe what happened in Mystmere was your fault, even if you taught her. You didn't know what she would become, and you didn't know my father would go into it, but he did that to save me." I paused, taking another breath. "You're not the monster, Ivarison."

I needed him to hear my words.

"You are not the monster," I said again. If he wanted me to believe in myself for what I could be capable of, he needed to see the good in himself and the changes he tried making to atone for what he had done. "You're not like them, and even if you were at any point before this, you're trying to change."

"I lost control many times when I looked for them. There were times Killian had been there to stop me, and I nearly hurt him multiple times. All I cared about was seeking revenge for what they had done. I turned into something horrible."

"Your parents and brother were murdered in front of you. What happened right after was a horrible accident. What happened to my family was not your fault. You did not kill them – Adriane and Ciaran did. And they will pay for what they've done."

His chest rose.

"I've not returned to Wildhaven since."

"You'll find your way back home, and you'll be a wonderful lord."

"I'm not sure I could go back," he whispered. "For a few reasons."

The horizon glistened in shades of teal, orange, and yellow as the sun set – moment of peace for us as we faced each other. I wrapped my arms around him tightly, his body stiffening under my touch.

"We will both get through this, one way or another." I paused, eyes staring up when he didn't move. "But I need you to pretend you know how to hug for one minute." I muttered. His body relaxed a fraction, and he wrapped his muscular arms around me.

Would I ever have a moment like this again? Watching the sunset as Bria began flying close to return to us. And if Ivarison blamed himself for what happened to my home, how would he feel when he saw whatever of it was left?

Chapter Twenty-Five

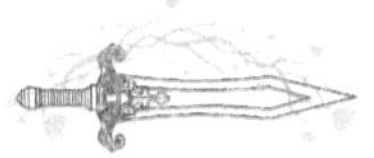

Mornwind was the last village before we reached Mystmere. If I had seen it when I was younger, it would have been in a better state. Now it was blackened and charred, as if set ablaze and left vacant. No living thing walked through the cracked streets.

Buildings were roofless, caved in by fire, with rubble strewn astray across broken stone paths. Grass and trees were charred. Fences were broken apart, as if animals and creatures had burst through to escape.

Silence was our only companion as we walked through. Not even birds were heard. If this was Adriane and Ciaran's doing, what possibly could have been done to Mystmere? Why desire to rule the land if destruction was the result? If we failed to end their reign, this could be Madora's fate. Life had once filled these streets; now, death stared us in the face.

"This is awful," Delaney muttered, breaking the hovering silence, as she looked through rubble. "It looks like it's been some time since this happened."

"Was this Adriane and Ciaran?" I asked, looking at the broken bits of buildings that may have once been a home.

"Without a doubt, they put their soldiers to do this. They relish in something like this," Killian answered somberly.

"Is this what Madora will end up being like if I fail? Will they ruin this land?" I asked, and I had stopped moving. Nothing grew, even if it tried. It lacked the nutrients and care, as if it had been sucked from the earth.

"Little Spark, you need to move." Bria's voice came on high alert. *"I spotted guards moving in from the west. I'm moving toward Mystmere to see what more may lie ahead."*

"Okay, keep moving. I'll alert the others."

She hissed, debating whether to listen. *"Be careful and stay alert. Something feels wrong about this place."* Worry and hesitation flowed through our bond.

"We need to move. Bria spotted guards coming in from the west," I said quickly. No point staying in a broken village.

During our travels and fights together, we'd found comfort in staying close. It helped us stay in tune with each other. We moved in the opposite direction of the guards. No sooner than I took a breath, we heard motion straight ahead.

Together, we huddled in the shadows of a half-decimated building. Dealla looked alarmed as she scanned our surroundings, not wanting to battle and draw more attention to ourselves.

Slowly, I peered around a partially hinged door. Dark Soldiers entered the streets from the opposite direction, cruel eyes searching broken homes. The guards were cornering us, knowing the way in and out. Dealla and Killian exchanged weighted glances and pointed toward the forest.

There wasn't another option, not with Bria so far away. I wouldn't let Dealla fade us out, not after what had happened in Ravenwick. We didn't dare separate, knowing guards would follow wherever I went.

"Ellowyn," Bria called as we moved out of a dark alley. *"What's happening? I can feel your distress. Do I need to return?"*

"No." I tried to catch my breath, having held it while running, fingers clutched to my sword. *"I think we're okay, just sneaking out."*

None of us spoke as we listened and waited. Distant enough, I was unable to hear what they were saying to one another as they searched for us.

"We need to find a way to go around rather than go straight into the guards," Killian hissed.

"What did Mornwind do to warrant this level of devastation?" Delaney whispered as we followed.

Could Adriane and Ciaran have done this because Mornwind had denied an allegiance with them? Would they burn the land to ash and not care as long as they ended up Queen and King? I looked at Ivarison, his eyes peering over an edge as he took in the village.

I took one of his hands and squeezed it, his attention falling over to me. This wasn't his fault, but I could see it. I could see the regret in his look as he looked around.

There was a blood-curdling scream that came from the forest. My hand fell from Ivarison's as my blood ran cold.

Was that my mother? The shrieking continued, and I knew that tone. There. My mother screamed my name. My eyes were darting so fast as my companions' eyes came upon me. I couldn't hear or focus on anything else that was around me as Dealla and Ivarison tried to speak. Their lips were moving, but I couldn't hear anything as my ears were ringing.

Where did the soldiers go? I didn't see them. My mind raced, and when I heard the scream again, I ran.

My legs moved faster than I had ever run before. The trees stretched upward as I reached the forest, different from the others. Footsteps came from behind me, voices yelling for me to stop.

The further I went, I heard faint growls, the screaming stopped, and I turned to look. Where was she? Where did they have my mother?

"*ELLOWYN!*" Bria was shouting, but I couldn't answer.

The hair on my neck rose, sending chills through my body as if I had dipped myself in an iced lake.

I stopped running, and the rest of my group nearly ran into me. I couldn't find her; she wasn't anywhere through the trees, and the screaming stopped.

"I'm sorry– It was my mother screaming," I stammered.

Something was wrong. I felt nauseous as Bria growled through our bond.

"*Where did you go?!*" Bria demanded.

I could hear our beating hearts as we stood in a circle. A ripple of air came crashing through, tree branches broke, and leaves scattered in circles above as we were thrown backwards, nearly landing on top of one another. The forest burst into pieces, and wind came tunneling through a clearing.

There. Just ahead were the nightmares that followed me.

The mist was appearing and growling, swirling as I could only watch while the others quickly stood with their swords in hand. For the first time, I had seen the mist form into something more.

"What's happening?!" I could hear my frantic voice as darkness grew impossibly darker. Ivarison's jaw tensed. Dealla and Killian's shoulders stiffened as Delaney moved closer, standing just ahead of me as she stared at the mist and started shaking her head. Ivarison grabbed hold of my arm to pull me back.

"We need to get Ellowyn away, now!" Ivarison turned to face me, his eyes frightening as his skin nearly glowed, magic filling his palms.

A figure began taking shape. Strikingly beautiful, but terrifying. Long dark hair fell to her waist; her black eyes were like tunnels to hell. Her pale skin and dark green attire flowed down her tall frame like a chest of armor.

A smirk stretched across her full lips, her eyes darting excitedly, while another figure appeared behind her. His dark blond hair was short and brushed over. His chestnut eyes narrowed as he came from the mist and stood next to the female.

The same female from the cottage.

The two Fae stood before us. Anger built through me as if I could take every bit of my power and strike against them.

Adriane and Ciaran.

"What a pity that your mother couldn't stay. I had to pull her away; her screams were rather annoying." Adriane blinked slowly, her grin only growing wider.

Then I saw the terrifying creature that lingered behind, emerging from the mist as it came through beside Adriane.

Starting at us, its faded gold skin weathered as if it had melted from its body. Battered wings with holes hung from its back. Red eyes watched hungrily, its nose slit like a snake with a mouth like a black hole. I couldn't see what lurked in its mouth, and I didn't want to find out.

"The Sleroka," Ivarison breathed. Even he looked nervous over the monstrosity.

"Oh, Ivarison. Haven't you learned your lesson by now?" The female's long fingers pointed as she stepped forward, inhaling and glancing at us. "Oh, how delightful." She clicked her tongue at him. "Have you had enough and are ready to come back to play?" Her eyebrows raised as she smiled playfully. Ivarison growled, stepping forward as beast claws unsheathed from his knuckles.

"It's been a task to keep tabs on you, half-breed Fae." The male spoke deeply, breaking Adriane's taunt. His eyes bore through me in disgust as he held his chin high. "We watched while we waited for you to come closer to Mystmere. To see what you were capable of, but we've yet to be impressed."

"You sure know how to make trouble like your mother, though, don't you? Poor thing thought she could hide you forever." Their voices made me cringe.

"Adriane and Ciaran," I said, not sure I truly believed they were standing before us. I had waited for this moment to occur sooner, and yet now I couldn't believe they were standing right there.

If anyone could throw daggers from stares, it would be them. Their eyes narrowed so tightly, they looked like slights.

"You'll address us as King and Queen," Adriane snapped.

"You are no King and Queen to me, and you never will be to Madora." Anger rippled through me. Bria roared, I could feel the powerful strokes of her wings as she flew back to Mornwind.

"I'm returning! I'm coming back for you!" she cried.

"No! I don't want them to see you, they will kill you!" I said frantically back to her.

"You are worth the risk!"

"As long as I'm alive, you'll never have our kingdom. I will not surrender it to you."

Adriane tilted her head with a grin. "We're not here for your blessing. I'm going to kill you, and now that you're near Mystmere, I will take what is mine."

Each of my companions moved closer, Ivarison's magic nearly shining through his skin as he waited to attack, welcoming a chance to end either of the two.

"Where is my mother?" My hands hummed as I demanded. Ciaran picked at his cloak, rolling his eyes as if bored. "WHERE IS SHE?"

My hands were heavy as they flew forward, palms out toward Adriane and Ciaran. Power emerging from me and throwing a ball of fire, and just when I thought it would strike, Ciaran swung his hand forward, changing its direction into a tree that blew in flames.

I would win this. I had to.

I couldn't let these two take what belonged to my family and turn it into what was left of Mornwind. I had to fight for what was left. Take control of myself and the power that stirred and yearned for escape.

"DO NOT DO ANYTHING RASH!" Bria roared in my mind, moving as quickly as she could. She would burn the forest to keep me away from them.

"My dear pet has waited so eagerly to sink its teeth in you," Adriane said with a laugh, her hand petting the monster's head and going down its spine. Her shrill laugh lingered as the Sleroka walked, paws ending with talons, digging deeply in the dirt. "You'll be joined by your mother soon enough, where we've left her to rot."

No. The words screamed in my mind. I wouldn't let them take anyone else. Not my mother. Not the ones who stood by my side, who had become like family to me.

Adriane's black mist began to grow behind her, darkness swirling as she looked back at Ivarison, an eyebrow arched.

"How embarrassing it must be after the years you've waited. Now look at you, about to watch her die." Ciaran said. Adriane took his hand, and they faded with matching cruel smiles.

The Sleroka moved out, standing yards ahead.

My hands shook as I gripped my sword. The world began to slow as I took it in. I could feel the flutters against my chest and rapid breathing.

Bria. Bria could fly us out. Would her fire burn this monster?

"BRIA!"

I could feel her pushing herself to move quickly.

"You must get out of there! I'm afraid I won't get to you in time!" Her roar vibrated through my bones.

"Ellowyn, love. Go, now." Ivarison growled, looking over his shoulder. I could sense everyone's fear creeping out. His body shifted, wings sprawling as he turned to his beast form.

"NO!" I protested, but Dealla moved toward me.

"Two thousand paces west – meet there," Dealla said, giving a nod to Killian and Delaney. The two shifted into their beast forms. Dealla grabbed hold of me.

"IVARISON!" I screamed, but the world spun. The Sleroka was gone, and we stood in another location. Walls were overgrown with vines and dead flowers. A gazebo overlooked a garden with a ruined cottage nearby.

Dealla released me, watching as she waited.

"What happened?!" I scrambled up from where Dealla left me. Two large animals arrived, transforming back into Killian and Delaney.

"We must keep moving now," Dealla said, ignoring me, her hand gripping her sword tightly.

"I heard my mother screaming, I have to try to get to her!" I demanded, but no one wanted to answer. "Where is Ivarison?!"

"We must keep moving. Mystmere is not far from here," Dealla said, her voice sharp as she looked at Killian, who wasn't making eye contact with me.

I refused to move. I couldn't leave Ivarison to fend for himself against such a vile creature. Not when it was me it wanted.

"Ellowyn, we are trying to keep you safe. Ivarison knows this," Killian said as Delaney shifted her feet.

"How can we leave him with that thing? You saw it! We left him there. What if he doesn't survive? It will continue coming after us! We are more powerful together."

"The Sleroka is Adriane's most vile creature. It travels through the mist, destroying everything in its path. That is her ability, and why others don't stand against her. There is no stopping it; you cannot kill it!"

"That thing took my father. I won't let it take Ivarison too!" I was screaming, searching for Bria, "You just haven't found a way to kill it yet! You hate him enough that you would let him die against it alone?!"

"This has nothing to do with hating–" Dealla began.

"Ellowyn –" Killian also said, but I held up my hand.

"No. I demand you take me back. That's an order from your princess. We cannot leave him to die."

"This is about protecting you! This is what we must do, I have to continue protecting you!" Dealla snapped.

"Bria, please, please take me back! Where are you?!"

"Dealla faded in the opposite direction. I'm drawing close now, but I cannot make it back to you and return to Ivarison quickly enough. Listen to them, Ellowyn."

No. No. No.

This could not happen. I wouldn't let him endure such a creature alone because of me.

"Ivarison!" I searched for him, hoping that I could hear his voice that annoyed and taunted me on most days. Anything to know he was still fighting.

"Dealla, please!" I begged, moving closer to Killian and her, grabbing her forearm. Their faces were grim as they dropped their gaze.

"He made his decision. He wanted to protect and save you." Delaney finally spoke, her tone off as if she too battled whether to go back.

I backed away. I would find my way to him. I doubted Bria would take me back once she returned.

I tried reaching for Ivarison again, but there was only silence. I focused on the streets, the broken streets of Mornwind, the death lingering through the village. The trees that looked different in the forest where Adriane and Ciaran had stood.

I had only tried once. Why hadn't I tried something more when they had been right in front of me?

My fingernails dug into my palms, magic flowing as I focused on where I needed to go, where my magic was calling for me to move. I could see Bria flying through the clouds, still a distance away. Her wings relaxed as she saw me.

"I'm sorry, I won't leave him," I said. I wasn't sure what I was doing as their eyes widened just before I vanished.

I hit the ground with a thud, catching myself before my head struck the ground. An eerie feeling lurked as I was near the woods' edge. It was quiet as my ears adjusted, and I knew I didn't have much time if Ivarison still fought the Sleroka.

How could such a vile creature be created and summoned? This is what would lurk in Madora. No Fae or creature had been able to take them down yet; humans wouldn't stand a chance.

"*ELLOWYN! Oh, you fool! Do not move until I'm with you!*" Bria shouted, having gone in circles trying to return. As sorry as I was, I didn't do what I was told to do.

"IVARISON!" I called out. I heard commotion in the clearing where we had been, horrifying roars of pain and screeching as I ran toward the noise. Even with Ivarison in his beast form, his paws larger than my torso and horns that could slice like swords, what could be done if a Sleroka couldn't be killed?

"Ivarison!" I stuttered, hand going over my chest as I stood frozen and watched the creature hold his neck. The Sleroka shrieked, red eyes blinking at me.

Its face twisted. It was a thing of nightmares. Ivarison immediately noticed the distraction that I had caused, his blue eyes finding me as he let out a painful cry. I couldn't think, couldn't breathe.

"You came back?! How wonderfully stupid of you," Ivarison snapped, trying to break free from the grip that was around him.

I couldn't reply before there was an echoing crunch as the Sleroka threw Ivarison across the clearing against a tree. He didn't move as his body shifted back to Fae form.

"IVARISON!" My body was burning. Was he breathing?

The creature reached an arm out, longer than any normal arm should reach, straight for me. I dodged, as its long legs leaped in my direction, missing me only by inches.

"Ellowyn, you better stay alive until I can get there!" Bria was furious; her voice echoed, and I thought I heard the sky rumble.

I had to get to Ivarison. The Sleroka shrieked again, taking notice that now Dealla had faded close by with Delaney. Within moments, Killian was approaching in his wolf form, shifting back to his Fae form.

They began to scream, begging me to escape. But I had to get to Ivarison as the Sleroka had turned back for me. I moved at the last second, avoiding another swipe. I reached Ivarison's side and grabbed and held him as screams escaped me.

"PROTECT YOURSELF!" Bria was at the edge of my mind. *"I'M NEAR!"*

My throat was on fire. If the Sleroka neared and took a swipe, we would both perish. I felt the wind, blue power surrounding and seeping from my skin that circled me. I would not be afraid. We would not fail now.

The Sleroka shrieked as it tried to reach, but the blue aura that exuded from me created a barrier around us. Ivarison had blood dripping from a gash across his temple, his skin pale as I pulled him closer, listening for his heart as faint heat hit my cheeks.

He was breathing. I laid him back on the ground and stood to face the Sleroka as it tried passing through my protection barrier.

I could hear Bria's roars to keep the monster at bay just a minute longer. There wasn't enough time, however close she may be. I didn't know how long my barrier would stay intact or for the Sleroka to turn onto the other three.

Was this, in fact, the same Sleroka that took my father?

"Come after him or me again, and I'll kill you." I seethed. There was such power that was emerging and vibrating against me. It was nothing I had felt before. I burned as if I could destroy the earth around me. The Sleroka kept forcing its way in, my palms raised, long talons scratched against the surface.

I focused on the words Ivarison had spoken during our training and battles. He thought I let the magic sit within me and fester. It needed to be released. My bones felt like they were burning, as if every fiber sizzled and burned away.

"DUCK!" I shouted. I didn't know if it would work, but I had to hope it would.

I dropped my barrier as the Sleroka lashed out. Power rushed out with such force that it nearly knocked me from my feet. Trees shook, the world grew quiet as I could only see the flash of blue and white power as it bolted from me.

The Sleroka blew into pieces, and the world spun.

Black surrounded my vision's edges as the ground shook with Bria landing, tree branches breaking as she cursed at me, searching the area for anything else that might attack and let out a roar that rattled the earth.

Dealla, Killian, and Delaney knelt together beneath broken bits of trees from the surge. They stared at where the Sleroka had just been.

My knees buckled as I slid to the ground next to Ivarison, Bria coming closer.

"Ivarison!" I checked his chest again. "Ivarison!" I looked at Bria for reassurance or at the others for help. "Don't die on me, you stupid prick!" My eyes blurred as I hit him hard on the chest.

"Ow," a soft noise came from his cracked lips. He took ahold of my hand before I could hit him again. "I'm injured and now you're hitting me." He looked through thick eyelashes, blinking a few times. "What did you do?"

The others stood stunned. The Sleroka remains had scattered across the ground and trees. Bria kept us surrounded, still shouting profanity for my stupidity.

"I don't know," I answered, taking a deep breath. "I knew I needed to kill it for what it's done, so that's what I did."

"Why did you come back?" he demanded, eyes dancing with questions as he looked at the others.

Dealla huffed, still pale and furious. "The princess decided to ignore direct orders and blew up the Sleroka." Her tone could freeze fire. "We'll discuss her definition of 'staying safe' later."

Delaney looked proud, patting me on the back. "What have you been doing during your training?"

Ivarison looked up to me, holding his head where the wound bled. "You killed the Sleroka. Next time, let me die. I'm not worth whatever guilt you'll carry."

I flinched at his words. He was worth the guilt that I had just before returning. "I'm sorry," I muttered as he sighed, trying to pull himself up. His eyes closed as his head fell back, the sun hitting his face.

Killian reached out, grabbing Ivarison's forearms.

"Come on, let's get you up."

"I'll be fine. I'm beginning to heal." He grimaced, reaching the side of his temple where the gash was. "Sleroka has poison in their talons, so it's taking longer to heal."

"We have to figure out what happened with Princess Alina. If they haven't killed her, they will do so soon if they believe Ellowyn to be dead. I don't believe there is a chance they will keep her alive now," Dealla said, lips downturned.

"They may still try using her as leverage," Ivarison muttered.

"They won't need to use her as leverage if they believe I'm dead," I said. Could this mean we were too late for my mother? But if the Sleroka didn't return to Adriane, she would have to know that her plan didn't work. She hadn't expected me to be capable of killing the Sleroka.

"Let's move from here. We need to make camp and get out of sight," Killian stated, holding Ivarison up. Dealla nodded, looking pale. She had forced herself to fade twice now, and it was taking a toll on her being.

"I will not be leaving again," Bria hissed. *"That was incredibly irresponsible. Senseless! What if that hadn't worked?"*

"I'm sorry, I panicked. I couldn't let him face that alone."

Bria huffed as I reached for her, and her head came closer, resting against me.

"We work together, Ellowyn. You must talk to me."

"Together. I'm sorry."

Chapter Twenty-Six

Delaney found a sloped area through the woods as Bria flew above, and Killian scoped the land. Checking for signs of Adriane and Ciaran, or the guards we had seen in Mornwind. None. As if they had disappeared again, with no sign of where they may have gone.

I hid in the tent Dealla had put up for me, seeking privacy. No one spoke during dinner; all were quiet, not wanting to speak about what had occurred. I couldn't figure out if Dealla was more hurt or angry that I hadn't listened. Bria's annoyance still tinged her voice when she spoke. Now she lay outside the tent, on the opposite side of the campfire, away from the others.

Dealla had a small tent that she had never used during our journey. Once she set it up and stated it was for me for the evening, I gathered she didn't want to speak with me.

I'd killed a Sleroka. The monster claimed to be unkillable. I didn't know if I'd ever be capable of pulling that sort of magic from myself again.

Part of me still couldn't believe what I had done. I closed my eyes, remembering a moment with my parents together, to rid myself of the thoughts of the Sleroka and what I had done.

I envisioned my father: the creases by his eyes as he smiled, sitting close to my bed, humming a beautiful lullaby that soothed my nerves with calming tunes. He whispered goodnight before kissing my forehead. Then he vanished, and I was forced to open my eyes.

"Ellowyn?" a deep voice came from outside the tent, interrupting the battle in my head. "May I come in?" Ivarison's voice vibrated in his throat. As he entered, I saw color had returned to his skin, and the gash on his forehead healed.

I lay on the cot as he closed the tent, darkness overtaking as I stared at his figure. The lantern near me lit, and I could see him more clearly as he approached, shadows under his eyes.

"I thought you healed instantly?" I asked, seeing the faint line on his forehead.

"The poison slowed the healing," he whispered. "I thought it was very foolish of you to return today." Bria snorted outside. Ivarison looked toward her shadow through the tent. "The Sleroka is a complex creature."

I nodded, knowing only what Dealla had told me after, lecturing me repeatedly about my foolishness. Ivarison came closer to sit on the cot's edge, careful not to hit my feet.

"Why did you do it?" Ivarison asked, his voice was still quiet, blue eyes never leaving my face. "Why did you come back?"

The feeling of certainty entered my bones. I couldn't explain why I had felt to return and help, but I knew it had been right. I had made the decision and faded before I could question myself.

"Why not? I wouldn't let you die so willingly for me. I care for everyone here, and that includes you, Ivarison. Even when you piss me off daily, might I add." I tried to smile, but my lips hardly curved. "You've saved me multiple times now – tell me you wouldn't have returned and done the same." My cheeks heated as I rose to sit. It wasn't a question, because I knew he would.

"Adriane and Ciaran know I'm a risk to them. You aren't the only reason they would like to see me dead. How did you know you'd be able to fade again?"

"I didn't. But I knew I couldn't let the Sleroka hurt you. I wanted to protect us, and I listened to everything you said during training." I paused, lost in thought. "I don't think I would have handled it well seeing you die from the Sleroka. It's what took my father."

His sigh was heavy as it filled the tent, hands gripping the cot's edge. "Thank you." A smirk crossed his mouth. "You must have a wonderful instructor."

"He is very arrogant, though." I grabbed his wrist before he could stand, afraid to touch his bare skin. "Please don't risk yourself like that for me again." My voice cracked with my plea.

His eyes widened slightly as his gaze fell to where my hand held him. "We're at the start of a war, Ellowyn. We will have to make decisions and sacrifices others may not like. Including losing others." His eyes returned to mine. "Don't let one victory go to your head, Princess."

As my hand dropped, he stood, flexing his hand.

"Get some rest. You look terrible." He grinned as I threw a pillow, and he caught it.

"As do you, ass." I said, catching the pillow back. Warmth built in me as his chuckle lingered in the tent where he left.

There had been no signs of creatures, soldiers, or Adriane and Ciaran as we neared Mystmere. If I went an entire lifetime before seeing another Sleroka, it would be too soon. Unfortunately, no one seemed to know if Adriane could conjure another.

"Adriane conjures creatures that look like they come from hell's deepest parts and controls them," Killian said after I asked what Adriane and Ciaran were fully capable of. "The Sleroka seems to be her favorite when she's in dire need. She uses the mist as a home for it, since it prefers the dark. We can only assume the worst when someone falls into it with an awaiting Sleroka. We've never known anyone who had escaped its grasp." He shivered, probably thinking of the devastation it caused. "And Ciaran can manipulate air and wind."

My father had gone willingly through that mist.

Delaney had been quiet since the attack, traveling ahead in her panther form, searching the ground as Bria did the same above.

The air continued to warm as we moved further from Northhorn. The grass grew in the prettiest shades of green, and flowers were blooming. I waited for Delaney as the sun shimmered through the wispy trees.

Bria flew as low as she could through the clouds, refusing to be far from me. She hadn't wanted to give up her search for her kind, but her discouragement was evident. But I wouldn't let her give up.

"I know there are more dragons out there somewhere, Bria. You'll find them." I whispered when I could sense her longing.

It was near afternoon when we stopped to rest. Delaney came running as fast as her panther legs allowed, flustered and panicked.

"The barrier is a few miles ahead. I can't move further on," she said, turning back to her Fae form, hands on her chest as she gathered air in her lungs. "I ran down the path toward Mystmere but felt like I was being pushed away when I tried entering."

"Lord Eirwen was right," Killian mused.

"Who could've done such a thing?" I asked.

Killian and Dealla didn't respond, unsure and just as surprised.

"There were enchantments King Everett knew. Perhaps they were placed before the attack. Ellowyn is the princess, so there could be a chance she could still get through?" Ivarison asked, studying each of us.

"What of us?" Delaney asked before taking a swig from her canteen Killian offered, then brushing the dirt from her clothes.

"We have to try. We've traveled too far to turn back now," Dealla said. Killian nodded. "We have made no progress learning where Princess Alina is."

It didn't take long to cover the distance to Mystmere. We stopped just before the spot where Delaney couldn't move through, hesitation in our steps. Mystmere was there, yet we could only see trees ahead.

"What should I do? Just walk forward?" I asked. None of us had moved as we stared, searching for anything abnormal. Dealla nodded, and I took a step, each of them near me. Bria landed, and I glanced over my shoulder, her eyes narrowing as she nodded.

"There was something that felt different, even in the air. I can't see the true identity of what awaits."

I didn't need to ask how far the barrier was. Within the first few steps, something pressed against my body.

"It's also pushing me back," I said. A groan escaped everyone.

"Focus on the barrier. You can create barriers, perhaps you could work your way through one," Ivarison said, urging me to try again.

"Think of anything you may remember when you lived here. No matter how small a detail, it may help," Bria said, nudging my back.

I closed my eyes, imagining I could see the barrier that stretched around Mystmere. A bubble had protected me. I envisioned walking with my father, my hand wrapped around his fingers. A balcony where my grandfather stood, lifting me in the air as we laughed together.

I put my arm out, palm forward. I demanded entry. I wanted to see what was left of my home, my kingdom, where I was supposed to have grown and lived alongside my family.

"Ellowyn!" Dealla cried as I stumbled forward, crossing through the barrier. I held onto those thoughts and beckoned for the others to come with me.

"Come quickly! I think I have it open!" I called Bria, who hesitated as she moved to walk with the others. She kept her head down as if she would run into something.

We made it through.

I turned back, and the world looked vastly different than it had moments ago. Grass shimmered against the sun and danced along the wind. The river that flowed ahead hadn't been visible just before. I inhaled, an exhilarating aroma filling me as my entire body warmed.

"We aren't far," I could hear urgency from Dealla. This had been her home too, and this was her first time returning in seventeen years.

Bria kept to the ground as we walked. The others were ahead as I stayed with her, ground rumbling from her steps. We took a turn on a bend in the road, and I could see radiance from Dealla's smile as Ivarison and she turned back to me.

"Welcome home, Princess," Ivarison said, guiding me to step forward.

Just ahead, my breath caught in my throat.

The attack happened seventeen years ago, yet nothing looked like Mornwind. The river went along the village edge, leading further beyond. The village was close enough that Fae could be seen walking through the streets and farmers in fields.

At the village's end, a path led toward a castle surrounded by gardens. Gray stone gleamed in the sun. Rooftops were a dark blue, with tower peaks and flags blowing in the wind. Countless windows and balconies were visible, and very faintly through one, I could see a figure, standing and watching.

I looked back at the grassy lawns where children played. Fae children who laughed and ran alongside together.

My chest tightened, and my eyes burned as I blinked tears away. I had missed such a beautiful kingdom and the memories I could have made. There were villagers with joyous smiles as they walked and greeted others. It was nothing like the human village.

I was in such a daze that I hadn't been aware of the sudden commotion. Soldiers rushed over with weapons pointed at us. Bria's legs straddled over me, as I stood just below the center of her chest.

"We do not know what to expect and who's living here now," Bria said, head close to mine, growling at the soldiers.

It was hard not to take notice of the dragon standing with us. Guards watched her move as Ivarison and Delaney stood on either side of me, between Bria's legs. Killian and Dealla stood at our front.

"How did you enter through the barrier? What business do you have here?" one of the soldiers demanded, keeping his distance from Bria.

Another guard walked past the others in line as he pulled his helmet off, revealing a tanned face and brown eyes.

"Dealla?" he asked. His gaze darted to each of us, "Killian?"

Killian and Dealla lowered their swords, bowing their heads to the male.

"Alix! I wasn't sure I'd ever seen you again," Killian said. The Fae moved in, and they embraced. "Brother."

"What has happened?" Alix asked, smiling at Dealla. "It's an honor to be back with you. It was hard not knowing what happened when you left." He turned to the other soldiers who stood behind him, signaling them to depart.

"We've been traveling through Madora as of late, searching for Princess Alina. We returned to Mystmere in hopes we would find more answers."

Ivarison," Alix said, spotting him standing by Bria and me, giving him a nod. "Who else do you have with you?"

Dealla sighed, extending a hand for introductions. "Commander, this is Delaney of Luminara." She moved closer. "I would like you to meet Princess Ellowyn, daughter of Princess Alina. As well as her dragon, Bria."

Alix immediately dropped a knee. "Princess, forgive me. I did not know it was you."

I had many things to learn and how to handle each one.

"Please don't do that!" I gestured for him to stand. "It's nice to meet you. Are we allowed to go to the castle? We have much to discuss."

Yes, but–" he glanced at Ivarison, then put his helmet back on, "I will have to take you directly, as there are matters to handle." He looked at Bria. "She won't be able to walk through the village. She can fly above and meet us in the courtyard."

"*I'll be directly above,*" Bria said, stepping away and ascending into the air.

Chapter Twenty-Seven

The air felt light while we walked through the village. Cobblestone paths led through every turn while villagers watched us pass. Muttering and pointing at us, and then at Bria. Some quickly entered buildings as they watched her fly above. Lanterns hung from each door, and some buildings were taller than others. Flowers streamed down archways, giving the village a beautiful color and a sweet, deep, earthy scent.

"It looks so familiar," I said to Bria, remembering glimpses of the beauty. How the sun set over the river, memories of me running down the riverbank with my mother behind me, rushing back. As I looked ahead, I remembered the black mist that had overpowered these streets and watched my father disappear.

The castle was more beautiful as we neared. Gray bricks stretched toward the sky, multiple keeps at corners, and the size seemed to double from what I had seen from afar. It was a place I could find myself lost in. The sun shone through the large courtyard as Bria descended and landed.

She tucked her wings tightly against her body and stood still. Her head lowered toward the stationed guards, showing she was not a threat.

"If you go through those walls and feel as if you're in danger, I will not hesitate to tear the walls down."

I smiled. *"I appreciate you having my back."* I knew she wouldn't hesitate. She gave me calmness that I focused on to keep myself at ease. Dealla and Killian looked around, completely serene.

They were home.

"This way," Alix called, stopping at the door for the guards to open. Once we entered, I watched the door shut, Bria and I staring at one another until it closed completely.

We're safe. We're safe. I said to myself. The rest of our group stood close by my side.

"The dragon has traveled with you?" Alix asked, walking a step ahead. I didn't immediately answer. "I apologize, Princess. I'm only curious. I've never seen a dragon up close."

"Yes, she is with me." I said in admiration. "Her name is Bria. I would appreciate it if she weren't disturbed."

"I'll let them know if they are disturbing me," Bria said with a higher tone in her voice.

Footsteps echoed in the foyer as we proceeded. Delaney, who took in every detail of the castle, kept a hand on her dagger's hilt. She looked pale.

The corridors were lit with lanterns hanging from the walls, allowing minimal light. We traveled deeper into the castle until light beckoned us further. A large bronze door awaited at the end of the hall once we turned a corner.

"In this room, please," Alix said, pushing open heavy doors. A large oak table sat at the center, surrounded by fifteen red, cushioned chairs with gold arms and legs. The chandelier hung above with more than a dozen lit candles. Just behind the table, windows gave a beautiful view of the courtyard where Bria rested, and a large mirror rested against the fireplace mantle, reflecting the room.

We each surveyed the room, expecting to see why we were brought here, but found nothing.

"What's this about, Alix?" Dealla asked, her eyes taking in every inch of the room.

"Pardon me, I shall return momentarily," Alix spoke quickly. "Please take a seat if you wish." None of us moved as Alix quickly crossed the room to another door in the corner. He left, the door closing behind him, with a resounding click of the lock.

"What is this about? Why's he locking us in here?" Delaney asked, stepping around the room. I paced with her, already planning to call for Bria. I felt her listening, prepared.

"There is nothing to fear. Be patient for his return." Ivarison said calmly, leaning against the back of a red cushioned chair, pulling his hood from his face.

"What was that about with Alix?" Dealla asked, turning to face Ivarison. "I didn't know you knew Alix. What have you been keeping from us?"

"Bria," I said, afraid this was another trap, and we were falling into something like the twins' manor again.

"I promise, I will be up the moment needed. They are watching me, I would like to see what the guard is doing."

Everyone in the room stared at Ivarison when he didn't answer Dealla. His brows furrowed as he avoided making eye contact.

"Ivarison," Killian called, voice deep. "Do you know what's going on?"

"I can't say," he finally answered, lips twisted.

"You can't tell us if you're leading us into a trap?" Delaney asked, pacing faster. She moved to the window, looking down at Bria. "Could Bria catch us?"

"Not comfortably." Bria huffed. I may have laughed if I weren't so worried.

"No, this isn't a trap. I can say that at least." Ivarison's jaw clenched as his lips pursed.

"What is it, Ivarison?" I finally asked. "Why can't you tell us?"

"He cannot say because he swore an oath never to speak of it," Alix said as he entered the room. "I would like to welcome our King." He gestured to the male, who entered through the door slowly.

His pointed ears peeked out from his tight, half-up hairstyle, which fell past his shoulders. The color I noticed was so similar to my own. His clothing in shades of green and black accented his eyes. His green eyes glimmered as he took us in. Dealla and Killian stared agape. I could hear their breathing quicken.

He was tall, muscular, and looked older than the rest, but I knew him. I knew his face.

"Everett – King Everett?" Dealla gasped, her eyes wide as she stared at him.

The face that had begun filling in missing memories. Memories of us walking together down corridors as he made little water figures with his magic that danced across our hands. Dealla looked ready to faint and grabbed hold of Killian's arms to steady herself.

"Dealla, dear," he spoke softly, as if she were an old friend.

"We were told that you perished alongside Queen Amelia. They stabbed you with a Riker blade," Killian said, but King Everett's eyes found me.

I stepped back, trying to remember all that I could of the male before me.

My eyes and nose burned as I tried to stop the tears. The hair on my arms rose.

My grandfather was alive.

"I was stabbed, and we did lose my beloved Amelia." His eyes never left me. "Ellowyn." My name came out as a whisper.

I felt the warmth of tears escape. The male in front of me had taught me how to ride a horse, fought with me using wooden swords, walked through corridors together, and taken me down garden paths with vines swirling in arches. I could remember.

"Grandfather," I said, my chest tightening and heart hammering as the one before me was supposed to be dead. A piece of my family was still here. Alive.

He came closer, hesitation bleeding through his steps before he embraced me tightly, arms wrapped with warmth and love.

"Oh, my sweet Ellowyn. Look how much you've grown. If Amelia could see you."

Delaney and Ivarison watched. Delaney smiled happily as she wiped a tear away from her cheek, and Ivarison's eyebrows wrinkled as he bit his lip.

"You knew he was alive?" I asked, eyes narrowing at Ivarison over my grandfather's shoulder. "We've been together for nearly two months, and you didn't think to tell me once?"

Ivarison's chest rose before he let out a breath. King Everett pulled from our embrace and grasped my hands.

"There were many times I wished I could have told you, Ellowyn. That I wanted to tell you," Ivarison said.

"It's not his fault, he took an oath with me to keep the secret that I was alive," my grandfather explained. "I had to ensure no one outside the kingdom knew. That is why the barrier has been placed around Mystmere. I didn't want to risk Adriane and Ciaran learning."

"Why him?" Dealla asked, her bottom lip trembling.

"You were where I needed you to be. When I learned Alina and Ellowyn survived, I knew that if anyone could find them, it would be you, Dealla. I knew you would never give up." My grandfather's voice was filled with pain, squeezing my hand together before letting go.

"I failed to keep her safe. She has been captured." Dealla kept her frown, bowing her head down as she stared at the floor. "I failed."

"You did no such thing," my grandfather said sharply. "You protect Ellowyn – you did not fail Alina. You did what she requested and protected her daughter. Come now, please sit." He motioned us to sit at the table. "There is still hope to bring Princess Alina home to us. We have much to discuss, and I know you must be famished. Let's eat, and I'll have chambers prepared so you can rest after."

"We don't have time to rest. We need to find my mother." I said, looking at the table he had put his hand toward for us to sit.

"Yes, we do, but we must discuss everything first." My grandfather stared at me, nodding his head.

"You need to eat, Ellowyn. Listen to what he has to say. I would love a few goats.." she muttered before her voice faded.

My legs felt heavy as everyone began to sit. I stared at the king, my grandfather. He was alive. He had been after all this time, while we had remained hidden in a human forest from the Fae world. Now, what would we do to bring my mother home? We had our kingdom and my grandfather at our side to find her.

Chapter Twenty-Eight

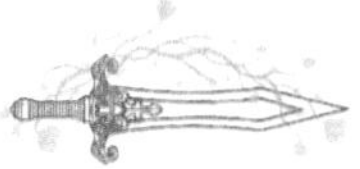

The silence was heavy through the room, making everything feel like it was spinning as I sat. My heart was beating fast against my ribs, waiting for the unknown. Did I call him grandfather or King? I ran my hand against the smooth table's edge, feeling uncomfortable. Still not used to being included in such conversations.

"Where do we begin?" I finally asked, breaking the silence. "I'm sorry, I couldn't handle the silence any longer."

Alix took a stand near the table. A female Fae entered, her dress falling to her ankles, and she wore a white apron, pushing a serving cart filled with food, pitchers, and goblets.

"There is no need to apologize. Let's get you food first, you must be famished," my grandfather said, as the female placed plates across the table: baked chicken, asparagus, potatoes, and pie. I inhaled the lovely scents, my mouth watering as my stomach ached in hunger.

My grandfather watched as we piled our plates with food, joy in his eyes as I tried not to notice his attention. I wanted to be happy that he was alive. I wanted to embrace the joy and excitement, but my mother was missing, and that ache felt stronger.

"Do I call you King Everett?" I asked once I finished placing my food on my plate.

He smiled, showing perfectly straight white teeth. "When you were younger, you called me grandfather. If you're comfortable, I would love such a title."

I nodded. It was as if we were the only ones in the room as I studied him. The others sat quietly, eating, enjoying perhaps the best meal we'd had lately. Maybe it tasted better because we were home and reunited.

"I remember some things about the attack, but not much of what happened to you." I paused, resting my fork and knife, wanting so desperately to bite into the food. "My mother made me forget what happened. Until recently, I couldn't remember who I was, where we were from, and that I'm just a halfling."

"You are as much Fae as I am, Ellowyn. You're not just a halfling." My grandfather blinked hard. "What do you mean your mother made you forget?"

Dealla cleared her throat. "Apologies, Your Majesty." She took a steadying breath before she delivered the news. "Princess Alina gave her Rikeroot and glamoured her while they were gone. She grew Rikeroot at their cottage."

He placed his palms on the table, going very still. "How did she grow Rikeroot away from the tree?" He pursed his lips, and I could see his mind racing behind his eyes. A hand of mine fell to my satchel at my waist. "That should be impossible. The implications..." His fingers tapped against the table. "Ellowyn, your mother may have been more desperate, or more resourceful than I realized."

I slowly picked up my utensils again and picked up a piece of potato, as I puzzled over my grandfather's questions in my mind. Why was it hard to believe that she grew Rikeroot in our garden? It was one of the best plants we had grown.

"I don't know much of the Riker Tree or what happened to us, but I would like to know," I said to my grandfather as we finished our meals. My stomach was as full as it had ever been in weeks.

My grandfather nodded, holding his goblet in his hands. "There is much to learn of the Riker Tree and its power. I would love to show you." He swirled the contents of his goblet before taking a swig. "Adriane and Ciaran had been brought in for the killings and conspiracy they committed against Madora. For the killings and schemes, even in their own land.

"As King, it was my responsibility to see that they were held responsible for their wrongdoings on my land. Your mother was nervous, and she had every right to be. We heard of a prophecy, but it had been quiet for some time, and we didn't know the full extent of it. I thought we had prepared well, but I was mistaken." He shook his head. "We brought them into the throne room to put an end to what they had done, but they struck first. They knew to attack Queen Amelia first; she was an incredible healer and master of healing. With the Riker blade, the wound was too severe, prohibiting her from healing as it traveled through her blood."

My grandfather took a breath, and I saw the pain flicker across his face. The same raw grief I had witnessed when Asher held Xantara as she died. My heart ached, understanding now what it meant to lose the person you'd planned to spend eternity with. He'd been alone all these years, carrying that loss.

"The battle began instantly. Our guards did not hesitate to attack, and they were ready. I had seen Alina running with you, Evander following, but I had been stabbed. They told me that you both would be next as I lay with my Amelia, waiting for death to embrace me with her. They thought I had died when they left to search for you. I was unable to do anything since my powers had been muted. I trusted Alix, and he took charge. It took days, but the guards and he were able to force Adriane, Ciaran and their Dark Soldiers out of the kingdom."

He took another sip from his goblet. "By that point, my abilities had returned, and I was healing. I was able to place a barrier over the kingdom, a spell that had been gifted to me by a witch. We let word spread through villages that they had killed their King and Queen, but did not mention Alina or you. I let the rest of the world believe that I was gone, trying to protect you as well as the Riker Tree.

"I knew Adriane hadn't reached you in time, because Alina would have taken much more than just soldiers down with her to keep you protected. I learned Evander helped you both escape, and that his sacrifice saved your lives." He paused at the mention of my father. "I'd like to discuss what happened when we speak privately. I believe it deserves a more personal conversation."

My hand covered my mouth as I remembered. My eyes burned with tears ago, remembering my mother panting as she ran with me in her arms, voice shaking as she spoke. Her cries and pleas rang in my ears when my father went the other direction. Tears streamed from my eyes, hitting the table. Everyone kept their eyes on their plates, unable to look at one another.

"What has happened since you left?" my grandfather asked, his eyes on me.

I took a breath, not sure where to begin. "We lived quietly in the human lands. Dealla trained me and kept me safe." I glanced over at her. "When my memories started returning after my mother's capture, my magic slowly manifested, and I knew nothing was ever going to be the same."

"She's been extraordinary," Dealla added. "You would be extremely proud of Ellowyn, King Everett."

"Once her abilities returned, I began helping her learn control," Ivarison said, not looking my way.

"How could you not tell me he was alive?" My voice snapped harsher than I meant. Ivarison glared at my grandfather as the lit candles on the chandelier flickered.

"Careful, Ellowyn. Your emotions are getting the best of you," Bria suggested.

"This is a lot to take in." I said, taking a deep breath to calm the tension in my body.

"You cannot break an oath with a king. If he found a way to tell you that I was alive, it would have killed him," my grandfather stated.

Heat flooded through and out of me. "How could you make an oath like that?" my eyes bounced between the two males.

"I had to know he could be trusted. I couldn't jeopardize the chance of the wrong one learning. I didn't force him; he chose to do it. He took the path willingly to show that he was faithful to Madora."

"Why did he need to take the path in the first place?" Killian asked, Ivarison's head fell back as he stared at the ceiling.

"We heard that my daughter had been captured. We didn't have information on Ellowyn's whereabouts, though. I know what was done to Ivarison's family and the error in his ways. He is one of the strongest Fae in our land. He wanted to make things right, and I knew he could protect Ellowyn once he found her."

Ivarison's throat bobbed as he breathed, still staring upwards.

"Alix requested him to Mystmere. He was brought here for me to ask for his assistance; find Ellowyn by searching for Dealla. If Dealla wasn't with Alina, then I knew she would be with Ellowyn. And if Alina truly had been captured, I knew Dealla and my granddaughter would search for her or return to Mystmere. We searched for some time. Our guards ventured in and out as much as possible to search. Finally, it was reported that Adriane and Ciaran were spotted in Mornwind, and we have recently learned where they are keeping Alina captive. As of just two days ago, she was still alive."

"W-what?" I shuddered, vegetables falling from my fork. "You know where the prison is? Why haven't you gone to her! Why hasn't anyone rescued her yet?" I tried to rise from my seat, but Delaney pulled me back down.

"Mystmere's patrol saw you coming. Alix has been waiting for you to arrive, and then we learned you were traveling with a dragon."

"Her name is Bria. She joined us after I helped her escape from poachers."

"You've connected with her?" He leaned in closer, interested.

"Yes, I can communicate with her. Lord Eirwen helped us with a saddle so I can fly with her too."

"This is incredible. I knew you would be extraordinary. Queen Amelia had a grandmother who connected with a dragon. Their bond was unbreakable, as was their power. They died together."

I bit my tongue, I had not told the group what Bria had warned me about our connection.

"Yes, Bria told me what our connection meant." I said quietly, not wanting to repeat the words. "Where is my mother, grandfather?" I asked, attempting to bring the subject back to where she was.

"Wait, what does that mean? What did Bria tell you?" Delaney asked, as Dealla and Killian stared, waiting for an answer.

"Bria told me that being connected to her could amplify my power."

"Why did you keep that from us?" Dealla asked.

"We were already connected. I didn't want anyone to fear me more since you already feared I couldn't control myself." I said, glancing at Ivarison, who didn't move. "After what happened when we did connect, I was definitely afraid to speak about it."

Dealla shook her head, wanting to know more, but I turned back to my grandfather.

"I apologize if what I told you causes strife between you and your companions. I could sense how strong you truly were alone. I felt you needed to know," Bria nudged through our bond.

"You do not need to apologize."

"Alina is at a prison that Ciaran built, and it's very unpleasant, from what guards have claimed. It's on a small island outside Ravenholde. We cannot figure out how the prison has gone undetected for so long, but we've found it. We cannot fade in or out; the only option would be by ship. If they know we are coming, they may kill her."

"Bria could fly us there," I said quickly, adrenaline hitting me. I would find and save my mother. Now was the time, and I couldn't wait any longer.

"You need to rest before you attempt anything!" Ivarison snapped, his tone catching me off guard. "You need to make a plan and decide who will go and what the plan shall be. One successful battle does not make you a hero."

I growled and stood from the table. "I'm going. I will go alone if I have to. I have to bring her home. I didn't train this hard to sit on the sidelines."

Ivarison pinched the bridge of his nose. He knew my stubbornness, and he wouldn't win, even with trying to be dismissive.

King Everett gave a soft smile, "You're so much like her."

"My mother?" I asked, groaning.

"No, your grandmother."

"Ellowyn," Dealla said, her chair scraping behind her as she stood. "Let's rest first and make a plan in the morning. You will not go alone. I'll go with you." Dealla looked at me with determination blazing from her eyes to her clenched fists. "We started this together. We will finish this together. I'm with you, always."

"You cannot go unprepared. Let's get the rest we need." my grandfather said. He stood from his chair and strode over to me. "The joy you've given me today with your return is simply everything I've wanted for the last seventeen years. I do not wish to lose you again. There is more that needs to be discussed. After we discuss a plan, I would like to meet with you privately."

I nodded as he cupped my cheeks and kissed my forehead. He walked from the room with Alix in tow.

My body was shaking. Perhaps from the need for sleep and a full stomach. Perhaps because I was home.

"We all need the rest. We will figure out our plan and rescue your mother. Sleep well, Little Spark." Bria said calmly, and I could hear her own voice growing tired as she spoke.

I admired the castle's beauty as we were guided to our chambers. There was something different as we walked, a warmth that hugged tightly around me. Arches connected to the ceiling, lanterns hung with warm lighting. How lonely the castle the castle walls must have felt, living without family as my grandfather had done these last years.

But tonight, for the first time in nearly two decades, the castle was full of family again.

Chapter Twenty-Nine

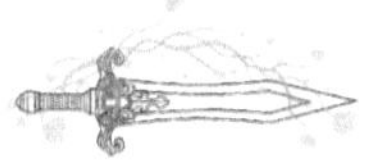

Warm streaks of light hit my skin as I woke. Unsure of the time, I groaned and stretched, soft sheets wrapping around my body. I was so comfortable, I didn't want to pull myself up.

"Finally, you're awake!" Delaney's voice came from the corner.

I jolted. Well, I was up now. Who knows how long she had been sitting in the chair with a book in her hands. After dinner the night before, Delaney, Ivarison, and I had been brought to rooms sharing a hall. Dealla and Killian returned to the room they had once resided in before their departure seventeen years ago.

Delaney sat across from the balcony opening, lush curtains dancing against the wind. Once I left my bed, I looked out of the balcony. Down below, Bria had nestled herself in the large garden, and she let out a small growl as she yawned.

I would have enjoyed the quaint moment if it weren't for Delaney's feet tapping against the shiny gray tile. I looked over at her, rubbing my eyes, still adjusting to the rising sun's brightness.

"Good morning to you. Why were you watching me sleep?" I asked, half laughing.

The book in her hands thumped shut. "I thought I'd have to throw you from the balcony for you to wake. I've been trying to wake you for a while now."

"What's the matter?"

"They've been waiting, but I figured you needed rest, so I wasn't trying that hard. King Everett wished to discuss plans for rescuing your mother." She watched me as I sat back down on the bed, resting my chin on my hand. She tilted her head like a curious owl. "How are you doing?"

I waved a hand, unsure of how to answer. "I'm still processing, I think. My grandfather has been alive after all this time, believed dead, and my mother ran because of it. Now he knows where she is. It just doesn't seem real."

"It must be a lot to handle. I'm here if you want to talk." Her voice was calm as she gave a tight smile. "I mean it."

"I know, thank you." I stood from my bed. "I appreciate everything you've done for me since we've met." She stood as I walked over and pulled her into a hug.

"That's what friends are for," she said, her voice soft against my hair.

"Exactly," I said, pulling away. It was too early to be so sentimental. "Let me get cleaned up. I'll be down shortly."

Delaney was my friend, something I longed for.

When she reached toward the door, she stalled and turned back.

"I wanted to ask you something." She looked at the door and then back at me. "In Mornwind, when the mist was in front of us, did you see anything through it? Other than the Sleroka coming out?" Her voice shook, gray eyes slightly wider.

I shook my head. "No, I think I only saw the Sleroka," I answered, trying not to rethink the moment.

Delaney sighed, rubbing her forearm. "I just thought I would ask. I think I was imagining things." She tried to smile, but her brows were pinched and her lips hardly curved into anything.

"Is everything alright?" I asked, seeing that something was bothering her. "I'm here for you as well if you need to talk."

"Yes." This time, she gave me a better smile. "I'll tell them you'll be down soon."

She left, the door clicking shut behind her.

I went to the balcony and looked over the beauty. Mystmere was magnificent. A smile crept across my lips as I said good morning to Bria. Warm air brushed over me, and for the first time in months, I *almost* felt relaxed.

I was going to find my mother and bring her home.

At the center of the courtyard, Bria and my grandfather stood facing each other. There was a short distance between them as they stared intently at each other. Her head moved closer, inhaling his scent. She huffed smoke, and he laughed.

"She's remarkable," my grandfather said, eyes never leaving Bria as I approached. "I had to see for myself once Alix told me that my granddaughter was with a dragon. Bria, it's an honor to meet you." His voice was soft as he turned to her, and she bowed her head. "I know you want to save your mother, Ellowyn. The others informed me of the struggles you faced while traveling."

"We faced many challenges while we searched for my mother," I said calmly. We each had our own struggles during our travels.

"I would rather send Dealla and a few other soldiers instead." He stood tall. Was he demanding that I stay behind?

"I will not stay behind." I was not going to back down now.

"Of course. Your father was just as brave." He paused. "Maybe foolish, but he was willing to risk everything to save who he loved."

My father. The comparisons had always been that I was so much like my mother. It was hard to swallow, being compared to him, who gave his life for us. My nostrils flared as I contained the stinging in my eyes.

"I remember some of it, the last moment I saw my father. He told us goodbye as they switched cloaks to confuse our scents, and that is how we were able to escape. I watched him run into the mist and vanish." My jaw trembled as I spoke.

"Your father was different. We knew that the moment we met him. Your mother was traveling when she saved him from a Norwag attack. She brought him here to heal him. I'm sorry for what happened to him, and we were unable to find him after the attack on the kingdom." He paused, glancing at Bria as he blinked. "For some time, I questioned if the same thing happened to Alina and you, but I could feel that you were alive. I could feel you were both somewhere. Alix told me Dealla and Killian had left the kingdom after the attack in search of you two. Alix stayed to keep me safe when I was at my weakest, as Dealla and Killian have done for your mother and you. I owe my soldiers everything for their loyalty."

I was silent, unable to find the words to say. He was right for everything that Dealla and Killian had done for us.

"Well," he clapped his hands together, "I would like to show you something before we discuss your mother's rescue mission."

My grandfather motioned for me to follow. We walked to the back of the courtyard to an entrance that led to the opposite side of the village. Bria's wings swooshed as I looked back to the gated entrance.

"The Riker Tree was one of the first living things in Madora. Many believe that it was once a goddess from another realm, cursed and sent here, and her mate forced to another part of the world. Together in the same realm but separated. Instead of being left alone, she drew her power and created this land and us. It's believed she hopes to one day find her way back to her true love. The Riker Tree has given power to the Fae and our land." He glanced at his hands, excitement twinkling in his eyes as if power flowed around us.

"We always kept the Riker Tree hidden so no one could access it. Its power has given us life, but in the wrong hands, it can also destroy. It was another reason why I placed the barrier over our kingdom. Adriane and Ciaran believed I was dead, and I could not risk them discovering the Riker Tree because it's on Mystmere territory."

"The Riker Tree is here? I don't know much of it apart from a few things I've been told the last two months," I said in surprise.

We walked through a mossy area near an ivy-covered woodbine that I remembered from memories with him. My grandfather reached toward the ivy and pulled it to the side, revealing a hidden pathway. Roots created natural arches above the pathway, while stones were embedded in the dirt, and grass and ivy wrapped around the edges.

"It's important to know why we've kept our tree hidden. There was another Riker Tree in Ravenholde, near the home of Adriane and Ciaran and believed to be the mate of our Riker Tree. When they began their rule, they started stripping their Rikeroot Tree. They embedded its properties in swords and made tonics to mix into food and drinks." He was still as he spoke, the pathway he revealed still open. "Some time later, after they had cut from the Riker Tree to use as lumber, their tree began to die, and the land around it started to die with it. Nothing would grow."

"If it died, couldn't they just have grown it like my mother had with the Rikeroot?"

"That's what is peculiar. No one has been able to grow Rikeroot like you say your mother could." He put his hand out." Come this way."

We didn't speak as we walked. Nearly midday, the sun shone on our faces, and the path opened up as we passed the last of the tree arches. I had never seen anything quite as breathtaking.

The tree looked to be twice the size of Bria, sitting beside a pool of sparkling water. The trunk appeared to be multiple trunks wrapped together, rising off the ground. Roots created large archways underneath, tall enough for Fae or humans to walk through. Even Bria may have fit.

Limbs grew tall, stretching toward the sky. Leaves shimmered like stars throughout the branches. Vines hung from limbs, and as more leaves hung down, they shimmered like light crystals at the bottom of the tree with Rikeroot growing heavily in the soil.

The old lady from the village had been right.

"This is the Riker Tree. This one was said to be the goddess, while the one in Ravenholde was her mate. Because of the beauty and life it provides, I couldn't chance Ciaran finding this one and destroying it as they had done to the other," my grandfather said, face stern and sharp.

"She's beautiful. Why can Rikeroot mute the magic and harm us?" I asked, starting at the massive tree. It was unlike anything I'd ever seen. Everything about Madora had been incredible, but as the vines and lights grew from the tree and brushed in the wind, it seemed to have its own story to tell.

"What gives life can also take. I'm surprised your mother could grow Rikeroot, I don't know how she obtained and grew it." He chuckled as thoughts of my mother must've flashed in his mind. "I suppose I shouldn't be surprised. She always found a way for everything."

"She gave it to me for seventeen years while we were gone. There are still holes in my memory, and I haven't fully learned to control what abilities I have." There was a hint of annoyance in my voice. I tried not to be angry with my mother, but sometimes I could feel it simmering. I couldn't help but think of the difference it might have made if I had been better prepared for my time in Madora. If I had known, trained with my abilities, Asher and Xantara may not have died.

Unless she had never planned on returning to Madora.

All we went through haunted me.

"Ellowyn–" He cut himself off, moving closer to the Riker Tree. The light vines moved again, coming forward as if trying to reach us. "Your mother should be the one telling you this, but you're special."

My shoulders slouched. I had this power within me and had seen some of what I was capable of, but that didn't mean I was different from any other. "You're supposed to say that. You're my grandfather." My voice fell flat.

"You don't understand. You're destined to be one of the most powerful Fae in our realm." he said so nonchalantly, as if we spoke only of weather.

I shook my head, "I'm only a halfling. Adriane, Ciaran, Ivarison, you? How could I be more powerful than anyone else?"

My grandfather looked at a particular spot near the trunk, his eyes wistful, as if he were transported into a memory. "Alina had a dream that woke her before you were born. For thousands of years, the Riker Tree has been known to exist, and no one has ever been born beneath it," He gazed at me. "Only you,"

I blinked. My throat tightened, but I managed to say. "I still don't understand what you're trying to tell me."

"The Riker Tree transferred some of her power to you when you were born," he explained, looking up at the tree's radiance. "If our power and what feeds our lands comes from the tree, you're destined to protect it. It wanted to ensure you would succeed in what is to come and gave you the power to do so."

I gulped.

This was not what I was expecting. Bria shifted behind us, her full attention on everything my grandfather said.

He stepped toward the tree, gesturing for me to follow.

"Take a step forward. She would like to meet you again."

I stared, truly pondering whether he had gone mad or if he truly believed the story he told. It was a tree. A beautiful tree that could light up as if the sun shone through its core in a magical land. If creatures roamed, Fae existed with magic abilities, and there were dragons, then a goddess in a tree should be believable.

As I stepped forward, the tree shook and its lights shone brighter as a branch of the tree pulled me in. I jumped, startled as vines began wrapping around my arms, moving to my stomach. Fear churned over what it would do and what my grandfather walked me into. But the energy that she emitted was smooth, warm, and gentle. I looked back over my shoulder at my grandfather, but he was gone.

My mother approached, her belly was round, with one hand placed over her stomach, tensing. Her other hand tightly gripped a handsome man. I gaped as I saw my father stand just before me.

Gooseflesh rose across my arms. I was seeing what the Riker Tree wanted me to see.

My father's sandy-colored hair was ruffled as if he had just woken. My mother's face was strained as she breathed heavily. I turned as I watched them approach the tree, my hands racing out to them. Our surroundings shifted as time passed. My mother lay on the ground under the roots of the tree.

Her screams of agony pierced through me as my father held her hand, rubbing her head and kissing the top of it. Another female, who looked to be a midwife, waited near my mother's legs.

I looked around – my grandfather was by the path, standing with a beautiful female in a green gown. I did a double-take, at first thinking it was my mother. But standing beside my grandfather was my grandmother.

My heart clenched, and my nose stung. My family.

My family was before my eyes as I tried to reach out for them.

Baby cries rang out. I turned back to see that my mother had given birth to me. My father held me in his arms, with tears brimming his eyes.

"It's a girl! We have a girl!" he cried out, kissing my mother profusely. "Oh, Alina, you're incredible. She's so beautiful."

The Riker Tree moved slowly, its wisps of light coming down gently to my mother, father, and me. The tree's vines touched the baby me, cradled in my father's arms.

"What's happening? What is she doing?" my father demanded, not letting me go as my mother tried sitting up.

The tree's glow brightened leaves and wisps reaching toward the baby me as my father refused to let go. The tree held as the baby of me cried. Light growing and glowing, I was lifted from my father's arms, wrapping in vines as my father shouted and begged. Light began fading as the vines returned me to my father's arms, releasing me. The vines guided my mother, tapping into her, and she gasped.

"Alina!" my father cried out.

My shoulders shook. I blinked a few times and was back to the present time, my grandfather standing in front of me.

"What did she show you?" he asked, helping me from the tree and out from the vines' grasp.

"The day I was born. What did she do to my mother and me?" I asked, still hearing my father's cries.

"The tree showed your mother what it had done and spoke to her. The prophecy is true, Ellowyn. The tree transferred some of her power to you, hoping you would save this kingdom when the time came."

More power. How much more could I handle?

"What if I have too much power? The power from the Riker Tree amplified by a dragon connection? What if losing control is what causes me to fail?" I asked. Bria's words of amplification often lingered when I used my abilities.

"Ellowyn, dearest. You must believe that you can wield the world. If you begin to believe that it's too much, that is when it will be." He hugged me. His embrace filled me with comfort, knowing that it was exactly what I needed as the heaviness in my breathing slowly subsided. "I believe in you. We just have to remember we do the best we can in that moment. Believe in yourself."

He held my hand as I looked back at the Riker Tree, branches moving as if it waved goodbye.

Chapter Thirty

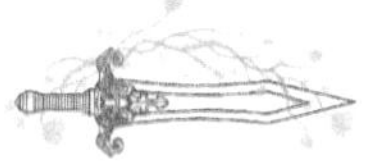

Chairs screeched as we took our seats. Alix stood beside my grandfather, who sat at the head of the table. Ivarison and Delaney sat on either side of me, while Dealla and Killian settled across from us. I hadn't had a chance to speak with any of them after my visit with the Riker Tree.

I could still feel the vines around me and envision my parents every time I blinked. Learning more about the truth that was hidden from me and how the Riker Tree gave me power. Did Dealla or Killian know? Did anyone else know?

Tension built across my shoulders. I bit my lip, trying not to let fear consume me. Ivarison's help with my abilities could only go so far. What I needed was years of practice and focus. Time I didn't have.

"While Ciaran has been preparing their soldiers, it seems Adriane has been traveling back and forth to a small island near their land," my grandfather briefed, his voice grim as Alix walked forward with a large map.

He unrolled it, covering most of the table. The map showed Madora and the surrounding lands across the seas. Through the terrain, I observed the woods that were the barrier of the human lands and Madora, where I once lived.

Madora was larger than Ravenholde. I took in the territory quickly, noticing villages we'd traveled through and seeing Dustvale marked.

"Adriane and Ciaran reside in Ravenholde. They have ruled for hundreds of years since Adriane's parents and sister were killed." I kept my eyes down, unsure if others knew what truly happened to Adriane's family. My grandfather pointed to a small island divided by water, north of Ravenholde. "The prison doors are located above ground, but the facility runs underground. We only know what is above. Once you're inside, we do not know what may lurk below."

"How long would it take by ship? We don't have time to waste. Bria could fly me there and back," I said, though I needed to confirm this was something Bria would be willing to do.

"I will do all I can to help save your mother," Bria whispered, just below the window.

"I would still prefer to send my best soldiers to retrieve Princess Alina. From what has been told, they don't keep the island heavily guarded since they kept it undetected," my grandfather spoke, his voice stern. I had a feeling he wouldn't easily let this go and give it another try to prevent me from going.

"I have searched for my mother since leaving home. With all due respect, grandfather," I said with a slight bow of my head before I met his gaze. "I will not stop now. As I told you before, no one will stop me." I looked around the table. "Wouldn't this set an example? I've been missing for seventeen years and just reappeared. It shows that I'm willing to put myself at risk for the sake of my family and my subjects. Bria could get there faster compared to soldiers on a ship. We do not have that kind of time. She has already been gone far too long, and now we are sitting here wasting time debating it." I gathered my thoughts, pointing out the flaws of the proposed ship plan. "They would see ships coming and take action before anyone could set foot on land. If you had that sort of time, you would have already sent them."

"I'll go with her," Ivarison said, watching my grandfather and me stare each other down.

"You have other tasks to complete," my grandfather said.

Dealla stepped up, hands clasped behind her. "I am more than willing to travel with Ellowyn and Bria as I stated last evening. I'm her guard, so I believe it makes sense for me to go." Killian, at her side, did not look pleased.

"I could go too," Delaney quickly chimed in.

"*We do not know your mother's condition or what we will face. The more we bring, the more attention we draw,*" Bria said.

"No, you should stay here," Dealla said, her voice booming.

"*Do you believe that Dealla and I would be enough?*" I asked. I knew Dealla was capable of anything, but it was my abilities I feared. I was afraid, and if I failed this could be the death of my mother too.

"*Yes, I believe you two are sufficient, and I will be with you. You cannot go into this mission having doubts about yourself, Little Spark. I'll also burn the entire island down if needed.*"

I closed my eyes, remembering my grandfather's words and now Bria's. I needed to believe in myself. I was capable of anything, and I could not start doubting myself after all that we'd accomplished.

I felt lingering eyes and saw Ivarison watching from my peripheral vision.

"*Stop invading our privacy,*" I snapped. He rolled his eyes, confirming he was indeed listening as his eyes returned to the map.

"*Believe in yourself, as I believe in you too.*" he said. When he said nothing else, I closed the mental shield, preventing more intrusion.

"Bria, Dealla, and I will go."

"I'm not pleased with the idea of you going, you don't have a personal guard yet either," my grandfather snapped, the vein in his forehead visible.

Another beat passed, and he gave a reluctant sigh. "I suppose you'll sneak off regardless of what I say."

"That is correct." I would not lie. I knew where my mother was now, and I wouldn't stop. My grandfather's eyes twinkled, a smirk hidden as he bit the corner of his mouth.

I might not know royal protocol or if crossing the king was wise, but I could be incredibly stubborn too. Dealla and I would rescue my mother, just as we'd planned from the start. I didn't want to anger my grandfather, but nothing could stop us.

"What of the rest of us? I suppose Bria couldn't carry us all?" Killian asked, his focus was on the map, not looking at Dealla.

"Bria doesn't recommend it," I muttered. My grandfather nodded.

"I will need Ivarison's assistance. He is one of the only who can fade longer distances. I will have him visit our allied lords and ask if they will assist us in war-and ensure they are ready," my grandfather said, looking at each of us. He sighed heavily as his fingers tapped against the table. "As the barrier is up and around our kingdom, you will be able to leave and enter freely now." He continued drumming his fingers, staring back down as his eyes drifted. "Once Adriane and Ciaran learn that you've rescued Princess Alina, they will make a move. And we must be ready."

Killian and Delaney were not pleased about being left behind. My grandfather was sending Ivarison away to the courts to have them prepare for war. It was something I hadn't wanted to think of, although I could feel others' worry.

"Ellowyn," Delaney called out, entering the courtyard. We had just left my grandfather, who once more tried to convince me to stay.

"Do try to keep Killian busy while we're gone. I'm afraid he may drive himself mad with worry," I said, Dealla's brows furrowed as her hands clasped her belt.

"Of course, don't worry about us. I'll ask him about the time he hung at Luminara's gates again." She rolled her eyes with a grin, her grip tightening around her wrist. "I wanted to give you this." She took the bracelet from her wrist.

"That's the bracelet your mother gave you. I can't accept that," I said, holding my hands up in protest.

"For luck on your journey. I'll take it back once you've returned home. Safely." She took hold of my wrist and slipped it on. "My mother stated it was enchanted for protection. Luckily, I was never hurt during our travels. I would like to think because of my great skill with my sword, but..." She shrugged, glancing down at the bracelet. "I know Dealla and you can take care of yourselves, but it doesn't hurt to have additional protection."

It was very thoughtful of her to let me borrow it.

"Thank you. I will return it as soon as we return."

It gave another boost of hope. If it were truly enchanted, I would return unharmed.

"Stay safe," she whispered in my ear as she pulled me into a bone-crushing hug. She glanced over at Bria. "Or burn whoever hurts our girl."

Bria made a low rumbling growl as she agreed, and Ivarison and Killian entered the courtyard.

"I thought you had left," I said to Ivarison, giving Dealla and Killian a moment together.

"I will once you're off. I couldn't leave without saying goodbye, of course." He moved closer, hesitating. Bria now stood beside me, waiting patiently. "Beware of your surroundings and keep your mental shields up at all times. I'm afraid you'll be walking into a trap. They may know you're coming."

"You're worried about me. That's sweet," I said, with a small grin on my lips as I stared into those blue eyes.

"Ellowyn," he said with a soft growl, rolling his eyes.

"Yes, I'll have Dealla and Bria with me. I'm not afraid. She must know by now that the Sleroka didn't kill me, but it was my fault my mother was captured. I have to try," I said softly, nerves building.

"It was never your fault, Ell. Adriane and Ciaran should've been stopped centuries ago. You have to stop blaming yourself for what was prophesied about you. Adriane and Ciaran will be stopped."

I bit the inside of my cheek. "I hope you're right." I couldn't look up to meet his awaiting gaze. He had been a rock – my rock – when I doubted myself, caved into my despair, lost control.

"Breathe, love," Ivarison reminded me. I checked my mental shields and made sure they were up.

I inhaled deeply and nodded, but his fingertips brushed against my forearm.

"If things go wrong, rush back to Bria to get away. Promise me," he said, his voice a whisper as he had come closer.

"I promise," was all I could manage to say before Dealla called.

"Ellowyn, let's go."

Killian glanced back once more, his jaw tense, before he left the court-yard as Dealla approached Bria.

Ivarison stepped back with Delaney. "Take care of her," he muttered to Bria as they bowed to one another, and we climbed onto the saddle.

It was nearly a half-day ride to the island. Wind pushed against us, Bria's wings beating hard as she tried reaching our destination quickly without draining herself. She stayed above the clouds, using them to prevent us from being seen.

I glanced back at Dealla, her face was pale as she watched the horizon ahead, gripping the saddle tightly.

"Are you alright? You look green," I called out over wind gusts, hoping she wouldn't vomit on me.

"Yes, I'll be fine. Of course, I've never flown on a dragon, and I'm not sure I enjoy the height." she shut her eyes.

"It's frightening at first, but you get used to it. What should we expect once we land?" We hadn't discussed a plan amongst ourselves. The island appeared small from what could be seen on the map, and we wouldn't be able to linger long. It would force us to move with haste; the longer we stayed, the more likely we'd be discovered. A chance we couldn't take.

"We need to find the prison's exact location. Once we do, Bria should land as close as possible without detection. Which I know will be difficult, being a dragon. We just have to move fast." Her eyes opened as her voice turned harsh. "Any Dark Soldiers spotted must be slain. Do you understand? I should have asked this before we left, but will you be able to do that?"

She hadn't known what had happened the first time I faded from Ivarison. The shock and panic that I'd experienced after killing the soldier still haunted me.

"Yes," I could only say, knowing it would happen. I had to face it.

"Keep on guard, always. We must try staying together. We need to find your mother and get out, so do not hesitate. If we're separated, you must continue, and you must remember everything you've been taught. Hell, even what Ivarison taught you. Our lives will depend on it today. Understand?"

I nodded. We were flying into enemy territory, and I had never seen Dealla as nervous as she seemed now. We were only one full Fae and a half Fae, amongst whatever lurked throughout the prison grounds.

"We are near," Bria said. I blinked a few times, hearing her growl as I could see her scanning ahead. *"The prison is north. There are guards at the entrance. I don't see any others on land."*

"How many at the entrance?" I asked, trying to squint to see what she could see.

"Four."

"Nearly there. Bria sees four guards at the prison entrance."

"I don't have a good feeling about this, Ellowyn. Why aren't there more guards here?" Bria's voice shook me. Her head swayed back and forth, searching. *"There is a ship further out at sea. I don't recognize it. If you move quickly, they wouldn't be able to reach land fast enough."*

"There is a ship further out in the sea. She's concerned about why there aren't more guards," I reported to Dealla, wondering the same as I looked down from the clouds toward the island.

Brown. The land looked dead. Not a hint of green from grass or trees. Life had been pulled from its essence, lacking any vitality.

"King Everett said this territory has never never been documented. Perhaps there is more that we're missing," Dealla said as she tried looking below, searching for anything.

Wind whooshed as Bria tucked her wings and squeezed through an opening of trees to land. Dead branches broke as she hit the ground with a thud.

"I'll fly above to stay hidden and keep watch. I'll warn you if I see something amiss. I cannot continue toward the prison without giving you away." She nuzzled closer. *"If something happens, I'll break through the ground to reach you. Be careful, Little Spark. You are almost there."*

Her voice roared through my mind as I nodded. The thought of her breaking apart and crushing any Dark Soldiers was a promise.

"I'll call for you soon." As we deposited back on the ground, and Bria launched herself away, I explained the plan to Dealla as we moved forward.

The ground was barren. Trees were rotten and broken, and no birds sang as we passed. There was no life on this island except the guards and whatever lurked below in the prison.

A large gate hung open with an iron flame. Two large Fae soldiers stood at the door. Behind the prison entrance, two additional guards stood at attention. The prison entrance looked like a dark tunnel that led through a hill and down below. We positioned ourselves away, behind dead trees and bushes, and watched.

"Take an arrow and shoot one," Dealla muttered, pulling her bow from her back. "I'll take the one on the right, you take the left."

The soldiers stood with blank stares, looking out from their helmets, lost to the world. I pulled my bowstring, drawing it close to my face as Dealla signaled to fire.

Our arrows flew true, striking their targets. My arrow landed in one's chest, Dealla's in the other's eye. Bullseye. The remaining two soldiers began shouting at one another, rushing out to the fallen.

"Ready?" Dealla asked, slinging her bow on her back, sword at the ready. "Do not hesitate. Remember, find your mother and get out."

My mind rushed through everything she and my mother taught me. The difference now was embracing all that I was capable of as my powers emerged from my fingers.

I was ready.

Dealla didn't have time to praise my improvement as we charged toward the remaining guards, determined to make it through the prison fast enough before we struck again. Their bodies fell beside the other two.

"Keep moving!" Dealla urged. I followed her through the gate, feeling the temperature drop as we traveled deeper into the tunnel, our path's light growing fainter. We walked side by side, our arms brushing against each other.

After being separated in darkness before, we remained close together. Our eyes tried to adjust to the blackness.

The callouses on my palm felt raw from how tight I held my sword's hilt. I was afraid that at any moment, soldiers would attack.

Chapter Thirty-One

The only noise I could hear was my heart hammering against my ribs and the blood rushing in my ears. Dealla's rapid breathing echoed around us. Shadows swallowed us deeper with each step, the musty scent of damp earth filling my nostrils.

"Light ahead," Dealla whispered. Small flames flickered in the distance. I tugged at my Fae senses, letting them help me scan for danger that could be coming our way.

The oppressive darkness made me want to reach for Dealla, ensuring that I wasn't alone. But just as I shifted toward her, boots scuffed against stone near a lantern hanging low on the wall. A pair of legs moved across our path, blocking the way forward.

"I could light us a path?" I breathed, grimacing as the stale air hit my throat.

"Wait until the last moment. At least two guards ahead, be ready." Her voice was barely a whisper, so quiet I wondered if I'd imagined it.

The sentries stood against the wall, closer to the lantern, swords drawn and ready. One lifted the light, casting harsh shadows across his grime-streaked face.

"Who's there?" he barked.

My breath caught. The smallest movement would give us away. I pressed my back against the slimy tunnel wall, my senses alerting me of another presence.

My mother.

She was close. So close that I could feel her presence urging me to continue. Instincts overrode caution. My sword ignited with blue flames, bathing the tunnel in ethereal light.

Dealla's eyes widened as the guards bellowed and charged.

I blocked the first strike, sparks flying as steel met magical fire. The second guard lunged for Dealla. These soldiers had tortured the innocent, stolen families, shattered lives. My fear of killing another Fae evaporated, replaced by cold determination. They would not keep me from my mother.

"I'm here if you need me," Bria whispered at the edge of my mind, her presence warm and ready. *"But you can handle this."*

The guard's blade rang against my flaming sword, unable to extinguish it. Vibrations shot up my arm as I blocked another strike, his steel missing my shoulder by an inch. I pivoted and thrust toward his heart. He dodged, but my flame brushed against his exposed forearm.

He screamed as the fire scorched his flesh off. While he stumbled back clutching his ruined arm, I spun away, avoiding his wild swing. Frustration made the soldier sloppy. I anticipated his next move, a desperate lunge to avoid my flames, and I raised my blade to meet him. The sword pierced deep into his chest. He crumpled without another sound.

"Ellowyn!" Dealla's voice cracked with frenzy. Shouts ricocheted off the walls from the path ahead. "Douse the light! We need the element of surprise! Are you alright?"

Her eyes raced over my body, looking for injuries.

"I'm fine," I breathed, putting out my flame, and darkness enveloped us once more.

"*Well done,*" Bria whispered with pride.

We felt our way forward through the suffocating black. Occasional candles guttered in wall sconces, wax pooled thick beneath them like frozen tears. A nauseating stench grew with each step as I took a whiff.

"What's that smell?" I covered my nose, fighting the urge to gag. My senses told me to run with every breath. A sickly sweet smell mixed with mold and rot.

Dealla tensed beside me. "Death."

A sudden rush of air swept through. Lanterns blazed to life around us, showing we'd walked into a circular chamber. I gulped.

We stood trapped in the center. At least fifteen guards stood against the walls, their weapons gleaming, and their yellow teeth bared in vicious grins.

"Dealla..." My heart plummeted.

"Light that sword and use everything you've got, Ellowyn!" she ordered as the guards charged.

I ignited my sword and roared my defiance.

I began to swing without fear. Fear would mean death – for both of us. Even Bria wouldn't reach us in time. Dealla fought like fury incarnate, sword in one hand, a dagger in the other, always aiming for vital parts as she carved through our enemies.

My head turned to see a Norwag crashing through a dark alley, right for Dealla before toppling over her. She hit the ground hard.

"Dealla!" I shouted, my sword against another soldier, just as I drove my dagger's tip into his chest.

The Norwag came above her, ready to strike. Time couldn't be wasted as saliva fell from its teeth. I threw my arm out toward the beast, the blue magic running down my arm and out of my palm, straight in the chest of the Norwag.

It shrieked in pain as the fire began to grow around its body. It moved backward, giving Dealla the opportunity to strike.

"Focus on our connection! Use our power!" Bria's calm voice anchored me in the chaos.

Another guard came, and I was surrounded. More guards poured in to replace the fallen. I reached for Bria, opening the door to our shared magic just as I had when we flew with Ivarison. Power flowed through me like molted gold, warming my skin and lighting my veins.

A guard pressed close, our blades forming an X between us. His malicious grin filled my vision as he bore down with his full weight.

Clang!

The sound filled my ears and ran through the chamber.

My sword blazed brighter, the glow spreading up my arms until my hands pulsed with the same blue fire. I felt our combined power building, stronger than ever before. I threw out my palms and released everything.

The blast erupted from my hands, hitting every sentry around me. They were thrown against the wall, skulls cracking against stone with a sickening finality before they slumped down.

Dead guards littered the floor.

Dealla was gone.

"Dealla?" I called out, but there was no response. I strained to hear something – anything – and there it was. The distant sound of a beating heart deeper in the prison.

"Continue, Ellowyn. We will find Dealla later." Bria said. *"Do not linger. Time is running out."*

The path I followed narrowed, the stench growing unbearable. I gagged and forced myself to breathe through my mouth so I didn't vomit. The thought of leaving Dealla almost stopped me, but I wouldn't allow myself to doubt. Dealla would be okay. She was Madora's most powerful soldier. She could take care of herself.

I had to find my mother. I would not lose one to save another.

My senses pulled me deeper. The faint heartbeat called to me through stone and shadow. Since she was taken, I could feel in my gut that she was alive. I was so close. She was here.

Open, empty cells looked as if they had been there for hundreds of years. Moss carpeted the walls. Something dripped from the ceiling that echoed through the empty cells. I refused to stop and look.

Clank.

There it was again.

Chain links scraped stone. Someone else moved in the shadows ahead. I closed my eyes and reached out with my senses, but something dark and hungry stirred in response. I was no longer alone.

Deep breath.

One.

Two.

Three.

I flicked my fingers to give myself light just as a Norwag lunged for me, yellowed fangs aimed for my throat. I slashed, finding the center of its neck. It screeched and crashed to the ground with a wet crunch.

I am strong. I am powerful, and I will not panic.

I will save my mother.

I repeated the words like a prayer, using them to shore up my confidence against the fear trying to seep through. I couldn't feel Bria at the edge of my consciousness, and I was growing tired. I had lost count of how many soldiers we had faced, but there had been no other way.

I was nearly running, twisting Delaney's bracelet around my wrist for luck. I had yet to be hurt. Maybe it truly worked.

Clank.

Rattle.

To my right!

I burst through the cell door, nearly toppling over it as I went through.

Blue flames at my fingertips revealed a figure hunched against the far wall. Chains around her wrists and ankles, matted hair hanging in bloody clumps. When she looked up, I saw the hollow green eyes in a face I'd dreamed of finding.

My mother.

"We have to get you out," I said, reaching for her chains.

"No!" Her voice cracked. She pulled away from my reach. "You–You're not real!" Her lips quivered. "NO!"

What had they done to her? Broken her until she couldn't trust her own sight?

"Mother, stop! It's me. It's Ellowyn!" Distant shouts echoed through the prison. No time. "We have to get you out of here now!"

She tried to strike me as I knelt by her chains. When she missed and hit the wall instead, stunning herself, I gently grasped her face, as carefully as time allowed.

"Look at me." My voice cut through her panic. "I'm real. Remember Dealla. Evander, my father. Me, your daughter. Please – please, let's go. We will not die here."

Recognition flickered in her eyes. "Ell-Ellowyn?" My mother choked on a sob as she reached for me. "I'm sorry–"

"We don't have time. We need to get out of here." I raised my flaming sword to the chains. "I lost Dealla getting here. We will have to find her and go."

I channeled the little power I had through the blade and struck.

Clank. Clank!

My mother collapsed into my arms, hugging me as tightly as her weak body could. For one heartbeat, I let myself feel the relief. Then I pulled her to her feet.

"I'm so sorry," she said in between her cries, her hands cupping my cheeks. "I didn't–"

I swallowed the lump in my throat. "We really need to go."

I feared the words, knowing that if I said anything else, I would mentally break down with her as she cried.

"There is a passage that's quicker to get out," she whispered between deep breaths, leaning heavily on me. "The guards have used it when they move in and out."

"After we find Dealla." I wrapped my arm around her waist.

I held my blade out, the flame helping us to see our way. My mother kept up, with a limp on her right side, but she didn't complain.

"I never wanted things to go as they did," she muttered. "I was lost. I know you must be angry." A flicker of anger burned beneath my ribs for what she'd done.

"We can talk about it when we're safe." I couldn't look back at her yet. Not fully. But I had her back, and that was what mattered now.

Chapter Thirty-Two

Prison reeking of death was not a place for the conversation my mother and I needed to have. We walked in silence, my arm supporting her weight. I held out my palm to light up our guide.

"*Bria?*" No answer. My heart raced – I hadn't been able to reach her since I lost Dealla.

The guards we had killed lay lifeless on the ground. My mother's eyes darted around, seeing the carnage in the little light we had. With Dealla still missing, we moved onto another pathway, hoping to find her.

I tried to listen, using my growing senses for anything abnormal. Around a corner, there were footsteps, followed by a faint whistle I hadn't heard since our cottage days. Blood roared in my ears as I whistled back in recognition.

Dealla jumped from the shadows near the steps, moving toward my glowing palm. I looked her over, checking for injuries. A shallow gash along her cheek, and a small line of blood dripped from her jaw, her fighting leathers soaked in crimson.

"Just a scratch. Already healing," Dealla said quickly, breathing hard as her gaze found my mother. Her blue eyes glistened with unshed tears. "I think we got most of the soldiers."

"Dealla," my mother whispered, falling into her arms.

"I was worried when we were separated. I stayed to take care of other soldiers instead of returning to Bria – afraid you would need me here." Dealla spoke over my mother's shoulder. "Oh, Alina. I'm so happy she found you." She pulled back from helping my mother stand as her nostrils flared. "But let's get you out of here for a proper bath." They both managed weak chuckles through their tears. "We can't linger. More are coming."

My mother leaned between us as we helped her up the steps Dealla had come from. The passage led us through packed earth, the escape route my mother mentioned. We moved quickly, knowing guards could appear anywhere, and not hearing from Bria had me worried.

When Dealla pushed open the heavy door at the top, fresh air hit like a blessing. But as the door shut behind us, a horn blasted somewhere on the island, and two soldiers raced through the dead woods toward us.

"Dealla!" I released my mother, letting her fall into Dealla's arms. My sword ignited with blue flames that rippled up the blade, making my hands vibrate with power. I narrowed my eyes, focusing on the approaching enemies. They smirked with dark confidence, heavy swords swaying in their grips, as their feet kicked up dirt.

"*Ellowyn!*" Bria's voice sent chills of relief through me.

I screamed as I raised my sword overhead, my blue flames brushing my skin with familiar warmth. The first soldier's sword crashed against mine. When our eyes met, recognition hit like a physical blow. He was one of the soldiers who'd destroyed my cottage and taken my mother.

My body shook with raging vengeance.

I shoved him away and raised my palm. A ball of fire formed, and I hurled it at the second soldier. His eyes widened just before flames erupted across his chest, and he became a human torch.

The soldier at my sword balked, just long enough for me to call on Bria's power. Our connection flowed through me as I gripped my sword and drove it deep into his chest. He dropped to his knees.

I ambled as he gasped in the dirt, my stomach churning. But I would not falter. Not for him.

"You filth," he stammered, blood staining his lips. "You will lose this war."

I bent down so he could stare into my green eyes. "Maybe. But not today." I grasped my sword still lodged in his chest as he wheezed. "This is for my mother." I pushed it further. His agonized scream pierced the woods before he collapsed sideways, the light leaving his eyes.

"Ellowyn!" my mother cried. She and Dealla moved closer. Dealla's sword was at the ready as my mother stared in shock at what I'd done.

"What the hell has Ivarison been teaching you?" Dealla stammered, looking between the burned soldier and the other one I'd run through. She shook her head, not looking for an answer. "Signal for Bria. We must leave before more arrive."

Dealla was right. My mother was too weak to fight, and even Dealla and I had limits while needing to protect her.

"We need open ground," I said, helping support my mother again. "*Bria!*"

"*I'm near Little Spark. To your right!*" Bria's voice came over again like a wave of relief.

She was safe, and she was coming. We were going to make it out alive.

"There! She's coming!" I called out. Dealla and my mother followed my gaze. Bria descended.

My mother gasped and tripped. Dealla caught her as I rushed over to Bria, who gently tapped my head, examining me over.

"I'm fine, no wounds that I can feel," I answered her unasked questions as she continued to look me over. If I were hurt, adrenaline had numbed the pain. My mother stared at Bria, her face pale as if she was about to hurt. "Bria, I would like for you to meet my mother, Alina."

Bria tilted her great head in a graceful bow.

"A d-dragon?" My mother's voice dragged with exhaustion. "She's a friend?"

"Technically, I'm her rider. But yes, I like to believe that Bria and I have become close friends, right?" I grinned up at her.

She rolled her eyes. *"Of course. Do you believe I would tolerate such a nuisance if I didn't find you at least mildly entertaining? And the chaos you attract is exhausting."*

I huffed a laugh and smacked her leg.

"There hasn't been a Fae rider in a thousand years." My mother whispered.

"Movement further north," Bria announced, her head swiveling over the trees. *"We must go. Now."*

"We need to move now."

We helped my mother in the saddle without hesitation. Once we were secured, my hands shook as I clipped the harness around my mother's frail body and reached for Dealla. The hair on my neck rose as the sound of horns began again.

Unwilling to wait to find what else came for us, Bria glanced and double-checked we were ready before she lifted us swiftly skyward. My mother rested her head against my back, between Dealla and me, looking down at the prison. I had to stop myself from asking Bria to set it alight.

Sentries moved through the dead trees, bows raised, and arrows whistled past us. They bounced off Bria's scales as she climbed toward the clouds. The ship we had seen at sea was now closer to shore, but we didn't linger to investigate.

The smell of blood, mud, and worse clung to my mother as we flew, her head heavy against my back. We didn't know how long she had been in prison. We only knew they had traveled through Madora before vanishing. Her screams from Mornwind still haunted me, but I wasn't sure I'd ever be able to ask if that truly had been her.

Cool air rushed past as I focused on the horizon ahead, not daring to look at the dark stains on my clothes from what I had done at the prison. I spoke with Bria as she asked questions about my mother.

We had been gone from Mystmere for a full day before reaching the kingdom's barrier. My heart soared when the castle appeared, gleaming in welcome.

"We made it," I whispered as Bria let out a soft roar through the clouds. We flew over the village, keeping our distance as villagers watched in wonder. The pressure in my chest was finally fading, and I was feeling more at ease.

"Your mother needs a healer immediately, she's not doing well." Bria spoke urgently as she landed gently in the courtyard.

"I can never repay you enough, Bria." I rubbed her back before Dealla and I began rousing my mother, who immediately sagged in our arms, her legs too weak to support her.

"We need to get her inside," Dealla said quickly. Alix rushed over with Killian in tow. "I'm fine! We need to get her to a healer." Dealla managed a soft smile for Killian as she held my mother up.

"The maids have prepared her chambers," Alix said, his eyes widening as he took in my mother's condition.

"Alix," my mother whispered faintly, her eyelids heavy as she looked around at our surroundings. "We're in Mystmere?"

His composure cracked. The setting sun revealed the green and yellow bruises covering her body, her once beautiful brown hair matted with blood and filth.

"Take her up. I'll fetch the healers," Alix said, gently clasping my mother's hands in welcome.

"How is the castle still here?" my mother asked, but her legs gave out. She cried as she collapsed. Dealla and I both caught her.

"Much has happened while you were gone, Princess. Let's get you healed and better, and then we can discuss." Alix squeezed her hand before letting go.

Dealla lifted my mother into her arms as if she were a child. "This way, Ellowyn."

I kept quiet as I followed, afraid to let my mother out of my sight. My grandfather waited somewhere in the castle for the news of our return, but my mother still didn't know of his survival.

But her health came first. The revelations could wait.

My mother was confined to her chambers for a week. She initially begged for different rooms, unwilling to stay where she had once shared with my father. She had been far weaker than we'd realized during her rescue. She hadn't told us how severe her condition was.

The magic she possessed had been so diluted that her natural healing abilities hadn't worked properly.

The wounds on her back and legs had festered into infections. The healer worked constantly with potions and ointments. It took nearly four days of intensive care before her magic began returning.

Dealla and I took turns keeping her company. Near the week's end, Delaney came to meet her. My mother rested mostly, with little to occupy her while we waited for Ivarison's return, which we hoped would come with promising news.

It grew harder to keep information from my mother. My grandfather was so desperate to see his daughter, but after my mother's ordeal, we weren't sure how she would take learning he had been alive after all this time.

As days dragged on with no word from Ivarison, worry gnawed at me. I knew he was capable of taking care of himself, but after seeing the prison and facing a Sleroka, fear crept in about what the coming weeks might bring.

Knowing it wouldn't be right to continue withholding information from my mother, Dealla and I decided it was time to tell her everything. She needed to know what had happened during her captivity.

"What's the matter?" she asked when Dealla and I entered together. Killian stood guard by the door with another guard. My mother rested in the large bed by her balcony, allowing her to see outside and breathe the fresh air her body desperately needed.

"We need to speak of something important." I sat by her bed, nervously playing with the armchair's edges as Dealla stood at my side.

"How long has it been since they took me?" my mother asked, staring as if she didn't fully recognize me. It had been a long time since she had seen my true form; pointed ears, taller stance, sun-kissed from flying with Bria.

My mother sat up straighter, her brown hair looking healthier. Her skin had more color to it, and her eyes weren't so sullen. Her pointed ears showed through her hair, and her features were sharper as I studied her healing Fae form. I had always thought she was beautiful, but now there was something softer about her too.

"Over two months. We've been traveling through Madora searching for you, and then we found our way to Mystmere." I swallowed hard at her sharp intake of breath.

"Oh, what was it you needed to speak about?"

I glanced at Dealla, who nodded encouragingly. "It's about your father, my grandfather. He's alive, and he's here."

Her eyes darted from me to Dealla, jaw slightly ajar. "That's not possible, you must be mistaken. They were both murdered in the throne room. I saw them. I took you and ran because they were killed."

"He is very much alive. Grandmother did die in the attack, but grandfather lives, and Alix helped him. He's been here protecting the kingdom and the Riker Tree."

"It's truly him, Alina," Dealla said softly, moving closer.

"He wants to see you when you're ready. He has asked every day since you've returned. We just didn't want to overwhelm you."

Her hands shook as she covered her mouth, tears forming as she gasped.

"No," she sobbed. "I thought – I ran because I thought he was dead. I ran to protect you! We could have stayed –" she broke down again, tears soaking the bedsheets. "That's why your father is dead!"

I bit my lip as my eyes burned. This was not the mother I had grown up with at the cottage. My mother had never cried in front of me, and now she sat before me, broken and needing to piece herself back together.

"That's not true. He died protecting us, and I know he would do it again if he were still alive." I scooted my chair closer, the sound echoing as I took my mother's hand. "I've started to remember things. Not everything from my past remains; some memories you forced me to forget. I remember running through the village, The Sleroka, and the black mist."

" I didn't want you remembering that about your father. You were so young, and you loved him so deeply." Her jaw muscles twitched as she breathed in a shaky breath. "You cried for him every night. You had nightmares."

"You could have told me as I grew older, instead of hiding and taking it all away. You took everything." I stopped the anger from snapping, straightening in my chair and releasing her hand.

"We encountered a Sleroka before we reached Mystmere, Alina," Dealla said, nodding in my direction. "Ellowyn killed it."

My mother gulped loudly, reaching for her water glass.

"A Sleroka has never been killed. We don't even know if Adriane had only one or if there were multiple like her other creatures."

"I watched it happen. She blew it to pieces and saved us."

She sighed, rising higher in bed. "Tell me everything that has happened."

We spent the afternoon explaining our journey. Dealla spoke most of the time, while I filled in the gaps from when Ivarison and I were together to how I met Bria and how we connected.

We didn't linger long on the prison and rescue, not wanting to dwell on those moments if my mother wasn't ready.

"I'm so proud of you. You've done so well." My mother turned to Dealla. "Your friendship and all that you've done for us, I could never repay that." Tears filled her eyes when she turned back to me, brushing her splotchy cheek. "I know you're angry with me, and I understand. I was foolish and broken over what happened. I know what I did was a cowardly thing to do, but I promise to try to do better."

I wiped my own tears, sinking into her embrace as she put her arms out. I was tense, but didn't want to ruin the moment for her. I had been so lost in this new world, but I knew that in time, it would get better.

Chapter Thirty-Three

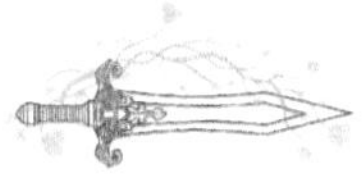

My grandfather's footsteps echoed throughout the corridor. I nearly had to jog to keep up with his pace. My mother's wounds were healing, her magic was returning, and she was ready. My grandfather had waited long enough to have their reunion.

I knocked on her door before entering. She stood beside the large canopy bed, her hair falling over her shoulders. She was dressed in a soft undershirt, tucked into trousers with a thick tunic embroidered with gold thread.

Moments of silence passed. My grandfather and mother stared at one another, eyes wide, mouths agape. I was still grappling with this reality. It didn't feel real, both of them alive and here in Mystmere.

Home.

I wanted to say something, but Dealla caught my eyes and nodded toward the door. She and Killian slipped out quietly, giving them privacy.

"Alina," my grandfather spoke with a shaky voice, "Oh, my daughter." He stepped closer. "You look like you're healing well."

When he reached her, they embraced, squeezing each other as tears spilled down their faces.

"I thought you were dead. I thought you died with mother." My mother's voice trembled, her body shaking in his arms. "I shouldn't have run. I'm so sorry."

"You had to keep Ellowyn safe. I will never hold that against you." He pulled back, cupping her face in his palms. I pressed against the wall, trying to disappear. "They were going to kill you both. We will end this, Alina. War is coming, but we will be ready this time."

I breathed in heavily as I left the room. We would talk another day. For now, she needed this time with her father. The conversation my mother and I needed about our life at the cottage could wait. They both deserved their moment together.

No words had come from Ivarison on the quest he had been sent on. Every day, I found myself looking out to the barrier, wondering if he would appear.

Mystmere's healers had done wonders with my mother. She slowly regained her strength while Killian and Dealla helped her rebuild lost muscle through training. She was determined to fight for our family when war arrived.

I trained with Delaney while my mother worked with Dealla. Delaney worked with shifting between strikes and moving quickly, bringing her claws into play while I dodged any attacks from her. I avoided using magic, working on controlling my emotions when my magic flared unbidden.

I took an afternoon off from practice, wanting to fly with Bria and feel air rushing through my hair. Fear had caged my mind. The worry about what was coming made the days feel endless. When I watched the horizon for Ivarison, I also dreaded the attack that would inevitably come.

I tried to push away the weight and recall memories from when I'd lived in Mystmere as a child. One resurfaced: my mother and I, walking together, my tiny hand wrapped around one of her fingers. She'd turned back with the biggest smile. Her face radiated joy as she laughed. It felt wrong to wish she might be like that again.

While we flew over the village, villagers looked up and waved. I grinned and waved back, catching sight of Alix in the crowd below, looking displeased.

As a princess, I was supposed to have a guard assigned at all times for protection. I had yet to have one assigned and did not feel the need, especially with a dragon at my side. But I had heard the disagreement that Alix had over the matter and wanted their princess protected at all costs.

Bria flew to a hill near the barrier that offered a wide view of Mystmere. The castle and village spread out behind me, while the boundary stood protected by sentries ahead. I could hear the gentle chatter below, harmonizing with the rush of the river.

I unclipped from the saddle and rested against a tree, pulling an apple from my hip satchel. Bria settled with her massive head beside my legs, our size difference causing me to chuckle.

"*Oh, it's so humorous,*" Bria said with a glare.

"Any luck with other dragons?" I knew if there had been sightings, I would already know, but I couldn't stop hoping for her. Ivarison had once said it was rare to see dragons in Madora, but I wouldn't allow myself to believe Bria was one of the last.

"*Unfortunately, not, though I know others exist. I've sensed them.*"

"Is it because of Adriane and Ciaran?"

"*They were the ones who began to kill my kind and encouraged the poachers. Poachers believe our horns, talons and blood are worth a fortune.*"

"Is that true?"

"*Of course it's true, we're magnificent.*"

I grinned, "That is true. I'm sorry, Bria. If I make it out of this war alive, I'll help you find others." I spoke softly.

"*You will survive this, Ellowyn.*"

Before I could respond, we jolted as sentries blasted a warning horn.

Something was approaching the barrier.

Bria's head snapped up as I spotted a large group began to enter through the barrier. My breath caught as I recognized dark hair and piercing blue eyes finding mine across the distance.

"*Ellowyn.*" His deep voice carried to me, and I was immediately on my feet.

Ivarison.

"Bria, could you take me closer?" I jumped back into the saddle, without taking my eyes off Ivarison as he led a group into Mystmere.

Some of the soldiers froze when a large dragon appeared.

Ivarison smirked and shook his head as we landed. I leaped from the saddle and rushed to where he waited. Alix appeared, directing the newcomers on where to make camp.

"You sure know how to make an entrance." Even exhausted, Ivarison attempted to sound amused. I clicked my tongue and embraced him. His body tensed under my arms before relaxing and wrapping around me tightly. His breath warmed the side of my face.

"*Don't you think that's enough?*" Bria huffed out, her hot breath washing over us.

"Were you worried about me?" Ivarison asked, eyes slightly narrowed as we pulled apart.

I shoved him lightly with a grin. "Of course not, I needed my trainer back. I don't enjoy setting anyone else on fire."

"Of course. We can't have you setting anyone else aflame."

I sighed. A hint of happiness flooded through me. "We found my mother and rescued her. I was worried when there was no word from you." Awkwardness crept in as I realized how close we still stood, and I stepped back. "The place they kept her was horrifying."

"She's back in the kingdom?" Relief crossed his features. "No one could give me updates, and I didn't want to risk giving away my location either. Information falls into the wrong hands too easily in times like this."

"Who are you traveling with?" I had much to learn about Madora's politics.

"We have more that are making camp outside of the barrier. Others will be here soon. Some here are from Lord Eirwen and Lord Durin. I've been traveling everywhere, seeking allies." He glanced around at those who had joined our cause, then brushed dirt from his leathers as Alix approached.

"I would like to clean up before we have a meeting," Ivarison said to Alix, not mentioning the King since the newer soldiers did not know of his survival.

"Want to fly back with Bria and me?" I asked. Bria snapped lazily toward Ivarison, annoyed by the suggestion.

"You know I can fly myself," he said, eyebrows raised as I told Bria to hush.

"Yes, but you look exhausted."

"Is that your way of telling me that I look like shit?"

"I'll not answer that." I chuckled. I'd seen him look far worse, and even then, he was still stunning.

We flew back to the castle in comfortable silence, the sun casting warm light. Ivarison sat behind me, arms wrapped around my waist, hands gripping the saddle horns. I felt at peace as I closed my eyes and sighed, letting my head tip back so the sun could warm my face.

Candles bathed the hall with orange light. The crystal chandelier hung from the center of the vaulted ceiling. My grandfather sat at the head of the long table while Killian, Dealla, Delaney and I waited for Ivarison.

Bread and cheese sat on the gold platters as I took a few bites. The large wooden doors opened, and Ivarison entered with Alix. After a bath and a change of clothes, the filth had been washed away, and his dark hair was pulled from his face.

Much better.

Ivarison bowed his head, addressing the king, "Your Majesty."

"It's a pleasure to have you back safely, Lord Ivarison," my grandfather said. "I wanted to meet with you as quickly as possible before meeting with the rest of the king's guards. Alix will be staying to listen."

"Thank you, Your Majesty." He nodded at the rest of us, a smirk playing on his lips when he looked at me, and then bowed his head again before taking a seat at my right.

The door opened again, and my mother entered.

"Princess Alina will also join us," my grandfather announced. "She needs to hear what has happened during her absence."

Absence wouldn't be the exact choice of words that I would have chosen.

"Are you sure you're up for this?" I asked, as she took the seat next to my grandfather. Her joining a meeting was not needed when she could be briefed privately later.

"More each day." she glanced between Ivarison and me, her nose wrinkling before looking at the others.

"Please proceed, Ivarison," my grandfather said, his arms crossed as he leaned back in his golden chair, his elbows resting at the armrest.

"I began at Northhorn. Lord Eirwen and Lady Serene will fight for us. They've sent soldiers ahead, and the rest will travel when they arrive," Ivarison spoke quickly, having much to cover.

"We passed other villages, and many residents, both in the villages and outlying areas, have agreed to follow us. At Luminara, Lord Durin had been traveling frequently between courts." Delaney frowned, her brows drawing together at the news. "I believe it's obvious they are willing to fight with us, as their daughter traveled with the princess and is here now. They have sent soldiers, with more arriving once they arrive too."

"What of your court?" My grandfather asked. Ivarison inhaled sharply, his lip twitching.

"I did not return to Wildhaven. I've not been there since the attack on my home. It is not what it once was."

My grandfather sighed. "I will send another in your place. We need every willing fighter. Tell me, what is troubling you?"

Dread emitted from him. I had thought it was exhaustion, but his blue eyes were troubled, and his shoulders tensed as he leaned forward.

"Lady Celia reported that her guards spotted Adriane and Ciaran. The guards had attempted to approach Luminara but were stopped. After the confrontation, Luminara believed the soldiers had returned to Ravenholde, but most of the land near their kingdom was vacant. We believe they are somewhere in Madora."

"What are you saying?" My mother sat higher, pointed ears visible through her golden-brown curls.

"They're coming with thousands. They will attack this kingdom and destroy anything in their path. Some smaller villages throughout Madora have already been destroyed."

"What of the human lands?" Killian asked, his cheeks heated with anger.

"I don't know, I doubt the Dark Soldiers would attack the human lands, at least not until Adriane and Ciaran were on Madora's throne. They'd believe themselves unstoppable then." He looked at my grandfather. "No one knows you're alive. Your majesty. It's only known that Princess Alina and Princess Ellowyn have returned to reclaim their home."

"Your Majesty, if I may," Dealla said, her hand hitting the table. Frustration exuded from her as she glanced at Killian. My grandfather nodded toward her. "I believe we should keep your survival secret for now. At least until the other lords and ladies have arrived. Let them discover the news together. That way, Adriane and Ciaran won't learn the information or have time to prepare."

Ivarison nodded. "I agree with Dealla. The element of surprise could benefit us. I'm still bound by oath, so I couldn't speak to anyone about your survival. I could only say that Princess Ellowyn was in the process of rescuing Princess Alina."

"Are they truly coming?" My grandfather's fingers tapped against the arms of his chair, his eyes staring out the window.

"Yes," Ivarison admitted. "I don't believe it will be long before they try to break into the kingdom."

"Then we must prepare. Anyone who wants to fight and has the right to do so must be ready. We cannot let them succeed on our land. This belongs to us. If we fail, Mystmere could cease to exist." My grandfather's gaze found mine, unblinking. I could sense the fear coursing through him. The same fear that ran through me.

"We must do our best. We can and will succeed." His voice echoed with determination, though I knew this kingdom might be relying on me because of some prophecy.

Chapter Thirty-Four

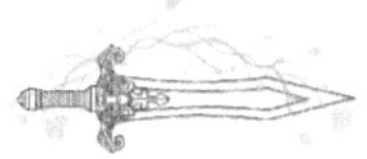

Our life at the cottage felt so long ago now, years even. I was a princess of a Fae realm, learning abilities I never knew I had, discovering more each passing day. The air seemed to tighten around my chest as we prepared for a battle.

The prophecy had been kept quiet; not everyone knew its contents or who it concerned. Regardless, the weight loomed over me like a storm cloud, waiting to release its chaos. I would be either the downfall or salvation against Adriane and Ciaran. If I failed, Madora surely wouldn't survive their reign. I couldn't keep those thoughts at bay, dreading I might let down the subjects of Madora and my family.

When I could sneak away, I would find Bria, and she would take me to the sky. Being with her helped clear my mind and calm my nerves. My grandfather and Alix were never pleased when I went, but I knew Bria would protect me if I couldn't defend myself.

After returning from a short flight, Alix waited to escort me to my grandfather.

"You left again." Alix said as I unfastened from the saddle and climbed down. I narrowed my eyes as Alix stood still and watched. "He is only trying to keep you safe."

"I've managed for the last seventeen years. He cannot keep me confined now." I crossed my arms, glancing back at Bria, who rolled her eyes and huffed in Alix's direction.

Alix sighed. "Well, come on then. The King is waiting for you." He motioned for me to follow him into the castle as he began to walk. "He is one of our best. I have trained him personally for many years."

"What? Who are you talking about?" I stopped, balancing on my heels.

"We've selected your guard. This way, please." He turned to continue.

I bit my lip, hesitating before following. The part of the castle was a section that I had not explored. Through a wooden door, my grandfather stood with my mother and Dealla.

"Why can't Delaney be my guard? I've managed fine without one for seventeen years, haven't I?" I didn't want another person to shadow my every move.

"You were hidden during that time, and you had Dealla for the past few years. During your travels, you had Killian and Dealla, who are guards," Alix said, trying to soothe my complaints.

"Okay, then let me have Delaney. I trust her."

"That isn't how it works. You're a princess, and it is protocol to have a royal guard. This should have been done sooner." My grandfather stated, "Besides, Delaney is Lord and Lady of Luminara's daughter. She cannot be a royal guard."

"There is always time for a change. I'm sure Delaney would beg to differ on what she can and cannot do. I'm with Bria most of the time, anyway. Are you saying a guard is better than her?" I picked at my fingernails in frustration.

"*The guard cannot follow you everywhere,*" Bria commented with a snarl. Unless the guard dared to jump on her back during flight, she was right. If Ivarison hadn't been a lord, I would have considered asking for him; his powers alone kept others at bay.

Alix huffed. "I would like you to meet Carwyn."

A figure strode down the stairs from the corner of the room. In the shadows, his heavy footsteps echoed until he stepped into the window's light, revealing a handsome Fae male. His broad shoulders filled an ivory tunic. His sharp jawline was tense as he looked across the room. His ash blond hair fell past his creamy skin, and when the light hit his silver eyes, they were like steel, he bowed to the royals.

"Carwyn has served in the guard for many years. I personally selected him for Princess Ellowyn," Alix said proudly. My jaw dropped slightly as I studied his tall, muscular frame.

"It's a pleasure to meet you, Princess Ellowyn," he purred, and I found myself squinting as I stared.

"The pleasure is mine," I said curtly, not letting my annoyance falter as I turned back to my grandfather and mother. Dealla grinned, but I ignored her. "Why don't I have a say in this?"

"Ellowyn, just for now, please," my mother pleaded. "War is coming, and we do not know what is to come. We need to take necessary precautions."

I pinched the bridge of my nose, feeling a headache coming, my temples pulsing.

"According to the prophecy and tree, I'm the one who will defeat Adriane and Ciaran, or perhaps ruin it all. But you don't believe I can protect myself? Will you keep me guarded while the rest of the land burns? What have I been doing since searching for you and saving you from that prison?" I paused, glaring at my mother. "I thought things were changing. Is this just another way of controlling me? Because this time, I *will* fight back."

My mother flinched. I turned on my heel, feeling their stares piercing my back as I left, slamming the door behind me. My heart pounded between my eyes. The headache lingered as I rubbed my temples.

I found Delaney sitting against a tree in the courtyard, using her beast paw to slice an apple. She tossed another apple toward Bria, who caught it in her mouth with a soft crunch before swallowing.

"I apologize in advance," I said as I approached, the grass brushing my ankles, and she looked confused. "I've been assigned a guard. I tried asking if it could be you instead, though." I looked from her to Bria. "I still don't understand why I need a personal guard."

"Protection, Ellowyn. We're protecting you. However, I don't believe it's necessary that he follows you everywhere," Bria soothed, shifting her position.

"You asked if I could be your guard?" Delaney's tone was unreadable. I couldn't tell if she was amused or honored.

"Yes." I looked over my shoulder as Carwyn entered the courtyard and took position by a wall. "Ah, there he is."

"Aldric was once my guard. After nearly a dozen escapes where he couldn't find me, my parents finally gave permission for me to train. Eventually I was allowed more freedom when they believed I was capable of protecting myself. His training was brutal, but worth it. I'm proud of where I am now,"

"Are you saying I should find hidden passages and escape routes?" I snorted a laugh. "We just rescued my mother from a prison and survived a brutal journey through Madora."

"Hey, I'm willing to help find those passages if needed." Delaney shrugged with a wry smile. "It's royal protocol, as you're the princess, though. I don't believe they doubt your capabilities. They just want additional protection. At least he's nice to look at," She looked at Carwyn and waved. A slight pink tinge colored his cheeks before he looked away. "Oh, look at that, he's playing shy. It would have been an honor to be your guard, but I understand why they declined. I am a daughter–"

"Of a Lord and Lady," I said with a scowl. "So they've also said."

Delaney nudged her shoulder into my leg. "Ive had training, but not royal guard training."

The village seemed distressed with more sightings near Mystmere's border. Courts joined our fight, camping around the barrier, some came through the barrier while others were stationed outside.

I rarely spoke to Carwyn and refused to ask where the library was. I searched the castle area by area, making him take every turn that I took. Eventually, I found two ivory doors, concealing a room lined floor-to-ceiling with hundreds of bookshelves. The smell of old pages emanated into the air, and I sighed as I began searching, feeling something calling to me.

Carwyn stood near the door, giving me the desired space while I explored the library. Old, tattered books with delicate pages hanging by a thread. As I opened and closed tomes, my nose wrinkled, and I sneezed from the dust. Feeling restless and eager to learn everything about the power of the elder Fae who lived before my grandfather, I settled at a table with a pile of books.

One contained stories of witches and Fae once living in peace. Humans traveled through Madora, unafraid of lurking creatures. Page after page, I learned of the power that could potentially run through me. As I turned the old pages, something called to me, and I felt eyes watching me.

"What?" I snapped, assuming Carwyn had moved closer.

Carwyn remained at the entrance. It was Ivarison who leaned against a nearby bookshelf. His hair hung slightly over his forehead before he pushed it behind his ear, smirking.

"I'm trying to read. I can't focus with you standing there, staring," I said when he didn't speak.

"You looked deep in thought. I would have hated to intrude." He produced a book from behind his back. "You should read this one. It has more information about your healing abilities." He placed the brown volume atop of my pile. Imprinted on the cover were outstretched palms and a tree growing in the center.

"What about you? You have healing abilities too," I said, reclining in my chair.

"Yes, but I've read it. Now, I'm passing it to you."

"Where have you been?" I asked, "I've not seen you since we returned."

"I didn't know you wished to see me." He leaned against the table, inches away. I could smell him as I looked into his bright blue eyes, then I rolled my own and pulled myself away to avoid drowning in their depths.

"I didn't say that. We just haven't trained. I've gotten used to our daily routine."

"You wound me. Did you miss looking into my eyes?"

"What?" My eyes narrowed. "Stay out of my head, Ivarison!"

"Another thing we should practice. Keep that barrier up at all times, love. *Anyone* could be listening."

"I look forward to it," I snapped, returning my attention to the book in my hand, flipping through the pages without another glance in his direction.

Luminara Court had arrived at Mystmere. My grandfather remained hidden, watching from a tower. Since King Everett was believed to be dead, my mother, next in line for the throne, was required to welcome our guests.

When we arrived, soldiers had already begun establishing camps around the area. I stood beside my mother, unnerved as I watched. Aldric stood near his Lord and Lady as Delaney made her way to her parents with a grim expression, offering brief, formal greetings.

"Lord Durin and Lady Celia," I said with a smile as my mother and I moved closer. They bowed their heads as Bria came closer. "It's a pleasure to see you both again."

"The honor is ours, Princess. Did you give it a name yet?" Lord Durin gestured toward my sword.

"I came across a name in a book I was reading, *Glaukos.* I thought it was fitting." My hand found the hilt of my sword, and it hummed in response.

"Perfect name," Lady Celia said with a soft smile.

"Other courts are to arrive shortly. May we escort you to the castle while we wait?" my mother asked, standing tall as she took my side.

"Yes, Princess Alina. It's an honor to be back in your presence," Lord Durin said warmly, studying my mother before taking her hand and kissing the top of it.

I hadn't seen much of my mother as of late, only during training. I watched carefully as she spoke with the others, knowing how she could hide herself behind a steel barrier. Avoidance was a harsh shadow between us. She didn't talk as we returned to the castle.

"We will dine in the hall tonight, and you're more than welcome to stay as our guests. I'll have our maids show you to your chambers." my mother said, turning to face Lady Celia and Lord Durin.

"I will be traveling back and forth to our soldiers," Durin informed. "Lady Celia will stay more frequently as she wishes to be closer to our daughter."

Delaney approached and let out a soft groan. Lady Celia's brows furrowed at the sound as Delaney smiled innocently.

Over the following days, villagers watched as more arrived outside the barrier, joining the growing collection of soldiers. Flying above the clouds on Bria's back, I could see how many Fae had joined recently. A lump formed in my throat. Soon enough, this could all be a battlefield.

One hot afternoon, Delaney and I were at the border with Ivarison, Alix, and Carwyn when a horn sounded. More soldiers appeared over the horizon. Ivarison stiffened mid-sentence, stopping entirely.

The approaching soldiers wore armor emblazoned with a winged lion. Though their numbers were small, they would still make a difference. A tall, muscular Fae led the group.

"What is it?" I asked Ivarison, who hadn't taken his eyes from the newcomers.

"My court." He frowned as they moved toward him. The handsome Fae leading them was taller than Ivarison, shoulders squared as he stopped in front of his lord.

"Keegan," Ivarison whispered. Keegan looked Ivarison over. He didn't appear much older than me. He pulled Ivarison into a tight embrace that was immediately returned.

"Brother, it's been too long. I wasn't sure I would see you since someone else came to collect us." Keegan spoke with a slight accent like Ivarison's, his voice deep and rumbling.

"Brother? Who-who is that?" Delaney asked, unable to take her eyes off the male. My mouth twisted to hide the smile. I could see why. He was incredibly good-looking, with honey-colored eyes and dark, messy hair.

"I think he's just a close friend from his court," I answered in a whisper, knowing the truth of Ivarison's true brother.

The other Fae began setting tents and campfires as Ivarison and Keegan returned to where we waited.

"Hello," Delaney said cooly, brushing silver hair from her face. "I'm Delaney."

I bit my lip, glancing at Ivarison. His eyes tracked the movement, heat rising in my cheeks as he licked his own bottom lip.

Ivarison cleared his throat. "This is Keegan. He's been a close friend since childhood, like a brother." He patted Keegan's back, breaking the stare between him and Delaney.

"It's a pleasure to meet you, I'm Ellowyn Kelgrove."

Keegan took a deep breath and looked at Ivarison, shaking his head before he returned his attention to me.

"The pleasure is mine, Princess. I heard quite a bit about you during our journey here." He took my hand and kissed it politely.

"I'm not sure what you could've heard." I said, surprised.

"All delightful things. Your beauty, how you've traveled throughout Madora, befriended a dragon–" he glanced at Bria, who watched intently, "And saved your mother. I look forward to hearing more."

I blushed. Those things had been necessary. My only goals had been the survival of myself and finding my mother. Finding and befriending Bria had been a wonderful bonus that I'd be forever grateful for.

"Yes, I'm a true delight," Bria snuffed, watching the soldiers around camp. *"Although, I'm not fond of crowds."*

"I couldn't have done any of it without help. Ivarison and Delaney were a huge part of it. I owe them my life." I rubbed Delaney's arm as she stood at my side, still staring at Keegan.

What was wrong with her?

"We're grateful for your mother's return and yours, Princess." Keegan looked at Ivarison and grinned. "The Fae of Madora are truly grateful and will do what they can to restore Madora to what it once was."

"Keegan took control of Wildhaven during my absence. My home may be gone, but some villagers remained and have rebuilt. He maintains order if anything is amiss," Ivarison explained, answering unspoken questions.

"Yes, though I speak for others when I say you're deeply missed in your court. They would very much enjoy having their Lord back."

"One day," Ivarison said, then cleared his throat. "I'll take Keegan to the castle." He pulled Keegan to walk with him.

I couldn't blame Ivarison for not wanting to return to Wildhaven after his family's death. My mother fled the kingdom after believing everyone she loved was killed. The village had been the last place my father lived. When I walked through it at times, I could still envision the black mist overtaking it and him running into it.

"Ellowyn," Delaney whispered. "Where is Dealla? I need to speak with her,"

I could sense her racing heart, her pale skin nearly white as she looked at me.

"Let's go find her," I said as I began guiding our walk back.

"What's the matter with silver hair?" Bria asked, as she let us pass before lifting into the sky. *"She's frantic."*

"What's the matter?" I asked, when her heart didn't calm.

Her voice caught as she cleared her throat. "I need to ask how she knew Killian was her mate. I can't ask my mother. She'll go into a frenzy of questions." Her voice was now nearly frantic. "I think I just met my mate. *My mate.*"

Keegan?!

Her eyes were wide as she looked through the village toward where Keegan and Ivarison had disappeared into the crowd.

Chapter Thirty-Five

My grandfather remained hidden in the castle as we waited for the remaining lords and ladies. Alix delivered news from a soldier who'd return from barrier patrol.

I had never seen Delaney in such a state. She picked at her fingernails and glanced at Ivarison, wanting to ask about Keegan but unable to find her voice. She knew he was her mate even without having the chance to speak to Dealla before the meeting had been called.

Carwyn stood near Alix as we sat at the large table with my grandfather. The soldier had spotted Adriane and Ciaran's force during patrol. They lurked east of Mystmere, in the mountains, hidden in the peaks.

Bria had flown over those very mountains when we traveled to the prison. If only we'd looked down during the flight, we might have spotted them. No word reached our ears about whether Adriane and Ciaran remained in Madora or their own lands. No sign of creatures or her mist. They were hiding, waiting to strike.

Once the meeting ended, I left Delaney to speak with Dealla, apologizing as I departed quickly. War was approaching, and my fear grew with each passing day. And now I saw that same dread in Delaney. She had met her mate. Though both could deny the bond, she didn't know him yet, but interest sparked, and she wanted to discover more.

I walked through the corridor after Ivarison. He had left the meeting quickly and remained quiet, now walking away staring at the floor.

"Ivarison," I called, hastening my pace to catch him before he reached the stairs. He turned, immediately noticing Carwyn, who took his place by the wall when I stopped.

"Hello, love," he said. My eyes narrowed. "What may I do for you?"

"It was nice meeting Keegan. I didn't know you had friends," I said, looking for his usual smirk.

He huffed as if he were hurt, then chuckled lightly. "Keegan is who I spoke to you about before. He's been a friend of mine since we were children." He paused, looking away and biting his lip. "I just hope we make it through this war. He has always been there, through the good and bad."

"I hope I can get to know him more. I'm curious, did he mention anything about Delaney?" I asked, but Ivarison didn't fall for the casual tone.

"Now, why would you ask such a question?" He folded his arms, looking down at me.

"Only curious, just something that Delaney may have mentioned."

"He suspects she is his mate, if that is what you're asking. But he's only just met her and wants to get to know her." He strolled, tilting his head for me to follow.

"What would that be like?" I asked quickly, looking around the corridor. Maybe that was too personal a question. "How do you know when you've met your mate?"

He halted, his gaze finding my face as if he were entranced, before he blinked. "It feels like your body is calling to them." He stepped closer. "There is a connection you cannot explain – you feel for them, long for them. A tug in your head and mind, like you're finding your equal. Home."

"Oh," I said, releasing a soft sigh. How intimate and intimidating. During my time in Madora, I had experienced all sorts of feelings as the Rikeroot left my system. Even tugging sensations when danger was near.

Ivarison coughed, noticing Carwyn still nearby. A low ruble emerged from his throat, almost like a growl, as he was annoyed by the other male's presence.

"Are you busy? Would you like to train with me?" I asked, thinking of an excuse before Ivarison could leave me standing in the corridor with my guard.

While training with Ivarison, Carwyn was dismissed. The only other times I escaped him were when I was in my bedroom. I hadn't completely ignored him, we spoke occasionally, but having a guard shadow my every movement was at times overbearing.

"I know you've been training without me, and you're doing well, I suppose," he said with a smirk. "What would you like to focus on?" Ivarison asked once we made it to an empty courtyard of the castle.

As soon as we entered, Bria swooped down and landed nearby, giving me a gentle nuzzle.

"I was wondering if we could focus on fading. I've done it twice but haven't figured it out exactly." I said, after Bria pulled herself away and gave us distance.

Ivarison hesitated. "Why would you want to focus on that now?"

"I want to see the mountains where the soldiers are camped." I wouldn't bother lying. I knew he could easily discover the truth if he wanted.

"You know damn well that isn't wise," he said, his posture shifting as Bria shook her head in agreement. "Why not fly with Bria instead?"

Bria snorted smoke at him, disagreeing with that suggestion.

"That isn't very wise either," Bria snapped.

"I need to practice. We've had to fade multiple times because of danger. It would be useful to know that I could do it."

Ivarison sighed, "You're right. But this plan of yours has many ways that it could fail catastrophically."

"Good thing I made up a plan for this to work," I said with a grin.

"Your optimism is either inspiring or terrifying, I haven't decided which." He rolled his eyes. "What is your plan?"

"Bria can fly that way, or you could come with me. If I can't return myself, Bria could pick me up." Bria rolled her eyes and rested her head on the ground in objection.

"That is your plan? You haven't been to the mountains," Ivarison countered. "How will you know where to go?"

"I don't want to land right in the middle of their camp. Just close enough so I can see what we're facing. I saw the mountains when we approached Mystmere."

"Let's start small, before you send yourself off on some quest. We know you're capable, we just need to master the technique." I watched his forearm muscle flex as he rolled up his sleeves. "Think about those times you've moved from one place to another. Last time, when you returned to Mornwind, what were you thinking?"

My eyes danced around, lost in thoughts as I remembered exactly what I thought and the horrifying creature we had left him with.

"You." I blurted out. I could hear my embarrassment as his brows furrowed. "I kept thinking of you, how wrong it felt to leave you to handle the creature. I had such an awful feeling, I couldn't accept it and leave you."

"Careful, Little Spark. Now you sound like you may care," Bria said, her voice crisp. The ground rumbled as she shifted. Ivarison ran a hand through his hair, his expression stern.

"All right," he said without looking at me. "So, you were thinking of *me,* which helped you fade. When moving between locations, you need to focus on that specific destination. Nothing else can cloud your thoughts, and you must move quickly. Think of taking that first step toward the location, and that's how you move. It's like walking through a doorway. Remember what I just told you and try moving closer to Bria."

I stared where Bria rested in the grass. Closing my eyes, I thought of the grass beneath her talons, her scaled body, and the leather saddle wrapped around her large torso – the feel of her scales underneath my palms. Air filled my lungs as I took a deep breath. Pressure pressed against me from all sides. I sensed a door opening and took a step, feeling the pressure building against every inch of my body.

I opened my eyes. Bria jerked her head around, startled to find me sitting on top of the saddle.

"I'm impressed. On the first try too," Ivarison said with an odd smirk. "Do it again, but return to where you were standing."

This time, with my eyes open, I thought of where I stood in front of him. He leaned against a brick wall, grass brushing his boots. I took another step through that doorway I'd opened, feeling the same pressure against my body, and found myself looking directly into his blue eyes. Just inches away, his breath warming my cheeks.

"Oh! I'm sorry, I didn't mean to come that close." I gulped as he let out a joyous laugh I had never heard from him before. A sound that gave me warmth and could chase away and kind of darkness that lingered above me.

"You should have seen your face," he said, straightening himself.

"I've never heard you laugh like that," I said, looking up at him. "It sounded wonderful." I immediately clamped my teeth shut as the last words left my mouth. I turned to Bria with wide eyes, her chuckle filling me.

"Oh, did it now?" He didn't move, and I could sense how close he remained behind me. "You never need to apologize."

"Shall I fly away so you can practice, or should I incinerate him?" Bria asked, making me jump. I moved away quickly.

"Yes, please go ahead," I said, distracting myself from the Fae behind me and not answering to which she could go ahead or incinerate him, as I felt the heat growing through my chest and arms.

Bria glared at Ivarison before she soared out, wind from her wings catching through my hair as I watched her disappear.

"Ellowyn," Ivarison said calmly, "There is nothing to be embarrassed about."

I glared, sneering. "Stay out of my head, Ivarison."

"I can't exactly do that when you're broadcasting your thoughts." Irritation filled his voice. "Fine, go ahead and try fading toward the mountain area that you remember." He grasped my arm lightly to draw my attention, then released it just as quickly. "Do not get too close. Keep your distance."

Beyond Mystmere's barrier, farther from where our soldiers were stationed, lay the mountains where Dark Soldiers hid. I thought of those peaks with a light dusting of snow.

Then I was gone. Ivarison disappeared behind me as pressure enveloped me. This was further than I had faded before, and my head spun as I regained my stability. I opened my eyes to the change of air. The wind blew harder, whipping my hair around my face. I turned and realized this was not the post I had intended to go to.

The mountain's edge was cold. Gray and black tents lined up to the peak, the mountain curving around in paths with trees scattered about as Fae walked throughout. I had faded much farther than intended.

How did I go so far?

"Oh, shit," I whispered. If I were able to see them, they'd spot me. I tried thinking back to the courtyard with Ivarison, but fear and panic wrapped around me. My only weapon was the dagger on my belt.

"*Ivarison. Ivarison!*"

Silence.

"*Bria, where are you?!*"

I screamed as loud as I could through our connection, but even if Ivarison could hear me, would he find me like he did last time? How had he been able to find me last time?

"*Oh, I knew very well this wasn't wise,*" Bria snarled.

I heard her cry from the sky. Soldiers looked up for the source as she stayed out of sight behind the clouds. She was near, and I thought all was well as I began running through the trees, downhill, twigs and leaves stinging my face as they struck me.

I thought I was safe with Bria close. Then a horn blasted through the mountain, echoing down the paths as shouts came from soldiers behind me.

I was spotted.

"*To your right, Ellowyn!*" Bria cried. I could see her form splitting the clouds and didn't dare look behind me at what was coming.

I went right as the ground shook violently under my feet. Running toward her, she landed, positioning me beneath her chest. There was a soft sound as Bria roared, then large arms wrapped around me and pulled me in close.

Ivarison had suddenly appeared. I could hear a deep, piercing noise and heat building from Bria's chest up her throat.

I covered my ears as I turned to see fire blazing from her, Ivarison's arms tightening around me. Smoke and flames now scorched the ground where soldiers had been, and my blue aura surrounded Ivarison and me, protecting us from the fire.

"*Climb on my back now,*" Bria demanded. "*Hundreds will be running down within seconds.*"

"Go! Oh, this was foolish," Ivarison said, helping me up onto Bria's back into the saddle. As soon as I was fastened, he wrapped his arms around me, and Bria's powerful wings thrust us skyward.

With an explosive burst of energy, Bria tore away from the mountainside, the force so powerful it left me queasy. Looking down, I saw rolling hills and the peak's view. Thousands of tents covered every inch of soil. Soldiers ran down the mountain to investigate the commotion while others stayed alert near a large black tent at the center of camp.

"*I can't believe I went along with this,*" Bria snapped furiously, but didn't slow as she headed back to the kingdom's barrier.

"I can't believe I did too," Ivarison muttered, shaking his head.

Out of the awful plan I had created, we learned Adriane and Ciaran were close to Mystmere, and no one had known. They were ready for war, and it was only a matter of when.

Chapter Thirty-Six

The tension in the room felt like ice. I couldn't sink any further in the chair without sliding to the floor. Ivarison sat at my side as we faced my grandfather in his ornate chair, while my mother paced behind him.

The trouble we'd caused was clear, but risking myself to learn what lay beyond the barrier had been worth it. My mother and grandfather were furious, and when they learned Ivarison had helped, it didn't improve matters.

"You're supposed to be helping this kingdom stay protected!" My grandfather's voice thundered through the room, the vein in his forehead bulging.

"What were you thinking?" my mother demanded. She walked to the table, her long fingers tapping hard against its edge. "Because it sounds as if you weren't!"

"Don't yell at him!" I shouted back.

Alix, Dealla, and Carwyn stood rigidly at the side of the room, staring straight ahead, not daring to glance in our direction, Ivarison gripped the armrest of his chair tightly.

"Instead of yelling and belittling me, why don't you ask what I discovered?" I asked furiously. They had not seen the number of soldiers Adriane and Ciaran had. I could still picture the faces racing toward me, the same ones who would have killed me if Bria hadn't arrived.

"You cannot go as you please. You're a princess of Mystmere and expected to set an example," my grandfather forced out through gritted teeth. Tension built in his shoulders as they rose.

My glare shifted to my mother. The discussion of what she had done still lingered undone between us.

"I will not apologize for who I am. Don't expect me to act as someone I was forced to forget suddenly. I am my own person outside of that title. There's a reason I don't know how to act as a princess." I stared at my mother. "I lived in that cottage, isolated from the world, from Fae and humans, unable to live like a child. Seventeen years, glamoured to forget. Have you forgotten that?"

Warmth flooded my face as anger grew. The room seemed to shrink, making it harder to focus on who stood before me. My hands rose dismissively. "Do not blame Ivarison. I asked him to help me. He's the one who has not sheltered me, who's shown me what I could be capable of, ways I could save this kingdom. That is what's expected of me, since no one else is doing that."

The only sounds in the room were our pounding hearts and birds singing from the open window, but even they seemed to have quieted. I couldn't stand the lack of communication any longer.

It was why we were in this situation to begin with.

I stood, grabbing hold of Ivarison's sleeve to pull him with me, and he didn't object.

"Neither of you has seen what I'm capable of or tried to understand. What it was like after the cottage being thrown back into a land that you didn't understand while being hunted. I don't even know what your own capabilities are because you hide them from me, as you have done with everything." I looked between them both. "There were thousands of tents on that mountain. Soldiers were everywhere. Adriane and Ciaran's tent sat at the center of the highest peak. I could have asked Bria to incinerate them.

I keep questioning myself if I should have. But that isn't the right way to win, is it? The prophecy states it is up to me, and I can't fulfill that if I'm constantly belittled and held against my will."

I took one last look at the two across the table before I nearly ran from the hall. Through the corridor to the courtyard, where Bria waited in her usual spot. Her eyes narrowed as we entered, knowing that she had heard everything.

My grip tightened on the soft cloth. I still held onto Ivarison's sleeve, and he hadn't once pulled to escape my grip as he followed.

Since the visiting Lords and Ladies did not know my grandfather lived, neither he nor my mother had followed me out. I pressed a hand to my chest, reminding myself to breathe, trying to dissolve the lump in my throat as tears burned my eyes.

Shit.

Why did this feel so complicated? This was not what I had wished for when I'd dreamed of leaving the cottage. My hands glowed as I tried to shake the emotions.

"Ell?" Ivarison whispered, his voice the only thing I could hear as I sat on a crumbling wall. He hadn't called me that since the first memory I remembered with my father.

"I'm afraid. Truly afraid," I said after a pause, unable to bring my eyes up to him. I scuffed my boots against the grass. "I'm afraid of how I feel and the emotions that I harbor inside me. Afraid I have no true control and might not be capable of what I'm supposed to do. I don't even know what that is! What if I become like them?"

He moved closer, kneeling before me and taking my trembling hands in his. His blue flames wrapped around mine.

"Through all the darkness we've faced, I believe you can find the light needed to bring to the surface. You're light, and they are darkness. Don't be afraid of that power, Ellowyn. Embrace it, even if you're afraid it may consume you."

Ivarison's eyes lingered on me, my reflection staring back from his piercing gaze.

"We will do everything possible to stand with you, every step of the way. Fighting both the physical and mental battles." Dealla's voice came from behind Ivarison as she approached with Delaney at her side.

"Did my mother send you to talk with me?" I asked, rubbing my nose.

"No, I came on my own and found Delaney along the way," Dealla replied, her lips pursed as she tried to smile.

"You will always be more than enough," Ivarison said, searching my face. "We are with you, *Princess* Ellowyn. You're more than any of us could hope for and have."

Tears escaped as I looked at the three of them and Bria, who bowed her head.

"*We stand together to the end, my dear Little Spark. I believe in you.*" Bria declared.

If our time traveling through Madora had taught me anything, it was that I was stronger than ever and capable of handling the inevitable. I had a dragon connection because she believed in me and saw something I hadn't seen in myself. There had to be a reason for everything we'd endured.

Unable to drift to sleep, I walked through the cloister to find Bria lingering on the grassy hill as the sun began to rise. She looked up at me and Carwyn, the distance obvious as he never came closer to Bria.

"She won't bite," I said as he positioned himself further away from Bria's tail.

"I don't recall promising that," Bria said, turning toward Carwyn with a lazy snap that caused him to flinch.

"Unless I ask her to or you anger her, of course," I corrected myself.

"Would you like to fly?"

"Are you trying to get away from him?"

"I've stated before that I don't believe you need a guard when you're with me."

"I'll return shortly, unless you care to join?" I asked Carwyn. Bria glared over, standing taller as if daring him to accept the offer. He gritted his teeth, unwilling to leave his post. "I'll return shortly then."

"Princess Ellowyn," Carwyn called sharply.

I didn't listen. I jumped into the saddle, and once I had latched the last strap, Bria was in the clouds before Carwyn could object. Loose strands of my hair whipped through the air as we soared above the castle, circling over the village as the villagers began to wake. Sunrise gleamed against Bria's dark scales, and as I brushed my hands against them, a roar sounded behind us.

Ivarison was in his beast form, large wings cutting through the wind to catch up with us.

"Couldn't sleep either?" I called out. Bria flapped a wing at him. He dodged it, climbing higher.

"Be nice!" I reminded her, laughing. Ivarison said nothing as he returned to her side, watching as if waiting for another strike.

The horizon painted itself in yellow and gold hues as the sun climbed. I closed my eyes, spreading my arms wide, feeling warmth hit my skin. My lips curved into a smile as my arms rose higher, like wings, feeling as if I were flying alongside them.

Through the mountains of green that lay behind the kingdom, a tall waterfall reflected the gold of the sky. Bria flew across the pool of water at the bottom of the waterfall, her talons playing against it as water splashed back at Ivarison.

I laughed as he dodged the water before Bria let out what sounded like a muffled laugh with me. There was a warm buzz moving through me as we began to fly through a field, and the pink and yellow flowers waved in the wind.

This was my home. I finally felt like I belonged.

Such beauty in every direction. If I had the chance to fly with Bria every day, I would do so. I could never grow tired of seeing this world.

As we made the flight back to the courtyard, the village bustled with early morning chores. I spotted Carwyn where we left him, arms crossed. His eyes darted from Bria to Ivarison as we landed. Ivarison shifted back to his Fae form.

"Princess Ellowyn," Carwyn growled, the muscles in his jaw clenched as he moved closer. "You've been gone half the morning."

I pushed my wind-beaten hair from my face as I slid from Bria's wing. "I have said it enough times: I don't need a guard," I snapped, stepping toward him.

Ivarison lingered back, wings still visible before they slowly faded from him.

"It's not my place to make that decision. The king requested that I be your guard, and I must honor that. You're being foolish going off on your own."

Ivarison stepped forward, a sneer played on his lips as he narrowed his eyes at Carwyn. "Might I remind you that you're speaking to your princess."

Carwyn's teeth grounded as he retreated a step, clasping his hands behind him.

"Forgive me, Princess. We're being summoned. Your presence is requested at the barrier. Lord Arran and Lord Eirwen have arrived, and your mother is waiting."

"Where have you been?" my mother hissed as I joined her. Behind me, Dealla, Killian, and Carwyn stood in formation. Ivarison was near Keegan while Bria lingered at the back with the other soldiers at camp. Delaney stood with her winged guards and troops.

I shrugged, not bothering to answer as Lord Eirwen and Lady Serene approached. He extended his hand in greeting, his fingers cold as they brushed mine.

"Princess Ellowyn, how lovely it is to see you again so soon," he said, tilting his chin upwards to admire Bria with delight. "And lovely Bria, how is the saddle serving you both?"

"It's been a wonder. We've broken it in perfectly. I will forever be grateful that you had this made for us."

"The honor was mine."

"It's an honor to see you again, Princess Alina," Lady Serene greeted, approaching my mother. She and Lord Eirwen both bowed their heads.

"Thank you. If you wish, we can escort you to the castle – we have had rooms prepared for you. If you continue with Alix here, he will guide you ahead while I greet our next lord."

I followed my mother to welcome a male with beautiful bronze skin. Broody and incredibly handsome, his broad shoulders and bare chest showed through an ivory tunic with buttons undone just below his sternum.

"Thank you for coming, Lord Arran," my mother said kindly. "Having you return as a friend is something I appreciate greatly."

He bowed his head slightly to my mother. "I was requested, but I am honored that I am still welcome to the kingdom." he stared at my mother, his face stern. "As a friend,"

"Let's get you to the castle with Lord Eirwen. We would like to welcome our guests with dinner this evening so we can begin discussing the future."

We left the barrier and traveled through the village while Bria flew above. All eyes watched her. Some were still shocked that not only was there a dragon in the kingdom, but she was connected to their princess.

Lord Eirwen stopped to observe the children who watched our procession. He wiggled his fingers and snowflakes appeared, floating above his head. He blew them upwards, and they drifted over to the children. They laughed and giggled, trying to catch the snowflakes before they melted.

Chapter Thirty-Seven

The balcony curtains fluttered as Bria flew over. I watched her disappear behind the castle grounds, birds fleeing as she approached and tried to catch them.

The Lord and Ladies of Madora were gathered in Mystmere. Tonight's dinner represented a special occasion. It would mark my mother's and my return. As I got ready for dinner, anticipation built for the surprise about to unfold. King Everett had planned to make his entrance during this meal and announce his survival.

Knock. Knock.

"Come in," I called out, my fingers nearly shaking with nerves. The first official dinner as Princess of Madora. Before, it had been family and immediate court members. There had been no judgement. I wasn't sure that would hold true this evening.

Carwyn pushed open the door and remained in the doorframe, finding me staring at my reflection in the vanity mirror.

"I was asked to escort you to Princess Alina. She requested to meet before dinner began," he said quietly, his hands resting on his sword hilt, unmoving.

I tried to take a deep breath. "You can come in. You don't have to stand there with my door open."

I glanced at the necklace my mother had left me, sitting in its black velvet case. The silver chain held pearls and a small blue pendant at its center. Carwyn's feet shifted as he entered and shut the door.

"Princess–" he began, but I stopped him.

"Please stop calling me princess. Call me Ellowyn, at least when it's just the two of us. I don't want to get you into any more trouble than I already have."

"Of course." His hands returned to their position as his silver eyes watched me, and he coughed. "I was spoken to about your ride this morning and your trip to the mountains."

"It wasn't my intention to get you in trouble, I'm sorry," I said, turning in my chair to face him.

"I understand your frustration. I'm sorry there is nothing I can do to change that, but I want you to know that I'm on your side." His voice was low, his head slightly bowed as he gazed through long lashes. Just for a moment I forgot he was my guard.

I realized I had been holding my breath and let it out. I took the necklace from its case and held it against my chest to fasten it.

"Thank you," I muttered, dropping the velvet box on the vanity and taking in my reflection as I stood.

As much as I loved the kingdom's beauty and finding home, being here as a princess was an adjustment I needed to master.

One of the maids had come to help with my hair and dress before Carwyn had arrived. She had pulled loose strands back and let the rest fall in soft, curling waves. After taming every unruly baby hair, she secured it with a jeweled comb in the back.

The dress I wore was designed with sleeves that ended at my shoulders, flowing down to a square neckline at my chest, and leaving the back open to expose my shoulder blades. Small dark gems embedded at the center of my stomach that twinkled like stars. The silk draped to the floor in blue that matched my magic, fading from the jeweled center to white at the hem.

"Y-you look radiant," Carwyn said with a stutter. As I glanced over, he averted his eyes to the ground.

"Thank you. Let's hope I still look composed after dinner." The pressure building in my chest made me want to hide in my room. "I suppose I should make my way before any more trouble finds me."

He nodded, opening the door and stepping ahead before allowing me to exit. The tension between us began to shift. I didn't mind having him follow me as much anymore.

My mother stared at a portrait as I entered the parlor outside the hall. Beyond the door to my left, I could hear our guests arriving, muted conversations as they waited.

"Where is grandfather?" I whispered, noting his absence.

"We will enter first and thank everyone for their arrival, then announce him. It may not be wise to have him appear immediately. I just need you there for support," my mother spoke without detaching her gaze from the portrait.

"You wouldn't want me to say the wrong thing, now, would you?" I snapped, and she finally looked at me.

"Now is not the time."

"It seems that it will never be the time."

"I know this is not easy for you; it hasn't been easy for me either. It's been an adjustment since returning." She paused, not elaborating further.

"Yes, but if you had prepared me for this life, things might be different. You won't even talk to me. We haven't discussed anything since *I* rescued you." My eyebrows drew together. "You kept me away, but I still found my way back. I was the one who found you and rescued you, and now it's like we're back at the cottage, but we are here instead! Now, I know more!

"You know how many times I've been asked how you even grew Rike-root away from the Riker Tree? What secrets are you hiding? What are you not telling me?!"

Her hands clasped in front of her olive dress, lips pressed so tightly they went white as she closed her eyes. "I didn't know what to do, Ellowyn! I still don't! We lost everything in moments from one ignorant decision. We must enter this dinner united and show the royal family lives. We must let them see we're well and prepared to fight for them."

"Shouldn't we be asking them to fight this war *for* and *with us?* My existence is the very reason we face this war."

She bit her lip, chest falling and rising with heavy breaths. I shook my head and gestured forward.

"Lead the way, Princess Alina."

Her eyes flashed with hurt before she walked ahead into the hall.

Dealla and Killian stood by the entrance. My grandfather had offered them seats at the table, but both declined, feeling it would be inappropriate as guards. Carwyn stood at another post near my empty chair. Chair legs scraped against marble as everyone stood to welcome us.

Delaney sat with her parents, the three dressed in matching pale blue attire. Her gray eyes brightened as she grinned and mouthed, "You look beautiful!"

"Welcome to Mystmere and our home," my mother said warmly. My mother motioned me to the chair to the right of the head of the table as she took the one on the left. "It has been some time since we've all gathered in one room."

The seating arrangement didn't go unnoticed.

"I'm sure you all have questions," my mother stated as she sat down and motioned for us to do the same. Lord Durin sat closest to her, taking in her pale complexion.

"Indeed. We met Princess Ellowyn and had the pleasure of hosting her in our court while she searched for you. I've also had the honor of meeting Bria," Lord Eirwen spoke, his voice filled with curiosity and determination. I sent a nudge down the bond to Bria. Though not in the room with us, I could sense her listening to every word.

"Unfortunately, Princess Ellowyn seemed to know very little, as we did," Lord Eirwen added. "Why weren't we able to enter Mystmere, and who protected it while you were away?"

"Perhaps we should address this directly," my mother proposed. "I'm honored you would dine with us as war rapidly approaches. There is much to discuss, which is why I hoped for you to join us now."

I remained in my seat as my mother stood, her serious expression moving across each face.

"Lord and Ladies, this evening is not only about Princess Ellowyn and my return." She looked at Dealla. "Dealla, if you could, please?"

Dealla turned on her heel, entering the parlor we had just left. My stomach dropped into a fiery pit of anticipation over what was about to occur. Dealla was gone only a moment before returning to her guard position. Alix entered and poised in front of us.

"I would like to welcome my father, King Everett," my mother said, nodding to Alix. The room went still, as if all the air had been sucked out. Every eye shifted from my mother to the male who had entered the room.

My grandfather stood tall, green and black robes falling past his knees, his chin high as he walked to the head of the table.

"Welcome back to Mystmere. I'm truly honored you're here and able to join us," he said with a faint, blissful smile. My grandfather stood at his chair while shocked faces stared back.

Lady Celia's hand covered her chest as she looked at Delaney, disbelief and confusion washing over her features.

Lord Eirwen didn't miss a beat. "Ha! This is absolutely wonderful."

"While the rest of your land has suffered, attacked, and destroyed, you've been alive this entire time?" Lord Arran spoke through gritted teeth.

Lord Durin stood from his chair. "Now you come forth because your daughter and granddaughter have returned?" He turned to face Delaney. "You've known that our king has been alive and didn't tell us?"

Alix stepped closer to the king.

Ivarison stood from his seat, daring others to say more, faintly, dark shadows were escaping his fingertips. "King Everett has his reasons for protecting Mystmere with a barrier. If you'd sit and be proper guests by shutting your mouths, you may learn of those reasons–" he cleared his throat, "now, or I can be honored by helping with that."

"Thank you, Lord Ivarison." my grandfather said, raising his hands for Lord Durin to return to his seat and Ivarison's shadows faded. The maids entered, pushing trolleys of food and drink.

"There is much to explain, and I hope you will help us in this war. If you're sitting at this table, you're an enemy to King Ciaran and Queen Adriane. They will not stop until their enemies are destroyed alongside this kingdom, or we annihilate them."

Mixed meats, vegetables, and potatoes were placed at the center of the table. Wine and water arrived in pitchers as the maids began serving, filling our plates. The aroma was divine, making my stomach growl as I waited to dive in.

"Please, eat. I'll get to the point of what you would like to hear," my grandfather said before sipping wine from his goblet. "Seventeen years ago, we requested Queen Adriane and King Ciaran to the kingdom as they traveled through Madora, attacking locations and massacring our lands and families.

"They were after the kingdom and our Riker Tree. Wanting Madora because they had stripped their own lands bare, leaving nothing but wasteland and death. They orchestrated an attack on our home by poisoning us and using Riker blades to render us powerless. We lost Queen Amelia that day–" he looked over at my mother and me, "and Evander and for some time, what we believed of Princess Alina and Ellowyn. It's a miracle I survived, but Alix protected me before they could finish me off."

No other sound filled the room as my grandfather spoke, not touching their plates as they listened carefully. My heart raced at the story, remembering sitting on the throne room floor at my mother's feet. It had been quiet when the screaming began as I watched my grandmother fall, blood covering her dress, her arm reaching for my grandfather, who'd fallen beside her.

"Ellowyn, slowly breathe in and out." I nearly jumped, hearing Ivarison's voice. He sat across the table, and I stared into his blue eyes. I blinked several times, following his breathing pattern. *"You look very beautiful."*

I could feel the heat grow in my cheeks. He gave a small smile before returning his attention to the king, while Keegan watched from the corner of his eye.

"My recovery took time. I was vulnerable, having barely regained my powers when I raised the barrier for protection, preventing them from returning in search of the Riker Tree. The Riker Tree is a power source flowing through Madora that Adriane and Ciaran must never find. Alix and the rest of our guards had managed to push our enemies from Mystmere before its location was discovered, but we lost many lives in doing so."

"Why keep your survival secret instead of revealing you had not perished?" Lord Arran asked, his voice clipped.

"You could have given others hope," Lady Serene added, not sharing her mate's enthusiasm. "I have seen hope lost in the eyes of others, Fae and creatures, who've lost homes and loved ones. They suffered, and you could have changed that."

My grandfather breathed deeply, his lips pursed, knowing well that chaos raged beyond the barrier. "My life wasn't what mattered. There's a reason Queen Adriane and King Ciaran began slaughtering halflings."

Keegan frowned. "Do you speak of the prophecy told ages ago?"

My mother placed her palms on the table. She slid her eyes to me as she recited the prophecy that had plagued our lives the day I was born. "Long ago, the witches foretold our land's fate: Two shall rise in shadow to claim dominion over all lands, but their reign shall be sundered by one born between worlds. There lies the fate of all, to restore what was lost, or watch all fall to endless shadow." It was the first time my mother had spoken since my grandfather entered the hall.

A shiver ran up my spine. Everyone in the room hung on every word my mother spoke. And ever so slowly, their eyes shifted towards me. I swallowed the bile that threatened me as I bounced my foot. I tilted my chin up, doing my best to project a noble expression or what a princess should look like.

"I will be Adriane and Ciaran's downfall. I cannot fail, or they will take everything from us." I tapped my fingers against the table in fury as my voice carried through the room. "They have already taken enough. We cannot let them take more from us."

Battles were coming, and I wasn't sure I would truly feel ready. I had to believe I was more than capable, or I would fail. Hells, after centuries of believing a Sleroka could not be destroyed, I had done just that. If I was capable of such a thing, I could take down two dark Fae.

The room fell quiet. My mother's sacrifice hovered in the air as I watched her stare around the table. I was thankful for Dealla's loyalty, coming to find us after my mother fled. She was not just a guard, but family.

"I understand why you believed secrecy was necessary, King Everett," Lady Celia spoke, rubbing the bridge of her nose with closed eyes before continuing. "We cannot deny we would also do what was necessary to protect our own court. We have kept unwanted visitors from Luminara for this reason. What the other Lords and Ladies do not know is what I witnessed when Princess Ellowyn and her companions arrived in Luminara; what I saw from Dealla when I touched her, and what Princess Alina sacrificed to save Ellowyn."

After another paused, she looked at Delaney and squeezed her hand. "I'm with our kingdom. I'm with you, Princess Ellowyn. I will support you until the end, should this be it."

Delaney squeezed her mother's hand back, admiration shining in her silver eyes, but Lord Durin stared blankly at the words of his lady.

"You should lower the barrier. With the soldiers now stationed in Mystmere, it is well protected. If they come, they will see us, and we will have the chance to strike." Lord durin stated, fingers brushing his chin. "It could give us an advantage."

"That is a foolish mistake," Ivarison snapped as Lord Arran nodded.

"They will come if you lower it, or they will continue destroying villages."

"I'll consider the request," my grandfather said as Delaney watched her father, though he refused to look in her direction.

Each Lord and Lady slowly voiced the same agreement, understanding, and having their king restored to Madora. Together, our courts and kingdom would fight as one united force. Light would triumph.

It had to, and I would make sure of it.

Chapter Thirty-Eight

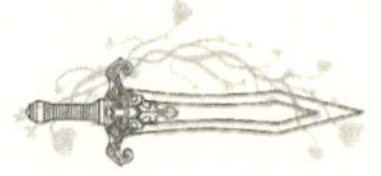

The barrier was lowered around Mystmere, despite objections to the decision. With the barrier down, Mystmere was visible and prepared, and the King was ready to begin our fight. Each of Madora's courts stationed themselves around the perimeter, prepared to fight at any given time.

Where soldiers weren't positioned alongside the border of Mystmere, they were sent through Madora, scouting for hidden soldiers or signs of Adriane and Ciaran from the mountain. Each day brought waiting for an attack, causing restlessness. Bria sensed trouble lurking nearby, but each time it seemed to come from a different direction. Whenever we flew reconnaissance, nothing was found. Not even another sight of a dragon.

Soldiers paced as we waited. My grandfather and mother stayed occupied with war strategies. While the sun hung high, Bria and I flew at the highest altitude I could handle, rolling through clouds as we tried to distract ourselves. It was peaceful, with cool clouds and the sun peeking through. Then Bria and I dared to fly past the mountain where Dark Soldiers had camped. I held my breath, staring below as Bria tilted for a better view.

Once occupied tents now sat vacant, some falling off their poles as canvas flapped in the wind. The thousands of soldiers once scattered across the mountain, gone. Fearful, Bria flew quickly back to Mystmere.

Where had they gone? How had they disappeared without our own soldiers spotting them?

"They're gone!" I breathed out, pushing open the heavy doors. My grandfather stood at the table's edge with Alix, the map of Madora, and the lords.

I hadn't stopped running since I jumped from Bria's saddle, rushing through the castle with Carwyn trailing behind, complaining that I had left again.

"Ellowyn–" My grandfather turned to face me. I could see my pale stricken face reflected in his eyes. "What do you mean, who's gone?"

"The Dark Soldiers. Tents were abandoned, and there wasn't a soldier left on the mountain." I said in one breath.

His shoulders tensed. "You went back to the mountain?" I held back my wince down as he peered over my shoulder at Carwyn. Ivarison and the other Lords stood still, listening.

"I was with Bria," I blurted, "Carwyn came with us and stayed in the clouds. There wasn't a single soldier remaining."

"*I don't recall him being on my back,*" Bria rumbled, but I shooed her off.

My grandfather turned to Alix and the rest at the meeting. "Send soldiers out immediately. We must find where they've gone. If they're on the move, they are planning to attack. We must prepare."

My grandfather dismissed the meeting as he walked closer to me.

"You left the kingdom again," he muttered under his breath, mouth twisted in a frown. "Do not think for one moment that I believe Carwyn accompanied Bria and you on your flight." He glared at my guard before leaving the room, Alix following.

Ivarison was the last to leave, studying Carwyn with pursed lips.

"You better be careful," Ivarison muttered, beginning to grin. "Next time, take me with you again. At least I could fly with you if Bria won't let me share the saddle." His voice lowered as he spoke, "Bring me the Rikeroot from your satchel. It's time we did something with it." With that, he also left the room.

"You shouldn't have done that, Princess." Carwyn whispered. He stood several paces behind me. "I could've accepted punishment. I believe you're safe with Bria and you trust her."

"Oh, he is smart after all," Bria remarked, pleased at his compliment.

"Ellowyn! Ellowyn! You must wake up. ELLOWYN!" Bria's voice roared. I rubbed my eyes, looking around the dark room. Near my balcony, her roars vibrated the windowpane and against my ears. I jolted upright from my bed, cold stone hitting my bare feet.

"Bria?" I asked, my voice hoarse and my eyes burning and blurred as I tried to wake fully.

"Soldiers are approaching Mystmere. It won't be long before they're here— Maybe before sunrise. I can warn others at the perimeter. You need to alert everyone in the castle. NOW!"

The exhaustion consuming me vanished. I rushed to dress in my leathers, sword, and dagger at my hip as I fastened my belt. Once I pulled my hair back from my face, Carwyn was at my door, eyes wide.

"I heard Bria and figured you may be trying to leave," Carwyn said, looking down at me, then back at my face. My shoulders tensed, and I could smell the lingering scent of fear in the air. "What's wrong?"

I explained what Bria told me, knowing we needed to move quickly. He left to warn Alix and my grandfather while I went to wake Delaney and Ivarison.

Ivarison's room was closer to mine, and I didn't bother knocking as I entered. My thoughts were in such a frantic state that I wasn't thinking clearly as I rushed through the middle of the night. Ivarison lay in the center of his bed, asleep.

He was beautiful even in slumber, dark hair partially covering his face. I noticed bed sheets were the only thing covering his naked body, his chest and legs peeking out. I stopped admiring the sculpted form before me.

We did not have time for this.

Stop it, Ellowyn.

"IVARISON!" I shouted as loudly as my dry throat allowed. I backed away, afraid he might attack while waking. "WAKE UP, WAKE UP!" I pushed a wave of magic from my hands toward him, afraid to physically touch him.

I pushed another as he began to stir, grabbing at the air with blue flames of his own, nearly setting his bed ablaze.

"Ivarison," I said more calmly so he could hear me. "Bria woke me and told me soldiers are coming toward Mystmere. We must move."

He didn't speak as he rushed from bed. I wouldn't dare peek as he moved, moonlight giving his skin a silver sheen as he hurried toward the closet.

"Ready?" He asked, fully dressed, with his sword at his hip. "Did you happen to enjoy the view?" He smirked as he opened his door, and we rushed down the corridor.

Not trusting my words, I ignored him. But my face betrayed me, flushing intensely as he went to wake Delaney. Once we reached my mother's chamber, she was already awake and moving with Dealla and Killian.

Time stood still since Bria had woken me. I could sense Bria's warning as she flew past soldiers' tents, her urgent roar warning the entire camp before they understood her cry and hastily prepared.

Our soldiers moved through the village, going to homes with warnings and instructions; barricade yourselves inside and don't open until ordered otherwise. Dark Soldiers were coming, but what those soldiers didn't know – Mystmere was ready for a battle.

The air thickened with anticipation. Fires were doused to keep the light dim. We stood under the stars with their meager illumination. Bria hid in the shadows of the woods behind the camp. When I looked for her, I could only see her golden eyes staring back at me. Her dark scales kept her invisible in the darkness.

Sunrise wasn't far as the night grew heavy and movement became scarce. No one dared to speak. We watched the horizon for what felt like hours before hundreds of soldiers slowly became visible, approaching silently, believing they had the advantage of surprise.

"Ellowyn," Bria growled quietly. I stood with my companions as my mother remained quiet at my side. My grandfather stayed at the castle for this fight. This was only the beginning, and if Adriane and Ciaran weren't in this battle, it was not the time to let the rest of Madora know that he was still alive. *"Get in the saddle. Let's surprise them as they tried to surprise us."*

"We should just light them on fire," I suggested, knowing Dark Soldiers would do the same to us, given the chance.

Was this what our lives would become? Waiting for attacks while we slept, until our entire army or theirs was eliminated? It made me miss the quiet cottage.

"There are too many. If I scorched them all, I may harm some of our own. Fire at that magnitude could become uncontrollable. We could try to take a few without risking others."

I left the line, some soldiers watching to see if I was retreating. Being Madora's princess, I needed to act as one, as my grandfather claimed. I was connected to a dragon, and if I wanted to battle on the back of her, I would.

The air felt still as soldiers drew near. Alix stood at the front with Carwyn, giving quiet commands. Their raised shields cast shadows in the night to avoid detection. It was only moments before the battle would begin.

It was easier to see from my position in the saddle, with a higher vantage point from Bria's back. Without the glint of moonlight and stars, we would have no way of knowing what was upon us.

Alix put a hand up.

With a flick of his wrist, war shouts erupted. Metal clashed against shields, and fires ignited. All at once, everyone charged forward. It didn't take long before Dark Soldiers hit the ground, some scattering in different directions, shock filling their faces.

Bria hadn't moved. No one knew she prowled by the trees, waiting for some to come closer. One by one, soldiers began falling. Screams echoed in my ears, and the stench of blood was overwhelming.

"Let's go," Bria spoke. Soldiers were close, and she took the opportunity to flap her wings and ascend. They balked, fear in their eyes as they watched the dark dragon soar through the air. I didn't need to guide her as she slashed through soldiers with her tail spikes and crushed others. The sound of bone crunching underneath made my stomach turn.

She roared as a large arrow came for her, missing by inches. Somewhere in the darkness, an archer was hiding and aiming for her.

Bria flew higher into the clouds, making it harder to target her as she moved with such speed that soldiers couldn't track her with the cover of the night. We blended into the darkness and would use it to our advantage.

We were night itself. Clouds covered the moon, and shadows surrounded us as we neared soldiers.

"*Ellowyn, where are you?*" Ivarison reached out, his voice breathless as he fought below.

"*On Bria! I'm safe.*"

I looked below, searching for the archer, seeing only bodies scattered where the barrier had been. Hundreds of soldiers had come, but where were the rest? This was only a fraction of what we had seen on the mountain.

"I can't see anything!" I called out to Bria.

"*No need to worry, I found him.*"

There wasn't time to ask where, as her wings cut through the wind, her throat warmed, and she roared with such force that I thought I would be thrown from her. Looking down, I saw the platform where the archer had stood, now devoured in flames with dark smoke. Bria incinerated several other soldiers in her path.

A blast of fire came toward us. Bria pulled away, the flames missing me by inches but hitting her leg as she roared in pain. Her head snapped toward where the blast originated.

"Bria!" I cried out, looking to assess the damage.

"*I'll be fine, Little Spark!*" I could hear her wince as she shook her leg. "*Be ready.*"

Her fury rushed through wing strokes as she moved. When soldiers saw Bria charging, they began running, knowing they were about to meet their demise. Blood painted the ground as bodies of soldiers lay face-first in the dirt. What occurred beneath us didn't seem real once she finished with them.

"*Bria, take me down!*" I called out.

"*You need to learn to battle and fight while riding me.*"

There was no time to argue as we quickly formed a plan, targeting a pack of Dark Soldiers fighting against our own. Bria tucked her wings as she dove, turning to her side and forcing me to rely on leg muscles as I squeezed tightly, thanking the clips that held me in place.

Bria leveled out on her side. My fingers gripped Glaukos's hilt, and I struck the first soldier, my sword piercing through one and then another. They fell, blood dripping from Glaukos.

Again and again, we tore through the crowd of attacking soldiers. Looking for my family and friends, I worried as I hadn't seen any since the battle began.

A horn sounded, and Madora's soldiers began to cheer. Victory belonged to us. Though if it hadn't been for Bria's warning, the outcome could have been drastically different. Some soldiers would've been slaughtered in their sleep.

Bria landed as the sun began to rise. Dark Soldiers lay throughout the field while some of our own nursed wounds. Assistance had already begun for the injured as aides and healers walked the area.

"Only a few escaped." I heard Dealla's voice, speaking to Alix as they gathered.

"Bria and I could go after them?" I suggested with Bria's approval.

"No, there weren't many left. Let them be the ones to spread word of their loss. Mystmere won the battle they attempted as an ambush and failed." Alix said, watching the horizon as if he could see the soldiers fleeing.

My mother rushed forward and embraced me, confirming I was unscathed. Ivarison, Delaney and Killian joined, nodding to one another that we made it through our first battle of the war.

We were safe.

For now.

Chapter Thirty-Nine

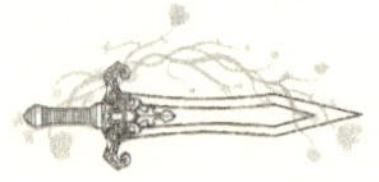

The morning, once our battle was over, was different than what I'd imagined. The aftermath stretched endless, soil painted red with blood, swords and broken shields scattered among arrows, all covered in dirt. Wounded soldiers lay helplessly, their faint cries cutting through the air, while others pushed wooden carts, bodies of the deceased piled together.

Even with cries of the injured and whispers of healers, everything seemed unnaturally quiet. Surviving a battle was one thing; witnessing the devastation was another. The sound rang in my ears. Some of Adriane and Ciaran's soldiers had carried weapons laced with Rikeroot, causing wounds far more severe.

My magic. My magic could heal the wounded. I stared at my hands, hoping they wouldn't betray me as they had done so once before. I pushed aside the doubt and took a deep breath.

There was a gaping wound that drew me to the male lying on the ground, blood flowing from his thigh as his hand kept pressure on it. Fae could heal quickly, but Rikeroot prevented proper healing as it lingered in the bloodstream.

"May I try to help?" I asked, not looking directly at the wound. The sight of so much blood made my stomach churn.

"Princess," he muttered through gritted teeth.

"I might be able to help. Could I try?" I knew I was capable of healing myself, and I had better control and understanding of my abilities. I had to try.

The Fae didn't answer as I knelt at his side and took his hands in mine. I shut my eyes, feeling his calloused hands beneath mine, warm blood and labored breathing.

"What's your name?" I asked, attempting to distract him from the pain.

"Malik," he answered with a sharp intake of breath.

Blue. Blue light danced in the shadows behind my eyelids, healing magic flowing as it had when I needed it most. Malik's breathing steadied, and a sigh of relief escaped him. I looked down at the wound, pulling our hands away from the gash as I watched it finish knitting together.

"That's incredible," Malik whispered as he pushed his upper body off the ground. He stared at the wound, watching the last drops of blood fall away from unmarked skin.

I helped nearly a dozen soldiers with various wounds before my body began aching and my eyes burned with exhaustion. Each healing took something from me, but seeing their relief made it worthwhile.

"You should rest, Princess Ellowyn," Carwyn said, standing behind me. His bloodied sheath caught my attention as I examined him for injuries, but he offered a gentle smile, "I'm unharmed, Princess."

"Other's still need help," I said, scanning the field where healers continued their work.

"There are other healers assisting," he said, extending his hand to help me up. "I watched you with Bria. You two were magnificent together."

"*Of course we were, sycophant,*" Bria said dryly. My eyes cut to her as I bit my lip to hide a smile. She positioned herself at the field's edge, staying close by.

Before I could respond, Ivarison approached, his jaw tense as he took notice of my hand in Carwyn's. Carwyn quickly let go once I was standing.

"I came to see how you were feeling," Ivarison said, shooting another pointed look at Carwyn before the guard stepped back.

"Exhausted. I'm thankful for Bria's warning," I answered, yawning.

"Yes, it wasn't the most pleasant wake-up call."

My cheeks heated, remembering how I'd woken him up and what the moonlight had revealed.

"You never answered my question when we left my room," he said, daring to glance at Carwyn. Was that jealousy in those blue eyes?

I smacked his arm and rolled my eyes, cheeks still burning. "Will you stop it?" I snapped. "I suppose I'll go back to the castle to rest." My eyelids felt heavy with the need for sleep.

"I'll ride straight to the castle with Bria. Please stay here to help," I told Carwyn as he moved to follow. I noticed my mother missing as I searched through the aftermath.

My entire body felt heavy as if I could sleep the entire day away. But not knowing where my mother had gone left me unsettled. I hadn't seen her since the end of the battle.

I walked through the castle's corridors, following voices that carried from a distant hallway. I found my grandfather and mother sitting together in what looked to be another parlor.

I found a new room each day that I was here.

"It's entirely my fault. She still has so much to learn," my mother's voice carried, stopping me at the doorway. "How can we place this burden on her? Isn't there another way?"

"Alina, it was prophesied centuries ago by the High Witch. The vision from the Riker Tree only confirmed the prophecy's truth. As much as I wish it were not her, we must have hope." My grandfather spoke softly.

"I won't lose her. I won't." The desperation in her voice made my chest tighten.

I was the chosen one. Only months ago, I'd discovered my true identity. My actions alone in this war could determine the survival or destruction of Madora and my family. What a terrible thing to have resting on one's shoulders.

The constant reminder of who I was and what I was supposed to do made my chest tighten and shoulders tense with the weight of expectation.

"We must do everything possible to prevent that outcome. I will not lose you both again," My grandfather continued.

My hand covered my mouth to stifle the sob I felt building. Such loss over seventeen years. The pain of not knowing the truth, of losing everything. My grandfather lost his mate, his daughter, son-in-law, and granddaughter in a single day, then remained trapped in Mystmere.

"You should have seen her riding Bria. Dealla trained her as best as possible, but seeing her in battle was different.. The way she was today and when she pulled me from the prison... She's different now, and that frightens me," my mother spoke, her words saturated with pride despite her worry.

"How so?"

"You can sense her power. She felt like the strongest presence on that battlefield today. I've never seen her like that before." My mother paused, and I could hear the tears in her voice. "She looked so much like Evander when he fought. Fearless. But I'm terrified that fearlessness will be what destroys her."

I pressed my back against the wall, tears sliding down my cheeks as I listened. My mother was proud, but terrified. For the first time, I could see the weight that she had carried through the years, not just the burden of keeping me safe, but the knowledge that my very existence meant I would one day have to face this destiny.

Chapter Forty

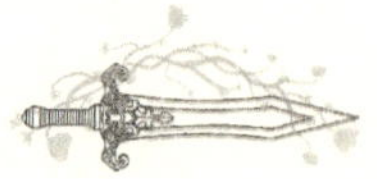

Unsettled dirt marked the remnants of our first victory through the field. The kingdom waited for signs of Adriane and Ciaran, but nothing came. A waiting game that caused tension throughout Mystmere.

I continued practicing with Ivarison as a way to keep both our minds focused and away from what could be happening outside our borders. Ivarison pushed harder each session, working on convincing me I was capable.

"Wait," he called out after practice. I turned to see him holding out a jar. "Your Rikeroot. Dip all your weapons in this. It will be absorbed, coating your weapons so when you strike, it will cause further harm. Be careful with this and tell no one you have this, keep it hidden." He whispered.

My hands brushed against his as I took the small jar filled with what looked to be fine powder.

"Thank you," I said breathlessly. His hand lingered, then he turned and left.

It was a warm afternoon, and I shared a quiet lunch with my mother in the courtyard. Bria flew away to give us privacy while my mother remained lost in thought.

"Will you ever actually talk with me?" I asked, picking fruit from the plate as we sat at a round table. My mother's head rose to meet my gaze;

setting down her glass of lemonade, condensation dripping as I watched it fall.

"We're speaking now," she said, leaning back in her chair, looking everywhere but back at me.

"About father. Our escape from the kingdom. The secrecy, the memories you stole from me, how you grew Rikeroot at our cottage," My voice stayed low, though anger still burned beneath the surface. I'd kept it caged while running for my life and searching for her throughout Madora, but now it looked for ways to escape, and I struggled to contain it.

"Deep breaths," Bria advised. *"Anger will not serve you."* I followed her counsel, while my mother continued to look away, her chin lifted as she sniffled and bit her lip.

"I don't think I can yet," she whispered. "I'm not ready to discuss what happened in the prison – what they did, what I saw." Her hand moved over her lips as she rubbed her face. "One day, I'll tell you everything I can about your father. How wonderful he was and how much he loved you."

I left lunch before Carwyn could follow, needing solitude. I didn't mind his presence anymore. When we were together, we conversed easily now. He had taken me on walks through the village, giving me tours of places he enjoyed.

Near another unfamiliar corridor close to the library, I heard muffled voices. I recognized Ivarison's immediately. Peering around the corner, I saw him with Keegan in a room, drinks in hand. When they began talking, I pulled back, pressing my spine against the stone wall and making sure mental shields were up.

How did I keep stumbling into private conversations?

"Just admit it, Ivarison. You've at least developed feelings for her," Keegan said with a huff. A glass clinked and liquid poured.

"Drop it, Keegan," Ivarison growled, his chair scraping against the floor.

"She's gotten under your skin, hasn't she? Maybe that cold, black heart of yours will beat once more."

"She's the princess, Keegan. I've been protecting her because I want her to survive. She deserves that after everything she's endured."

"I don't think that's all, and you know it as well as I." Keegan paused. My back remained pressed against the wall, my eyes closed as I listened.

"I've been spending time with Delaney, getting to know her. She's shared some interesting details about what happened during your group's travels."

"Oh, and how is *your* mate?" Ivarison asked.

"She's magnificent." Keegan chuckled. "I could spend every moment with her, and it wouldn't feel like enough. But don't change the subject. She's told me things."

"What does that have to do with anything?"

"You've been protective of her since the moment you met. Don't forget, I know you well, Ivarison. I may know you better than you know yourself."

Ivarison growled as glass shattered. "It doesn't matter, Keegan. There is nothing in this world I deserve after what I have done! I won't force anything to be accepted."

Accept what?

"Ellowyn," Bria said softly. I nearly jumped out of my skin. *"What am I going to do with you? You shouldn't be eavesdropping on their conversation."*

"You shouldn't be either!" I snapped, trying to steady my breathing.

Bria was right. This was private, and Ivarison wouldn't appreciate knowing I was listening.

"You'll never know if you don't try," Keegan said, breaking the silence. "You deserve more than what you believe. We all do, and we will find it one day."

There was a pause between the two males, and I could hear their hearts racing from both being tense.

"Tell me, Ivarison. Will you return home after this? Where is home for you?"

Ivarison didn't immediately answer, then I heard a weary sigh. "Anywhere that smells of amber and honey," he muttered.

I pushed off the stone wall, leaving as quietly as possible. Why would he think so poorly of himself? He tried – he was trying to be better. I collided with something solid as I turned the corner. Carwyn looked down at me, annoyed that I'd once again slipped from his watch.

I smiled, trying to push the conversation between Ivarison and Keegan from my mind as I left with Carwyn in the opposite direction.

"Something is happening," Bria announced. She had stayed close to the castle, afraid to venture far. For days, her senses felt disrupted, magic drifting differently through the air. Even the ground was quiet to her.

How quickly that changed.

Midday, Mystmere's horns went off, signaling spotted soldiers. This was what we had waited for as we watched the horizon, and they began appearing.

My grandfather remained hidden with his soldiers, concealed by a cloak and hood. When the time was right, he would reveal himself. Perhaps it would give them a moment of pause.

Row after row, Mystmere's soldiers stood in formation, awaiting battle. It was intimidating to see so many of us assembled. Lord Arran commanded the east side with his court, while lord Eirwen was stationed in the west. I stood with Bria while my mother positioned herself ahead of me and

Ivarison to my left with his court behind him. Lord Durin's winged guards formed legions in the sky, watching as Dark Soldiers crossed the distance.

The large field stretched open before us, some of Mystmere's woods nearby where Bria and I waited. I could see the group of Fae marching in dark armor, their swords clanging against shields they carried.

"Be prepared for anything, my Little Spark. This may be our final test. Something still doesn't feel right to me," Bria said, shifting her feet, golden eyes wide as we watched.

The air shifted as Dark Soldiers advanced. Darkness filled the field, not just the temperature that Bria could sense, but something more sinister. Oxygen felt sucked from the surface, and the ground was turning black. Creatures began emerging from the shadows amongst the Dark Soldiers.

Norwags.

They moved faster than average Fae, could slash through flesh effortlessly, and were disturbing to look at. Soldiers backed away, unnerved by the sight of them.

"There are so many! Can you do anything?" I asked Bria urgently, seeking comfort for my pounding heart. It raced, feeding the heaviness in my stomach.

"Not without taking many others into the flames. You might be able to. You can control and direct fire in ways I cannot when I breathe it."

"I could hurt someone just as easily. What if I can't do this?"

"It is too late to be doubting yourself now!" Bria shouted just as more shouting began.

"Take your mark!" Alix hollered, his voice echoing down the formation. Following the line, I spotted Delaney with her father, then Carwyn beside Alix, who stood in front of me. Dealla and Killian stood together opposite where my grandfather and mother stood.

Ivarison moved closer to me. "I'm staying near to help protect you. You pull those bastards from the shadows and destroy them. You *can* do this."

I nodded. I should've known he would be listening, causing me not to feel so guilty about overhearing the conversation between Keegan and him.

"We'll both be there," Carwyn said, his expression grave as he looked at me, then back at the soldiers.

I could hear hearts racing, blood pumping as swords began clattering against shields. My grandfather walked ahead, putting himself at the front line, and threw off his cloak, revealing his face.

Some of the soldiers looked surprised seeing the King before them. Others appeared disgusted and truly prepared to fight and kill.

"I, KING OF MADORA," he shouted, thrusting his sword above his head before bringing it to his chest, "Order you to stand down from this attack or die. This will be your only chance to surrender yourself before you begin a fight you shall not win!" My grandfather's voice roared across the hills.

Not one left their ranks. The Dark Soldiers stood united with Norwags at their sides. I rocked back and forth, dirt crunching beneath my boots, the only sound I could focus on. Not the snarls from enemy soldiers or hissing from the Norwags. Not the beady black eyes of creatures watching through shadows, waiting to be unleashed.

They would not win.

I felt the ground vibrate under my feet as Bria towered over our soldiers, the trembling intensifying. Her shadow enveloped those standing close. It did not stop the Norwags or Dark Soldiers who charged toward us, swords raised, shouting, and screaming. Yet somehow, amid the chaos and horror, I felt calmness rise within me as I reached for Bria.

Battle broke out in an instant.

Swords clashed. Norwags shrieked as they slashed their way in, but our kingdom held their ground, standing stronger and pushing them back.

I reached for the power between Bria and me, like a rope that pulled and bound us together. Our magic collided, and I felt the roar sitting in her throat within my own chest. Dragon power merged with mine, beating heavily and aching for release as my heart pounded with anticipation.

The growing power was frightening. My hands and arms glowed with a blue aura as we became one. Mystmere's soldiers kept clear of us while Carwyn and Ivarison fought to prevent Dark Soldiers from reaching us.

My palms rose as Bria took flight, her talons and tail striking and hitting targets. I couldn't see where my mother and grandfather had gone. I couldn't afford to worry as our battle commenced.

I reveled in our power, something that could easily lead me astray if I wasn't careful. I moved faster than ever before and roared as if all our kingdom's strength flowed through and out of me.

I wanted the soldiers to fear us, to fear me. To understand they'd made a catastrophic mistake attacking Mystmere, my family, my friends. As I engaged several soldiers, blood dripped from my sword, which now contained Rikeroot powder.

One of Adriane's terrifying creatures lunged. What should have been fingers were blades. One wrong move and they would slice through my flesh.

Carwyn and Ivarison were still nearby, Ivarison shifting between his beast form, using it to grab and hurl soldiers as far as possible through the trees. I could hear bodies crack against bark and thud as they hit the ground.

It was the creature and me, face to face. There were no eyes to meet, only blackness like deep tunnels in the underground prison. A raspy sound came from its mouth, waiting to devour me as I took my stance.

I reached for Bria, her power still surging, needing to know she was still flying above. Thousands of soldiers appeared to be beneath her. There on the sidelines of Dark Soldiers, archers stood ready to aim with large arrows. They had no time to react when a loud rumble came from her throat.

All that was left of them was ash.

My hands shook as rocks beneath my feet vibrated, power surging up through me, exploding through my veins. I focused on the Norwag, narrowing my eyes. Sword in hand, I screamed and charged the creature. Gripping Glaukos's hilt tightly, the Norwag's claw tried slashing at my throat, but my sword met its head first. Magic poured into my blade with the next strike as I twisted away, letting it slice across its neck. Its gurgling screams rang in my ears before it collapsed.

Dark blood stained my front as I continued fighting. I wanted to search for my family, but I couldn't risk the distraction.

"Bria! Where are Adriane and Ciaran?" This battle had already gone on long enough, and I hadn't seen either of them.

"I cannot find them. I don't believe they're here."

Not here? How could they not be?

Bria's powerful roar shook the sky as the ground trembled with her landing. Dark Soldiers were crushed under her feet and wings. Ivarison and Carwyn continued fighting against the Dark Soldiers with ease.

I climbed onto her back, fastening myself just as she took to the air. I needed to locate the King and Queen of Ravenholde. Through the breeze, air cooled my heated skin. Before, smoke and ash filled the air amid battle cries as swords met throats, and the sound of flying soldiers' wings echoed. Soldiers blocked the village, preventing dark forces from entering.

I spotted Dealla and Killian fighting near the woods. Norwags at their backs along with soldiers, but nothing could stop the pair when they fought together. Lord Arran wielded a dark sword in his hand, swaying as yellow energy emanated from him, creating a golden blade that slashed through Norwags, making them screech just before incineration.

Lord Eirwen was further away. I could see him freezing soldiers as his sword crashed against their ice figures and shattered them into pieces.

But Adriane and Ciaran were nowhere to be seen.

"Bria, this isn't all their soldiers. We saw more on the mountain."

Fear filled me. Bria didn't speak as she searched. The mountain had been covered with their soldiers, and even with the fallen below, the numbers didn't seem to match.

Her wings spread wide as she climbed higher, avoiding an arrow that flew past. The higher she went, only her wing strokes and my heavy breathing could be heard. I took deep breaths, perhaps the first since our battle began.

"They are coming from the water." Her voice was urgent, and I had to squint to see as far as she could.

My heart sank before it lodged in my throat.

Ships.

They knew where the Riker Tree was.

"QUICKLY!" I screamed, I had to land. I had to find the others and warn them that Adriane and Ciaran were targeting our power source. Soldiers surrounded the village, but it wouldn't be enough to stop what was coming if they reached our sacred tree.

Chapter Forty-One

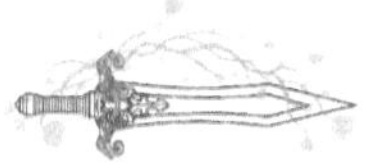

Bria landed in a clearing of her own making, Dark Soldiers crushed beneath her. Something she was growing fond of doing.

Ivarison and Delaney were the first I spotted once I leaped from the saddle, slashing at another soldier who came for me. Bria followed as closely as she could, swiping at enemies. The swish of her tail sent loose strands of my hair dancing around my face.

Delaney shifted back into her Fae from upon seeing me. Ivarison raised his hands, shadows seeping from him and pursuing Dark Soldiers nearby as their bodies lay in twisted heaps. It was gruesome watching the pair, Ivarison's power frightening, and Delaney's beast from only slightly less terrifying than her Fae capabilities. They could eliminate many Dark Soldier's, but there was no time to admire their brutality.

"Ivarison! Delaney!" I shouted, breathless as I reached them, keeping a ready stance in case others dared to approach us. "Adriane and Ciaran are on Mystmere's far side, coming from the water. I have to stop them. They're going for the Riker Tree." I spoke rapidly, yelling over the battle's chaos and surrounding screams. I couldn't find my mother or grandfather, but we couldn't wait as more and more soldiers closed in.

"I'll find King Everett and your mother. You go!" Carwyn called, approaching my side, his sword and leathers dripping in crimson. "We will be right behind you."

Aldric had soared above with several guards, grabbing and tossing Dark Soldiers groundward while others shot arrows at them. He descended and landed, leaving a crater in the dirt. He scanned Delaney's body for wounds.

"I'm fine!" Delaney said. "We must reach Mystmere's far side. Adriane and Ciaran are coming from there."

Aldric paused, biting his tongue. "Yes, my lady. King Everett and the Princess are ahead by the wood line, taking out those vile creatures. I can't locate your father in this mess. I'll search for the others to let them know."

"You can't find my father?" Delaney asked, but Aldric already returned to the sky, golden wings shining in the sun as she surveyed the carnage.

I didn't watch as Carwyn found my mother. I couldn't handle her reaction to learning where I headed. I needed to stop them, or Mystmere would meet its end.

Soldiers were stationed throughout Mystmere, but not many near the Riker Tree and docks. They had been in ruins and abandoned since the attack seventeen years ago.

I climbed onto Bria as I looked at my personal guard.

"Tell every available soldier to head that direction. We must move quickly. They've nearly reached land." Carwyn nodded and departed. I turned to Delaney. "Will you stay here or come?"

"I'll help alert others and head your way. Now go!" She transformed back and raced off. It was difficult to meet Ivarison's gaze as Bria's tail swept aside more soldiers.

"Typical. The princess thinks she's the only one who can save everyone." Ivarison snarled, the claws of his beast form swiping against a Norwag that tried to approach.

I rolled my eyes. "Try not to miss me too much while I'm saving the kingdom, then."

"I'm not leaving your side. I'll fly with you," Ivarison declared.

"I'll be with Bria, help Delaney and Carwyn!" I finished strapping myself in Bria's saddle.

"No, I need to know you're safe, I would prefer to accompany you," he paused, his wings spreading wide from his back. "I'll fly with you."

I could only nod as he then shifted to his magnificent beast form and Bria and he took flight together.

I couldn't look down at the battle below; the damage below was too much to bear. Screams faded as we ascended, Bria's wings flapping hard while the soldiers followed, some shifting, others running.

I couldn't spot my mother, grandfather, Dealla, or Killian anywhere once I looked back down. My heart hammered in my throat as the enemy ships came into view.

The hair on my arms rose. Ahead, Adriane's dark mist swirled ominously while Dark Soldiers waited for the King and Queen's commands. The soldiers we had stationed there; gone.

"Bria," my voice was sharp, "burn them."

"*With pleasure.*"

Her neck shifted as she adjusted, her belly growing as she inhaled deeply and released a terrifying roar and stream of fire against the front lines of the Dark Soldiers that had hit land. They hadn't even had a chance to scream.

The remaining Dark Soldiers had pulled back, regrouping further from shore, but it was temporary. They'd advance again soon, and in greater numbers. Adriane's mist was already reforming, darker and thicker than before.

A large beast flew toward us, its shape resembling that of a bird, with a beak and feathers flowing in different shades of blue, gray, and silver. My eyes widened as it landed, and my mother shifted with my grandfather nearby. I jumped from Bria as Ivarison shifted to his Fae form at my side. His eyes filled with desperation as he looked at me. I couldn't bring myself to keep eye contact any longer, afraid that this would be our last moments.

"We have minutes at most," Ivarison said, scanning the enemy forces. "They're waiting for reinforcements from the ships."

That's when his fingers found my face, tracing my jawline, gently guiding my chin back to look at him. The weight of minutes, at most, hit us. His blue eyes glistened and danced as he stared into my soul. Unfolding every thought, the troubles, fear, and adrenaline flowed through me as I gulped. My fingers curled into his leathers as I stepped closer.

There was fear. So much fear that my breathing caught. This could be my last moment with Ivarison and with everyone around me. I'd hardly lived, hardly seen Madora, and what my life was supposed to be. I wasn't ready for it to end as I looked around. Chills ran down my arms as I stared back at the male before me, wanting to know more of him.

The one who helped me believe in myself. Who saw me.

"I'm afraid," I whispered, noticing the dark mist traveling with growing numbers of Dark Soldiers.

"I won't let you face this alone." He gripped my hand tightly. "I will follow you into the darkness, Ellowyn. I'll follow, and if we can't escape, I'll die with you. Remember your light – you're the light in my darkness."

A lump formed in my throat that I couldn't swallow away, "Ivarison." My voice broke as I looked down at our clasped hands, both covered in blood.

"You deserve to live. Survive this," he whispered. His thumb brushed away my tears, and for a heartbeat, the world narrowed to just us. His eyes held mine, and his touch anchored me. I wanted to memorize this moment, this feeling of being seen being loved, being –

"Ellowyn!" My mother's cry shattered the intimacy. She crashed into us, weapons still in her bloodied hands, and suddenly, I was drawing in the weight of everyone I might lose. Ivarison's hand found mine behind my mother's back, squeezing once before letting go.

"I can't let you go," my mother sobbed against my shoulder. "I can't."

The words I'd longed to hear, now breaking my heart. I looked over her head at Ivarison, whose eyes promised everything we'd never have time to say.

"I know, I know." My mother sobbed as I called for Bria. Our minutes were running out. "I just can't bear to lose you."

" I don't want to die," I admitted, but none of us would survive if I didn't end this. "I will survive this."

"You are Ellowyn Kelgrove," my mother began, gripping my face in her palms as her weapons fell to the ground, lips quivering. "You're the daughter of Evander and Alina. Chosen by the Riker Tree and prophesied for reason. You're stronger and braver than anyone I know, just as your father was." She took a breath, eyelashes wet. "You're so capable, I wish I had recognized it sooner. I have faith in the gods that you will survive because you have so much more to live for."

"*Breathe,*" Bria said softly. She was right, I had stopped breathing.

If I couldn't make it through this, I would go down fighting for the sake of those surrounding me. I smiled at my mother, pulling her hands away, and climbed back on Bria.

"Stay safe. I love each of you," I said, looking over them. "Take care of each other." I had to know they would if I didn't make it.

"I have faith and believe in you. Be careful, Ellowyn." my grandfather said, walking closer to Bria.

The mist near Adriane's soldiers' formation grew thicker. Her figure appeared with what looked like a white panther forming and sitting at her side, nearly as tall as her in height, as Adriane's slender hand ran across its fur. She looked ahead, directly at me, grinning.

"No," I stuttered, my heart feeling like it stopped breathing. "No!"

That couldn't be Delaney standing with her, the same female who had been at my side for these past months, who had fought alongside me, winning my trust and friendship. But I hadn't seen her since I left the battle at the border of Mystmere.

I felt sick. This couldn't be real. Bria began growling.

"Ellowyn–" Ivarison shouted, but I watched as the panther began shifting into a Fae – a male. Lord Durin stood at Adriane's side.

"I'll kill him!" A familiar female voice brought instant relief, drawing me back to the present. Delaney, Dealla, and Killian, and Keegan pushed through our soldiers to join ranks with my mother. Delaney's face was red as she nearly sobbed. "I knew it! I knew he was up to something," she screamed as her father looked her way. Keegan stepped up, holding her arm gently as if afraid she might charge.

It wasn't Delaney. It wasn't Delaney.

"Ellowyn," Delaney said roughly. "I saw him in the mist with the Sleroka in Mornwind. He planned this. His disappearances. He was the one who suggested lowering the barrier!" I glanced at her father as the knowledge of what needed to be done hit me, her fragile voice breaking. "He caused this, he doesn't deserve to live for what he's done."

I couldn't kill her father. My heart raced as memories of my own father running through black mist flashed through my mind. Ivarison looked at Delaney, understanding where my thoughts went as she covered her mouth, hiding escaped sobs.

My mother, grandfather, Dealla, Killian, Delaney and Ivarison. They were who I fought for, along with Madora. We were together, and this wasn't where our story would end.

Bria ascended before anyone else could speak. Adriane vanished, leaving Durin with the soldiers. Bria flew to the clouds, climbing higher for a better view before diving down to search for Adriane and Ciaran.

Soldiers from both sides began charging. Bria dove through a crowd of Dark Soldiers, twisting to her side, talons lashing as I swung my sword and attacked multiple enemies from the other side.

"Get me closer to Durin," I shouted.

"*Are you sure?*" Bria asked. My hesitation was for Delaney, but we knew he had to be stopped. He'd persuaded to lower the barrier and revealed the Riker Tree's location. She knew my answer, finding him back in his beast form and diving toward him.

As we descended again, everything accelerated. Delaney and Ivarison were nearly side by side in their beast forms, fighting toward the same enemy I approached, determined to carve through the hordes of Dark Soldiers. Their roars echoed with Bria's as they swiped and killed every enemy that opposed us. Shadows seeped from Ivarison, choking every soldier they could reach. Keegan battled farther down, fighting more Dark Soldiers as he tried to reach Delaney.

Bria and I were moving closer, almost at Durin's side, but we were not the only ones. Delaney made it to her father first, back in Fae form and ready to deliver a killing blow. One she would never forgive herself for, no matter the betrayal she felt.

I ignored the sounds filling the sky. Battle cries, swords clanging as screams of the injured rose. My eyes caught sight of ground covered in red stains, a shade I would never view the same, flowing like a stream. My thighs clenched tightly in the saddle as Bria twisted through the crowd of soldiers once more. My hand glistened blue with flames, and for the soldiers I couldn't reach with my sword, I pushed my palm forward, guiding the blue fire to engulf them.

Wind blew against me as Bria dove, keeping soldiers from the village. I glanced around to see my mother fighting with Dealla and Killian. Ivarison and Keegan were near each other, close to Delaney, taking down soldiers as she faced her father. Her battle cry echoed as their swords clashed in the unfolding scene. Delaney's sword met her father's. She had the upper hand, and for a split moment, the chance to strike a killing blow. But hesitation flashed across her as she stared her father in the face.

She couldn't do it. She couldn't thrust her sword into his chest as panic filled her, realizing her mistake. Her father wasn't loyal to her and he was going to kill her. As he began gaining an advantage, he faltered, limbs going rigid as blood swelled across his leathers. Delaney gaped as Keegan appeared from behind Durin, pulling his sword from Durin's back.

Durin fell in a heap. Delaney's eyes widened as she gripped Keegan's arms, collapsing as he caught her, and I could read the apology he offered.

Before I could process it, a flash of black caught my attention. My eyes darted over to see Adriane, farther from her soldiers, nearing the Riker Tree's path.

No. She couldn't reach it.

Just as Bria was about to dive down and intercept, she cried out in agony as I felt pain rush down our bond. Adriane grinned as she watched and waved. There was a howling noise down the sloped area by the entrance.

Ciaran.

He stood with hands extended, gripping a large arrow. I could see a second arrow already embedded in Bria's back leg. Ciaran's hands circled as the howling began again, his body turning as he released the projectile. The arrow rushed past us, just missing.

"Bria!" I cried out, wanting to heal her. "You must land away from him before he shoots again!"

The landing was rough as she tried to avoid putting pressure on the injured leg. She swiped at soldiers with her tail as I unfastened from the saddle, rushing to her back to pull out the arrow. Her roar turned to a scream that filled the sky like thunder. Her tail thrashed at soldiers.

I tried to pull again, my hands wrapped around the wooden shaft. I pulled and she roared, then I found myself thrown onto my back with a scream that could have blown my eardrums. I rolled in the dirt, quickly enough to miss the swipe from a Norwag that tried to slash my flesh open.

I spun, grabbing Glaukos. The Norwag released a horrible laugh and spat at me.

It gained on me as I waited for another strike. Warmth in my arms traveled down my hands as my sword burst into flames. Bria twirled, keeping weight off her injured leg as Dark Soldiers surrounded her. Iron chains were thrown over her body while I dealt with the Norwag.

"NO! BRIA!" I screamed. Bria tried attacking, snatching several soldiers in her mouth with a sickening crunch as she attempted to incinerate others. As she did, her fire weakened and vanished from her throat.

"Who would've known that Rikeroot affects dragons the same way!" Adriane screeched. I could see spikes connected to the chains, blood dripping. "Why won't you die?!" She looked at the Norwag. "KILL HER!"

I stood still, knees bent as I waited. The Norwag bolted and jumped, sharp fangs coming for my face, and I struck. The screams bounced through the sky as it rolled. Adriane left in a hurry as she dashed to the Riker Tree's path. I hesitated, seeing Bria completely wrapped in iron, body pressed down to the ground, her wounded leg unable to lift herself.

I seethed. I screamed. My Fae canines were sharp against my lips as the injured Norwag came for me again. It jumped as I feigned right, then swooped left and pierced Glaukos where its heart might once have beaten. Black blood oozed before its body collapsed.

"Go, Ellowyn! I'll free myself!" Bria roared, I didn't want to abandon her like this.

"No, we work together!"

My knuckles turned white as I clenched them, watching the battle play around us. My ears rang with clashing metal, beating hearts, and warrior cries. Ivarison, Keegan, and Delaney had fought their way in, starting to battle toward me.

Carwyn was closer, fighting through the Dark Soldiers, one by one. Blood dripped from his leathers and sword.

"Help her!" I demanded of him when he found me through the carnage. "That's an order, soldier!"

"Ellowyn," he snapped. He took a hard stare at me before he let out a heavy snarl, his sword swaying against others as he went toward Bria.

"Go, Little Spark. You must stop her before it is too late." Bria said, her voice soft as I found her gaze, and we stared at one another. I wouldn't allow myself another moment to consider. I rushed after Adriane, stopping for nothing. The arches that had created the path to the Riker Tree burned as vines and flowers shrieked in flames.

"You won't win this!" Adriane shouted as soon as I entered the clearing.

The tree glowed in beautiful orange light, water beneath shimmering and flowing with color. Long vines hung from the tree, brightly illuminating the space and moving in an invisible wind. But Adriane hadn't moved closer to the tree just yet.

She wielded her sword, trying to strike. I moved just in time to block as she attacked repeatedly. Each time I blocked, her frustration showed. Eyebrows furrowed as she tried laughing, as if this were merely a game. A game she wasn't winning as easily as she expected.

"Little child. I've existed far longer than you." She laughed, the noise making my shoulders tense. "Don't worry. I'll let you suffer and kill you slowly."

She moved again. "I could let you watch as I kill everyone you love. I'll start with your mother. After that, Ciaran will make sure the king is truly dead, and I'll hurt you most with your ma–"

"LIKE HELL YOU WILL!" I exclaimed, exhaling deeply as I darted from her strike. Piercing sounds of metal filled the air as our swords collided. Feeling the magic, I let it wrap through and around Glaukos. I went for Adriane as my power bursted forth like lightning.

Adriane wouldn't fight fair. She screamed, striking with such force that my feet dug into the dirt. Our crossed swords pressed against our chests. Her sneering smile appeared between the blades, eyes shining. She truly believed she would win.

Adriane may have had raw power, but she didn't have my training. I'd learned from one of Madora's finest. She relied too heavily on her conjured creatures to learn how to truly fight.

My magic wrapped around my sword, emerging in blue fire. Adriane could feel it as I began to flow in green and blue. Around us, the others fought closer. Delaney, Ivarison, and Keegan carved through enemies while my grandfather battled Ciaran, wings blocking wind strikes. Chains rattled through my bond with Bria as she tried breaking free. Carwyn and other soldiers with her trying to help.

"I have more than just a kingdom to fight for," I snarled, and drove my power through our locked blades. Adriane flew backwards into some of her own soldiers who came. Her sword fell from her hand, dust circling as it landed on the ground.

Adriane rose, fury radiating as she shoved aside her own soldiers. Her eyes went black, palms skyward, and shadows poured from her hands. She was pissed and did not care that it took her own soldiers down.

"*ELLOWYN!*" Bria's roar came with rattling chains that hit the edge of my mind.

The Riker Tree swayed furiously as a conjured mist enveloped us.

"NO!"

Ivarison.

I spun toward him as Bria's anguish flooded our bond – then nothing. Darkness slammed me to the ground. Blood filled my mouth. My hands tightened around Glaukos, determined not to let go of my sword. In the darkness, a hit struck me, and I was down again. Pain burned and radiated at my side as I stood, feeling the gash on my abdomen, while something gripped my ankles, preventing me from moving.

Sleroka. Adriane was gone.

"Pathetic that you must hide in the shadows because you can't manage this yourself!" I screamed. If I provoked her enough, maybe she would come. I gasped, pressing my palm on the wound, blood seeping between my fingers. Blue light pulsed from my hand as flesh began mending.

"How very clever." Adriane's voice came, sounding deeper and darker. "I should've known you would inherit your grandmother's ability. Just so you know, I enjoyed stabbing and watching her take her last breath. Maybe that is what I'll do. I'll let your mother live so she can find you when this is over."

I could hear faint roars and cries from Bria. I could sense Ivarison pounding the barrier, trying to break through the darkness surrounding me.

My sword lit as I stared down at black shadows, wrapping like vines around my feet. I squinted, adjusting my eyes to the darkness as I searched for the Sleroka and Adriane. Then I found Ivarison pushing and pushing through the mist, his skin ripping and healing as he moved.

"NO!" I cried out at his agonizing roar. The darkness whirled and tried to swallow him. He was on his knees, hands digging in the dirt beneath him as he moved, pushing himself forward and crawling toward me.

"Ellowyn, no!" His cry shook me to my core as I found his blue eyes, brightening my magic to see him.

Oh, those blue eyes stared back, and in that moment, they were all I could see.

"I told you. I'll pull you out or die with you," Ivarison said, pulling himself off the ground. The Sleroka tried to strike, but Ivarison was faster to move. I shot my hand up, creating a barrier to protect him.

There was rumbling ahead, and I ducked as Adriane emerged, trying to strike while I was distracted. My ignited sword met her blade as she pulled back, hiding in the darkness once more. Ivarison was there, trying to move closer but unable to move through the darkness that wrapped around him.

I couldn't let him risk himself after all that happened. Adriane and Ciaran had taken so much from both of us.

"Take my hand." his voice broke on his words. "We die together."

Blood streaked his face as he reached for me, fingers trembling. I couldn't breathe. Couldn't think. Those eyes held everything we'd never get to say.

My chest cleaved in two. His pale skin, blood glistening from his head to his battle leathers. His hand still reached for me as my barrier protected us from the Sleroka again as it pounded against it.

I leaned toward him. I reached for my power, ready to burn everything around me so he could move through the mist.

"Thank you," I whispered, reaching toward him until our fingertips almost touched.

His face transformed – from confusion to understanding to horror. "Ellowyn, no–"

"I'm sorry," I sobbed, slamming my power against his, shoving him beyond the mist. "Live for me."

If death called for me, I wouldn't be afraid. For my family, friends, for Ivarison? Losing him was now one of my deepest fears, and I was not ready for such a thing.

I couldn't dwell on the thought that he may never forgive me for using all of my will to push him free from our darkness. Out of the mist we were in.

And just as he was there, he was gone.

Ivarison was gone.

His anguish slammed against my mind. Raw, desperate, furious with Bria's roaring cries. Both tore at the darkness, trying to reach me. I could not bear it as I threw every mental wall I could, cutting myself off from their love, their terror, their refusal to let me go.

I closed my eyes, and lowered my barrier, and embraced the darkness. My flames flowed through the blade as I listened.

The Riker Tree. I sensed it calling me. The power moved, and it needed a place to go.

Alone in the crushing dark, I knelt, pressing my palm to the earth and whispered, "This is what you made me for, isn't it? Please, help me be enough."

The ground trembled. Power stirred.

"Yes." I heard a female voice. Faint, soft, like a dance through the wind.

I focused on each sense. Crunching dirt to my left. My hair blew in a soft breeze as I twisted and struck my sword true.

The Sleroka released a horrifying scream. I grimaced as it pierced my ears. I punctured through its putrid flesh. Warm, thick blood poured over my hands.

Through the silence, Ivarison's voice echoed: *You're the light in my darkness.*

I closed my eyes, feeling power rise from the earth, from the tree, from the very heart of Madora.

Light. I would be the light.

Chapter Forty-Two

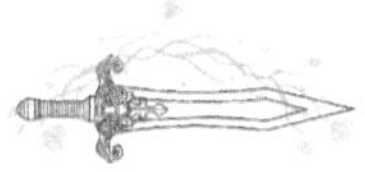

My sword slashed what felt like stone. The wounded Sleroka lunged again while Adriane kept hidden, waiting for her creature to finish what she'd started.

Glaukos shook in my grip, my arms aching from its weight. Adriane came from the darkness to strike, then disappeared before the Sleroka took another swipe, its razor claws grazing my leathers.

They attacked in succession, trying to exhaust me. It was working. My body ached, slowing with each parry. The moment I faltered, either would gain the advantage.

My mind drifted to what my life might have been like. Our cottage, seventeen years of memories now reduced to ash because of this creature and its maker.

My skin warmed as I listened for movements, reaching for the Riker Tree, for the goddess within. I tried blocking the mental pounding from Bria and Ivarison.

The hair on my neck rose, sensing an attack. My skin began shining, becoming the light Ivarison told me to be.

I twisted away from the Sleroka's slashes, breaking free from the restraining mist. I moved as if I danced across the battlefield, my growing light making the Sleroka flinch. Its black mouth gaped, revealing sharp teeth.

I was unafraid. A battle cry tore from my throat, leaving it raw. I threw my weight behind the sword, slashing through leathery skin as blue flames burned through flesh.

The creature dropped with a heavy thud, its mouth still hanging half open.

Adriane's mist began faltering as I searched for her. She stood in dark leathers that made her eyes appear heavier, darker like the shadows she fought in. Her piercing stare held a cruel smile.

Oh, she was pissed.

"I may not have accepted it immediately," I snarled, meeting those soulless eyes, pulling my feet free the mist that held me, and stepping toward her. "But I am Princess Ellowyn Kelgrove. I will not bow or fear you. You've taken everything from me. And I will not stand for it any longer." Thank the gods my voice held steady.

Adriane stepped into the ring created by her mist, showing herself. I gripped my sword, ready for her next move.

"*Bria?*" I called through the dissolving mist, seeking connection for what needed to be done.

Her roars echoed around me. I raised Glaukos as Adriane stalked closer. The darkness diminished, light breaking through and exploding, demolishing the remaining of her dark walls.

Adriane's overconfidence was her disadvantage that I could exploit. As she swung, my sword rebounded with power, lightning rippling through the blade and striking her. She was thrown through the air, crashing into a copse of trees, knocked away from the Riker Tree.

The battlefield surrounded us. The stench of blood and sound of clashing metal ricocheted through the trees. Banners lay trampled and torn, still clutched in dead hands. Soldiers fought desperately to break through the darkness that had trapped me.

I spotted my mother standing and protecting a fallen figure, my grandfather. Hands pressed to his abdomen. Ciaran was gone, but I could sense him close, lurking through his wind magic. There he was, walking in front of me. Foul hatred and smugness played across his face, approaching for the kill.

He was frightening.

Then he disappeared. My eyes darted, searching. My heart pounded as I tried to catch my breath.

"ELLOWYN, BEHIND YOU!" Bria roared, trying to blast flames from her throat, knowing very well she was too far. Chains were still around her as she tried to break free.

"ELL! NOW!" Ivarison shouted. My mental shield dropped for him as he tried to break through. His face went pale when he found me, shifting to Fae form.

Something else seized control of my body. I ducked from Ciaran's sword. He retaliated, his fist slamming into my jaw. Pain radiated through my skull as I stumbled back. I thought I heard my mother screaming, but my vision blurred, and I couldn't find her.

Ciaran was determined to end this now. Because of me, they hadn't achieved their goals in two hundred years. His sword sliced the air as I moved, grazing my skin before I hit the ground.

His hand curved as if to choke me. Pressure closed around my neck, cutting off air as the tip of his sword touched my throat.

Death had arrived.

Warm blood trickled down my throat as I stared death in the face. Death was no longer something to fear, but to welcome as an old friend. I knew what the Riker Tree demanded.

"Bria?" I called out to her again. If her voice were the last thing I heard, I'd be at peace. Her soothing tones could put me to sleep.

"I'm here with you until our end." Her voice trembled. Chains clanked as she struggled, blood streaming from the spikes that held her down. I was not ready for our end, but I would accept it if others survived.

Tears fell down my cheeks as I surveyed what was left of the battle. Bria crushed soldiers as she fought against the chains. My mother and Dealla moved like deadly dancers, protecting my grandfather. Killian in wolf form, shredding soldiers.

Delaney, with claws and a sword, blood-covered, Keegan fought to reach his mate and keep her protected.

Then there was Ivarison. He was in and out of his beast form, hands extending power as shadows danced from him, crushing anyone who approached. He was coming for me, but soldiers came from every direction.

Blood dripped from countless swords. Time felt suspended, silent. Ivarison found me, his sudden roar of panic filling the skies as he saw Ciaran's blade at my throat. He was screaming as he tried to make it through the soldiers.

"Bria," I whispered. Her eyes closed as her power merged with me. My shoulders rolled as her roar filled my chest. The ground shook as I focused on our bond, my hands pressed against the earth. Brightness flowed from under the Riker Tree, vibrating the earth, toward me.

I closed my eyes and breathed. Was this what dying felt like? I saw a female before me. Her golden blonde hair flowed in the wind. Her entire body was glowing. Her white gown shone with light, a silver belt of beads under her breastbone. She offered her hand to me, lips curved upwards.

"Focus, and be our balance," she whispered, her voice sounded like a soft melody.

My eyes shot open. The female had vanished. I focused on the momentum I felt. Ciaran would be first. He pressed his sword deeper into flesh. I would go to any end to stop my kingdom's destruction, even if it meant going with them.

More power came. Darkness. It came through the cracks of my mind and soul. Ivarison channeled strength to me, a soft nudge through our bond. My skin nearly burned as my surroundings were set on fire.

The power shook my core, a source I had never felt before. Darkness engulfed me, but I would not fear it. I was the light, and the fire running through me would burn this darkness away.

I could no longer hold onto the pain in my bones. I couldn't hear anything over my screams, the fury I felt for these two who'd caused so much death and loss. My family. Asher and Xantara. So many more. All the halflings that had been destroyed.

My eyes narrowed on the male before me. I ripped my sword as my barrier wrapped around me, his sword crumbling up to the hilt. Fire pushed out, wrapping around the rest of my sword, traveling to his hands until he released me and dropped what was left. I rose from the dirt, my feet inches above ground as fire continued growing around me like a rope.

"It's only fair that I don't offer a chance for you to surrender, since you weren't going to do the same for me," I said in a voice I didn't recognize, booming across the battlefield.

Everything within me sprang forth. I lifted my hands toward Ciaran. Adriane appeared from where I had thrown her, her mouth opened in a scream I could no longer hear as she tried to rush for Ciaran.

I spread my arms wider as blue, white and yellow flames poured from me. I pushed out my palms, trapping Ciaran, letting those flames explode like lightning.

Ciaran gasped, trying to grab me, eyes widening as his jaw unhinged. He clutched at his own throat with burning hands.

More screams. I realized they came from my raw throat. Power ran through my very soul, nearly blinding in pain. Dark Soldiers that were close by burst into flames. I was determined not to let this end until I watched Ciaran fall to his knees. His golden skin turned a pale gray as the edges of his face began to whiten. Eyes still wide, he stared, forever burned into my memory, and he began dissolving. His entire body turned to ash, ceasing to exist as the wind from the Riker Tree carried away his remains.

I turned to nearby Dark Soldiers, raising my hands as they tried to run. My flames were quicker.

Everything around me burned as my skin turned blue. My hands fell to my chest as I gasped for air, feet returning to earth. I tried filling my lungs while the ringing in my ears subsided.

Adriane's black hair ruffled from Ciaran's death wind, her horrifying screams stopping others to witness what had happened. She reached me, fists finding my jaw as she swung repeatedly, knocking me down.

"You're next," I said, grinning at her with blood on my teeth. I knocked her off, finding Glaukos while trying to fill my desperate lungs.

Adriane's eyes glistened as I blinked, clearing my vision, and the flames covering my body faded. I refused to feel remorse for what I'd done to Ciaran. For all they had caused, for everything they had taken.

"I'll kill you," Adriane screamed. "I will kill everyone that you love!" Her voice rose to a higher pitch as she attacked with such force that my ankles nearly gave out as I blocked the strike.

I huffed, "You've been trying for some time now, but haven't been doing a very good job," I said, wiping the blood from my mouth.

Again and again, she struck.

Bria roared, trying to break free. My mother, Carwyn, and Killian were back at her side, striking the chains.

"HELP HER!" My mother cried.

I felt exhaustion hit. My body was screaming from fatigue. I tried calling for Bria or Ivarison, but the bonds were muted.

Attack after attack, I blocked. I twisted, seeing over her shoulder, Ivarison in beast form, blocking a fatal blow meant for Delaney as Keegan rushed to her. When Ivarison turned back to Fae, shadows rippled from his arms and shoulders, eyes darkening.

He stepped in front of Delaney and Keegan, wings opening around them protectively. Both ducked as he slapped his hands together, and corpses of soldiers fell to the ground.

Adriane slowed, stumbling as she frantically tried pulling back the darkness I had destroyed. The monsters she'd created vanished, erased, no longer hers. She screamed, realizing what I had taken.

Her eyes darted through what was left of the battlefield, her soldiers facing defeat. This was the end. She had lost. She stepped back as I lifted my sword, tip pointed with blue flames.

It was my turn to be the predator.

"I'll find a way to kill you." She threw her sword at my feet as mine came for her. "Don't worry." She flashed a sly grin as the ground rumbled. "I'll find a way to see you again. I promise."

Just before I swung, Ivarison and Delaney rushed toward us. Bria's chains broke, and she bolted skyward to cross the battlefield. Adriane wouldn't stand a chance once either of them reached us.

"You won't get another chance." I gripped Glaukos tightly, swinging it over my shoulder to strike. But before the blade made contact, she vanished.

"NO!" I screamed as Bria landed. The Dark Soldiers, realizing their Queen had abandoned them, fled. Bria chased after them, her mouth and talons taking out as many as she could get.

"Ellowyn!" My mother's weight crashed against me as I stumbled backwards. "You're okay. You're alive. We're alive." Her eyes watered as she pulled my matted hair from my face.

"I thought she could only fade with the mist!" I shouted, but Delaney was rushing over.

"Your grandfather," Delaney said as she and Keegan neared. My mother and I rushed to where the king rested, Killian and Dealla knelt beside him.

He coughed as my mother sat and brought his head to her lap.

"I'm so happy you're both home, and that I was able to see you again," my grandfather said, voice breaking as he winced, hands pressed to his chest. Blood seeped from his ribs as he coughed, crying in pain. "You're just like your grandmother, Ellowyn."

I fell to my knees, hot tears running down my face. He took hold of my hand and gripped it weakly.

"No, no," I cried as his grip began to falter. We had reunited after being apart for so long. It couldn't be time to say goodbye again.

"Ellowyn." My mother's voice came out strained. I knew she would tell me to let go, try to pull me up. To let him die with his soldiers. His wound was deep across his chest. "Ciaran stabbed him with Rikeroot. It reached his heart."

"I have to do something." My hands shifted from blue to green, colors engulfing my fingers as exhaustion weighed heavily.

I focused on the wound slashing from his chest to abdomen. If Ciaran's sword came from the Riker Tree, I had power from the same source. I could heal this wound. He had to survive.

I worked around the wound, stitch by stitch, restoring the magic with his veins.

"Ellowyn." Ivarison whispered in my ear. I could hear myself crying out as I worked to pull the poison from the wound, vision blurring with black spots. My head pounded as I tried to remain focused.

"Ellowyn, you're going to harm yourself," Bria said, but her voice sounded distant.

My body vibrated, hands burning as I tried to heal the wound. My grandfather's blood stained my hands, my teeth gritted as I shouted through them. My arms burned, as if sand was running through my veins.

My eyes shut as everything screamed and ached. My body was drained, and my bones felt like they were breaking.

Who was screaming? There was so much screaming.

Warmth. A gentle pressure on my shoulder.

Ivarison's hand squeezed my shoulder once more as his magic helped guide what I was missing. His hands traveled down my arms, calloused fingers brushing mine before he laced our fingers together.

I could feel his exhaustion, how drained he was as he connected with me again. His magic flowed through me differently than Bria's, and my grandfather's wound began sealing. I whimpered as my grandfather started breathing deeply. His chest began to rise and fall. I slumped as Ivarison held on, looking pale.

I watched my grandfather's eyes flutter open, wincing at the brightness. We had healed a Rikeroot blade wound. We had saved him. His hands came up to where the wound had been, searching for any trace.

It was the last thing I saw before blackness pulled, and I fell into Ivarison's arms.

Chapter Forty-Three

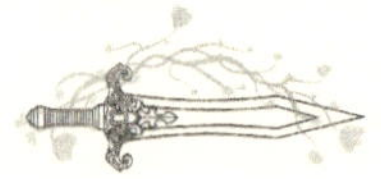

Deep, creamy sweetness of amber, leather, and wood. The calming scent enveloped me as I stirred awake. My fingers traced a soft surface, and relief swallowed me as I realized I was no longer on the battlefield.

My eyes adjusted to the tall ceiling of rafters above. I inhaled deeply, now catching the metallic scent of war on my leathers. I shifted in the bed, bumping into someone else. Ivarison. His eyelids twitched open, bright blue eyes adjusting to the light as he looked around.

"What happened? Where are we?" My throat felt like sand.

"Inside the castle. We must've both fainted." he answered with uncertainty, rubbing his tired eyes as he twisted onto his back.

"Ivarison," I whispered, closing my eyes to stop them from watering. Seeing him go through the battlefield, moving against Adriane's mist, willing to die so I wasn't alone.

"There is no need to say anything." He paused, closing his eyes. "Next time, perhaps warn someone before attempting to become a mystical light source, though."

But in his voice, I could sense there was more. Was it anger? Worry? I lay on my back at his side, lips quivering. I didn't want to start sobbing in front of him, but it felt nearly impossible after what we had just gone through. And Adriane had still escaped.

"Yes, I do. I'm sure it was reckless, but I had to try saving my grandfather too. Just as it was reckless of you to come through the mist, and for me to push you out. I'm sorry." I sobbed, hands covering my face. "I'm so sorry."

The mattress shifted as he moved closer. I looked up, hands still partially covering my face. His eyes darted over me, from my eyes to nose to lips. His hand rose with hesitation, finding my jaw and stroking my skin, sending those zapping sensations through me as my hands fell at my side. His thumb brushed tears from my cheeks.

"Ellowyn, love." His voice was raw and drained. "I will always choose you. To help you, and to give you whatever you need from me."

Another tear escaped from the corner of my eye as I smiled, holding his hand.

"We won, and you're the reason," he whispered. His face was so close to mine. I rested my forehead against his.

"It isn't over, Ivarison. Adriane is out there, and she's going to come back for me. She promised as much when I killed her mate." But today, I would not let the fear overpower me.

"You didn't die with Ciaran. I suppose that's something." He smirked, as he threw a hand up as if in surprise.

"You have such a way with words. Be still, my beating heart."

"If your heart stops beating after everything we've been through, I'm going to be very irritated."

Darkness flashed across his blue eyes, but the door burst open before he could say more. My mother and Delaney entered, hesitating at the sight of us. I jumped at their sudden appearance, and Ivarison's hand dropped.

"Way to ruin the moment," Ivarison said, his voice harsh.

"Is my grandfather okay?" I asked, realizing I did not know what happened after I fainted. Where was Bria?!

"Are you all right?" my mother asked, chest heaving, desperation in her voice as my eyebrows rose in protest. "He will be. The wound is healed. You healed him as if it were just a simple cut. Are you okay?" she asked again.

"Where is Bria?" I nearly jumped out of bed. "I'm fine. We just woke up. Where is she?"

"I'm here, Little Spark, and I'm doing well. I didn't want to intrude on what was occurring between you two." Relief washed over me when I heard her voice.

"She's resting near the courtyard. She is doing well." Delaney answered. "I was with her for a bit while you were resting here."

I felt as if my mind and body were fracturing. I pulled my knees to my chest and sobbed. I could still hear the rattling of chains wrapped around her, the sound of her fear when she couldn't escape. How I'd watched each of my family members and chosen family, battle and save one another.

Ivarison had saved Delaney. My mother, Dealla, and Killian had protected my grandfather. Keegan killed Lord Durin to spare Delaney the guilt of doing so. The trapped pain and remorse came pouring out. Delaney was pale, her gaze distant as she had to adjust and learn to live with the fact that her father betrayed their kingdom and her.

Ivarison rubbed my back before embracing me, holding me tightly as I sobbed in his arms. My mother and Delaney joined us, making Ivarison tense, which only caused me to laugh through my tears.

Bria sat quietly outside the tower of my room, her golden and purple flecks catching the light as I walked out to join her, unable to keep my emotions from showing.

"How are you?" I asked. Her head came closer, nuzzling against me as I hugged her.

"I am well, just as I was the other times you asked. My wounds have healed; my leg is well."

Her wounds hadn't even needed healers' help. Once the spikes and arrow had been pulled from her scales, she began to heal. I had been stuck in the castle, being checked over, and my grandfather and others were visiting. I hadn't been able to see Bria as much as I wanted.

"It's believable when I can see you with my own eyes." I did one more scan, confirming for myself that she was well. "I can never thank you enough for what you've done for me, Bria."

"I will not be ready to say goodbye to you for a long time. Do you understand? It's not your time to go."

"Well, what do we do now?" I asked quietly. Adriane's threat haunted me. And even though it was a waiting game, I could not stay here and dwell on it. Bria helped me on my search for my mother, and now it was my turn to help her.

"I hope to find others. I can still sense others out there." She paused. *"Don't worry, live this day in happiness, Ellowyn."*

"I love you, Bria." I said quietly. I placed my hand under her chin as I rested against the side of her face. "I appreciate you not burning me the day we met."

Light smoke escaped her as she chuckled. *"As I, you. I'm grateful I didn't either, although I considered it. How is the King?"*

"He is well, back to being the King and grateful too. He's trying to grant me everything and more for saving him."

I sat at her feet as she settled next to me. Talking to each other, learning things we failed to learn about each other before. She told me of different dragon species she had known of. I was determined to help her find others, sensing her loneliness without a companion of her own kind. If I could do anything for her, I hoped it would be this.

We walked through the castle, down a corridor to a spiral staircase. The air cooled as we descended further. At the corridor's end stood dark oak double doors. Carwyn opened it, revealing my mother standing with my grandfather.

"Ah, there you are!" my grandfather said, rubbing his hands together as his jaw tensed. "Both of you, follow me, please."

"What's this about, father?" my mother asked, glancing at me as her brow pinched together.

We followed him through the large room. Small trinkets lined the shelves while some portraits hung on the walls and others sat on the ground. I didn't recognize anyone in the portraits.

"Just back here," he said, taking us further.

Our footsteps echoed off the stone. Large items wore dust covers. Various jewelry hung from shelf hooks: diamonds, rubies, gems of different shapes.

"I have something I wish to show you both. I have wanted to for some time now. It never seemed to be the right time. Now I must, so I don't regret it."

My grandfather took another step, pulling a white dust cloth off a concealed item. It fell to the ground, revealing a large portrait of a beautiful female sitting on a throne. Her brown hair was pulled back in a diamond clip, looking so similar to my mother's and mine. Her eyes shimmered in the painted light.

Queen Amelia. I had only seen glimpses of her from the Riker Tree's memories and my own vague recollections.

"Your grandmother, Ellowyn," my grandfather spoke softly, sadness shone through his eyes as he tried smiling at the portrait. "She loved you both very much. She truly was magnificent, and I'll forever hold on to that. I wasn't afraid to die, knowing I would be reunited with her." He pried his eyes away and looked at me. "Your healing abilities came from her."

"She's beautiful," I said, stepping closer. It was hard not to wonder what it would be like if she had survived and stood with us.

"There is another portrait I wish to show." He took hold of another dust cover next to my grandmother's portrait. His chest rose before he pulled it off.

My mother gasped, hands covering her mouth, tears formed in her eyes as she inhaled harshly.

My mother stood in the portrait, holding a small child. Me. With bright green eyes and brown hair. She looked happier than I had ever seen her. It was strange to see myself so small, staring happily at the man beside us.

Such a handsome man. His golden hair and eyes shone brightly as he looked at me in the portrait. He was taller than my mother, one hand wrapped around her back, the other holding my little hand.

"This was your family portrait, painted just before the attack. It was finished after you left, and it was the only thing I had of the three of you. I often found myself standing here while you were gone, wishing for a miracle."

My mother's hand fell from her mouth to her chest, covering her heart. She approached the portrait, fingers grazing over my father's image. Evander. Her sobs bounced off the walls as she stared at our family portrait. Warm tears streaked down my own cheeks as I joined her, my arms wrapping around her shoulders in an embrace.

One of our last moments together as a family, smiling happily and enjoying our lives. Not knowing it would crash down only days later.

Chapter Forty-Four

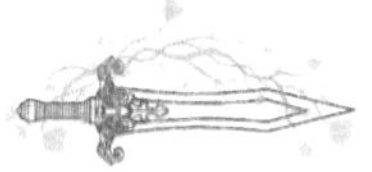

The kingdom felt different in the weeks following our victory. Where Adriane's shadow had once lingered, cautious hope now filled the courtyard of Mystmere. The courts helped restore what Adriane and Ciaran had nearly destroyed, though the memories of fallen soldiers and twisted creatures still haunted our dreams.

As visiting courts prepared to return home, a tentative freedom settled over Madora. Something we had missed for the last seventeen years. Adriane may be alive, but without Ciaran's presence, the fear felt different, manageable.

Others throughout Madora believed Adriane wouldn't stand a chance now that the kingdom stood united and the royal family returned. Lady Celia stayed longer than the other courts, hoping Delaney would return with her after losing her father. Without him, Luminara would need to adjust.

"Please return home," Lady Celia begged.

"I'm enjoying myself here and finally happy with where I am, mother." Delaney said, rubbing her mother's shoulders. "Everything will be alright, I promise."

"I'll keep her safe and take care of her. Luminara will be in good hands with Lady Celia," Aldric said, stepping forward. "With the journey you find yourself on, remember all you were taught, and you will do well. I'm proud of you." He tucked his golden wings against his back.

Delaney hugged her mother tightly, then pulled Aldric into the hug with them.

After their farewell, Lady Celia and her soldiers departed. The castle grew quiet as the courts began to leave. Ivarison's court was one of the last to go, and I dreaded the moment.

"Ivarison," I called out, finding him in the castle corridor. His shoulders tensed when I spoke his name, my breath nearly caught in my throat. "I've been looking for you. Have you been hiding from me?"

His expression was grim as he turned. "From you, never. Were you missing me already?"

I shrugged, shoulders sagging. "Perhaps I was. I haven't seen you."

His eyes lit as he smirked. "Keegan has forced me into making plans."

"Oh, what sort of plans?"

"It's time that I return to Wildhaven. They'll be expecting their Lord to return."

I gulped. I knew his return was coming, but my heart cracked at the thought of him leaving Mystmere.

"Oh," I paused, trying to gather my words. "You could always return or stay here."

"I'm glad to know I would be welcomed." he paused, taking a hard swallow. "Ellowyn, take care of yourself." he stepped closer, his breath hitting my cheek before he leaned down and lightly kissed my cheek. I froze at his touch, my eyes closing as his face lingered for a moment.

Then it was gone as he began to turn. I couldn't stop myself. I grabbed his hand; his fingers immediately laced through mine.

"Wait, Ivarison," I said quickly. Our goodbye didn't feel right. "Please tell me you'll return." I gripped his hand tighter, my skin feeling like it was burning. "It's hot in this corridor."

"All you have to do is ask, ask me anything, and I'll submit," he said breathlessly.

What? Ask him what? What did that mean? Submit to what?

I could hear Bria snapping her jaw shut, blocking herself from our conversation. I couldn't bring myself to ask him to stay. He needed to return to his home, even if it were temporarily. I couldn't be so selfish as to ask him to stop fulfilling his duties.

Instead of asking, I pulled him to me, tightly embracing him. His height towered over me as I wrapped my arms around his torso. He didn't react immediately, startled by my touch, but then his arms wrapped around me as if he might never let go. I inhaled his scent, knowing I would miss it when he was gone.

"We can stay in touch while I'm away. Just write," he said, pulling a piece of parchment from his pocket as he pulled away.

His eyes closed as he took a step back. "Hold out your hand." he whispered. His nose scrunched as the parchment in his hand faded, and I felt the edges scrape against my palm.

"How did you do that?!" I asked, staring at the parchment.

"Focus as if you were fading. Think of wanting it to move from one place to another."

He held out his palm, waiting. It thought of my hand in his own, brushing against his calloused skin, the claws that lay just beneath the surface.

My hand was empty as I watched his grin spread across his face. The parchment was now back in his palm.

"It's a royalty trick, I suppose. King Everett taught me that trick, wanting me to send letters during our travels once I found you. Apparently the witches long ago taught him this. The late Queen and he used to communicate that way when they weren't together, and that is how he communicated with the courts before the attack seventeen years ago. I taught Keegan and Delaney so that they can communicate now too."

My heart felt light as I smiled. So devastatingly happy as I squinted to stop the tears from forming.

"Thank you," I moved closer, his hand dropping to his side with the parchment clenched in his palm. I didn't know what I was doing as my fingers reached for his cheek, feeling smooth skin as my thumb grazed the edge of his lips, and they parted. He was so much taller than me, but he didn't object as I stood on my toes, his lips so close to mine. His ember smell filled my nostrils as I leaned in, wanting to smell nothing more. I leaned in further, and his soft lips touched mine, and a shock went down my spine.

My heart raced as my breathing stopped at the realization of what I was doing.

His scent was driving me crazy.

My eyes widened as I saw Ivarison stiffen when I pulled away quickly, his eyes still closed. My fingers grazed my lips where his had just been, and I wanted to kiss him again.

What was wrong with me?!

"I'm sorry, I don't know what came over me." I was ready to flee the corridor, but Ivarison snatched my wrist before I could, forcing me to look back.

"I'll come back." His voice was deep, his accent rolling off his tongue as his chest rose quickly and his grip tightened. "I'll be back."

A sense of longing ached inside me. I missed him already and wished he wouldn't leave. I may have killed Ciaran, but I wouldn't have accomplished anything without Ivarison. He taught me, made me believe in myself, showed me control, and even through his worst tactics, he gave me the hope that I never had.

He'd pushed me and proven I was capable of anything when I tried. He'd given me the confidence I had desperately needed. Without our group, I wouldn't have survived.

Ivarison was feared due to his past and abilities, which I didn't fully know. His power and healing made him nearly impossible to defeat. But I wasn't afraid of him, so I pushed back. He was my friend, yet so much more. And I wasn't ready to let go of that.

Most mornings after Ivarison left, Delaney pulled me from my bed to get me out of my room. We went to a private area for practice, and occasionally my mother, Dealla and Killian joined. I worked on channeling my magic through my sword to master it.

My mother and I spoke more. She told me about life as a princess, the kingdom and how my grandfather and mother had met. I never pushed her for more about my father or the prison, knowing she would share when she was ready.

When there had been sightings of Adriane in Ravenholde, we relaxed knowing she wasn't lingering in Madora.

Carwyn guided me through the village, showing me the land and more of Mystmere. Bria traveled occasionally, searching for other dragons that might be hiding throughout our kingdom, but never stayed away long.

"Ivarison returned to Wildhaven?" my mother asked when Delaney, Carwyn and I returned from the village, where locals welcomed us warmly with baked goods.

Why was she asking? Of course she knew that he had.

"Yes," I muttered, my eyes wincing at Delaney, who was still adjusting to her mate having to leave with Ivarison.

"Oh," My mother clicked her tongue, beginning to mutter something under her breath. I shrugged my shoulders.

"Don't do that. What is it?" I snapped.

Her head tilted. "I knew he would return, it's just–" she shook her head, staring off. "It's nothing."

My eyebrows shot up as I grabbed her arm to stop her. "No, I thought we agreed to no more secrets," I said forcefully.

She looked uncomfortable, glancing at our guards who stood farther away.

"I thought you liked Ivarison. It must've been difficult to say goodbye." Her feet shifted as she looked back at me.

I tried to swallow the lump in my throat at the sound of his name, but it didn't stop the ache. After everything that happened, I felt we understood each other. I learned to get past my emotions and control my power. I'd seen him for who he truly was and knew my hatred had been for the wrong reasons.

It wasn't difficult to admit that I was attracted to him. I'd caught myself in those feelings countless times. He was incredibly handsome, smart, witty, and maddening. During our time together, we'd faced enough obstacles to know I could trust him with my life. He had saved me countless times, and I had saved him.

"I-How could I not? He had been willing to die with me. It's difficult." I finally said, trying to control the higher pitch in my voice as my cheeks flushed. My mother tried to smile but failed, catching the shift in my mood. "But he left. I don't know when I'll see him again."

"You'll see him again," She squeezed my hand. "In the meantime, I know there's work between us, Ellowyn. I want to earn your trust back, so you know you can rely on me."

I could understand the heartache and pain she had felt and experienced. I knew things would be different, and we would make a difference if I could fully forgive her for taking those years away from me.

Chapter Forty-Five

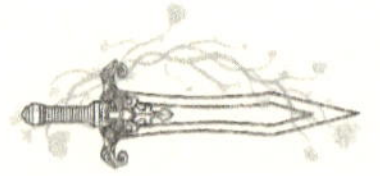

"*It's quiet without you bossing me around.*"

Ivarison's note landed in my palm as I rested in bed. The night breeze drifted from the open balcony, cooling my flushed skin as I heard Bria yawn just outside. My fingers brushed across the cursive writing.

"*Another one?*" Bria asked, "*Goodnight, Little Spark.*"

I held the note tightly in my hand, trying not to smile as if he would be able to see it. "Yes," I said out loud to Bria. "Goodnight!"

"*Oh, do you miss me?*" I wrote back quickly imagining his hands, his ivory skin brushing against mine to receive the note.

"*It's much more peaceful without your particular brand of chaos.*" His handwriting was so neat on the parchment. I shook my head, writing back again.

"*That's a yes,*"

"*...That's a yes.*"

I chuckled, my hand shaking with nerves as I wrote back.

"*You could return to Mystmere, and I could create some more chaos.*"

"*Are you asking for my return from missing me too?*"

He didn't miss a beat. I wished he were here, so I could crinkle the note and throw it at his forehead.

"*You're a much better trainer than the one I have now.*"

"Oh, is that all you miss me for? You don't enjoy setting any of your other trainers on fire? What are you working on?"

"My mother wants to see if I have transformation abilities like her and my grandfather. So far, it's not going well."

He didn't reply immediately. My fingers drummed against the sheets as I watched the twinkling stars through the window.

"It's complex, but I'm sure you're capable. Your subconscious will guide you into what you can do. Your mother can help with the rest."

"What if that never comes?"

There was another pause before he responded.

"Don't begin doubting yourself now. Nothing has stopped you yet, love. You've proved over and over that even without a transformation ability, you're one of the strongest Fae that I know."

It had been a month since he left. Notes appeared here and there, and I would respond as quickly as I could.

"Ell…" another note appeared, and my heart hammered before I continued reading. *"Even if you won't admit to it, I do miss you. Goodnight."*

I could sense his smile as I started at his writing, and my heart hammered so fast. I closed my eyes, placing the note in the side table drawer with so many others. I wasn't going to reply, I shouldn't. But I moved quickly to send a response, my hand shaking as I wrote.

"You're right. I miss you, and I look forward to seeing you again."

I didn't wait for a response, unsure if he would send one. With Delaney and him, I had developed the friendships that I had desperately wanted when I was at the cottage. A life that seemed so long ago. Now that I had it, I was so terrified that it would be taken away.

I didn't want to express how I felt over a note. When I saw him again, I would find the courage.

My grandfather sat at the long table in the great hall. My mother and Delaney sat opposite of him, while Alix, Dealla, and Carwyn stood nearby as I took an empty seat.

"Our sources have confirmed Adriane was spotted again, still in Ravenholde. I expect she will remain there for some time as she grieves," my grandfather spoke gravely, looking over the map of our land on the table. "Delaney, your mother sent word that they are adjusting in Luminara." He cleared his throat. "I'm certain Adriane will eventually plan to retaliate. For now, we must show Madora there is nothing to fear."

My mother nodded as I waited for what my grandfather had called this meeting for. Delaney sat with us as my support, per my request. We were nearly always together.

"Proceed as if nothing has changed? Do you believe that to be wise?" My mother asked.

"Yes, we will have additional guards, and I know other courts will be willing to supply them just as they did in the past."

"What are you talking about?" I asked between the two, not understanding.

"A royal ball. Our first one in over twenty years now," my mother answered, a small twinkle in her eye. "They were a bit enjoyable, once upon a time."

"A ball?" Delaney winced as she stared at me. "I was too young for the last one. I'm sure my mother will be very excited."

"It was once a tradition for the kingdom, and it brought the courts together," my grandfather said. "It helped gather the courts for meetings and diplomacy. After everything that has happened, it may be nice to have one. It will show Madora that we continue to stand together and will not live in fear."

I was silent, flashes of the battles playing in my head, Bria pinned down by heavy iron chains.

"Adriane will strike again. You don't think she will try to attack? A ball would be the perfect opportunity." I countered, not looking up from the section of the map labeled Ravenholde. I had nightmares of Ciaran burning to ash and what I had done to The Dark Soldiers. "She promised she would find a way to make me suffer."

My mother's fingers gripped her chair.

"She would be foolish to strike during it. With other courts attending, she would know the risk to herself. She wouldn't make it out alive," my grandfather stated. "We would be heavily guarded, as I said."

"I don't believe she would care. What about the twins? They aren't with the kingdom either. They didn't offer assistance for our war and haven't been seen since our last encounter. They are the reason we were attacked in Dustvale," I said through clenched teeth. "They were working with Adriane and Ciaran."

"We have begun to track their whereabouts to learn what they've been planning. Their actions will have consequences for defying the crown."

I huffed, not believing that was good enough, and I was also not agreeing to the dance. "I don't know how to dance." I muttered, and Delaney nodded in agreement. Dancing hadn't been on my training schedule.

I wasn't sure I was willing to make a fool of myself in front of Mystmere. If the courts came, Ivarison would come too. I wanted him desperately, my chest aching for his return, but I was petrified for the day I would see him again.

"Don't worry about that, dear." My grandfather stood, ready to dismiss us. "We have much to plan and prepare for, along with dancing lessons."

I stared at my mother with wide eyes. How had we gone from searching all of Mystmere for her, fighting a war, to dance lessons? I still had so much I wanted to learn about Madora, discussions about our lost time, and the village of humans we had lived near, and what it meant to be a halfling Fae. I ached for answers.

"All of the courts are invited," my mother said as she stood as my grandfather left the room. She quietly followed him, Dealla behind her.

I looked over at Delaney.

"If Wildhaven comes, Keegan will return," I whispered, with Carwyn still standing with us. I leaned closer in my chair toward Delaney.

"Yes," she whispered, a smile growing on her face. "Oh, he's lovely. It's an odd feeling, but if we have the chance to see each other again, I'll be happy to attend a ball."

"What was it like?" I asked. I hadn't had a chance to know Keegan as well as I liked. I only learned so much about him during occasionally brief conversations, and what I'd overheard with Ivarison and him.

"When I met him, I had this feeling like I had never felt before. As if all the wrong things were suddenly right. I could see him clearer than anything, and his scent? I can't get enough of it. It drives me insane, but it was all I wanted to smell."

"His scent?" I wasn't sure I had noticed his scent other than Ivarison's, but I had noticed that I picked up on scents more and was more sensitive. "What do I smell like?" I said half-jokingly, sniffing my arm.

Delaney leaned in, a grin on her face. "I don't just go sniffing others, you know. But his just overpowers everyone." She paused. "I suppose you smell like honey and something sweet, maybe amber?"

I froze in my chair as I watched Delaney continue to speak. Keegan's words echoed as I remember the conversation I overheard.

'Tell me, Ivarison. Will you return home after this? Where is home for you?'

'Anywhere that smells of amber and honey.'

Delaney was still speaking, and I missed most of what she had just said.

"--I also had a pull toward him, and I can connect with him when he's near."

I shook my head. "What does that mean?" I felt my heartbeat in my chest as I gripped my armchair tightly. I think it may have been breaking under my grip.

"What?"

I looked over at Carwyn, remembering he was still lingering nearby. "Carwyn, could I have a moment alone with Delaney?"

"*Why is your heart racing so incredibly fast?*" Bria asked, listening.

"*Not now!*" I snipped back as Carwyn hesitated, looking between us then nodded.

"I'll be right outside the door," he said, before he exited.

"What's wrong?" Delaney asked.

"What do you mean by the pull and connecting?"

"After we had spoken more, we could communicate mentally. Only when we're near each other, though. Since he has been gone, we've had to communicate through our notes."

My heart beat faster, and I felt like I could vomit. Delaney's eyes widened as she stared at me, hearing my heart and seeing my face growing paler.

"You look like you're about to vomit. What is the matter?"

"I can connect with Ivarison. We can communicate like I do with Bria too. He taught me how to put shields in my mind to prevent it. He knows my scent, and his own drives me crazy. I kept feeling something right before we met him too," I said it all so quickly, I wasn't sure if I was making sense.

"Oh, I knew it," Delaney whispered, nearly grinning from ear to ear.

"Knew what?"

"I had suspicions he was your mate, the scent between the two of you together, and I sensed something was different. Not to mention the way he's so protective over you. He isn't like that with anyone else." She twisted in her chair, arms resting on the table. "You have no idea how he was when you were in that mist during the battle. Once you threw him out of it.." she paused, shuddering. "It was absolutely terrifying, Ellowyn."

I shook my head, not wanting to remember his face when he realized what I was about to do.

Mate.

I had a mate?

Another word I didn't fully understand. What mate meant for Fae and the depths of their bond Accepting a mating bond was unbreakable, the strongest bond known to Fae kind. That alone was frightening, knowing what it had done to my mother when my father had been killed.

"Ellowyn?" Delaney waved her hand in front of me. "If you could talk with him, what did he say about the connection?"

"He said he had the ability but didn't tell others of it," I whispered. It wasn't my place to share his secrets. "Is this why it hurts so badly that he's gone? Does it hurt like this with Keegan?"

"Well, there have been Fae with that ability. Keegan and I haven't officially accepted our bond, but there is still an ache when we're not together."

My hands covered my face, fingertips rubbing my temples. Why didn't he tell me? That pulling sensation I had the night we met, how it disappeared when he arrived.

But that conversation with Keegan still lingered in me.

"He's never going to tell me. He doesn't believe he's worthy and thinks he doesn't deserve it," I whispered. Those blue eyes that watched me often, those fingers brushing against my skin that always sent a zapping sensation down my spine.

"If you want to accept the bond, speak up for yourself. You just saved your kingdom. I think you could tell him how you feel." She stood from her chair, palm against her chest. "We deserve our happiness. *You* deserve it."

"Could I blow some flames on him to move you faster?"

I bit my lip to hide my chuckle as I stood in the north courtyard of the castle.

Carwyn was trying to stop me from going on a flight, but Bria wasn't having his nonsense. I never listened to him; I wasn't about to start now.

"Bria said she could light you on fire as an excuse for not being able to stop us?" I shrugged as he stood in front of me, arms crossed.

"We truly need to work on your spokesperson skills when you're speaking for me." Bria glared, huffing smoke at Carwyn. It was her pleasure during the day to irritate him.

"Fine. I'll wait here," he said, taking a step away from Bria.

"Well, where else would he wait?" Bria snipped out as I climbed into the saddle.

"Unless you care to join?" I called out as I stared at Bria from the corner of my eye.

"Excuse me, pardon me?" Bria yelped, snapping her mouth as if to dare him.

Carwyn didn't respond as he took another step away while she shook her wings, readying herself.

"ELLOWYN, STOP!" a voice carried across the courtyard. I turned to see Delaney in mid-jump from her panther form, shifting to Fae.

Carwyn's hands immediately went to his sword as he looked around the area. "Why are you screaming and running?!"

"Stop," she breathed out, ignoring him as she gasped for air and looked at Bria and me. "It's Wildhaven." She took another deep inhale. "It was attacked."

ACKNOWLEDGEMENTS

My husband, who never reads, always listened when I needed to talk and figure things out with my story, and was someone I could read it out to. You always tell me to reach for the stars, but I would never be able to do it if it weren't for you.

My children. My pride and joy. I love you all so, so much. Even when I said you wouldn't be able to read this book because it's an adult book, you were still so proud and told everyone that your momma was writing a book! I do this for you, and I hope you know, you are capable of anything you put your mind to.

To my parents and family. The ones who were there giving me support from start to finish. Your encouragement pushed me through the moments I was down.

To my best friend, who cheers me on with everything I have ever done and shows me love and support from the moment we met. Nikki, I love you, my dear friend. Your support and encouragement were always given at the right time.

To my Hilt group ladies, finding each other on Instagram chat was a blessing. Our passion and love brought us together. I may not be where I am if it weren't for our chats and the help that you've given me. I'm so thankful to have had your encouraging words and push to finish and do this! The love that you've shown through the process has been a grace.

To my incredible editor, Laura. Thank you so much for your eye and for loving my story. You made the editing process enjoyable and lovely, and

I am so thankful to have met you! This book would still be in shambles if it weren't for you! I will be forever grateful and look forward to future projects and working with you again.

To my cousin Misty Dawn, who had the love for fantasy and dragons. Even though you aren't here with us physically, I know you would have been here cheering for this book. The kingdom name Mystmere, comes from you as well as the title 'Dawn'. So you could live on in a world of fantasy and dragons.

To two important teachers I had that made a difference to me while writing and showing me the love with writing and reading, Cindy Young and A. Moreno. You may never see this, but I still want to thank you for the encouragement and kind words that made me feel that I had a chance.

Lastly, to my readers who gave this book a chance and read it. You granted me an opportunity to share my story with you, and I thank you. This would not have been possible without what you have given and helped me with along this journey.

ABOUT THE AUTHOR

Shaina Parks lives in Southern Maryland, where she enjoys her time with her husband and children. Her nose is often in a book or against her laptop, working on her next project.

She has always had a love for all things fantasy. Fae, dragons, witches, and wizards. It was a dream to finally create a fantasy novel and for others to read it.

For more information about her work, please visit her website!

Visit: www.shainaparkswrites.com and sign up for her newsletter to receive upcoming news!